AFTER SHOCK

Sam Fisher is the pseudonym of thriller writer Michael White, author of the acclaimed international bestsellers *Equinox* and *The Medici Secret*. *Aftershock* is the second book in the E-Force series.

Visit his website at www.michaelwhite.com.au.

Also by Sam Fisher

State of Emergency

AFTER SHOCK

SAM FISHER

PAN BOOKS

First published 2010 by Bantam, an imprint of Random House Australia Pty Ltd

First published in Great Britain 2011 by Pan Books
an imprint of Pan Macmillan, a division of Macmillan Publishers Limited
Pan Macmillan, 20 New Wharf Road, London N1 9RR
Basingstoke and Oxford
Associated companies throughout the world
www.panmacmillan.com

ISBN 978-1-447-20149-6

1 3 5 7 9 8 6 4 2

A CIP catalogue record for this book is available from
the British Library.

Printed in the UK by CPI Mackays, Chatham ME5 8TD

The story so far . . .

'The world needs an organisation that can go into disaster zones and save lives, superfast,' declared Colonel Mark Harrison. And he was a man who made things happen.

It took him a year to get anyone to listen to his plan and then a further three years before his dream became reality. But when it did, he found himself leader of a team that could go into any emergency situation anywhere in the world and save lives. He called his team E-Force.

E-Force is fronted by the six key members: Mark Harrison, Peter Sherringham, Stephanie Jacobs, Maiko Buchanan, Josh Thompson, and Tom Erickson, but they are backed up by 1300 others – techs, engineers, maintenance, medical and comms people. Their main base (Base One) is the tiny Pacific island of Tintara, a little under 2000 kilometres south-south-west of San Diego, but there are several other bases dotted around the globe at secret locations.

Although Mark, Steph, Josh, Pete and Mai are at the sharp end of any mission, they could not operate without Tom, the team's cyberguru. Wheelchair-bound after a childhood road accident, he is a world-class hacker and has an intimate relationship with the 'seventh member' of E-Force, Sybil, the world's only quantum computer. Sybil operates all the E-Force systems from Tintara and is the computer nerve centre of the operation.

During the team's first mission, they were called in to rescue Senator Kyle Foreman who was trapped in a bombed-out building in Los Angeles. The team had not yet completed their training, but were catapulted into action regardless. Since that first operation, E-Force have conducted more than a dozen separate missions and become globally famous. The world now knows the faces of the team members, but the locations of Base One and the other E-Force hubs remain a closely guarded secret.

It is now almost six months since E-Force's first mission. The team have gained a great deal of experience since that excursion to rescue Senator Foreman. They are as ready as ever, and waiting for action.

E-Force personnel

Mark Harrison
African American.
1.90 metres, 95 kilograms.
Greying black hair, dark brown eyes.
Born: Houston, Texas, January 1969.
Areas of expertise: Team leader, IT expert, experienced pilot.
Experience: Rhodes scholar, mathematics major, Oriel, Oxford 1987-90; PhD in
Computer Science; four years with IBM, 1990-94; US Special Forces, 1995-2000
(retired with the rank of colonel).
Other talents: Fluent in four languages including Mandarin and Russian; marksman
(distinguished expert class); judo master sixth dan; first African American Oxford
rowing Blue.

Peter Sherringham
Caucasian European.
1.8 metres, 84 kilograms.
Red hair, green eyes.
Born: Newcastle, England, March 1973.
Areas of expertise: Explosives, engineering.
Experience: NCO in British Army 1991-98; served in Northern Ireland and Iraq.
After retiring from the Army, Peter founded Globex, now a leading specialist
in commercial demolition.

Stephanie Jacobs
Caucasian Australian.
1.7 metres, 65 kilograms.
Blonde hair, green eyes.
Born: Sydney, Australia, June 1975.
Area of expertise: Medical doctor.
Experience: Completed medical training in 2001; specialised in burns treatment;
made consultant at Royal North Shore Hospital, Sydney, 2007; headed internationally
renowned team at the cutting edge of burns treatment.
Other talents: 100 metre and 200 metre freestyle gold medallist in both 1996
and 2000 Olympic Games.

Maiko Buchanan
Asian American.
1.63 metres, 54 kilograms.
Black hair, black eyes.
Born: Kyoto, Japan, May 1974; emigrated with her parents to Boston, Massachusetts,
in 1984.
Area of expertise: NASA space shuttle pilot.
Experience: Flown three missions, one as commander.
Other talents: Engineering major at UCLA; excellent soccer player.

Josh Thompson
Caucasian European.
1.96 metres, 110 kilograms.
Black hair, brown eyes.
Born: London, July 1973.
Area of expertise: Encryption.
Experience: Wrote *The Theory and Practice of Cryptography*, 2008, the standard
text on the subject; formerly Professor at Columbia University, New York.
Other talents: PhD in Cryptography, King's College, London, 2002. Served in SAS
until 2007, as an SAS encryption specialist (retired with the rank of major).
A triathlon gold medallist at Olympic Games, 1996.

Tom Erickson
Caucasian American.
1.75 metres, 58 kilograms.
Brown hair, blue eyes.
Born: Baltimore, May 1992.
Area of expertise: World-class hacker.
Experience: E-Force's wheelchair-bound computer guru; served one year of a
six-year sentence in Aldermont Correctional Facility, New York State, for internet
fraud. Other talents: IQ of 202 (four points higher than Stephen Hawking).

E-Force Equipment

E-Force's equipment is at least 20 years ahead of publically known cutting-edge civilian or military technology. This is because it is supplied to them by an organisation called CARPA (Civilian Advanced Research Projects Agency). CARPA coming out of universities and industry. It is a clandestine organisation that is funded by a multinational group through the auspices of the UN. The *quid pro quo* for the arrangement is that, in exchange for the use of this technology, E-Force act as guinea pigs to test the innovations and help in perfecting CARPA's gadgets. Here is a list of some of the key pieces of equipment used by E-Force.

BigEyes

E-Force are given warning of any potential disaster thanks to a network of 32 highly advanced satellites which girdle the earth in geosynchronous orbit. These satellites are called BigEyes and they are fitted with supersensitive detection equipment that can pinpoint any sign of impending trouble anywhere on the planet and communicate the information to Base One on Tintara.

Sybil

The world's only quantum computer. Because it makes direct use of quantum mechanical phenomena it can operate millions of times faster than the most powerful supercomputer in service. Sybil is the cyber nerve centre of E-Force. The computer core is located at Base One, the primary operations platform for E-Force on the island of Tintara, 2000 kilometres south-south-west of San Diego. However, it is linked with a network of subsidiary bases around the world.

Cybersuits

Each operational team member wears a cybersuit. These are made from a blend of manmade polymers and carbothreads. They are wired for comms and internet connection to Tintara base. The wearer can be supplied with nutrients to last a week. The suits protect the team from extremes of temperature and toxic and corrosive environments. The suits are also fitted with nanobots that can repair injuries and fix the suit if it is damaged.

Implants

Another important aspect of E-Force technology is more personal. With the exception of Tom, all the team members have undergone surgery to have implants and enhancements fitted. These include alterations to their eyes to expand their visual range, and cochlear implants to enhance hearing.

Silverbacks

These are Mach 10 jets capable of reaching anywhere in the world within two and a half hours. Like all E-Force aircraft, they are powered by next-generation scram jets and are Vertical Take Off and Landing (VTOL) planes. They carry a pilot and navigator, but may be flown solo if necessary. E-Force have a fleet of eight Silverbacks, six based on Tintara – *John*, *Paul*, *George* and *Ringo* (along with two backups, *Dylan* and *Eric*). The remaining two, *Mick* and *Keith*, are shared by the other, smaller E-Force bases around the world. Along with all E-Force equipment, Silverbacks are painted with Camoflin which confuses cameras and video recorders to produce a blurred image.

Big Macs

These aircraft are the workhorses of the organisation – huge transport vehicles in which heavy equipment is delivered to operation sites. There are two Big Macs in service, both based on Tintara Island. Each is capable of flight at Mach 6 and has a range of 20,000 kilometres.

Hummingbirds

Seven of these aircraft are in operation. They are large passenger planes, each capable of carrying 22 passengers at speeds up to Mach 6, and with a range of 20,000 kilometres.

Drebbel and *Narcis*

Nuclear-powered submarines used to carry survivors of marine incidents. The optimum crew is six, but each sub may be piloted solo. They can each carry up to 23 passengers in comfort and may stay submerged indefinitely. Top speed is 100 knots. Transported aboard a Big Mac.

Hot Dogs

These are mini-subs. There are six in service. Each carries up to two people. They can descend to a depth of 6000 metres and are powered by a 600 horsepower engine. Top speed is 150 knots.

Hunters

Autonomous, self-powered moving sensor devices, these can be pre-programmed to conduct a mission, or may be piloted by a human operator with a two-way audiovisual feed. They are used primarily to enter unstable buildings and to conduct reconnaissance.

Prams

E-Force's key High Speed Ground Transporters (HSGTs). Loosely based upon the design for the hovercraft, Prams are each capable of transporting six passengers and approximately 100 kilograms of equipment at speeds approaching 300 kph.

Moles

A 2000 horsepower burrowing machine used to carry a single rescuer into seemingly impossible places. It consists of two integrated parts: a massive drill bit and, behind that, a cabin and control module called the Bullet. The Mole is protected from extremes of temperature thanks to cooling and heating webs integrated within its superstrong infrastructure. E-Force have three moles and like all its vehicles, the Mole is made from Maxinium, an alloy five times stronger than the toughest titanium-steel composite.

Sonic Drills

These lightweight drills can be used on a stand or held in both hands. The size of a rifle, the Sonic Drill can cut through 5 centimetre thick steel in seconds using ultrasound in the range of 35 kilohertz.

Vasjets

A needleless injection, the Vasjet is used to supply survivors with pain relief or other drugs. A microspray is directed through the skin and the blood vessel wall for immediate response.

1

The St Maria Nuclear Power Station, Paraguay, 15 May, 5.02 am

'Sure as hell hope this ain't no wild goose chase,' Robbie Valentine said, swinging a length of electrical cable in his right hand.

'I wouldn't be too surprised, my friend,' Mario Alves replied. 'We've had two false alarms this week.'

Valentine, an American night-shift tech, led the way along a low-ceilinged tunnel lined with heavy duty electrical cabling. After 20 metres the two men came to a hatch. It swung open onto a broader, higher tunnel. They could just about walk upright. At the end, they reached the main power conduit. Valentine dropped the cable to the floor and tapped in an alphanumeric to unlock the inspection cover. The metal door levered outwards and the tech shone a torch into the opening.

At first, everything seemed fine, then Valentine noticed the copper contact on one of the main cables had slipped from its socket. He flicked off the power to the circuit and leaned forward to grasp the cable. As he stretched into the box of electronics, his right elbow nudged the main power switch he had just flicked off. For a second the switch hovered between 'on' and 'off', then slipped a centimetre downwards. Two hundred amps of electricity with a potential difference of 50,000 volts shot through the

American's body. It travelled the length of his spine in under a microsecond, frying his nervous system, killing him faster than a bullet through the brain. Valentine's body flew out of the junction cupboard, through the air and landed in a smoking heap 5 metres along the tunnel. En route, the dead man knocked his partner off balance. Alves stumbled backwards over the electrical cabling Valentine had been carrying, and landed badly, his right arm fracturing under the weight of his body.

One hundred and 27 metres away from the charred remains of Robbie Valentine, the main operations room of the St Maria Nuclear Power Station was quiet. Of the three nightshift engineers on duty in Main Control, two had gone off for a coffee, leaving behind the new boy on the job, Fernando Guitica, who had only qualified from the University of Asunción a month earlier. The master controls were entirely automated and had a German-designed self-diagnosis backup system in case any faults occurred in the complex network of computers and electronics that monitored the power station. The job of the engineers was really just to babysit the machines, unless, that is, something went very badly wrong.

At the precise moment technician Robbie Valentine was barbecued in the maintenance tunnels, Fernando Guitica was engrossed in a thrilling game of *Mario Kart* on his new DS. He failed to see the red warning light flashing on the electrical systems monitor. By unfortunate coincidence, the cable that Valentine and Alves were supposed to repair was a multifunction conduit. Its main purpose was to send electricity to a digital thermocouple that regulated the temperature of the main pumps keeping the reactor cores cooled with water. A subsidiary cable in the conduit powered the audio alarm systems for Main Control. So, as Guitica entered the final lap of a nail-biting race on the DS and moved up from third to second place, he was blissfully unaware the internal temperature of Pump Number 4 on the east side of the power station had already gone critical. As a consequence, the first warning he had that something very bad was happening was when the sound of a massive explosion reverberated through Main Control.

The shock of the blast threw Guitica from his swivel chair. He went sprawling across the highly polished floor and only stopped when his head made contact with a leg of one of the computer cabinets. Dazed, he shook away the pain surging through his head and scrambled to his feet, searching for the nearest computer screen. What he saw sent a wave of panic through him. The monitor displayed a schematic of the power station, and he could see immediately a flashing red symbol. One of the four enormous pumps cooling the radioactive core had been obliterated.

His body froze, his mind racing. There was an acid taste in his mouth and his right hand was clenched so hard his nails cut into the flesh of his palm. He span around as the other two engineers, Dominic Xanando and Kurt Fritzer, dashed into the room from the corridor, their faces ashen.

'What the fuck's happened?' Fritzer screamed as he rushed over to the console. Guitica stepped aside as his boss surveyed the monitors, looking on dumbly as the man stabbed at a series of buttons. 'Holy Mother of God!' Fritzer exclaimed.

A second loud explosion shook the room and instinctively the three men dived for the floor. Xanando got up, shoved Guitica aside and found Fritzer scanning the controls, his breath coming in loud gasps. 'It's going critical. Fuck! How can this happen? How come we had no warning?'

'That's what the techs were sent in for,' Guitica managed to reply. 'A fault in the cabling, they thought.'

'This is in a different league, Guitica,' Fritzer yelled, his face lathered in sweat. 'We thought everything was okay, but the whole fucking warning system must've been down for hours. Christ . . . the station could go critical. It'd make Chernobyl look like a fart in a jacuzzi.' He ran his hands through his hair and stared, slack-jawed, at the computer screen.

Smoke began to rise from the console. 'What the . . . ?' Xanando began. Then came a fizzing sound followed by a brief flash of light from inside one of the monitors. All three men sprang back from the desk and a second later the computer screen died. They turned in unison as a grating sound came from the other side of the room and the main door slid shut. A red light above the door started to flash.

'Containment,' Fritzer announced. And they heard a heavy, lead-lined radiation door slam into place a few metres along the corridor. Without waiting a second, Fritzer ran over to a second computer console, stabbing at a red button – the emergency alarm. Before he had lifted his finger from the control they heard the alarms kick in outside Main Control. Their own audio systems were still down, but alarms on a different circuit were blasting out around the station. In all main corridors, containment doors were slamming down, secondary coolant surged through pipes around the massive pumps and through backup tubing around the gigantic coils of the pumps. But the damage to the reactor had already been done. There was nothing they could do . . . except pray.

2

'Pete? What's your ETA?'

Tom Erickson's voice resonated in the tiny speakers positioned close to Peter Sherringham's ears. He flicked his gaze to one corner of the holographic image in his headset. 'Three minutes, 10 seconds, Tom.'

'Copy that.'

Pete ran his fingers over the plastic control panel in the cockpit of the Silverback jet, *George*, and the plane ascended 400 metres on a sharp incline. At Mach 10, it covered the distance in a fraction of a second. Glancing back at the holoscreen, Pete could see two traces – two planes behind him – another Silverback piloted by Mai Buchanan, and the larger bulk of the Big Mac, the E-Force workhorse, with Stephanie Jacobs and Josh Thompson aboard.

'Okay, guys.' It was Mark Harrison, the team leader, speaking from where he stood next to Tom in Cyber Control at the E-Force base on Tintara Island. His voice could be heard by all four E-Force members in the three planes. 'As we have a few minutes before you reach the target, I'd like to bring you up to speed. The BigEyes tell us the situation at St Maria is deteriorating fast.' A schematic of the plant appeared on the team's holoscreens. 'As you know, Pump Number 4 blew. We're not sure how or why. The engineers on site are unable to increase the flow of coolant to the core.

11

Coolant is getting through from secondary backup systems, but it's way too little, too late. The core housing has ruptured and the outer casing of the reactor itself is exposed. There's been a very small radiation leak from this, but it also means we have a way of cooling the thing externally.'

Tom broke in. 'The quencher tanks are on "max", Steph. That means you have 50,000 litres of Quenchex to smother the flames. You then have a further 20,000 litres of liquid nitrogen to dump on the core itself. As you can imagine, you only have a small margin of error. Miss the flames and the liquid nitrogen will be ineffectual. Putting the fire out is only half the job, so both drops have to be within a metre of the target.'

'So, no pressure then,' Steph, in the Big Mac, laughed. 'How long do we have?'

'Tom reckons we have nine minutes until the reactor blows.'

'Wonderful!' Josh said. 'Our ETA is six minutes 35, so we'll have no more than two and a half minutes to get the core temperature down.'

'I know,' Mark responded. 'Mai and Pete, you should be there a few minutes ahead of the Big Mac. You have to get a clear picture of the critical drop areas. Use the full spectrum analysers that've just been installed. Here's a schematic of the plant.'

A 3D image of the St Maria Nuclear Power Plant appeared on the Silverback holoscreens. Tom described the layout. As he spoke, the image shifted perspective and different parts of it became enlarged to show more detail.

'There're four pumps,' he explained. 'In most reactors, failure in one or even two of the pumps would be manageable, but this place is old. In fact, it was due to be decommissioned a year ago, but the Paraguayans managed to push it back. All four pumps need to be working at a constant 80 per cent plus efficiency rate to maintain stability for the core. Pump 4 has vaporised and the core temperature has risen rapidly. I can't understand how it was left to get so bad. The warning systems must've also been offline. Anyway, the explosion has done us one favour. It just fell short of ripping open the reactor core itself, but it's exposed the housing. This is the primary drop area. There's a serious fire raging all around the Pump 4 module, but there's also a very hot fire all over the core housing.'

'How hot?' Josh asked.

'It's a chemical fire, outdated insulation and piping material. We're looking at 6000 degrees in places.'

Josh whistled.

'And that, my friend, is why we only have . . .' Tom paused for a second, 'seven minutes 50 to put out the fire.'

3

Pete swooped low in the Silverback. Turning a tight circle 300 metres above the gutted building, he could see the extent of the damage. The power plant consisted of a square concrete block, six storeys high. Next to this, on the eastern side, stood a stumpy cylinder with a domed roof – the reactor itself. The entire east side of the main building had been ripped away by the explosion and a great tear was visible in the dome covering the reactor.

As Pete banked around, Mai came into view aboard the Silverback, *John*.

'Looks so much worse in reality,' Mai commented through her comms.

'Yep,' Pete replied. 'I'm running the spectroscopic analysis now.' A moment later, the information appeared on his holoscreen. It was a multicoloured image showing the thermionic conditions 2000 metres below the plane, highlighting the hottest parts in red and running through the spectrum to the cooler green regions. The same images appeared on the big screen on the wall of Cyber Control on Tintara, some 10,000 kilometres away. Tom's voice came over the comms.

'Josh, Steph. We have the images from the ground.' He sent them over to their holoscreen. 'The real hot zone is at grid reference 21.456 by 33.788. You copy that?'

'Copy,' Steph replied.

'There it is,' Josh said through the comms. 'We have a visual.'

The Big Mac was a gigantic machine, a heavy plane. But for all its size, it could be thrown around like a conventional fighter plane. It dropped 3000 metres in a few seconds and made a preparatory approach over the burning reactor.

'Three minutes nine seconds, guys,' Tom said over the comms.

The Silverbacks took up a holding pattern hovering 7000 metres above the nuclear power plant. Pete and Mai could both see the massive disc shape of the Big Mac below. It was turning, getting ready for the first drop.

Banking around to the west, Steph brought the plane down to 700 metres above the building. From this height they could see, unaided, the tangled metal and charred plastic. Intense purple and blue flames rose 20 metres above the reactor casing. Things would have been easier if the Big Mac could have been put into a hover position over the burned-out reactor, but it was too hazardous. Instead, they had to swoop in and get out quickly. Two seconds before they came overhead, the onboard computer systems set the drop sequence in motion and with an accuracy of one hundredth of a second, 50,000 litres of Quenchex sprayed from the underside of the Big Mac. Two sheets of white liquid cascaded down onto the wreckage.

Quenchex was a new material invented by the eggheads at CARPA, the organisation that supplied E-Force with all its hi-tech equipment. It put out fires at least a hundred times faster than any conventional methods. The material landed in a coating several metres square. Spattering onto the superheated metal of the reactor, it instantly sent a grey mist hundreds of metres into the air. The Big Mac banked around and prepared for the second run to drop the liquid nitrogen that would cool the reactor.

'Nice one, guys,' Tom's voice came through the comms. 'Direct hit.'

Steph and Josh could see through the windows that almost all the flames had been quenched. A few small fires continued to burn at the periphery of the drop site, but these were far enough away from the reactor to present little danger.

'We're prepping the liquid nitrogen,' Josh said.

'Advise using half on the first run, just in case.'

'How long do we have?'

'One minute 40 seconds. Sybil reckons you can do two runs with a 45 second margin.'

'All right, we're going in.'

The Big Mac came around from the west again and the automated systems on board calculated the precise moment to release the chemical payload. Liquid nitrogen, cooled to 50 Kelvin, well below its vaporisation point, streamed out from underneath the mammoth aircraft, dropped the 650 metres to the devastated building and smothered the reactor housing.

Stephanie pulled the plane up and around, racing to prepare for the final run.

'How'd it go?' Josh asked.

'Just getting data,' Tom responded. 'Goddamn it!'

'What?'

'It's only lowered the temperature of the core casing by a couple of hundred degrees.'

'We're ready for the second run,' Steph announced.

Mark Harrison's voice broke in. 'Hold, Steph. Repeat. Hold.'

'But time's running up,' Josh blurted out.

'Just a second.'

'We have a problem,' Tom said. There was an unnatural silence over the comms. 'The rip in the roof is too small.

The liquid nitrogen only covered about a quarter of the core housing. It's not enough.'

'You want us to go lower? Swivel the emission jets to get under the remaining roof?' Steph asked.

'No. Won't work.'

'Pete? Mai?' Mark called through the comms. 'Who's closest to the building right now?'

'I am,' Pete said immediately.

'Right. I want you to get down to 80 metres above the roof. Use the onboard laser cutters to open up the roof. Get the hell out the instant you have it ripped. Steph, Josh, you need to be a few seconds behind the Silverback and drop the remaining liquid nitrogen into the gap. You got that?'

'Loud and clear,' Pete responded as he banked the Silverback and plunged towards the earth at incredible speed.

'Steph, Josh,' Tom said. 'You'll need to shift the drop site 10 metres north, 6 west.'

'Affirmative,' Josh replied, and set the controls.

Timing was critical. They had only a couple of seconds between Pete cutting the roof away and the Big Mac coming down for the drop. Then, in the remaining 20 seconds, both planes had to get as far away from the site as possible.

The Big Mac started to make its run. Steph and Josh could see Pete had taken up position ahead of them, extremely low over the flames. From their angle it looked perilous – the flames seemed to be lapping at the underside of the sleek plane. An intense blue beam shot out from the front of the Silverback, a neodymium yttrium-aluminium-garnet (Nd-YAG) laser that could cut through several metres of lead-lined steel and concrete like a hot knife through butter. The laser made contact with the remains of the dome covering the reactor, and the outer shell dissolved, exposing the metal framework beneath. The steel beams crumbled like heated sugar.

One glance told Pete the roof had been split open, and he engaged the forward thrusters. At that precise moment, the Big Mac came in 600 metres overhead and dropped its payload of liquid nitrogen. Pete banked hard, but before he could pull up and shoot off to the east, a geyser of super-heated vapour from the reactor housing shot up, cascaded onto the wing of the Silverback, and was sucked into the starboard engine.

The plane rolled 360 degrees. Pete could see the Big Mac high overhead swooping away in the direction he had planned to go. With lightning reflexes, his hands flew over the control panel, stabilising the plane into horizontal flight. Then he pulled *George* around, bringing the nose up. He felt a jolt. The 3D schematic of the plane in his visor showed a malfunction in the starboard engine. A red icon started to flash. The starboard engine exploded and the wing vaporised. The Silverback went into a tailspin. Fighting the controls, Pete tried to bring back the stricken plane, but it was hopeless. He pushed the eject button, heard the canopy of the Silverback rip away and felt himself thrust upwards into the morning sky. In that moment, Pete Sherringham knew it was too late.

4

New York City, six weeks later

On days like today, Madame Zavarelli really hated her job. She knew she was devoid of any real talent. So different to Grandmamma back home in Casoria. She would never forget how the old woman terrified her with her prophesies. There was the time the old man in the village suddenly dropped dead the day after Grandmamma said he would. And then there had been the incident with Maria Bellini's dog. That had been horrible. But no, Madame Zavarelli told herself for perhaps the thousandth time, she did not have 'the gift' – although that hadn't stopped her. The sad truth was, she had no real talent for anything. If she hadn't become a palm reader in a travelling circus, she would have been forced to sell her body. She didn't even have the looks to snare a decent husband.

Most of the time, things were okay. She made a respectable living, got to see places, had a few good friends and she had long ago accepted the fact that she was merely a performance artist. She had no qualms about it – it was a job. But today she felt uncomfortable and she had no idea why.

Drawing on an illicit cigarette – her employer would have dropped her like a hot potato if he had caught her – Madame Zavarelli saw the flap over the tent entrance twitch. She stubbed out the cigarette and hid the evidence, as a tall, thin, elegantly dressed man in his thirties appeared. He was extremely good looking with carefully sculpted eyebrows, big brown eyes and fashionably tousled black hair. Too handsome to be straight, Madame Zavarelli concluded immediately.

'Good afternoon, young man,' she said, fixing him with her piercing black eyes. Her voice was heavily accented. 'You wish to know the secrets of your future?'

The man nodded.

'What is your name?'

He told her.

'Well, Jim Kemple, my standard consultation fee is thirty dollars,' Madame Zavarelli said. 'But you're my first customer in New York, so I will charge you only twenty.'

Jim had been walking through Central Park and had noticed Rinaldo's Circus tents. By serendipity, he had only that morning read an article in the *New York Times* about Rinaldo's, one of the few remaining old-school circuses playing the nostalgia ticket. Jim had almost walked straight past a sign carrying the picture of an elderly woman in gypsy headdress staring meaningfully into a large crystal ball. Inside the orb, strange ghostly shapes were frozen, mid-swirl. Over the picture was written: 'MADAME ZAVARELLI – CLAIRVOYANT AND FORTUNE TELLER. BE ASTOUNDED!'

Jim pulled out his wallet and handed over a couple of bills. 'Believe,' he told himself. He did believe in clairvoyance and prophesy, but he was also aware that most 'Madame Zavarellis' were little more than vaudeville acts.

'Sit,' the woman said, and indicated a chair on one side of a small folding table. The table was covered with a purple velvet cloth, and in the centre sat a crystal ball on a wooden stand. Madame Zavarelli lowered herself into a chair across from Jim and indicated he should place his hands on the table, palms up.

The old woman took his hands in each of hers and peered down at the lines and furrows in his skin. 'You are a happy man,' she said without looking up at Jim. 'You are balanced. You enjoy your work and your love life is good.' She looked at him, then back down at the hands. She ran a finger along the hollow of Jim's left palm. 'Your health is also good. But, you have a bad left knee, yes?'

Jim was startled. He had indeed been suffering from carti-lage problems in his left knee. 'Yes,' he said. 'That's right. How . . . ?'

'Sssh,' Madame Zavarelli said. 'You are worried though. What are you worried about?' She traced a finger along a line close to Jim's wrist. 'Money? No, you're fine there. Ah . . . your partner.'

'Alfred?'

'He is a lot older than you,' Madame Zavarelli said.

'Yes. He's 60 . . .'

'Ssh,' Madame Zavarelli said again. She was on a roll. She had noticed Jim's very slight limp as he entered the tent, spotted his Rolex and diamond ring. He was clearly wealthy. She had taken a punt on the man's partner being older based on the guy's old-fashioned name. Three out of three. 'You are concerned about Alfred's health.'

'Erm . . .' Jim hesitated wondering if he was going to be admonished again. 'He has been unwell, tired . . . But?'

'You must not worry, Jim. I think Alfred's health will soon improve. You both need a holiday.' And she smiled at him. 'Now, let me consult the ball. Place your hands flat on the table and pull your chair close. That's it, good.'

Madame Zavarelli leaned in towards the crystal sphere, her eyes narrowing to slits. This was the part of the 'perfor-mance' she enjoyed the most. She could let her imagina-tion run free, make up wonderful scenarios, weave a web of intrigue and mystery that must always be fun, always positive. The last thing anyone wanted was to leave her tent under a black cloud. Sometimes she really did see things in the crystal, images conjured up from the depths of her memory and her subconscious, images she could twist and distort to offer the punter a lively tale.

'The mists are beginning to clear,' she said, her voice ascending half an octave as she spoke. 'Yes, yes. Goodness, yes, colours. Orange.'

'Is that good?'

'Yes, that is good. A fish. Many brightly coloured fish.'

'You said I needed a holiday,' Jim quipped.

Madame Zavarelli ignored him. She felt odd suddenly. What was wrong? She was feeling strangely nervous. There was a tingling in the pit of her stomach. It rose up and rippled towards the base of her skull. Something was taking shape in the crystal, but she could not make it out. She could feel it, feel its darkness, its dull weight. She tried to look away, to break this weird connection, but she was held there, gripped by an invisible force.

The blackness swirled and then she saw something unspeakable, indescribable . . . and froze. With a huge effort, Madame Zavarelli broke free and pushed herself back in the chair.

'What's wrong?' Jim exclaimed.

'Noth . . . nothing,' the woman stuttered. She ran a hand across her forehead, it came up wet. She took a deep breath and brought herself under control. Forcing a thin smile, she said, 'I'm sorry, young man. I feel a little sick. A headache, it's nothing. Now, where was I?'

Jim felt his momentary panic pass. Poor woman. She just had a cold or something, he told himself. 'Fish,' he said.

'Ah yes.' Looking back into the crystal ball, there was

nothing to see but clear glass. 'A holiday,' Madame Zavarelli said breezily.

Five minutes later, the old woman had ushered Jim Kemple out of her tent and made her farewells. Then she threw herself onto her sofa, trying desperately to stop shaking and to force out of her mind the terrible thing she had seen in the crystal. 'That poor young man,' she said aloud. 'That poor young man.'

Jim Kemple had tried to put the whole thing out of his mind, but the more he thought about Madame Zavarelli, the more he worried about the way the old woman had behaved. At first, he had wanted to take her comments at face value. All was well, and she had merely felt suddenly sick. But maybe there was more to it than that? After all, she had been right about his knee, *and* about Alfred. Maybe she was for real. Maybe she really had seen something – something terrible.

Walking along the path that led to Eighth Avenue, he almost turned back. He stopped on the gravel. Two cyclists passed him. He looked back towards the circus, now lost behind a line of trees, then carried on towards the road, forcing away unwelcome thoughts. He brought his partner Alfred to mind. Then he made himself think about work, and all the things he had to do today. Jim had one of the finest collections of occult books in Manhattan. At 35, he was the most respected arcane book dealer on the East Coast. The little shop he had set up with Alfred in the East Village was a Mecca for anyone interested in any alt-culture subject, from trepanning to alien abduction. Jim's particular obsession was Atlantis, and the concept of advanced civilisations existing before the dawn of recorded history. He had collected over 200 books on the subject including some very rare and very valuable ancient screeds. His most treasured possession was an early copy of Plato's dialogues *Timaeus and Critias*, originally written during the 4th century BC, in which the Greek philosopher made the first known reference to the mythical land of Atlantis.

It was all a long way from the days, almost 20 years earlier, when he had moved to New York. Stepping off the Greyhound from Avon, Illinois (population 915), he had arrived in the Big Apple for the first time as an impressionable 18-year-old literature student. Although he had quickly fallen in love with his adopted city, the Mid-West boy remained buried below many layers of sophistication and education. He had hated Avon, not least for its homophobia. But for all the romance of his first five years in the city – the parties, the clubs, an endless stream of guys – he considered that life had really only begun when he first met Alfred. They had clicked instantly and had remained inseparable.

Back at the apartment on West Sixty-fifth, Jim turned the key in the lock and opened the front door. It was quiet in the apartment. Prada, the cat, brushed himself against Jim's calves and he crouched down to stroke him.

Alfred was sitting, sound asleep, in front of the TV. Jim crept towards him, looking down at his partner's soft features. 'You're suddenly an old man,' he thought to himself. Despite the age difference, Alfred had always been a catch. Virile. Fit. 'What has happened to you, Alfred? What's wrong?' he thought.

Alfred stirred suddenly. He opened his eyes, and for a moment he seemed to be in a different world, then he smiled. Jim flicked off the TV and sat in the chair next to his partner.

'Hey, Jim,' Alfred said, now fully awake and his face alight with excitement. 'You won't believe what arrived in the post.'

Jim pulled off his coat, placed it over the chair and sat back down. 'Must be exciting,' he said. 'I haven't seen you this happy in ages.'

'Just look,' Alfred said and handed Jim an envelope. 'Isn't that fantastic?'

Jim said nothing for a moment. He read the note through again, hardly believing his eyes. It was an invitation. It said: 'You are invited to attend the star-studded Grand Opening of The Neptune Hotel, Fiji.'

'That's in eight days time,' Jim said, his excitement matching his partner's. 'Wow! But how come?'

'I didn't tell you. It was a shareholder's lottery. I put us in for it months ago. Forgot all about it. And we only have a few hundred shares. Can you believe that?'

'Amazing,' Jim said. 'We need a holiday.'

5

Hollywood, the same day

Danny Preston sat in his agent's office and waited for the secretary to place the cup of peppermint tea he had requested on the desk. The secretary smiled politely and crossed the vast expanse of carpet that stretched from desk to door.

Danny felt jumpy this morning, but he couldn't quite put a finger on why. At 71, he was still fit and still working. His skin was deeply tanned, almost as though it were a continuous brown tattoo covering him from hairline to toe tips. He had worn the same style of suit for 50 years, made by his favourite Savile Row tailor, and the waist measurement hadn't changed in 25 years. He had the same hairstyle he had when he was 35 and in his heyday. It was coloured fortnightly now, at Rick's on Rodeo Drive, but that was a mere detail. His personal trainer, Stanley, had assured him only this morning that he would live to be at least a hundred.

Sure, he had sacrificed much to reach the peaks he had scaled. His three marriages had followed roughly the same arc – infatuation, then a brief stability, followed by rapid disintegration. Three of his four children had claimed publically that they hardly knew him, and Tabitha, his favourite, had died of breast cancer at 29, only five years ago. But it was none of these things that troubled him today. He still had self-assurance in bucket loads. He had once been the highest paid, most successful actor in Hollywood. He could no longer command big bucks and he had not had a lead in a movie for over a decade, but that didn't matter a jot. He knew he was the best, knew he was one of the immortals. He was idolised by generations who had seen him evolve through bit parts to three Oscar nominations, and then on to the lofty heights of celluloid elder statesman. He was happy with that. Most importantly though, he was on the cusp of a career renaissance. Only a week before, he had agreed to work with Sigmund Dunning, the hotshot British director behind Dreamworks' new half billion dollar epic, *The Old Testament,* for which Danny had been offered the plum role of Moses. So what the hell was eating him up?

'What you got for me then, Charlie? You look like your fucking house just burned down.'

Charlie Hudson, self-styled 'über-agent', looked uncharacteristically grave. Danny Preston felt his stomach knot and realised what had been disturbing him. In the twelve years he had worked with Charlie, Danny had never once been asked to come into the office on Wilshire at an hour's notice.

'I would've come over to you,' Charlie Hudson said, his voice the free-rolling and languid Californian that Danny had always hated. 'But it's already turning into a bastard of a day.'

Danny said nothing and waited. Part of him knew what was coming.

'Okay, I'll cut to the chase, Danny. Dreamworks have pulled Dunning.'

The two men stared at each other, expressionless, across the table. Finally, Hudson said, 'They're replacing him with Simon Blackburn.'

'Oh fuck.'

'Yep.'

'Well that's that then. That bastard queer hates me.'

Hudson was nodding, letting Danny have the floor.

'This is a disaster, Charlie, a disaster.'

More nodding. 'I know,' Hudson managed.

Danny Preston looked away through the 10 metre high windows, out to blue sky, chrome and concrete. *This never happened in my day,* he thought to himself. *Never. No one would have dared dump the real directors, the men who had made Hollywood what it was. Who would have had the nerve to squash John Huston or David Lean like a beetle? No one. Now, some little shit in a Dolce and Gabbana suit could command ridiculous budgets and believe they were Eisenstein.*

'So what you going to do about it, Charlie?'

'Danny, my hands are tied.' The agent put his wrists together on the desk to emphasise the point.

'Oh, don't give me that crap.'

'Dreamworks have offered a generous compensation package.'

Danny Preston was shaking his head. 'The money is irrelevant, Charlie. You know that.'

'I know, I know.' Hudson had his hands up now. He pushed his chair back, folded his arms and looked out to the view Danny had been gazing upon a few moments earlier. A commercial jet swung behind a tower block and started dipping sharply towards LAX, glinting as it caught the morning sun.

'Do you want me to call Blackburn? Sound the guy out?'

Danny waved a hand dismissively at his agent. 'No, I don't Charlie. God, I would have thought you had more pride than that.'

The agent bridled. 'I was thinking of you.'

'Yeah, I know. Apologies. I'm just so damn angry. Is there anything we can do to get Blackburn out of the deal? Okay, we probably couldn't get Dunning back in, but . . . stupid bastard must've really pissed someone off. Is there *anyone* else?'

Charlie Hudson was shaking his head. 'Don't you think I thought of that, Danny? I heard first thing this morning and I've been on the phone ever since.'

Hudson could hear the older man's breathing. Beneath the surface, he was quietly pleased with the morning's news. He had every respect for Danny – they went back a long way, the actor had been best pals with his father, Jack Hudson, who had founded the agency. But he could not let sentimentality cloud the fact that he knew Danny Preston was way over the hill. So far over the hill, he was outta sight. The man had once been a fine actor, but those days had gone and Hudson had been secretly worried that Danny would be fired from the job or turn in a horrible performance and embarrass himself. This way was better, cleaner, and the old boy would never know how his agent felt.

'So, what do we do now?' Danny asked and fixed the agent with tired eyes. 'Please tell me there's something else. Some good news would go down very nicely right now.'

'Well actually,' Hudson said, his face brightening. 'One thing has just come up. It's a bit wacky, but . . .'

6

02 Arena, London, the same day

Wearing a flowing silk top over black satin pants, and thigh-high boots with 10-centimetre heels, Kristy Sunshine stood still, arms in the air, as a lemon spotlight swept jagged patterns across the huge video screens dominating the back of the stage. Twenty thousand voices screamed in unison, the sound deafening. Waving to the adoring ocean of humanity, her band bowed and trooped off, stage left.

'Thank you, London. I love you!' the girl shouted, and waved one last time. Then she was gone.

'Kristy, honey, that was . . . man, I'm lost for words!' Kristy Sunshine's manager Brett Littleton, towel held out for his protégé, made to hug her but saw the expression on her face and thought better of it.

Ignoring him completely, she snatched the towel and whirled on her lighting tech, Jenny Svetzel, standing to Littleton's left. The singer's face was like thunder. 'What the hell were you doing in the last number?' she screamed. Two of the band standing close by melted into the shadows, and the hangers-on milling around Kristy fell silent. Out in the auditorium, the crowd was still braying for more.

Jenny Svetzel was nonplussed. 'What?'

'You had the yellow beam on me, not the blue, you retard!'

'Kris . . .' Littleton began.

'Shut the fuck up, Brett,' Kristy Sunshine yelled. Turning back to the hapless lighting tech, the pop star bellowed, 'That's the last time I put up with that shit! You're fired. Get out of my sight or I'll call security.'

Jenny Svetzel turned pale and stepped back as Kristy charged past, almost knocking the woman off her feet.

'And get me a decent towel,' she hissed, flinging the 200-dollar piece of Egyptian cotton to the floor.

No one approached Kristy as she stomped away from the backstage area towards a long corridor leading to her dressing room. Some of her entourage knew her better than others. They knew this behaviour was nothing unusual immediately after a show – that the adrenalin of the gig couldn't be drained away straight off, that Kristy was a ball of energy when the lights went up and she had to decompress. But even her most loyal friends knew the singer was also a spoilt brat with an over-inflated sense of her own worth. Fame and fortune had come easily to Kristy, and she was far too young to deal with it. She had very quickly come to believe she could do no wrong, that everyone around her belonged to an inferior class of human being. She had yes-men catering to her every whim. All she had to do was keep singing and keep looking pretty. There was only one person to whom she deferred. Only one person who could tell her what to do.

Reaching the door to her suite of dressing rooms, Kristy began to calm down. She took deep breaths, letting the tension flow out of her as her Pilates instructor had taught her. Inside, the room smelled of jasmine and her private spa had been prepared. Brett Littleton followed her into the room, closed the door and pointed to a coffee table. 'Everything's arranged, Kris.'

She silently perused the items on the table. A bottle of vintage Krug, a tray of handmade Belgian chocolates on a silver platter and three lines of the best Bolivian cocaine. Neither Kristy nor Littleton had noticed they had company until they heard a brief cough.

Kristy turned and saw her uncle, Freddy Tomenzano, sitting in a leather chair on the other side of the table. 'Nice show, Kristy,' he said, his voice like hot gravel.

She produced a vague smile. 'Thanks.'

'Brett? Could you leave us for a moment? I need to have a word with my niece.'

Brett shot Kristy a quick, questioning look. She nodded and he left.

'What is it, Freddy?'

The man looked at her, his face totally devoid of expression. He was a small man in a dark, sharply tailored suit, crisp white shirt and red tie. With slicked-back black hair and finely chiselled cheekbones, he looked like the CEO of a multinational or a financial minister from a small European state. He was, though, one of the most powerful men in the entertainment world, a feared agent and Svengali. He had made Kristy a global star. Other singers – the likes of Bethany Shakespeare and Mary Casey – were snapping at her heels, but thanks to Freddy's business genius and ruthless scheming, Kristy was staying top of the pile. And, as much as Kristy hated to accept the fact, her uncle was the only person in the world who could pull her strings and make her dance.

'You seem a little defensive, my dear.'

'I've just come off stage.'

Freddy nodded sagely. 'Yes, I apologise. I meant it when I said it was a nice show.'

'Thanks again. But what do you want, uncle?'

'Okay, you obviously have pressing matters to attend to,' he said, eyeing the goodies laid out on the table with a contemptuous half-smile. 'I'll come straight to the point . . . the Neptune gig.'

'The what?'

'The opening of the Neptune Hotel? Remember? You weren't keen. We agreed to disagree and you said you would give it some thought. I said, you have a week, honey. The week is up.'

Kristy threw herself into a chair and let out a weary sigh. 'You're not going to let this one go, are you, uncle?'

'Er, no,' Freddy replied sarcastically.

Kristy was silent for a moment, staring at the ceiling, her jaw clenched. 'I told you I don't want to do it. It sounds creepy.'

'They're offering a million dollars for three songs, Kristy.'

'So?' She could sense him looking at her. She hated his icy stare, but somehow she found the will to ignore him.

'It's not so much the money. It's going to be a big media event. Don't you get that?'

'I get it. I just don't want to do it.'

'Why?'

'I told you. It sounds creepy.'

He was staring at her again and this time she couldn't fight it. She turned away from the ceiling and met his gaze.

'I have the contracts in my bag,' Freddy persisted.

'When is the gig?'

'Next Wednesday. You really weren't paying attention, were you, Kristy?'

She let her gaze fall on the items spread out on the table and started to feel angry. She resented this. She had just performed in front of 20,000 people, and put on a fabulous show. She deserved her rewards. For a second, she considered simply giving in to her uncle, doing whatever he asked to get him out of the place. Then she could have some fun. Wasn't that what she had always done? But then a new voice butted in, a voice of defiance. She stood up. 'I need more time,' she said.

'Not possible,' Freddy said quietly. 'I've promised the promoters I would have an answer for them tonight.'

'In that case I'm saying no.'

Freddie held her with his intense, dark eyes. They sent chills down her spine. She had heard all the stories, of course. About how Freddy had killed at least one man, about his Mafia connections, and the sort of people he employed to ensure he got his way. Her own father, Vincent, Freddy's brother, had been terrified of him. Vincent had not wanted his only daughter to go into the entertainment business, but then he had gotten himself killed in a motorcycling accident on the Ventura Freeway. By that time, Kristy had developed an untameable desire for fame. She had won singing competitions and had begun to get noticed, and Freddy had become involved. After that, she had never looked back.

'I'm not doing it,' Kristy added, surprising herself.

Freddy stood up. He was at least 8 centimetres shorter than his niece. 'Very well,' he said. Bending down, he picked up a metal attaché case and turned towards the door. Kristy stood rigid, watching him silently, barely able to believe she was going to get her way.

Freddy stopped at the door, his tiny hand gripping the handle. Without turning, he said, 'I'll contact the promoters right away, my dear. They've let slip they have a backup. Apparently, Bethany Shakespeare is *very* keen to do it.'

7

Base One, Tintara Island, the same day

'Rewind to 15.16 please, Sybil,' Pete Sherringham said to the air. Sybil was the base computer, the world's only quantum processor. It, or 'she' as the team liked to think of Sybil, was the nexus of a vast network that kept all the systems running smoothly at Base One, the command centre of E-Force.

'Ready,' Sybil replied.

'Play.'

Pete sat back in the leather chair in his quarters and watched the holoscreen on his laptop. With amazing clarity it showed the three-dimensional images he had seen at least 20 times before: a Silverback, the dark blue hull of *George*, six weeks earlier. The plane was swooping low over a burned-out shell of a building when suddenly the starboard wing was hit by something. The engine exploded and the aircraft nosedived. Then he saw himself, a tiny figure in a cybersuit, rocketing away from the cockpit in an ejector seat. But he was too low. The chair plummeted and the chute opened no more than 10 metres above the ground.

Then the image changed to a different film sequence shot from a cybersuit helmet. The camera stabiliser technology worked well, but the person filming was running over rough terrain and the image wobbled slightly before the screen was filled with a man lying twisted on the floor. One severed leg dangled from a thread of suit fabric, the other was twisted and shattered under his body.

'Stop, Sybil.'

The screen flicked off and Pete suddenly felt the stillness of the room, the silence broken only by his own steady breathing. The doctors had offered him antidepressants, and Stephanie Jacobs, the team's medical expert, had talked to him about the psychological impact of what had happened. But he had decided against taking the drugs. Right now though, he wondered if this had been a wise decision. Instead, he seemed to have developed an obsession with watching the accident over and over again. A part of him kept insisting that the more he saw it happen, the better he could assimilate the reality of it.

The same thoughts kept going around inside his head. How on earth had he ended up in this position? A year ago he had put the action-hero life behind him. He had served his time in the British Army, given it eight years of his youth. He had faced death many times as a bomb disposal expert and had come through the first E-Force mission seven months earlier after surviving a powerful explosion that no one would have thought it possible to walk away from. Now, here he was, six weeks after another near-death experience.

Using the most advanced surgical techniques on the planet, his body had been repaired. When they found him – unconscious, thankfully – he was as close to death as it was possible to be and still survive. Both his legs had been so badly damaged nothing other than E-Force technology could have saved them. As well, one arm had fractured in six places, he had a punctured lung, a skewered spleen and his heart had stopped. But somehow, the team's medics had kept him alive and he had been placed in an induced coma for two weeks. In that time, he had undergone 15 separate operations. All of those had been conducted by nanobots supervised by a medical group led by Stephanie Jacobs. The bots had repaired his internal organs and some of his bones. Tissue had been cloned from his own cells and blood vessels, and severed nerves had been knitted together by billions of bacteria-sized nanobots all working in unison.

Following the surgery, he had gone through three weeks of intense physiotherapy while he adjusted to his new body. He had hated every minute of it. The therapy was repetitive, painful and boring, but Mark, Tom, Josh, Mai and Steph had been incredibly supportive. The lowest point had come when he had been forced to quell his natural impatience a week into physio. The team had been called out to avert a potential disaster when part of a subway in New York had caved in. Seeing the team live on the big screen in Cyber Control had given him a perspective he had never experienced before. Beside his chair were his crutches. He glanced over at Tom Erickson, the 20-year-old cyber genius confined to a wheelchair since childhood. Tom was at a nearby console, lost in concentration as he relayed detailed data to the Big Mac hovering over the East River. Tom had turned, seen Pete staring, and given him the thumbs up.

It had made him feel terrible, adding to his depression. After a catastrophic accident, he was on the mend. He would soon be back in action, but a similar medical miracle was still a long way off for young Tom. He had talked about it with Steph – it was one of the first things to occur to him when she had explained what they had achieved in surgery. Sure, they could clone new tissue for Tom and they could reroute some of his nerves, but his spinal cord had been severed in the childhood accident that had led him being wheelchair bound and which had rendered his lower body useless. Even for the techno wizards at CARPA, fixing snapped spines was still some way in the future.

The buzzer to Pete's quarters sounded and he heard a voice on the intercom.

'Hey, Pete, my man!' It was Tom.

'Let him in please, Sybil.'

The door slid open and Tom wheeled in, seated in his motorised wheelchair. Walking beside him was Josh Thompson, the team's tall, dark-haired encryption expert.

'How you feeling?'

'Fit as the proverbial fiddle,' Pete replied, a trace of his Geordie accent just discernible in his voice. He stood up and did a little dance. 'See.'

'Promise me you'll never dance like that again, Pete,' Josh deadpanned.

'So, you two here for a reason?' Pete said, tilting his head slightly.

'Tom wanted to show off.'

'It's not showing off. It's passing on information,' Tom retorted. 'I've got the CyberLink to work.'

'You have? That's excellent.'

'Thank you, thank you,' Tom replied, nodding and twirling his hands in the air as though accepting applause.

'What was it again?' Pete asked.

'Oh, for God's sake, dude.' Tom sighed heavily. 'I've been working on it for three months. It's pure genius.'

'Is this the gizmo that allows you to hook up with any computer and get inside it as though it were a real object?'

'Super-hacking, dude. It's called super-hacking. It's . . .'

'Even I know more about it than that,' Josh interrupted, frowning at Pete.

'All right, all right. So, it's worked, yeah?'

'Yes, it has worked, my friend. I just had a quick stroll around the Pentagon's mainframe. So cool.'

'When you say stroll . . .'

'Look, it's like this. Every computer in the world has a virtual counterpart, or cyber twin, if you like. Think about it. On the web there's every piece of information about any computer. The manufacturer has its design spec, the very components that went into making it, and their serial numbers are all online. We can find its IP address in a flash. We know who operates any given computer, where it is in the "real" world. And naturally, every piece of software running on it and every piece of hardware attached to it.'

'Yeah, but that's a lot of information. Most of it irrelevant . . .'

'No, nothing is irrelevant. Every jot of knowledge about a computer helps build the cyber twin.'

'And Sybil does that?'

'Of course. It would be impossible without a quantum computer.'

'And a genius like you, Tom.'

'Yes, well that goes without saying.' Tom grinned.

'So, you hacked into the Pentagon?'

'Super-hacked, Pete. Learn the term, dude. There's a big difference. No more machine code, no more finding passwords or breaking through firewalls. I just walked in, had a little nose around, got what I was after and left. Not a trace of a cyber footprint. No one knew I was ever there.'

'Actually, that is pretty impressive,' Pete admitted, looking at the young computer whiz with genuine admiration.

'Yeah, and it would be even more impressive if it came with a little humility,' Josh said and sat down.

'I don't believe in humility,' Tom replied.

'Obviously.'

'What you got there?' Pete asked noticing a rolled up magazine in Josh's hand.

Josh handed it to him and he opened it out.

'Now that's what I call fame,' Tom said.

It was a copy of *Time*. On the front cover was a picture of the six members of E-Force. Tom was in his chair at the front, and the others, wearing their cybersuits, stood or crouched around him, each staring at the camera with serious expressions. Over the picture it said: 'MEET A NEW BREED OF HERO'.

'Well, isn't that something?' Pete said and held the magazine at arm's length.

The picture had been taken just before the mission to the stricken nuclear power station. The journalist had not been allowed on Tintara, but the team had convened at the Beverly Hilton in Los Angeles, not too far from the site of their first mission together when they had rescued Senator Kyle Foreman in the bombed-out shell of the California Conference Center. Immediately after that first mission it was decided that E-Force would not behave like caped crusaders and try to hide their identities. Indeed, it was already too late for that. Their hi-tech equipment was concealed from photographers or anyone with a camcorder thanks to Camoflin, a special paint used to scramble any image taken. But the members of E-Force had all been seen by the public, their pictures taken, their identities known.

Going public had been a major decision and it had repercussions. The original plan for the team was that they would each return to their normal lives after the initial three-month training period the year before. But they had quickly realised this would be impossible. For a start, they were needed far more often than they had originally believed. Hardly a week went by when they were not called out. And second, having their faces splashed all over the media immediately after the LA rescue mission meant that even if they had wanted to, they could hardly go back to their 'normal' daily lives.

One or two of the team had secretly wondered whether this had been E-Force founder Mark Harrison's intention all along. In the beginning, he had hand-picked the team based on their extraordinary abilities and adaptability, but he had also chosen people who were not in long-term relationships and whose lives or careers had stalled in some way. Each of them had been bitten by the E-Force bug, and none of them could have contemplated opting out.

'Do you think they've caught my best side?' Josh asked, pointing at the magazine.

'Do you have a best side?' The voice was Steph's. She had just come through the door and they all turned to watch her approach. 'Just came to remind you, Josh. We leave in ten minutes.'

'Leave?' Pete asked. 'Where you going?'

'The rolling hills of Semja Alexandry,' Josh said.

'Polar Base?'

'Yep. Ten-day training course.'

'Nice! Just the two of you?'

'Yeah! Wonderful, isn't it?' Steph said, rolling her eyes.

Tom laughed. 'Come on! It'll be cosy.'

Josh looked from Tom to Steph and back again. 'And I thought you two were my friends,' he said.

'I am,' Steph replied. 'But I'm not sure I will be after next week.'

8

Sydney, a week later

An alarm . . . fantastically loud and growing louder. It filled his head, crashing through his skull. He was wading through water, trying to reach the source of the sound, but he was being pulled back, dragged down. He was suffocating.

Harry Flanders broke through to consciousness, but it still took him a few moments to realise the bedside phone was ringing. He scrambled to reach it, missed and knocked a glass of water to the floor. Cursing, he pulled himself up as far as his screaming headache would allow and grasped the receiver. 'Flanders,' he croaked.

'Morning, Harry.' There was a slight delay – long distance.

For a second, Harry could not recognise the voice of his producer of eight years, Natasha Young, the woman who kept his BBC3 program, *The Buzz*, on track week after week back in London. Last night had been a doozy. He had stayed in the hotel bar until they kicked him out at 3 am. Even after that he had emptied half the minibar in his room. The last thing he could remember was sitting at the desk and composing yet another weepy letter to Jane. Jane, his ex-wife whom he could not stop loving, even though she had walked out on him a year ago and was now pregnant with another man's baby.

The neurons clicked into place and Harry Flanders began

to focus. He reached for his spectacles, glanced at the alarm clock and groaned into the receiver.

'Is it sunny there?' Natasha asked brightly.

Harry felt like screaming, but he managed to keep a lid on it.

'Gone nine there, right?' Natasha went on.

'Seven.'

'Oops.'

'What do you want, Nat? Please tell me it's big – another 9/11 or a Jacko.'

'You've heard about the Neptune Hotel, I take it?'

'What? Nat, I hardly know my own name right now.'

She explained. He let her talk.

'They've given us the exclusive, provided we give it a primetime slot on BBC1. So Robert Jenkins was en route,' she said. 'Collapsed in Jakarta. It's touch and go.'

'Shit!' Harry said, suddenly awake. 'I like Rob. What's wrong with him?'

'Not sure, looks like a heart attack.'

'Shit!' Harry repeated, pulling himself up and resting his back on the headboard. Robert Jenkins was the presenter of a high-profile BBC program, *The World at Large*.

'Yeah, so the Controller, no less, has passed the slot on to us.'

'But what about the election story?' Harry went to take a gulp of water and realised the glass had gone. He cursed again.

'What's up?'

'Nothing.'

'Look, Harry. The Neptune story has to take priority.'

Harry winced. He had been in Sydney for a week covering the federal election. He was a political journalist, not an editor-at-large, and between marathon sessions in one

Sydney bar or another, he had put a lot of work into the story. It was a snap election, a close-run race between two party leaders who hated each other's guts.

'But I've done the research for a 20 minute segment, Natasha. Tom and Andy arrived last night to start filming.'

'I'm sorry, you're the only one I can rely on. And Harry, this is a *major* story. Did you hear what I said just now . . . *an exclusive*. Forget the damn election.'

'But . . .'

'No buts, Harry. Christ. I wish I was there, it sounds fantastic. It's done nothing but rain here – British summer, right!'

Harry wasn't listening, just staring into space, barely taking in his surroundings. The room stank of booze and unwashed socks. Then he saw a glass on the other side of the bed. It contained a finger of brown liquid. Gripping the phone in his left hand he stretched over and pulled the glass to his mouth, downing the liquor in one.

'Harry?' The tinny sound of Natasha Young's voice came from the receiver. Harry stared at it and sighed. He could feel the wonderful burning sensation of whisky in the back of his throat, and remembered there was still a shelf of miniatures left in the little fridge under the TV.

'Harry?'

'Yeah?'

'Terry will meet you at 10 am. He mentioned a café, The Beach. Know it?'

'I'll find it.'

'Oh, and Harry? You can swim, can't you?'

9

Sydney, the same day

Harry sat at a waterfront table in the Beach Café at Circular Quay in the heart of Sydney. He was early for his meeting and was already onto his second black coffee, trying to blunt his hangover. From where he sat he could see the Opera House directly ahead, and to his left stretched the black expanse of the Harbour Bridge. It was a warm winter day, the air still. He could let his mind wander as he watched the crowds pass by, their backdrop a perfect blue. Growing bored, he flicked on his phone to get the latest from the BBC website.

The only story was the building tension between China and the US. In fact, it was all anyone seemed interested in right now; even here, in Sydney, a week before a general election. It was a scenario everyone had dreaded for decades, prompted by the spectre of Taiwan. The Chinese had perceived the American president as a soft touch and upped the ante by deploying a dozen warships anchored just outside Taiwanese waters. But the leader of the western world had shocked the old men in Beijing by ordering the Third Fleet into position for a short ballistic missile flight from mainland China. The Chinese had then started flying planes into Taiwanese airspace, trying to push them into launching a Patriot missile. When one was launched, and shot down a Chinese fighter, the world had held its collective breath. That had been 24 hours ago.

Since then, there had been nothing but an ominous silence hanging over Beijing, Washington and Taipei.

Harry had just finished reading the latest report when his producer Terry Mitcham arrived, a folder under his arm.

'So what's the story?' Harry asked, taking off his reading glasses and pulling on his shades as Terry tucked in his chair and placed the folder on the table.

'Here's everything I've managed to unearth,' he replied. Harry pulled the folder towards him, opened it and extracted a dozen sheets of A4.

Terry studied his colleague. Harry Flanders was wearing his perennial outfit – a shabby cream linen suit, white shirt with the top button undone, brightly-coloured tie loosely knotted, scuffed brown Doc Martin shoes, and three pens in his breast pocket. At his side was a well-worn brown leather satchel with one clasp broken. This morning he was unshaven, his receding hair dishevelled. Even in shades, he appeared washed out. 'You look terrible, by the way,' Terry added and signalled to the waitress.

'Thanks.'

Terry ordered a large latte. 'The whole thing beggars belief,' he said as Harry read. 'Two brothers – the ambitious and hyper-intelligent Michael, now in his late forties, and his clearly dimmer, slightly younger sibling, Johnny Xavier. They shared a childhood fantasy of creating a hotel on the ocean floor. As kids, they grow up in an ordinary lower-middle-class family home in Hampshire, share a room and plaster the walls with pictures of submarines, sci-fi designs for underwater bases, and presumably they watch every episode of *Stringray* ever made. Michael becomes an incredibly successful business-man, the head of a global media corporation which he started as a student at Cambridge selling advertising time on his own radio station. He carries young Johnny along with him, and

46

by the time he's 35, Michael is a billionaire and decides to start living out the fantasy.'

'Reminds me of Richard Branson and his bloody space hotels.'

Mitcham laughed as the waitress placed his coffee on the table. Harry looked up and ordered a third black for himself.

'So, anyway. Ten years ago, Michael and Johnny form a company, bring in a raft of investors ranging from futurist nuts to some heavy players,' Terry went on. 'Branson included, I believe,' he added wryly. 'They decide to locate the hotel off Fiji and call in the best marine engineers, architects, designers and materials experts to help them draw up a feasibility plan. It takes even a Michael Xavier five years to get the financial backing, the permissions from the Fijian government, clearance from environmental agencies, the UN, you name it.'

'You have to admire the chap for his perseverance.'

'Too right. But then, the crazy bugger actually goes and builds the thing!'

Harry flicked through the contents of the folder. 'Not a lot here, is there, Terry?' he said.

'That's all I could get from Google and everything that's on file in London. Natasha faxed it over. The Xaviers have been as secretive as they could be. Understandable really. Part of the appeal is the wow factor when it's done.'

Harry nodded and scanned the pages. The first contained an artist's impression of the Neptune, labelled 'The World's First Ocean Floor Hotel'. It looked like three anthills placed in a line and connected by tubular passageways. The next page showed a schematic of the building along with a set of floor plans, all copied from originals in the offices of the International Forum for Oceanic Development (IFOD), a sub-subgroup of a UN department to which all parties interested in commercial exploitation of the world's oceans must apply. These plans had been lodged almost eight years ago. Under them were a few grainy clandestine photographs taken during construction of the hotel. The next three pages were a set of legal documents outlining the structure of the companies involved in the project and how they interacted. The last couple of pages contained potted biographies of the key players involved in the scheme. Harry sped through the biogs and flicked through half a dozen short articles about the brothers from popular magazines including *GQ, Harpers* and *Newsweek*.

'So there's no hint of anything dodgy about the project?' Harry asked.

'None at all, by the look of it. Sorry!'

Harry smirked. 'So, we have to fall back on the sheer wonder of the project and the engineering miracle of it all?'

'Spoken like a true political journalist.'

Harry sighed. 'Must say, it's really not my cup of tea.'

'No?'

'To be honest, the whole thing pisses me off. I'm supposed to be here for the election. I've done a whole shitload of work on it. As have you,' he added quickly, seeing Terry's expression. 'But no, I'm sent to some fucking fantasy hotel on the ocean bed. I'm a *political* journalist, for Christ's sake. If London doesn't consider the Australian election worthy of its time, I should at least be given a crack at Beijing right now. That's where the real action is.'

Terry gave him a sympathetic glance and took a sip of coffee. 'Maybe you should think yourself lucky, old boy. A night in a luxury hotel, a night that may turn into a media sensation.'

Harry shook his head dismissively.

'Oh come on, Harry. Where's your sense of adventure?'

Harry gazed around the sun-dappled harbour, squinting behind his sunglasses. 'That, my friend, was lost a long time ago in a bottle of bourbon. Which reminds me . . .'

10

Nadi Airport, Fiji, the next day

Michael Xavier met the two TV journalists at the main doors to the airport. He was all smiles and exuded a relaxed air, belying the fact that he was in charge of a five-billion-euro project just about to be unveiled to the public. But then, he was well practised in putting on a brave face – it came with the job. He had been the one to dream up the Neptune, the world's first deep ocean hotel, a pleasure palace to accommodate 100 guests, each paying up to 50,000 dollars a night for the best suites. The project was a monumental undertaking that used cutting-edge technology and employed brand new materials and construction techniques. And, as chief executive of the corporation undertaking the job, he was responsible for the billions invested in the scheme.

Xavier strode forward to shake hands with the journalists. He was tall and gangly, with thinning black hair that had once been a luxuriant mop in the days when he played bass in a band at Cambridge. His big hand enveloped that of a middle-aged man in a crumpled linen suit. 'Michael Xavier,' he said.

'Harry Flanders,' the man in the suit replied. 'This is my producer, Terry Mitcham.'

'Delighted you could both make it. I was very sorry to hear about Robert Jenkins,' Xavier said. A Fijian chauffeur in a dark blue uniform approached, pushing a trolley. He started loading the visitors' bags. 'This way,' Xavier added. 'The car is just outside.'

A few minutes later, the limo pulled onto the main highway leading from the airport to the capital city, Suva. It was raining hard, drenching the lush tropical forest that lined the highway left and right. The sky was heavy with dark grey, low cloud.

'This is supposed to be our drier season,' Michael Xavier commented wryly. 'But of course none of that matters a bit where we're going!' He handed a brown plastic folder to each of the visitors. In the back of the limo, the three men were seated in oversized leather seats. Each of the guests had a drink on walnut side tables attached to their chairs. For Harry, this was a godsend – he hadn't had anything alcoholic for almost an hour.

'You've both signed the contract agreeing to the press embargo, so I'm happy to let you see these now. They contain the basic facts behind the Neptune. Let me talk you through them.

'The Neptune is the world's first true sub-aquatic hotel. It's been built at a depth of 100 metres, 12 kilometres off the coast on the edge of the continental shelf, in what is known as the neritic zone. Half a kilometre beyond the Neptune, the ocean floor starts to drop away almost a thousand metres. The reason this location was chosen is because 97 per cent of marine life lives in the neritic zone, and the variety of this life off Fiji is particularly remarkable.

'If you turn to the schematic, gentlemen. On page seven, you'll find the layout and stats for the hotel. The Neptune is a complex of interconnected domes made from super-strong micro-alloyed glass. There are three main domes: Alpha, Beta and Gamma. Each is 60 metres high and 50 metres in diameter. Each dome is topped with a thick

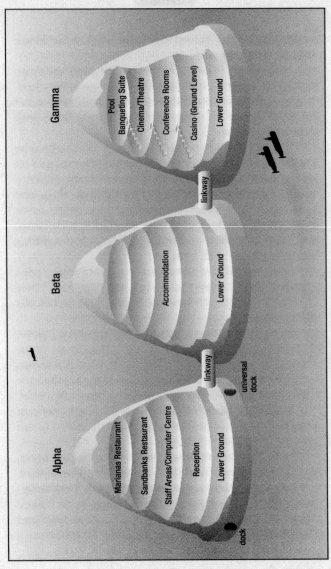

Alpha

Marianas Restaurant
Sandbanks Restaurant
Staff Areas/Computer Centre
Reception
Lower Ground

dock
universal dock
linkway

Beta

Accommodation
Lower Ground

linkway

Gamma

Pool
Banqueting Suite
Cinema/Theatre
Conference Rooms
Casino (Ground Level)
Lower Ground

The Neptune Hotel

metal cap. Alpha contains the main docking area and air locks for receiving the submarines that transport guests from the surface. Above this is the reception area, and on the top level is a restaurant with a wraparound view of the ocean. Beta consists of three floors of luxury rooms on the periphery of the dome, each with a view to the ocean. At the top of the dome is the Presidential Suite, more fish bowl than hotel room, actually. Dome Gamma also has four floors. On the first level is an enormous casino. On the second floor we have a conference suite. Above that is a 100-seater theatre, a cinema and two restaurants.' He glanced quickly at his guests. 'And on the top floor, there's an incredible pool and more restaurants. The administration centre and the power station and communications hubs are housed in separate, smaller domes linked to the main hotel complex. You can see them on the edge of the diagram. Any questions?'

'This is amazing,' Harry said, genuinely impressed. 'They sent some stuff over from London, but you've been understandably circumspect about what you've let out. I never dreamed it would be on this scale.'

'Thank you,' Xavier replied, clearly delighted. 'And, yes, we've had to be very careful. We want to make a big splash. If you'll excuse the terrible pun.'

'What about safety mechanisms?' Terry asked. 'Is it completely self-contained?'

'No, that would be too risky. The hotel has a double redundant backup system for power, oxygen and communications. But on top of this, it is linked to the mainland by a submarine cable for emergency power and communications.'

'So what's the budget for this?'

Michael Xavier took a deep breath. 'Five billion euros.'

Harry whistled. 'Christ! And how was that raised?' He knew the basics from the rather scant file Terry had compiled, but wanted more, and from the horse's mouth.

'A consortium called BHL – Bathoscope Holdings Limited – owns the project. There are 600 shareholders – some very big players, but quite a few small investors. The complex was designed by Felix Hoffman, a true genius. It's been almost 10 years in planning.'

'How on earth do you get to it?' Terry asked.

'Well,' Xavier replied, 'you're about to find out.' As he spoke, the car slowed and they could all see through the windows that the rain had cleared to reveal the ocean 70 metres below the road. Hugging the beach was a line of elegant steel and glass buildings. A huge sign over the main doors said: 'SUVA SUBAQUATIC PORT'. In the water just beyond the buildings lay the long, narrow shape of a submarine. Some 30 metres in length, it was low in the water and glinted in the weak sunlight. 'Gentlemen, the *Cousteau*,' Xavier said proudly, as the car swung onto the steep road leading down to the water. 'Your subaquatic taxi.'

11

Fiji

'I wish I'd told him I suffer from claustrophobia,' Harry announced.

'What!' Terry Mitcham exclaimed as they strapped themselves into the seats.

'Lighten up, Terry. I'm kidding!' Harry said, rolling his eyes.

It was surprisingly quiet inside the *Cousteau*. They could just hear a slight lowering in the note of the engine as the submarine dipped beneath the surface. They had been left in the main passenger compartment which could hold 20, in five rows of four, while Michael Xavier joined the captain on the bridge at the front of the vessel. There were no portholes, but the two journalists could view outside the craft on seatback screens. As the submarine descended, the murkiness clouding the external cameras began to clear and the gorgeous vista of the Fijian coastal seabed and crystal clear waters of the Pacific Ocean came into view. 'Certainly beats the London Aquarium,' Terry Mitcham said.

Five minutes later, the submarine reached cruising depth and levelled out. A hostess in a red uniform came round with drinks and canapés. The voice of the captain announced that they would be arriving at the Neptune in 10 minutes.

As the submarine docked, the passengers felt a gentle nudge and heard a hiss as the locks were sealed. Michael

Xavier appeared from the bridge. 'Well, gentlemen, I hope you had a pleasant trip,' he said. 'We've docked. If you would come this way.'

The airlock of the *Cousteau* opened onto a narrow corridor surrounded by concertinaed reinforced rubber. It was brightly lit and carpeted. Emerging into the hotel proper, the two guests met a man who looked strikingly similar to Michael Xavier. He had his hand outstretched.

'My brother, Johnny,' Michael Xavier explained. 'Johnny is Head of Operations here. The man at the sharp end.'

'Pleased to meet you,' Johnny said and indicated they should follow him.

The group passed along a short passageway and saw ahead of them a bank of elevators. They ascended, the elevator drew to a halt and they stepped out into a wide corridor. Johnny Xavier led the way to the main reception, explaining how the place was constructed and going through some of the mind-boggling statistics associated with the project.

The two newcomers stopped, stunned, and looked around the huge space, mouths agape. It was truly awe-inspiring, a reception that would perfectly suit a major five-star hotel in any city. An expanse of white marble stretched from where they stood to the perimeter of the circular room. Several passageways led off the space, and directly ahead stood a wide opening that connected with the next dome, Dome Beta. Beside this was a curved reception desk made from exotic dark wood. The ceiling was four storeys above their heads, adding to the sense of vast open space. A square arrangement of four gigantic crystal-and-brushed-steel chandeliers hung from the ceiling, and in the centre of the room stood a massive sculpture of the god Neptune, rendered in steel. His muscular metal arms stretched upwards, catching the light from the suspended illuminations. But perhaps the most impressive feature of the place was the perimeter of the room. It was a circle of clear glass, 6 metres high, opening onto the natural glory of the ocean beyond. The visitors were struck dumb.

'Good God!' Harry said simply.

'Pretty impressive, isn't it?' Johnny Xavier said. 'I still get tingles when I walk in here and I've been living with it for what seems like a lifetime. It all looks a bit sterile right now, but in under 24 hours it should be buzzing.'

'The Grand Opening.'

'Correct.'

'What's planned?'

'Should be quite an evening,' Johnny Xavier remarked. 'As journalists, you're very privileged to be coming,' he added with an air of self-importance. 'We've had to turn down several A-listers. But we should have enough celebrity glamour to please your cameras. Kristy Sunshine is performing and Danny Preston will be cutting the ribbon, so to speak.' He gave his guests a brief, rather patronising smile, and Harry suddenly got the distinct impression Johnny did not have much time for journalists. Or else the man felt insecure about something. Either way, Harry had taken an instant dislike to him. 'Danny Preston?' he said. 'I thought he was dead.'

Terry stifled a laugh.

'How many guests are expected?' Harry went on.

Johnny Xavier fixed the journalist with an unfriendly stare. 'Ninety-six,' he said crisply. 'A gala dinner, followed by the official opening. The guests will all be staying at the hotel of course. It marks the launch of a massive global media campaign, of which you are at the forefront, and we plan to be welcoming our first paying customers in two weeks.'

'Exciting.'

'Yes, it is.'

'All right, let's continue the tour,' Michael Xavier said, and led the way across the echoing marble floor. The visitors gazed around them, paying little heed to where they were going. They could see circular galleries on the floors above the huge girdle of glass.

'Above us, around the rim on the first floor, are staff areas, offices, computer control centres,' Michael Xavier said. 'Above that, on the second and third floors, are two of our four restaurants, Sandbanks and Marianas. If you come this way, the main corridor ahead leads into Dome Beta, the accommodation area.'

A huge spiral staircase dominated the centre of Dome Beta. It swept around in a swirl of marble and chrome. Looking up, Harry and Terry could see three circular balconies. Bridges stretched from the spiral staircase to the balconies on each of the floors. The top of the dome was capped with a steel hemisphere.

Through a pair of 8 metre high doors, the journalists were led into Dome Gamma. 'This is the recreation dome,' Michael Xavier explained. 'The top floor is a huge pool area with a ballroom and a restaurant leading off of it. The whole area can be opened up as a single, free-flowing entertainment zone. On the second floor is the cinema and a theatre, on the first are a set of conference rooms and here on ground level we have the casino. The floors are connected by these escalators.' He pointed to a bank of three oversized moving staircases. 'There's also a bank of elevators over here.' He led the others to the east wall. 'Let's start at the top.'

The elevator took just a few seconds to ascend from ground to the top floor of the dome where it opened directly onto a vast open space. The pool ran the circumference of the massive room, and it was easy to imagine that swimming in it would at first be a disorientating experience. The walls were glass, offering a view onto the ocean over 50 metres below the surface. Swimming in the pool would feel like you were bathing with the fishes. In the centre of the room were the dining areas and the ballroom, all open-planned, ready for the big event.

'It's spectacular,' Terry Mitcham declared.

Taking the escalators down to the second floor gave the men a true sense of the scale of the place as the glass roof slipped away behind them. Stepping off the escalator they found themselves in a large rectangular space. Several sets of doors led off, left and right.

'To the right is the theatre,' Johnny Xavier said. 'It seats 100, and we have some major shows booked, including some acts that have just completed residencies in Vegas. To the left,' and he indicated a couple of opened doors, 'is the cinema. Here . . .'

A incredibly loud bang resonated throughout the dome, followed by a high-pitched whine. Harry Flanders dived to the floor, his hands over his head. Terry Mitcham froze in terror. Another tremendous bang hit them and a burst of lemon light shot from the opened doors to their left. Then silence.

Johnny Xavier bent down to help Harry to his feet. 'We are a little jumpy, aren't we, Mr Flanders?' he grinned. 'It's just the techs testing the cinema system!'

12

The Neptune Hotel, Presidential Suite, Dome Gamma: grand opening night

'You really should take a look at this, Kristy. It's amazing!'

Brett Littleton was standing, hands on hips, staring through the 3-metre-tall window girdling the room. He felt as though he was standing in the centre of a vast fish tank. The outside of the hotel was lit up by huge floodlights embedded in the ocean floor. A giant turtle swam past, gliding low over the soft coral that burst into random red and orange shapes close to the north-facing panel. A school of tiny, silver fish – there must have been a thousand of them – wove a path close to the window and then dashed away like the swish of a curtain. 'I've never seen anything like this,' he added.

'Yeah, yeah, blah, blah,' Kristy Sunshine retorted.

Littleton sighed and wandered over to the sofa, picked up a remote and pointed it at a screen on a wide column in the middle of the room. The TV burst into life. It was set to *Fox News*, and the first images were those of grey warships cutting through the ocean, followed by a close-up of a sailor in combat gear manning a gun station on the deck. An American jet, an F18F, swooped down, seemingly out of nowhere and drew to a dead stop on the deck of an aircraft carrier. Then the images changed to the inside of a vast government chamber in China. The grave face of a minister reading something aloud. Brett stabbed the remote and the sound came up.

'In Beijing, the Military Commission, the official security branch of the government, held a special meeting this morning . . .'

'Oh please! Turn the thing off, Brett.' Kristy stood up and snatched the remote from her manager's outstretched hand. 'That's the last thing I wanna hear right now.'

Brett Littleton glared at her, but he had learned long ago that when it came to Kristy, resistance was futile. It boiled down to a simple choice: keep quiet, or get fired. He kept quiet, sat down and stared at the blank screen.

Glancing over, he watched as she lowered herself to the thick cream carpet close to a coffee table. Snatching up a 100 dollar bill, she stuck one end up her nostril and ran the other end over the smooth varnished surface, hoovering up a line of white powder as she went. Placing a finger at each nostril in turn, she produced a brief indecorous snorting sound and wiped her nose with the back of her hand. Littleton watched the girl's movements and thought for maybe the thousandth time what a terrible life the poor kid had. Sure, she was worth, what? Fifty mill? But on the way to such riches she had lost more than she could ever have hoped to gain. She was completely controlled, a slave to the media, a slave to cocaine, a slave to fame and adulation. He had never felt so sorry for anyone in his life.

She caught Littleton staring. 'What's up, Brett? Still off the shit for a while?'

He nodded. 'I think it's best I stay level-headed, don't you?'

She shrugged. 'I hate this place. Gives me the creeps. Knew it would.'

'God, I think it's fabulous.'

'You would!'

He stood up and stared out at the panorama of the ocean again. He had never seen such diversity of life before, even in an aquarium. And this building . . . what a feat of engineering. It was a technological miracle, barely conceivable.

Kristy Sunshine ran a hand across her forehead. 'For God's sake. Can you pull the curtains. All that blue is giving me a headache. Not what I need, baby.'

'There are no curtains,' Littleton said, a touch more bite in his voice than he had intended.

'There are no curtains . . .' Kristy mimicked. 'There must be fucking curtains.'

Littleton had paced over to a panel close to the TV. 'The glass can be polarised to filter out the light,' he said. 'Look.' And he depressed a button on a control panel fixed to the wall. Slowly, the glass darkened. 'Weren't you paying any attention to Johnny or Michael when they escorted us up here, Kris?'

'Well duh! Obviously, that would be a "no".'

The singer pulled herself up from the coffee table and walked a little unsteadily towards a cabinet a few metres from where Littleton was standing. On top of the cabinet stood a small case containing more cocaine. She opened the lid and started to spoon some onto a tray as though it were sherbet.

'Kris, do you really . . . ?'

The girl whirled on her manager. She opened her mouth to speak just as the door buzzer sounded. Brett Littleton strode across the room. A young man with the face of a jaded angel, all cheekbones and black rings under his eyes, appeared at the edge of the door. He cleared his throat. 'One hour to stage call, Miss . . .'

'Thanks, Trent,' Littleton said and closed the door on the kid.

13

The Neptune Hotel, Room 307

Hilary Xavier sat in front of the TV in the family's suite in the magnificent edifice her husband Michael had built and let the effects of the vodka soak through her. She blew a strand of peroxide blonde hair away from her face and when it fell back, she pulled it behind her ear irritably. She felt fat, but then she always felt fat, even if her doctor kept telling her to put on weight. She knew she drank too much, but she made up for it by not eating. That was supposed to keep the weight off, or at least that's what she'd read. She was always tired these days, and she felt old, much older than her 36 years.

She could hear her nine-year-old twins, Emily and Nick, in the next room, playing with the Wii. She was no longer paying any attention to the TV show, a rerun of *Will and Grace*. Her mind had started to wander, and when it wandered it always alighted on the same subject – her miserable life.

'What the hell went wrong?' she said aloud to the room, her voice drowned out by the TV and the noise from next door. 'I was clever once. Yes, clever. A First at Oxford, no less. Plenty under the bonnet, people used to say. *And* I was beautiful. Brains and beauty, a rare thing, not just a Porsche without an engine. But now . . . now what? Here I am, mid thirties, a mother of twins, married to a billionaire. I have homes in London, New York, Santa Barbara and Monaco.

I've had a racehorse named after me, for Christ's sake. I had the Rolling Stones perform at my thirtieth. The diamond of my engagement ring is the size of Madagascar, and yet I'm so unhappy I contemplate suicide *every single day*. How does that happen?'

She refilled her glass.

Yes, she had every material thing anyone could ever wish for, and more, and she loved her kids. But her marriage? That lay in tatters. Michael was a good man. Everyone loved Michael, but he was a lousy husband. She said it aloud. 'Michael, you're a lousy husband.' That made her feel a little better. Once upon a time, they had been close, a great unit, a unit that had been fantastic for both of them. She had given him the stability he needed and she had been a damn good mother. 'I'm a damn good mother,' she announced to the TV. But this, this *place* had taken over. Michael had effectively divorced her and married the Neptune Hotel. 'Well, I hope it gives a good blow job,' she blurted into the glass and laughed loudly.

And then there was Johnny. Oh shit, Johnny. Why? Why had she done that? She suddenly felt an overwhelming wave of sadness hit her. She swallowed hard and gazed around the room. Her focus wasn't too good suddenly. A tear rolled down her cheek. She brushed it away with an angry swipe of her palm, smudging her makeup.

She refilled her glass.

All this was becoming so familiar. She drank to forget and then she had to put on a big act to make her kids believe she was sober. But sometimes, sometimes, she just wished she could really let go. 'But what would I do?' she asked the TV. 'Run away?' She started to giggle. 'Oh, yeah!'

She went to refill her glass and realised the bottle was empty. Flinging it to one side of the sofa, she stood up.

Reaching for another bottle on the cabinet, she slipped on a slice of lemon, started to crash forward into the array of bottles and just caught herself in time. At that moment, the door opened and Michael Xavier walked in.

'What're you doing?'

'What does it look like, Michael?'

Xavier sighed heavily and walked over to his wife. He went to put a hand on her shoulder. She flinched. He took a step back, looked at the floor and said, 'Did you have to? Tonight?'

'Tonight? Oh yes, it's your night of triumph, isn't it, my darling?'

Michael Xavier gave her an exasperated look that made her feel like a 10-year-old schoolgirl. It infuriated her. To cover her anger, she laughed, lost her balance again and gripped the edge of the cabinet to steady herself.

'For God's sake, Hilary. What about the . . . ?'

She glared at him. 'Don't dare say: "What about the kids?" You wouldn't be that big a hypocrite.'

He gave Hilary another pitying glance, and the dam burst. She stepped towards her husband and went to slap him across the face. Catching her hand before it made contact, Michael tried to guide her to the sofa, but she pulled away, seething, her eyes aflame. 'Don't!' she screamed. 'We don't need you here, Michael. Go off to help the crews, help the staff, do something, anything, except be with us. The kids hardly know you anyway.'

Michael stared at her, expressionless. 'This isn't the time . . .'

'No, no, of course it isn't, dear. Never is the time, is it?'

'Hilary, please.'

'Please? Please? You don't need to say please. Michael dear, you do what you want. You always do. You don't need me. You don't need us.' And she waved her hand towards the next room.

Michael Xavier exhaled again. He felt exhausted. He knew he had been ignoring his family. Especially Hilary. He knew he had gone too far – knew their 11-year marriage was over. There had been no conscious decision to sacrifice it. Perhaps some subconscious impulse had driven him to choose the Neptune over her. But he never really had a choice. The two, the hotel and Hilary, had been mutually incompatible. Always would be. 'I'm sorry,' he said, quietly.

Hilary turned away and refilled her glass.

14

The Neptune Hotel, Room 320

Johnny Xavier opened the file on his computer. In it were half a dozen emails from the past three months, all but one saying basically the same thing: 'Stop construction.' The last one, sent a week earlier, was slightly different. It read: 'Stop now. This is your last warning.'

He had told only one other person about the messages – his lawyer, Chuck Warberg. He certainly hadn't breathed a word about them to his brother. Chuck had, as always, advised caution. But, when it came to self-preservation and retaining power, Johnny was a very cautious man. Chuck had advised him to go to the cops, but to Johnny it was obvious this was the last thing he should do. He did not like the messages, but equally he could not hold up the project because of them. And so he had decided to say nothing.

The warnings had begun to appear as the hotel infrastructure was completed and crews were starting to fit out the interior. He had employed some tech guys to trace the emails, but they had drawn a total blank. It was then he had turned to Chuck, and been given the advice he did not need.

He called Chuck's mobile number. He was in London on business. It was early morning there, but he knew his lawyer would be working even if he was in his hotel room. He was always working.

'Chuck, I've just been going through those emails again.'

'For Christ's sake, Johnny. I'm shaving. Can I call you back?'

'No, I've only got a minute.'

Xavier could hear his lawyer produce a resigned sigh. 'I told you to go to the cops, didn't I?'

'That was not an option, Chuck.'

The lawyer said nothing for a moment, then produced a small cough. 'Johnny? Have you thought about ducking out of tonight?'

Xavier laughed. 'Chuck, for a smart guy, you can sometimes say the most fucked up things.'

'Okay.'

'By the way,' Johnny Xavier went on, '*you* are conspicuous by your absence here tonight. You're probably the only person to turn down the invitation.'

'I couldn't make it.'

'Whatever,' Johnny slurred. Years of living in California had polluted what had once been the crisp British private school accent his older sibling still retained. 'Anyway, as if I would duck out and let big brother take all the credit! So, what are you going to do about these messages?'

'What do you expect me to do?'

'Jesus,' Xavier hissed. 'Sometimes I wonder why I pay you.'

'Oh please. Don't give me that BS. You know why you pay me. Don't forget who's covering your arse, Johnny boy. Don't forget who's cleaning up the money for your little hedge fund. Don't forget who's keeping nosy parkers off your case.'

'So you're saying there's nothing you can do about these emails? Is that it?' Xavier snapped.

'Got it in . . . what? . . . Three.'

There was a pained silence from the other end of the line.

'You tried the tech guys?' Chuck Warberg offered.

'Yes. I tried the fucking tech guys. They were about as useless as you.'

'Okay, Johnny. Gotta lot of work to do. I'm not going to stand here and let you insult me.'

'Well go stick your bald head up your fucking arse then, you . . .' But the line was dead. Johnny slammed down the phone and looked up as the doorbell sounded.

'Yeah?' he called.

'It's me.'

Xavier sighed, pulled himself to his feet and strode to the door. Hilary pushed her way into the room and Johnny closed the door quickly.

'Hilary! We're supposed to be downstairs in 20 minutes. What the hell are you doing?'

She turned to him, swaying slightly.

'Oh fuck, you're . . .'

'Yes, Johnny. I'm drunk.' She flopped onto the sofa and buried her head in her hands. Johnny looked around the room using all his reserves of patience to control his anger and frustration.

'I just don't know how that man does it.'

'Which man?'

'Your damn brother. Who else?'

'What do you mean?'

'I can't help but love him, even though he ignores me, ignores the family, cares only for this,' and she waved her hand in air. 'This . . . place.'

Johnny looked down at her. She used to be a really beautiful woman, he thought. Sexy, intelligent. He suddenly felt a wave of revulsion.

Hilary gazed up at him, makeup smeared across her face, tear streaks staining her cheeks, her hair a mess. She stood up. 'God, I'm so fucked up,' she slurred and made for the drinks cabinet.

'I think you've had enough,' Johnny said and took Hilary's arm.

She turned. 'Oh, Johnny. You do care about me.'

Still the old acid tongue, even half-cut, Johnny thought to himself and smiled. Hilary fell into his arms and he held her, breathing in her perfume. In spite of himself, he started to harden. Hilary felt it too.

'Oh my,' she whispered in his ear and dropped backwards onto the sofa, pulling him on top of her.

15

Computer Centre, first floor, Dome Alpha

Ralph Gafton was alone in service conduit Number 6, running off the computer centre. His Puerto Rican boss, Miguel Bandonis, had sent him in to check on a set of relays the diagnostic systems had identified as malfunctioning. He suspected a short in one of the circuits. He unscrewed the panel and lay it on the floor of the conduit. It was a tight squeeze in the narrow passage and he had to twist his body round to get the torch into the opening so he could see what was up. He flicked the light around inside the wall unit, a box about 2 metres long and a metre wide. He could see nothing at first, but on the third sweep of the torch he caught sight of a small bundle of components covered in melted plastic. 'Yep,' he said aloud. 'That would be the blown relay.'

He started to pull his head and arm from the opening. There was a flash of light and a loud pop. He jolted back, banged his head on the rim of the wall unit and cursed. A sheet of flame flew across the space inside the box.

Gafton reacted quickly. He crawled along the conduit and tugged on the extinguisher attached to the wall, span around and headed back to the hole. Just as he pushed on the release button, a voice came through the radio attached to his shoulder. 'Ralph, you okay? Just got a warning light.' It was his boss, Bandonis.

'Yeah, everything's cool,' Gafton responded. 'There's a small fire. I'm putting it out.' And he shot foam into the box of electrical circuits with practised ease. He had been an electrical engineer for a dozen years, including a spell on North Sea oil rigs. He knew what he was doing.

'I'm coming down,' Bandonis said.

'No need,' Gafton replied, but the line was already cut.

Gafton let the foam settle, then stuck his arm and head back through the opening. He flicked the torch beam around the cavity and had just pulled away, slipping back into the conduit, when Bandonis appeared at his side. 'Let me see,' he said. Gafton sighed and crawled along the passage to give his boss space to check on the problem. Bandonis waved a torch around inside the unit, then pulled back and leaned against the conduit wall. 'Seems all right,' he said. 'It's the secondary relay for the emergency escape doors, right?'

'Yeah,' Gafton replied. 'The primary circuits are further back in the next conduit.' He nodded towards the wall. 'They're well protected with sensors around them.'

Bandonis paused for a moment, a stab of anxiety in the pit of his stomach. They would be well protected, he thought, if the sensors were reliable, but he couldn't be sure they were. Bandonis had been on the engineering crew from the start of the build. He knew every nook and cranny of this place. More importantly though, he knew enough about how much Johnny Xavier had been cutting back on materials and skimming the building budget to line his own pockets.

'Okay. We need to get a repair crew down here. And Ralph, don't make a fuss about this. I'll call Mr Xavier, but he's made it clear any problems stay with the systems staff, capiche?'

Bandonis crawled back along service conduit Number 6, leaving Gafton to replace the metal panel. He had no intention of phoning Xavier – he would go to see him in person. Drag him away from the table if necessary. He could do nothing about the man ripping off his brother and the other investors, but his own life and those of nearly 200 staff and guests would be on the line if this small incident got out of hand.

And that is exactly what was starting to happen – it was getting out of hand. A strip of printed circuits to the rear of the wall unit had remained untouched by the extinguisher foam. A wire from a transformer less than 2 centimetres away from this strip slipped from its plastic cradle. The wire touched the hot chip and a spark jumped 7 centimetres, igniting a tiny rectangle of paper on a metal case. The flame slithered through an opening in the back of the wall unit.

According to the original design of the hotel, a sensor system was designed to pick up any temperature rises inside electrical units. To save money, Johnny Xavier had cut two-thirds of the sensors. This meant each unit would have only one-third of the necessary sensors throughout the hotel or that two-thirds of the component units would be completely unprotected. Johnny had gone for the second of the two options.

Unfortunately, service conduit Number 6 contained electrical units that were unprotected. So, when the fire in the wall unit caught hold and started to eat away at the primary emergency door circuits themselves, no one knew about it until it was much too late.

16

Dome Gamma

Jim Kemple surveyed the scene and thought for perhaps the tenth time that he had never seen anything quite so awe-inspiring. Their table was close to the centre of the vast top floor of the dome. All around them, the ocean flowed. Jim couldn't comprehend how the dome could have been constructed even though before dinner he, Alfred and the other guests had listened politely as Michael Xavier explained how the project had come to fruition. Xavier mentioned something about a new material – micro-alloyed glass – that had been used to construct the domes. Apparently it had a thousand times the strength of normal tempered glass so that it could withstand the tremendous pressure at this depth.

The floor had been opened out. There was a stage at the north end encircled by a gantry of lights. At that moment, a contemporary dance troupe was performing a specially commissioned piece, and in a few moments Kristy Sunshine was due to walk on. Around the circumference of the banqueting hall ran the swimming pool, 6 metres wide, a ribbon of aquamarine that hugged the micro-alloyed glass dome. Eight large round tables had been arranged in the middle of the space, accommodating a dozen guests each.

Jim noted there was no head table, no hierarchy; celebrities and major shareholders intermingled with ordinary folk like him and Alfred. He scanned the table. Beside him sat a middle aged man in a rather scruffy dinner suit. He had introduced himself as Harry Flanders, a journalist who was making a TV report about the gala night. Next to him was a young couple from Boston. He was a computer whiz, his wife an anthropologist. Going round the table from them, Jim glanced at the Xavier children, the nine-year-old twins, Nick and Emily. Nick was wearing a dinner suit, white shirt and bow tie. His dark hair was slicked back. He looked like a miniature version of his father. Emily was a rather precocious little girl, Jim thought. But she did look pretty cute in her green silk ballgown. Next to Emily, her father was engaged in an animated conversation with the man to his left. Jim half-recognised him from the pages of the *New York Times* financial section. He was a banker, he recalled, someone important at Deutsche Bank. Next to the banker sat Hilary Xavier. She had arrived 10 minutes late. Jim thought she looked ill; her face was unnaturally gaunt as though she hadn't slept properly in a long time. Alfred sat to her left and had been trying hard to make conversation, without much success. On Alfred's other side was Johnny Xavier, dressed in an immaculate dinner suit. He was a good-looking man, Jim thought, but he had a hard face and an unpleasant air of self-absorption. He looked like a bad actor. Johnny, Jim decided, had secrets – nasty secrets.

Jim turned from Johnny Xavier to the person who sat between them, an elegant woman in her sixties. She had told him her name was Sheila Hoffman and that her husband, Felix, was the architect who designed the hotel. He had been involved in a car crash a week earlier and, as much as he would have loved to be here, his doctor had forbidden it.

'So, shouldn't you be out in front of the camera, Harry?' Jim asked, turning to the journalist on his left. The man, he noted, had single-handedly demolished two bottles of red over dinner.

'Later,' Harry replied, draining his glass and refilling it. 'My crew are busy though. See over there?' He pointed to a spot on the far side of the stage where a cameraman was filming the room.

'Must be a very glamourous job,' Jim said.

Harry raised his eyebrows. 'Can be, but not often, truth be told. Mainly involves a lot of sitting around and waiting, then a quick burst of activity *and* you're supposed to remember your lines.' He laughed good-naturedly. 'Mind you,' he added, 'can't complain about gigs like this.' And he raised his glass, clinking it with Jim's.

Jim turned to Sheila Hoffman and was about to say something when he realised the music for the dance troupe had faded. A moment later, a familiar voice came over the PA.

'Ladies and gentlemen. Good evening.' There was a murmur from the diners and all heads turned towards the stage to see Hollywood legend Danny Preston dressed in an elegant tux and holding a microphone.

'God! It's a talking fossil,' Harry said in Jim's ear.

Jim produced a faint smile and sat back in his chair, arms folded.

'Well, ain't this something? I always wanted to play a part in a sci-fi movie,' Preston said, and beamed at the audience. 'The closest I got was in my first film, when I played the part of a telepathic cactus. Even I've forgotten the title of that one.'

The audience laughed. Preston gazed around at the guests, pausing for a moment. 'But this.' And he waved towards the expansive view beyond the glass walls. 'This is science fiction come to life. I've been here most of the day, ladies and gentlemen, but I can still hardly believe my eyes. It truly is a new wonder of the world.

'Now, I won't prattle on. My job here is to introduce the star of the evening and then buzz off. I'm told a glass of Dom Perignon awaits.'

A ripple of laughter.

'Ladies and gentlemen. There are few stars who can claim to be truly global superstars, but tonight, the Xavier family have arranged a special treat. A young woman, who had her first hit when she was just 16. It is hard to believe that was only three years ago because it feels as though her name has been known around the world for so much longer. I give you . . . Kristy Sunshine!'

There was a sharp tap on Johnny Xavier's shoulder. He turned to see a short, solidly built man with greying hair and a lined, tanned face. It was one of his senior engineers, Miguel Bandonis.

'Sorry to bother you, sir,' the man said. 'I couldn't reach you by phone.' He waved a hand in the air to indicate the noise.

'What's up?' Xavier responded, standing up and escorting the engineer away from the table. He glanced back at the guests and then led the way over to the edge of the circular pool. Kristy Sunshine's intro music began with a throbbing drum and bass rhythm. Xavier cursed under his breath and was forced to shout to be heard. 'Well?'

'We've had a minor incident in one of the conduits, sir,' Miguel Bandonis shouted back above the noise.

'What sort of "minor" incident?'

'A relay blew. One of my men was repairing it and a small fire started inside the wall unit. It was extinguished almost immediately.'

'What's the damage?'

'Nothing really, sir. We replaced the relay, patched up some charred circuitry. One of the secondary systems is out of action, but . . .'

'Precisely which secondary system, Bandonis?'

'The emergency doors. But the fire was a long way from the primary door system. I'm just worried about the sensors around them.'

'Why are you worried?'

'They were one of the . . . er . . . cutbacks, sir.' Bandonis gave Xavier a meaningful look.

'Cutbacks? What do you mean?'

Bandonis decided tact was essential if he were to keep his job. 'I heard, er . . . a while back, there were some budget cuts.'

'Don't be absurd,' Xavier retorted.

Bandonis was smart enough not to push it. If Xavier wanted to play innocent, fine. 'Okay, sir,' he said. 'If the primaries for the emergency doors showed any problems we'd know about it immediately.'

Xavier looked around the room. The guests were on their feet, clapping excitedly, but nothing could be heard over the pulsing beat. Lights swept the stage. There was a palpable sense of expectation in the vast room. He looked away towards the ocean. 'Yes. I think we would know about it, Bandonis,' Xavier said dismissively. 'Keep me informed.' And he turned back to the stage as the engineer retreated.

The music reached a crescendo and the lights snapped on, full power. Kristy Sunshine was standing centre stage, arms raised, head down. She was wearing an ABBAesque silver jumpsuit, long tassels hanging from her arms. Her hair was pulled back, partially covered by a sequinned bandana. The opening notes of her first hit single, a ballad, 'You Are My Everything', spilled from enormous speakers at the sides of the stage, and she began to sing.

The audience moved to the hypnotic throb of the bass line. The sound grew as the first verse ended and the band crashed into the chorus. Kristy's voice soared above the music, a melody that had blasted from a million radios three years earlier, a hooky tune that had girdled the world. The sound reverberated around the dome, soaring and swooping into a solitary synthesiser riff. A hush as Kristy's voice came in again, quiet and pleading.

BOOM.

For a second, everyone thought it was a bass drum. Everyone but the drummer, that is.

BOOM.

The room shook. The music stopped. The high-pitched hum of powerful amplifiers bounced around the glass dome. Then came a solitary shriek of feedback.

Screams.

BOOM.

Screams.

The room shook again. A lighting rig tumbled forward and smashed across a table.

The entire dome shook.

Screams.

BOOM. BOOM.

A metal beam crashed to the floor, crushing a score of people. Tables flew through the air, bottles and plates cascaded onto the carpet. Two huge chandeliers plunged to the floor, each smashing into a thousand pieces. Human bodies slammed together. A man somersaulted through the air and landed on a metal post, the pole skewering him. Blood spewed into the air.

BOOM.

The crash of breaking glass. Metal grinding against metal.

Screams.

BOOM.

A massive rumble. The dome shuddered. The vast banqueting suite looked as though it had been filmed and the celluloid strip had caught, juddering, in an old-fashioned movie projector.

BOOM.

Silence.

17

Base One, Tintara Island

It was close to midnight at Base One. The night shift was manning their stations in Cyber Control. Tom was in his motorised wheelchair studying the holoscreen on his laptop. He looked up as a loud buzzing sound reverberated around the room and zipped over to the control console where two techs were running some software checks.

'What's happened?' he asked.

'BigEye 9.'

'On the main screen. And get the others here.'

The screen was filled with a green smudge, but gradually it cleared. The image was coming from BigEye 9, one of 32 satellites in geosynchronous orbit about the earth. Each BigEye was loaded with detection equipment supplied by CARPA. They could detect any form of what was designated as an 'unconventional' disturbance on the planet. They were also programmed to act intelligently – that is, to filter out any 'disturbances' that fitted acceptable parameters and analyse any form of explosion, landslide, seismic or volcanic activity, any unregistered troop massing, gunfire or other military signature. If anything untoward was detected, the BigEye raised the alarm and transmitted the information to Base One.

The screen began to show the outline of an island. It resembled a larger version of Tintara. As the camera on BigEye 9 zoomed in, the image moved to a spot a dozen kilometres off the north coast of the island.

'Sybil. What are the coordinates, please?' Tom asked.

'16' 46" 39.9"' North, 179' 14" 31.8"' East. A point 12.2 kilometres off the north coast of Fiji in the Pacific Ocean.'

'Zoom in.'

The middle third of the screen expanded and the outer edges of the image fell out of sight. The picture was now an unbroken blue.

'What are we looking at, Syb?'

'The Neptune Hotel.'

'The what? Info on screen, please.'

A block of text appeared.

The Neptune Hotel. Construction recently completed. Designed by Felix Hoffman. Owned by an international consortium known as Bathoscope Holdings Ltd. CEO is Michael Xavier. Hotel is due to open in 24 hours.

The Neptune Hotel is located 12.2 km off the north coast of Fiji. Grid reference: 16' 46" 39.9"' North, 179' 14" 31.8"' East.

Structure stands 100 metres below the surface.

'Do you have a schematic, Sybil?'

Two diagrams appeared, artist's impressions showing the view from above and another from the side. The first showed three circles in a linear arrangement. They were linked by passageways approximately 20 metres long, 5 wide. To the north of the middle circle lay two smaller circles with a channel running from each to the central dome. The side view was from the south and portrayed the three huge domes constituting the hotel. It offered no sense of scale.

'How big are those things?' Tom asked.

'Each dome is 60.34 metres high and 51.2 metres in diameter.'

He whistled.

At that moment, Mark and Mai strode in. Mark looked tired. He had just finished a double shift. Mai had been in the shower when the alarm sounded. She was in a fresh jumpsuit, her jet black bob still wet. Without makeup, her high cheekbones were even more striking than normal. She somehow looked younger. Pete arrived a few moments later, dumping a backpack on the floor. He had just returned from a training exercise on the other side of Tintara.

'What's happened?' Mark asked.

'Not sure yet. The epicentre of the trouble is this place.'

The three new arrivals stared at the screen. 'What the hell . . . ?'

'A hotel complex 100 metres beneath the Pacific. Quite amazing,' Tom replied. Then he turned to the two technicians. 'Anything more from BigEye 9?'

'Just in.'

The screen lit up with a live image of the Neptune Hotel. It was obscured by churning water and sediment, but it was obvious something terrible had happened to the building. The most easterly dome was tilted as though its foundations had been damaged.

'An earthquake?' Mai queried, standing next to Mark.

'Anything?' the E-Force leader asked, turning to Tom who had returned to the main control console. 'Data are coming in now,' he said and tapped at his laptop. Numbers and symbols skittered across the holoscreen. 'Looks like a quake,' he said after a moment. 'Sybil? Project data from BigEye 9 on the screen.'

A set of coloured graphs appeared. Pete took two steps towards the screen and scanned the information. 'Hard to tell from this if it was a quake or a bomb, to be honest,' he said. 'Could be both of course. A bomb that caused a quake.'

'I seem to remember Fiji sits on the boundary of two tectonic plates,' Mai said. 'Sybil, show the plate arrangement on screen.'

The screen split. The graphs moved to the left, a new map appeared on the right. The map showed Fiji and the ocean around it. Superimposed onto this was a series of jagged lines.

'Fiji is located at the boundary of the Australian and Pacific plates,' Sybil said. 'These two plates are opposite-facing subduction zones.'

'Meaning?' Mai asked.

'The plates move in opposite directions which means their movements have caused transform faults in the past. Fiji was also once a volcanic island but has been inactive for a long time.'

'Seems like an odd place to put a hotel, don't you think, Sybil?' Tom remarked.

'I would have to disagree,' the computer replied. 'My analysis shows that the region to the north of Fiji where the Neptune Hotel has been constructed is, in fact, unusually stable. The ocean floor in this region is known as the Fiji plateau, a relatively flat and rocky area formed millions of years ago. Furthermore, the nearest fracture definitely produced by tectonic activity within the past million years lies approximately 298 kilometres to the north.'

'Well, what about a quake some distance away that caused a disturbance under the hotel?' Pete asked.

'BigEyes 9, 16 and 21 confirm no sign of seismic activity within a 1000 kilometre radius of the site during the past 48 hours.'

'All right,' Mark said. 'Tom, we need more information on this place. Was anyone in it at the time of the shock?'

Tom touched the keys of the virtual keypad – a strip of lights on a plastic plate under the holoscreen of his laptop.

Mark ran his hand over his cropped hair and turned to the techs. 'I need a full infrared scan asap,' he said. Then he glanced back at Tom. 'Anything?'

'There's almost nothing online about the place. Just permits for construction, design drawings and schematics. There're a couple of very vague articles about the Xavier family, the bunch behind the scheme, plus lots of hits for the designer, Felix Hoffman. But he's put nothing on record about working on the project. It's sealed pretty tight.'

'Fantastic,' Mark retorted and whirled towards the techs. 'Guys? Anything from BigEye?'

'Coming through now.'

A black outline appeared, superimposed over the distorted live image. It was a computer-generated image of the way the structure of the hotel should have been. They could see how all three domes were now misaligned and how the top of the most westerly dome to the left of the screen had shattered. Then, as they watched, scores of red dots appeared within the outline. Most of these were concentrated at the top of the dome on the right of the screen. Each one represented a warm human body.

'Hotel staff and guests,' one of the techs commented gravely. 'Some alive and some newly dead.'

18

Dome Gamma

When Harry opened his eyes, he thought he must be dead. All he could see was a blurred yellow light. It took his eyes a moment to focus, and his brain a few more to process the fact that he was actually looking at a flame, a couple of centimetres from his nose. Then he felt the heat. He recoiled, and realised he was lying on his side. Rolling over, he felt a stab of pain in his left arm and shoulder. He kneeled up and wiped a hand across his face, and it came up wet with blood.

The room was almost black, the only light coming from fires dotted about the vast expanse. Then, as Harry tried to see through the gloom, the emergency lights flickered and stuttered into life. They cast a greenish, unhealthy aura over a scene of abject horror.

There was dust everywhere. It fell like fine rain drifting down onto twisted human shapes. There was debris scattered all around – paper, tablecloths and cutlery, pieces of crockery, food, smashed wine bottles, shards of glass and lumps of twisted metal. Harry had been thrown against a column, and remembered how he had grabbed at it as the room swayed and the world seemed to be ending. Now he pulled himself to his feet, using the column to steady himself. He was covered in fine powder, from head to toe. His jacket was ripped to pieces and there was a gouge in the leather of his right shoe. Something had cut through it, narrowly missing his foot.

He tried again to rub the dust from his face, but only succeeded in driving the powder into his eyes. He blinked away the pain and felt again a sharp stab in his arm and shoulder. He pulled off his jacket and his shirt sleeve was red with blood. He tore at the sodden fabric and saw a deep cut in his upper arm, just above the elbow. It jolted him. He felt a rush of adrenalin, snapping him into the moment.

'Help me, please.' The voice came from behind him. He turned and saw Jim Kemple. He was pinned under a table.

Harry crouched down and tried to pull the table away, but it was too heavy. 'Can you push up, Jim?'

'Yes.'

'On three. One, two . . .'

The table began to lever up and Harry suddenly felt the weight lighten.

Turning, he saw Jim's partner, Alfred Taylor. He had his shoulders under the edge of the table. 'Got it,' he said. 'Get Jim out.'

Harry ducked down, squeezed his hands under Jim's shoulders and dragged him to his feet as Alfred let the table go with a dull thud.

'You okay?' Harry asked.

'I think so.'

Alfred stepped over and hugged his partner. 'Nothing broken?'

Jim patted himself. 'Nope. Just the usual maddening knee,' Jim replied, rubbing where his cartilage hurt. 'You?'

Alfred looked down at the fabric of his trousers clinging wet to his right leg. 'Cut leg and a few bruises but otherwise . . .'

They turned in unison as a horrible scream cut the air. In the half light they could just see a figure a few metres away. The person sat up from a prone position on the floor, convulsed then fell back, lifeless.

Harry was first over there. It was a woman who had been at a nearby table. He didn't know her name. She was dead.

He stood up. 'What the fuck happened?'

'No idea. A quake?' Alfred offered.

Their eyes had begun to adjust to the light and now they could see the whole room, albeit through a haze. The stage had collapsed, and the lighting rigs had crashed down onto it. The dance floor was dotted with shattered bodies. Harry jumped back suddenly as he realised the lumpy object at his foot was a human arm, mangled, red and grey. 'Fuck,' he exclaimed.

'Okay, what do we do?' Jim asked.

Harry was about to try and answer when they heard another sound, a child.

It came from their left, near the edge of the circular pool. They made their way towards the source of the sound, picking a route through the mess. The light was fractured, a pallid, sickly glow. A few moments later, they had reached the edge of the pool. There was nothing there but piles of debris. Then they heard the voice again, a child calling for help. They edged their way along the rim of the pool, the green glow producing a sinister pallor in what they knew had been pristine water just a few minutes ago.

They heard a groan and Harry almost tripped over the small boy huddled against the edge of the pool. He was shivering and sobbing. It was Nick Xavier. Jim crouched down beside him. 'Nick,' he said.

The boy looked at him uncomprehending.

'He's in shock,' Harry said. He turned to the boy. 'Nick, come on. Up you get.' He made to lift him from the low wall at the water's edge, but the kid pulled back.

'It's okay. We're here to help you. There's been some kind of terrible accident. Are you hurt?'

Nick shook his head, but stayed silent. His eyes were huge in the green half-light.

'Come on. We've got to get out of here.' He took the boy's arm, and this time the kid did not resist.

'How's that?' Harry asked when Nick was standing up. 'Everything working?'

The kid nodded. 'Where're my mum and dad?'

'I'm sure they're not far,' Jim said reassuringly. 'Where did you see them last?'

'They were close by at the table. Some of the others had gone up to dance. I went up there. My sister stayed behind. Then . . .'

'Okay, Nick. Okay.' Jim gripped his shoulder.

They made their way back towards where they had been eating, stumbling through the wreckage.

Alfred made them stop. 'Hang on. What're we doing?' he asked, turning to Jim, then Harry.

'Hello?'

They turned at the sound and saw two shapes approaching. In the dim light they could make out little more than the outlines, but as the pair drew closer, they recognised them. It was Danny Preston. He had his arm around the shoulders of a young woman, Kristy Sunshine.

'Are you hurt?' Harry asked.

'I'm okay,' Danny said.

'And you?' Harry asked, stepping forward to look at the singer. He lifted her chin and saw that she had a cut on her forehead. Blood ran down her right temple. She was in shock. 'Nothing too serious,' Harry concluded and helped the two of them back to the others.

'Did you see anyone else?' Alfred asked the new arrivals. Kristy looked at him, speechless, her eyes slightly glazed.

'There's a group over there,' Danny said.

'Did you see my mum and dad . . . and Emily?' Nick asked, his eyes desperate.

'I think I did,' Danny replied. 'There was a group of about 30 people. They were nearer the stage. Kristy and me were separated from them when the first lighting rig collapsed. Kristy ran stage right. I was in the wings. We dashed this way because it seemed the safest place to be. Not sure why now.'

'All right . . .' Harry was about to say something else and stopped suddenly, mentally checking himself. What was he doing? What had come over him? Why was he playing the leader all of a sudden? He hadn't behaved like this in years. But a second later he was stepping forward, doubts swept away by the desperate urgency to survive, to get out of this place at any cost. 'Follow me,' Harry declared and headed into the murk, back towards the wrecked stage.

It was hard going. The floor was slick with liquid. Metal beams and chunks of plaster had scattered at random. As they approached the stage they could hear moans and cries for help. From further off came an ominous creaking, the sound of the infrastructure of the dome reacting to the strain.

Then they saw the main group of survivors. They were close to the devastated stage, around 30 of them huddled together. But as Harry and the others drew near, they were pulled up short by a great fissure in the floor. It ran across the room, 3 metres wide.

Harry edged towards it and looked into the opening. Through the gloom, he could see lights. Flames were licking up from the third floor, some lapping over the edge of the fissure. Jim approached and stopped a metre or so behind him.

A figure appeared on the other side of the chasm. It was Michael Xavier. His suit was in shreds, his face smeared with blood and dust. 'We can't get across,' he called.

'Isn't there an emergency exit your side?' Harry shouted back.

'It's sealed shut.'

'What!'

Nick took a couple of steps towards the fissure.

'Nick,' Michael exclaimed. 'Thank God. I thought . . .'

'I'm okay, Dad. Where's Mum? And Emily?'

'They're here. They're fine.'

'Are you hurt?'

'No, son.'

'Dad, what do we do?'

'Look, everything will be all right, Nick. Trust me. If there is any problem in the hotel an emergency signal goes out to the surface and the authorities on Fiji will know about it straight away. Help will already be on its way, I guarantee it.' Then he turned to Harry and the others. 'You have to get to the other side of the dome. Over there.' He indicated the far wall, back the way they had just come. 'Try the exit there. If that doesn't work, there's another staircase. That will get you to the very top of Dome Beta – an observation deck on the mezzanine.' He pointed up to a gallery some 10 metres above the floor of the dining hall. 'You'll then have to work your way down the back stairs. There's a set of emergency subs on the lower ground floor. It's the best chance you have.'

'Isn't there another staircase your side?' Jim asked.

'It's blocked. We're working on it.'

'But, Dad . . . ?'

'No buts, Nick. We'll be okay here. You have to get out your side. I'll get everyone to the other subs here in Gamma.' He turned to Harry. 'Look after him please, Mr Flanders.'

At that moment Harry could barely imagine how he was going to look after himself. He turned and led the others away.

19

Michael Xavier stumbled back towards the small group of survivors. He had not been entirely honest with his son. He was hurt. He had a nasty cut running from his ankle halfway up to his knee, and he thought he had broken a rib because there was a terrible pain in his left side.

This end of the main hall was more badly damaged. There were holes in the floor and several large girders from the top of the dome had crashed down. Through the murk, he could make out the shapes of the other survivors. There were perhaps 30 of them, huddled together just beyond the edge of the stage. The pool ran in a sparkling curve behind them.

His mind was racing. The numbness of shock was passing, being replaced by a maelstrom of emotions – fear, anger, disbelief, and a churning confusion. What the hell had gone wrong? Had they been hit by an earthquake? Was it a bomb, for Christ's sake? And the emergency doors? Why wouldn't they work? The doors were supposed to be protected by a double redundant system. They couldn't have just failed. But they had.

He was so lost in thought it took a second for him to notice the grinding sound coming from close by. He looked up and saw a beam slide from its housing high up at the top of the dome. A metal bolt whistled past his ear and slammed into a table top, punching a hole right through it. He ducked instinctively. But as he came up, he saw the beam plunge through the air, and stood powerless and paralysed with horror as it dropped 9 metres. The beam, a hefty chunk of steel, sailed down, tipping end over end. Three metres above the ground it had rotated into the horizontal. The people on the floor of the dining hall saw it coming and scattered, but not everyone was quick enough. Covering the final 3 metres of its fall in a microsecond, one end of the beam brought down at least 10 people. An elderly man who had been slower to respond than the others was decapitated, his body crumbling as his shattered head rolled away. Another, a young woman, had her back ripped open by the leading edge of the beam. Almost split in two, she crashed forward, face first, hitting the polished wooden floor with an obscene squelch.

Michael snapped back to reality and ran as fast as his injured leg would allow. He reached the remaining survivors, dust and clouds of metal slivers still falling from the ceiling. Instinctively, terror building inside, he scanned the faces for his loved ones.

'My God,' he exclaimed, as Hilary and Emily ran towards him. He held them and kissed them. He welcomed the dust on them. Beneath it, their skin was warm. They were alive. He looked around and saw Johnny stumbling his way. His face was cut, a gouge from temple to nostril, blood running down his neck. They looked at each other in disbelief.

Suddenly they heard a cry from under the metal beam. Michael rushed over. A young woman was alive, but her legs were trapped. He recognised her through the grime and blood. It was Samantha Braithwaite, the daughter of an old college friend.

'Johnny,' he called. The younger Xavier picked his way towards them through piles of detritus. Michael crouched down beside the woman.

'Sam,' Michael said again, trying hard to keep his voice level. 'Sam. Can you move at all?'

She looked up at him, barely able to focus. 'No. I can't feel my legs,' she said, her voice verging on hysteria.

Michael looked at his brother, who crawled to the other side of the beam. From there he could see the lower part of the woman's legs through her ripped ball gown. Her left leg was mangled, the right torn to shreds from the knee down. Johnny met his brother's gaze and slowly shook his head.

'Okay,' Michael said. 'We need some more help.'

As Michael turned, two men appeared. He knew them immediately – the engineer, Miguel Bandonis, and the American financier, Sigmund de Silva. 'Miguel, Sigmund. Get to the end of the beam. Johnny, go with them. Try to lever your fingers under the rim.' Then, turning back to Samantha, he said, 'Sam, we're going to get you free. Don't worry. We have three strong chaps here. When I tell you, I want you to try to push back from the beam. I'll pull.' He tucked his hands under her shoulders and turned towards the three men at the end of the beam. Johnny nodded. Groaning loudly, they just managed to lift the huge chunk of metal a few centimetres, and Michael yelled, 'Now, Sam.'

Michael stumbled back and Samantha Braithwaite almost landed on top of him. She had just cleared the metal beam when it came crashing down again, the sound reverberating around the dome.

'Is there anyone with medical training here?' Sigmund de Silva asked, as he knelt down beside the injured woman. Michael turned to his wife. 'Do you know, Hilary?'

'The only doctor here was Simon Frasier. But, he's . . . ' And she suddenly crumpled, sinking into a heap on the floor, sobbing loudly.

Samantha gasped and gripped Michael's arm. He looked

down at her. The woman's eyes were wide with terror. She started to shake, and Michael held her tight about the shoulders. He looked across to Sigmund. His face was a mess of small cuts, rivulets of blood smudging the dust, his eyelashes white with powder. The injured woman exhaled loudly and went limp.

Michael lowered Samantha to the ground, pulled off the remnants of his dinner jacket and covered her face with it. Taking her hands from her face, Hilary looked at her husband and screamed, throwing her head back down into her hands. Michael walked over and sat beside her, putting an arm around her bony shoulder.

'I've seen Nick,' he said quietly. She looked up, her eyes red raw, tear streaks lining her cheeks. 'He's okay. He's with some of the others, the journalist Harry Flanders and some people from our table.'

'Where?' Hilary asked, barely able to contain herself.

'There's a huge chasm in the floor, near the stage. Can't get over it. They're on the other side. I told them to get up to the mezzanine and try to reach Dome Beta. I think things might be better there.'

'And what're we supposed to do?' Johnny asked, turning from the dead woman, a look of desperation on his face. 'The emergency doors are screwed. We've gotta do something.'

'I need to see what shape these people are in first,' Michael replied. He walked over to a small group of survivors, huddled together close to the edge of the stage. Most of them were in shock, their faces pale. Everyone was injured in some way, bloodied, their clothes ripped. They had the hollow-eyed look of those suddenly transported to a real-life horror movie.

Michael crouched down beside a young girl. Her arm was bleeding. Then he moved on to an elderly man, one of the major shareholders from an American bank. His suit was ripped and he had a deep gash across his forehead. Michael stood up. 'Okay,' he said to the group. 'This is the situation. The floor has been split in two. There's a 3-metre-wide fissure back there and flames are shooting up into the opening. I don't think many of us could get across in our condition. We've tried the emergency doors. There are two on this side of the chasm and two over the other side. They appear to be out of action. I guess the servo-systems have been knocked out by whatever caused this. I think the best chance we have is to try the stairs up to the mezzanine. I've seen a group of survivors on the other side of the fissure and they're trying the stairs. I think you should all wait here and my brother and I will try the door to the stairs.'

'I'll come with you,' Miguel Bandonis said.

'Me too,' another youngish man offered. Michael recognised him. He was one of the security team from the hotel, an Australian, Craig Deloray. His left arm hung limp at his side.

'Craig. Your arm.'

'I'm okay,' Deloray said. 'It's not broken.'

Michael looked at him doubtfully. 'Glad for your help,' he said.

'No worries. Lead the way, sir.'

20

Semja Alexandry, Arctic Ocean

The island of Semja Alexandry is a deserted strip of rock about 60 kilometres by 15, located some 700 kilometres due south of the North Pole. During the Cold War, the Russian owners of the island built a radar station there. Today the derelict building looks like a rotten molar half-buried in the snow. Close by lies a potholed airstrip. When the UN-affiliated group who created E-Force first approached the Russian government to investigate the possibility of leasing Semja Alexandry, it took three weeks to find someone who actually knew where the island was.

Now, three years after the lease was signed, a circular metal platform 40 metres in diameter stands close to the radar station. The Silverback, *Paul*, with Josh in the pilot's seat, landed vertically on the platform. Josh recited a coded alphanumeric into his comms and a voice came over his headset: 'Welcome back, Josh.'

The platform descended on a single gigantic hydraulic support, lowering the slate-grey Silverback 40 metres into the frozen tundra. A few moments later, it stopped, the hydraulics emitted a loud hissing sound, and Josh popped the canopy.

The hangar lay at the northern edge of the underground base. The entire complex, all 1.6 hectares of it, had been carved out of solid rock, making it virtually untouchable and unobservable by anything but E-Force's own detection equipment, the BigEyes. Designated Polar Base, 50 men and women worked there. It was one of seven stations dotted around the globe, each serving a multitude of tasks. These included processing data from the BigEyes, repair and maintenance of the vast array of hi-tech equipment used by E-Force, and acting as the location for training programs that could not be conducted on Tintara.

Steph met Josh as he climbed down onto the floor of the hangar. 'How'd it go?' she asked.

'Good. The modification to the remote guidance system works a treat.'

They had been on the island for over a week and it had been hard. This was their first day of relative calm. The rest of the time they had either been up to their necks in freezing water, abseiling down an icy cliff or trying to catch food on a two-day total immersion survival exercise, which had started with them being dumped in the middle of the island without cybersuits, without food or water, without a radio, without even a map or a compass.

'You enjoyed a morning off?' Josh asked.

'It was hardly a morning off. I had to reconfigure the computer systems without a manual, and then I had a really fun two-hour simulator course. I feel bruised all over.'

Josh laughed and gripped her shoulder.

'Ow!'

'Come on, let's grab some lunch.'

Josh led the way along a metal gantry. A flight of steel stairs took them down to a long passageway. At the end of this was a glass-fronted elevator. They stepped in and Steph pushed the button marked 'Level 3'. The elevators stood at one end of a vast opening in the earth. Around the other three sides were gantries on each of the 14 levels. On some of the levels they could see windows opening onto laboratories, service areas and workshops. Next to these, passages led away to accommodation and recreation areas.

The cage stopped and the door opened automatically. A short, brightly lit corridor took them to the mess hall. Here, everything was automated. One wall consisted of a bank of food dispensers and plasma displays. Josh walked up and touched a screen. The computer chirped up.

'Luncheon selection today: 1. Roast chicken with vegetables of the season, roast potato. 2. Sea bass with beans and mixed salad . . .'

It went on to list 10 more dishes. Josh listened carefully then asked for selection Number 6 – lasagne. Walking along the row of machines, he reached a service hatch. Steph placed her order. They picked up their trays and ambled over to a table close to the far end of the canteen.

'This lasagne isn't half bad,' Josh said after a couple of silent spoonfuls.

Steph had a mouthful of food and just nodded, waving a fork in the air above her plate.

It was then that Josh's comms sounded. 'Yes,' he said.

'Josh. Is Steph with you?'

'Hey, Mark. Yeah, she's sitting across from me stuffing her face with clam chowder.'

'There's been an incident. We need you there, asap.'

21

Steph and Josh were back in the hangar in under three minutes. On the way, Tom filled them in on what they knew of the disaster near Fiji.

'And there's no definite cause?'

'Not yet.'

'What's the team status?' Steph asked.

'Pete and Mai are in the Big Mac, left about two minutes ago. Mark's just boarding *Ringo* now. He'll be there before them, of course. His ETA is 21.57 local time.'

Josh paced over to the crew who were refuelling and checking out *Paul*. Steph went to get suited up.

'We'll be ready in under five minutes,' one of the techs told Josh.

'Make that four,' he retorted.

Steph appeared a minute later and they stood beside the craft watching the techs finish off. An engineer in a black boilersuit approached. 'So whose turn to pilot?'

'Mine,' Josh and Steph said in unison. The tech looked from one to the other, not sure whether to say anything.

'I think if you look at the log, Dr Jacobs, you'll see that you commanded the last mission.'

'Okay, Professor Thompson,' Steph responded. 'I refuse to play silly games. The keys are yours.' And she gave Josh a sweet smile. He turned and climbed the steps up the side of the Silverback and lowered himself into the pilot seat. Steph followed him up and jumped into the copilot's seat directly behind him.

A few moments later, the chief engineer shouted to the others and they all headed for the control shelter at the far end of the hangar. As he went, he gave Josh the thumbs up. Josh glanced at his watch. The engineers had prepped the plane in three minutes 55.

Paul ascended on the hydraulic platform, the floor of the hangar dropping away beneath it. A slit appeared in the ceiling. It grew larger as the two hemispheres of the landing pad separated. Above the plane stretched clear blue sky. The lift took the Silverback through the opening and stopped at ground level. Josh and Steph looked around them at the frozen wasteland. Close to the pad lay a few wiry, sorry-looking scrubs, but apart from these the view consisted of granite escarpments, and beyond that a scarred and rutted strip of tarmac. This was all that remained of the airstrip the Russian military had slapped down almost 60 years earlier. Beside the strip, they could see the ugly squat shape of the radar station. Rust lines ran down its concrete sides and not a single pane of glass had survived the years.

'Polar Base. We're making a final preflight check,' Steph announced into her comms, and she ran her fingers quickly over a control panel.

In the front seat, Josh adjusted his holovisor and made a tiny adjustment to his earpieces. He could see a 3D representation of the island of Semja Alexandry. 'Lay in a course for Fiji,' he told the computer. A panel of lights flashed on his control panel. 'You got that, Steph?' he asked.

'Perfect,' she replied. 'Flight time, one hour 37 minutes.'

'Okay, let's go.'

'Polar Base . . . ready for takeoff.'

'Copy.'

Josh tapped at the plastic panel in front of him, and he and Steph heard the engines fire up. He surveyed the parameters moving across his field of vision in his visor and ran his fingers over the panel again. The plane began to lift into the cold, crisp air at 300 metres per second, then gradually accelerated until it had reached the optimum cruising altitude of 20,000 metres above the Tundra.

'Okay, what's your tune?' he asked Steph as he simultaneously ran the flight schedule through a final check and prepped the engines for horizontal flight.

'My tune?'

'Yeah. What do you play on takeoff?'

'I . . .'

'Oh never mind,' Josh shot back. 'You'll have to put up with mine.' And he snapped the plane into horizontal flight mode, the engines began to change tone and the Silverback shot forward, accelerating to Mach 10 in a matter of seconds. Lynyrd Skynyrd's 'Freebird', Josh's favourite, burst through their headphones.

At an altitude of 20,000 metres, very little detail of the land below could be distinguished by the naked eye, but *Paul* was packed with the most sophisticated detection and analysis equipment coming out of the CARPA labs. Passing over the north-east coast of Siberia, Josh and Steph could have picked out individual hairs on a yak's rear end if they had wished to. Instead, Steph was refining the flightpath to get to Fiji in the fastest possible time, but avoiding hostile airspace.

E-Force had a special arrangement with the former Soviet states and had automatic clearance to fly over Russia, Georgia, Ukraine and the others. China, though, was a different matter. Beijing had not been involved in the creation of E-Force and they had refused to cooperate fully with the UN, only allowing E-Force to enter Chinese airspace in dire emergency. Since the recent heightened tension between Beijing and Washington even this small concession had been withdrawn.

Steph had felt the Silverback turn sharply without warning. 'What're you doing, Josh? . . . Josh?'

'I'm taking us directly south.'

'But that's . . .'

'Yep, it's over our friend's precious airspace.'

'Josh, you can't do that.'

'What? You think they have anything that can outrun us?'

'No,' Steph snapped. 'But they could fire at us.'

'What? And risk an international incident?'

'Too damn right they would.'

'I'm sorry, Steph, but I'm the one piloting this aircraft. It's my decision. We have to get to Fiji. Lives are at stake. You know that.'

Steph said nothing. She was trying to steady her breathing, trying to keep her mental balance. 'I don't think you've thought this through, Josh.'

'Oh, I have.'

'If the Chinese kick up a stink, the UN are not going to be happy with us. You could be forced out of the team.'

'I'll take the chance.'

'At least let Base One know.'

'Don't be ridiculous. Mark will have a coronary. We can be in and out of Chinese airspace before anyone even notices.'

'I'm against this, Josh.'

'Course plotted. It'll get us to Fiji 20 minutes faster.'

'No!' Steph cried. 'Please, Josh. Don't do this.'

'Too late. I'm sorry, Steph.'

Steph watched the display in front of her. Light patterns shifted across the highly polished plastic. The new flight-path was programmed in and would take them straight over the Gobi Desert, then out over the East China Sea. Josh had locked in the command.

There was an ominous silence between them. Steph was boiling with rage but she knew ways to force herself to remain calm. Years of yoga and practising meditation techniques had their uses. 'On your head be it,' she said, unable to keep the anger out of her voice. 'You can unlock the controls, Josh.'

The plane ascended another 3000 metres, rolled and swerved randomly to confuse any radar tracking that might break through its camouflage. The Camoflin coating made it almost completely radar-invisible, but a Chinese satellite might pick it up.

On the holodisplays in their helmets, Steph and Josh could see the terrain 23,000 metres below. It began to change, turning from rocky high ground to the orange wash of desert. The guidance system flashing across their visors told them they had encroached into the northern region of the Gobi Desert, a vast wasteland that stretched into the heart of northern China.

They flew on in silence. Steph was still too angry to accept fully what Josh was doing. She knew his heart was in the right place and that, in some respects, he was a better E-Force member than she was. He always put the mission first. But she also knew that she was the more disciplined person, respectful of the rules and regulations, someone more bound to protocol – and she believed in her approach. She could not admit it right then, but she knew Josh's individualism and self-belief got things done. She just didn't like the way he went about it.

A voice broke over their comms. 'Unidentified object approaching at high speed.' It was the onboard computer.

'What!' Josh exclaimed. 'On screen.'

'What is that?' Steph said.

'Unidentifiable,' the onboard computer responded. 'Object now 4.9 kilometres due south-south-east. It's falling away from us.'

'Good,' Josh said.

'There's a second object,' Steph announced.

Josh was silent, dumbstruck.

'That's falling behind too. Some sort of missile by the look of it. It came into range briefly.'

'Warning. Warning.' It was the metallic rasp of the onboard computer again. Three rows of lights on the control panel began to flash. The sound of the engines changed pitch, descending rapidly. The plane began to rock on its axis.

'Switching to manual,' Josh said. 'Steph. Anything more on what those things are?'

'Hang on. Picking up a low frequency emission from the second object. It's not a conventional missile. It's . . . damn!'

'What?'

'Just got a momentary sensor reading from the limit of the range. It's not an explosive device. It's some sort of probe. The first object must be a jet. The probe is emitting low frequency electromagnetic waves.'

'You put the shields up?'

'Yep. It's cutting straight though.'

'I can't believe that.'

'Chinese . . . clever people.' She resisted the urge to say *I told you so*. 'I'm modulating the shield randomly.'

'Just what I was about to suggest.'

'Oh good!'

The plane rocked violently. Josh and Steph were pushed forward, their bodies straining against the safety restraints. The lights flicked on, then off. They stayed off for three torturous seconds before coming on again at half power.

'Steph? You okay?'

'I've been better.'

'The modulation isn't working.'

'No, and the whole shield system is now offline. Engine two is working at 40 per cent efficiency, and . . .'

The lights went off, and stayed off. The tone of the engines changed again, shooting up through several octaves. The plane shuddered.

'Ninety per cent of the electrics are out, Josh,' Steph shouted above the screeching of the engines.

'Copy that. I'm going to try to land.'

Josh ran his fingers over the controls. Almost nothing worked. He grabbed at the emergency joystick, a design feature added in case all other control systems failed. With the engines working at low efficiency, it took all Josh's flying skills to bring the plane down to a lower altitude. He was also worried that without the servos and antigrav systems on board, the plane would be unable to handle the ridiculously high speed they were still travelling at. He glanced at the control panel to check their speed and altitude, but nothing was working.

'We've got to bail,' Steph screamed into her headset. But comms were down. She glanced out the window. The plane was banking hard. She could see the orange sand thousands of metres below. Then the Silverback rolled again. They were falling at an incredible speed, the sand rearing up towards them. She felt sick and fought it down.

The plane was shaking so violently it felt like it was about to shatter into a million pieces. Steph jolted in her seat as a crack appeared in the carboglass above her head. The crack slithered along the smooth parabola of the canopy and she could hear the air rush from the cabin as it decompressed. Her cybersuit was still functioning normally. She could breathe and she could withstand the cataclysmic drop in cabin temperature.

'Steph,' Josh called, his voice desperate. 'Don't think you can hear me, Steph, but I'm going to try to land in the desert. Hold tight.'

Josh leaned on the joy stick and the plane surged into an even steeper descent. Then, with expert timing, he pulled it back, praying the servo mechanism of the manual override could handle it. It was like the power steering in a heavy car. He needed it if he was to have any hope of landing *Paul* in one piece. The landing gear was offline. Through the window, the sandy terrain, featureless except for the shadow cast by the Silverback, seemed to rise up at him. It was almost impossible to get his bearings, to gain any sense of distance or scale.

Seconds before he had expected it, the plane touched the ground. Josh reacted with lightning speed, bringing up the nose of the jet, letting it skim along the sand. He knew they would survive just so long as the infrastructure held. It was an incredibly strong plane. But something like this had never been tested before.

Josh focused all his attention on steadying the Silverback, letting the underside of the plane take the strain. He had to hope the Maxinium would survive the landing. Josh was thrown around in the seat, the safety restraints screaming. The sides of his helmet smashed against the head rests and ear guards. He felt his guts churning.

The plane hit something and shuddered. There was an explosion to port. Josh could not turn to see, but he knew what it was. The engine had gone. Debris slammed into the canopy. Then the canopy itself shattered. Pieces of carboglass flew outward, propelled by the internal pressure in Josh's cabin. He heard a second explosion. This time from under the plane. Something seemed to be coming up through the floor. He couldn't quite believe it. Couldn't understand what it was. Then he realised it was a section of undercarriage sheared clean away from its support bracket. It emerged from the crumpled steel under him and then flew up, missing his face by a few millimetres before shooting out into the freezing air.

22

Hang Cheng, Gobi Desert, summer 1988

Chief Scientist Mengde Sun pulled down the bottom of his tunic and ran a hand over his bald head. There was a brief rap on the door and a voice said, 'Sir, it is time.'

Mengde opened the door and saw the guard standing to attention. He nodded and let the man lead the way. They were in the east wing of the base. It was hot and tiny particles of sand had somehow found their way through to the interior of the base. Funny, Mengde thought to himself, it was so easy for such a simple thing as sand dust to get into this place, a place otherwise impregnable.

They turned a corner. The guard opened the door for the scientist and he stepped into a narrow room. One of the long walls was a single sheet of glass. It was dark behind the glass. The room was filled with computer equipment. A row of desks ran along its centre. Each had a computer placed on the middle of the desk. An operator sat at each of the terminals. The operators were wearing headsets and mouth mics. To each side of the computers lay clipboards, papers and piles of floppy disks. The room was overlit, almost dazzling, and there was dust here too, suspended in the air, flecks lit up by hundreds of watts of power.

Mengde was led to the back of the room where there was a large leather chair. Beside the chair stood a low table with a glass and a decanter of water. He sat down.

It had been such a long journey, he thought to himself. A long temporal journey, but it had covered almost no distance. For he had been born within half a kilometre of this room. The date had been 2 October 1949, within hours of the birth of the People's Republic of China, the day Mao Zedong had ascended to the highest office in the land.

Mengde Sun had grown up with the Republic, his childhood had been spent in the tiny village of Hang Cheng in the southeast corner of the vast Gobi Desert, a frontier settlement in the middle of nowhere. His father, Mengde Zhui, had been the village leader, but he had been a weak man. When Sun was seven, his father was blackmailed by a business rival who had photographs of the village leader *in* flagrante *with the baker's wife. When Mengde's father decided not to pay the blackmailer, his infidelity was exposed. The baker tried to knife Zhui, and Zhui's wife, Sun's mother, was disgraced along with her perfidious husband.*

The incident could have ruined Mengde's life, but instead it changed it incalculably for the better. He was shamed and had become an outcast along with his parents, but he learned a great lesson from the experience. It taught him the power of blackmail, the power of coercion, the attractiveness of corruption. And besides, he had already been something of an outcast in the village. He was a mathematical prodigy, mastering calculus by the age of four, working through elegant solutions to problems of binomial expansion before his fifth birthday. Aged eight, he was packed off to Beijing, Technical College 18. He never saw his parents again.

'I'm sorry, sir, there has been a very slight delay,' a voice said at Mengde's side. He was so lost in memories that for a second he barely heard the man. He turned and looked up at a very nervous technician in a white lab coat. He had an ID pinned to the collar: Yung Sing. Mengde stared at him for long moments, then waved the man away.

He had not seen his parents again, but he had returned to the *village. Just once. In June 1986, two years ago. He had watched as troops stormed the town meeting hall where a few stubborn citizens had remained protesting against the destruction of their village and the planned relocation to tenements in Fung Ching Wa, the nearest town.*

By that time, Mengde had become a high-ranking official of the Communist Party and the government's Chief Scientist. He had reached this pinnacle by virtue of a peerless scientific brilliance, but had consolidated his position by whatever means necessary. He was ruthless, amoral and totally corrupt.

He had been given complete control of the project to build Scientific Base 44 and allowed free rein to choose where it was to be located. He had picked a 1000 square kilometre scrap of land on the edge of the Gobi Desert. No one in Beijing cared about the village of Hang Cheng or its handful of citizens.

From a sun-parched hill at a safe distance from the village, Mengde had witnessed the explosives being laid around the buildings. He had watched with growing contentment as the old stone homes, the town meeting hall, the shop and the school collapsed in a most orderly fashion. Then, as a group of a dozen red bulldozers rumbled over the desert, heading for the ruins left by the TNT, he had stood up, rubbed the sand from his hands and turned his back on the place.

'Sir, we're ready.' It was the same technician as before, Yung Sing. The man was standing close to the arm of the Chief Scientist's sumptuous leather chair. Mengde did not move a muscle, but stared straight ahead. The lights in the room dimmed as others brightened behind the wall of glass.

'Experiment 1,' Yung said.

Behind the glass was a small stage 2 metres square. On the stage stood a chair. A man was strapped to it by restraints at the wrists and ankles. It looked very similar to the apparatus used for execution by electric chair except there were no wires connected to the contraption. The man looked petrified, but resigned. Only his fingers twitched.

'Healthy man, aged 22,' the technician said. 'Prisoner AMV45.'

Mengde looked at the prisoner. He knew what should happen. He had conducted earlier trials. He knew the math. But even so, he felt a certain thrill of anticipation. Long ago he had read about the early Chinese alchemists – innovators and leaders of course, like so many other Chinese thinkers and warriors. The alchemists of the Qin Dynasty had conducted experiments on prisoners. He was part of a fine tradition.

The technician nodded to a man at one of the computers and he depressed a succession of keys. 'We are using a pulse at 2 hertz, with a wide dispersal, low intensity beam. Please observe.'

There was a momentary squeal from the other side of the glass. The man began to shake, his eyes widened in horror. He strained against the restraints, the metal edges cutting into him. Then his eyes exploded. The spray hit the glass and the techs the other side recoiled instinctively. The man's head slumped forward and he started to scream.

Nobody moved, no one said a word. The screeching metallic sound of the beam stopped abruptly, but the dreadful screams remained, cutting the hot, dusty air.

'Very good,' Mengde said after several moments. He was looking at the blinded man on the other side of the glass. The man was convulsing, covered in blood and vomit. 'Let's try the other setting – 7.5 hertz, and narrow the beam to 13 RDF.'

Yung Sing took a few steps across the room and whispered in the ear of one of the men at the terminals. The man tapped the keys and the technician walked back to stand beside Mengde's chair.

'Whenever you are ready, sir.'

'Yes, yes,' the Chief Scientist said slowly. 'There is no need to hurry, is there?' And he looked round at the technician for the first time. 'I'm rather enjoying myself.'

They all waited another 30 seconds. None of Mengde's subordinates dared move a muscle. The man behind the glass kept screaming. Then the scientist lifted a couple of fingers and the technician shouted to the computer operator, 'Align the beam.'

The sound started again, but this time it was a higher pitched shriek that sent shocks along the spine and resonated far into the inner ear.

Yung raised a hand. 'Now.'

The computer operator hit 'return' on his keyboard, and the man behind the glass turned to powder.

23

Fiji

Mark's Silverback, *Ringo,* slowed to Mach 2 and dropped 10,000 metres. Eighty-two kilometres, and two minutes later, he pulled his speed right back and descended to an approach altitude of 3000 metres. Beneath the jet, the calm waters of the Pacific lay like a mottled black carpet.

Details of the E-Force mission had been sent ahead to the Fijian authorities and to a Royal Navy frigate currently 40 kilometres north-west of the island. The ship, the *Essex,* had immediately set course for the disaster zone at full speed. Mark could see it now on his sensor display as it steamed south.

Ringo came in low over the patch of ocean directly above the Neptune and Mark made a preliminary sensor sweep of the area. He was just about to read the results off the screen when his comms sounded. A man's voice came over the system. He spoke English with a mellow Pacific Islands accent. 'This is the Fijian Naval Authority, Suva calling E-Force jet designation E991.'

'Hi, Suva. This is Mark Harrison aboard E991.'

'Sir,' the voice said. 'I have the supreme commander of Fijian national armed forces, Admiral Sir Joni Madraiwiwi here.'

'Admiral,' Mark said.

'Good evening, Mr Harrison,' Madraiwiwi replied. His voice was deep, almost a growl, but refined. Mark surmised the Admiral was an Oxbridge man. 'The speed at which you chaps travel never ceases to amaze me.'

'We try our best, sir.'

'I just wanted to let you know that you have our full coop-eration. My government will provide you with any materials or personnel to assist you.'

'We are very grateful,' Mark responded. 'I think at this stage we will be fine. We have to do a preliminary analysis. But I will certainly keep you and your government fully informed.'

'Very well, Mr Harrison. We have two ships en route to the disaster site and I understand a Royal Navy vessel is on its way.'

'That's correct. We are always grateful for any local assis-tance, Admiral. But if I may, I would like you to ensure your ships adopt a holding pattern no closer than 10 kilometres from the hotel site. It's a safety matter for you and for us. The commander of *HMS Essex* has agreed to this.'

'I see no problem with that. Keep in touch.'

Mark broke his connection and heard the familiar rumble of the Big Mac as it descended to hover over the water a short distance from his Silverback. It was staying just high enough to prevent its massive engines churning the water too much.

From the main control panel of the Big Mac, high up in the top bubble of the aircraft, Pete and Mai could see the surface of the water dotted with shapes. Cutting the engines to minimum power and dropping to 50 metres above the surface of the ocean, Pete flicked on the powerful front beams and a hectare of black water lit up. The surface was strewn with debris – sheets of plastic, metal cylinders, food and other organic material.

Mai stepped down from the guidance module on the flight deck and strode into the adjoining room to check the computers that operated the outboard equipment, leaving Pete at the main panel. He looked around the now empty deck and took a deep breath. He could hardly believe he was back on operational duties again. He felt a thrill of excitement. The old adage was spot on, he told himself: to get over any traumatic experience, you had to get right back in the saddle.

Mai came back just as a buzzer sounded and Mark's face appeared on a screen above the console. He was seated at the controls of *Ringo*, a short distance away, hovering 30 metres above the waves.

'I've run a scan,' Mark said, and touched a couple of keys on the panel in front of him. Multicoloured images appeared on the Big Mac screen. 'As you can see, the shock was pretty serious. According to the design plans, the three domes are called Alpha, Beta and Gamma. Alpha is the most westerly, there on the left of the screen. As we saw at Base One, the top of Alpha has shattered, but the rest of the dome seems amazingly intact. It looks like there are some pretty heavy-duty bulkheads that seal off any section of any dome if there's a major breach. Ironically, apart from the top floor, Alpha is the least badly hit, whereas the whole of Gamma has been shaken pretty bad. The top of the dome is holding so far, but it's under a lot of stress. I want you to launch a Hunter to get close to the wreckage.

'Right.'

'Tom called in a few moments ago,' Mark added. 'He's managed to explain why there are so many people at the hotel, a day before it's due to open.' He sent Pete an image that Tom had found on the web. It was from *Entertainment Today* – an article about the Gala Night at the Neptune Hotel.

Mai stared at it and sighed. 'If I believed in such things, I would say that was very bad luck.'

'Yeah, Mai, but I think you believe in luck about as much as I do.'

She turned away for a moment. Something on another screen had caught her eye. When she looked back to Mark, she was grimacing. 'Mark, take a look at the surface. Coordinates, 619.3 by 342.1.'

'What is it?' Mark said as a fuzzy image appeared on one of his monitors. The high-sensitivity camera on the underside of the Silverback automatically honed in and refocused, showing a dark shape – a badly charred body floating face down. 'Okay, Mai. Bring it in,' he said heavily.

24

Dome Gamma

Harry had to force himself to slow down. There could be no telling what dangers lay a step away. But the urge to just run, blindly, was powerful. It seemed that now he had snapped out of his usual torpor, his mind had slipped into overdrive.

The strange dull light threw confusing shadows everywhere, but in this crazy topsy-turvy world it was impossible to know what was what anyway. A few minutes earlier, all had been ordered, normal, everything under control. Now? Now, the world had collapsed.

He led the others towards the north end of the vast ballroom. Or at least he thought that was the direction. It was hard to judge which end of the room was which. All the normal landmarks were distorted.

There was a loud crack. They all froze. The sound seemed to have come from directly overhead. Harry looked up.

'That was the cap at the top of the dome,' Jim said, his voice hollow.

'Can you see anything?' Danny asked. He was squinting up at the apex of the dome.

'Too much dust and the emergency lights are too dim,' Jim replied.

'Come on,' Harry said, and he pointed towards the emergency exit. 'I can just see the sign. Directly ahead.'

Harry weaved a path through the debris, watching for stray electrical cables and live wires. They crouched to get under a collapsed girder covered in a mess of metal sheets and lumps of concrete. Reaching the far side of the obstruction, Harry made them all stop for a breather.

'How are we?' he asked and looked at each of them in turn. Nick Xavier's filthy face was streaked with tears. He wouldn't meet Harry's eyes. Alfred and Jim nodded. 'Okay, I guess,' Alfred panted and winced.

Danny Preston leaned back against a wall and took long, deep breaths. Kristy Sunshine looked completely dazed. She stared around at the five faces and burst into tears.

'Time to go,' Harry said and squeezed the girl's shoulder. 'This way.'

They reached the exit a few moments later. Harry leaned on the metal bar across the door, but it was locked. He pushed harder. Nothing. Alfred and Jim joined him and they all pushed together. Still nothing.

'Locked or blocked,' Jim said. 'Either way, it's useless.'

'My dad reckoned there was a staircase,' Nick said.

'He did,' Harry replied.

'I think it's over there,' the boy added, pointing towards the west.

Getting over to the staircase was slow work. The floor was slick with liquid and strewn with lumps of plaster. Harry was in front. He stopped abruptly. Jim was immediately behind him. He almost crashed into the journalist.

Harry crouched down. At his feet lay a vaguely human shape. The others caught up. Danny knelt on one knee next to Harry and stared in silence as the Englishman pulled a swatch of fabric from the face of a dead man lying on his back. The victim's face had been sliced vertically almost in two. Sinews and lumps of muscle hung limply. One eye was pulped, teeth smashed to shards. Harry emitted a low moan and jumped up, throwing back the material to cover the face of his friend and producer Terry Mitcham.

Jim stopped Nick from looking at the remains, turning him away and guiding them around the body towards the foot of the emergency stairs. Harry stared blindly into space, his hand clamped tightly over his mouth.

Suddenly Kristy Sunshine screamed, a piercing ear-shattering banshee screech. 'I can't stand this!' she cried. 'I can't stand it. I have to get out.' She swayed on her heels, her eyes huge dishes in the half-light. She span round, looking like a cornered animal. The terror poured out of her.

Alfred took a step towards her. 'Calm down, Kristy,' he said gently.

She glared at him almost uncomprehending. Then she screamed again, louder, more guttural, from the pit of her stomach. Alfred went to touch the girl's shoulder. She jolted, whirling on him. 'Leave me alone, you old fuck!' she yelled.

Stunned, Alfred took a step back. Kristy started laughing hysterically and dropped to her knees, grabbing fistfuls of her hair. Alfred stepped forward again and pulled her up. 'Get a grip, young woman,' he snapped, his face close to hers. Kristy fixed him with a totally blank look and started screaming again. Alfred slapped her, hard. She froze, took a deep breath and seemed to suddenly wake from a dreadful nightmare. 'I'm sorry,' she said quietly.

They stood in silence for a few moments.

'The stairs are there,' Harry said, breaking the tension. 'They're blocked. Jim, Danny, Alfred. Help me.'

Harry led them over, leaving Nick and Kristy to follow. A huge metal strut and a mass of ragged chunks of tile and plaster lay between them and the staircase. The four men took up positions at each end of the beam. On Harry's command, they swivelled it away from the stairs. It was incredibly heavy and they could only shift it a short distance at a time, but after three goes they had moved the beam far enough away from the side of the stairs to squeeze past. They then set to work on the chunks of rubble and other debris.

'Okay,' Jim announced. 'I think we can get through.' He crouched down under a girder and could see a route to the steps. From there, the path was clear as far as the light would allow him to see. 'Not sure we can reach the top, but we should be able to make some headway.'

Jim took the lead. Then Nick. Kristy ducked under the girder and crawled through the opening, Danny close behind. Alfred and Harry were last through. Emerging on the far side of the blockage, they could see the way to the mezzanine was clear. To the west, they could just make out the shape of the doorway through to Dome Beta.

'Let's go,' Harry called from the rear of the group and Jim took the stairs two at a time, the others close behind.

Alfred was panting heavily and Harry stopped him a moment. 'You okay?' he asked.

'I'm fine,' the elderly man gasped. 'Fine.'

'No you're not. Here, let me help you,' Harry said, and got Alfred to lean on his shoulder.

'I'm all right,' Alfred grunted.

'Shut up.'

Alfred looked at him and produced a small laugh. 'There was a time I would have punched you out for that.'

'I'm sure there was,' Harry replied and heaved them up three more steps.

'Stop a second,' Alfred said. 'Just need to get my breath back.'

Harry wanted to press on. 'Of course,' he said heavily, and they stopped a few steps from the top of the staircase.

Alfred leaned on his knees and took several deep breaths.

'Better?'

'Much.' Then Alfred looked up at Harry. 'I feel bad about slapping the girl,' he said.

Harry stared back at him. 'It was the right thing to do, Alfred,' he replied earnestly. 'The kid was hysterical.' Then he produced a crooked grin. 'Besides, I've been wanting to slap her since I heard her first single.'

25

Pacific Ocean, Fiji

A sensor on the retraction unit lowered from the underside of the Big Mac spotted the dead body floating in the water and moved into position a few centimetres above it. The unit was a cylindrical object about a metre long. Operating under its own power, it was remotely controlled by the Big Mac and could not stray far, but it was an incredibly strong machine equipped with an array of grapplers, pulleys and platforms.

Pete was controlling the device using a synapsecap. It consisted of a close-fitting plastic mesh which covered the top of his head. Two flaps hung down over his ears. The synapsecap took impulses from Pete's brain and translated them into electrical impulses that controlled the retraction unit. Under his instructions, a pair of grappling arms extended from the sides of the machine. The arms lifted the body a metre or so above the surface of the ocean. Once satisfied the weight was evenly distributed, the unit indicated to Pete that it was ready to return. He guided it back into a holding bay under the Big Mac.

Pete could hear Mai's voice through his comms. 'God, what a mess!' she said, as she stared at the mangled body in the holding bay. This was the part of the job she found the hardest to deal with. She was a pilot, a scientist, with no inclination towards what she had been trained to think of as the 'soft sciences' like medicine and biology. Ironically, she was filled with admiration for her team mate Steph, E-Force's brilliant doctor, who coped so easily with the damaged living and the dead. That was certainly not 'soft'. But Mai knew her own skills centred on her ability to control machines. She felt comfortable solving problems that involved metal and plastic, data and mathematics – not human flesh. But she had been forced to overcome her squeamishness. What use was an emergency rescuer, she had told herself a hundred times, who felt uncomfortable around dead bodies?

'Please tell me he didn't drown,' Mark said, his voice coming through Mai's wrist communicator and breaking her train of thought. He was still aboard the Silverback watching Mai through the videolink as she turned the body over.

'Don't worry, Mark. This person was dead long before they reached the surface. Getting here a few minutes earlier would have made zero difference. They must have been on the top floor of Alpha.'

Mai crouched down beside the blackened form. The face was unrecognisable and the corpse's clothes were little more than seared fabric. She could just about tell the victim was female, and from the tattered remnants of a red, braided tunic, she was clearly one of the hotel staff.

'Any ID?' Mark asked.

Mai moved some of the charred fabric to one side and found a melted plastic tag on a narrow chain. She turned it over and wiped the surface with her gloved hand. Using the optical implant she had been given when she first joined E-Force, she was just able to make out a few words on the plastic. 'Michelle Lambert,' she said. 'Assistant Concierge.' The photo of the woman was as disfigured as the real thing.

'All right Mai. I'm sure poor Ms Lambert won't be the only floater we'll get tonight. Pete, keep scanning and bring the Big Mac down to the surface, I'm coming over. We need to get this show on the road.'

'Okay,' Mark said. He was standing close to the big screen at the far end of the conference room on the Big Mac, pointing to Tom's latest schematic. 'This is the Neptune.'

Knowing it would take precious time to cut through the red tape and secrecy of Bathoscope Holdings Limited, the corporation who had financed the building of the Neptune, Tom had simply hacked into their systems. It took him less than three minutes to find the files he wanted – the latest plans for the hotel complex, showing every aspect of the building's infrastructure down to the last conduit and junction box.

'As we learned from Sybil and Tom, the hotel is located approximately 100 metres below us on the continental shelf,' Mark continued. 'Half a kilometre north-east of here the ocean floor starts to drop away a thousand metres. We're using everything we have to get sensor readings of the ocean floor for a kilometre around the hotel, but at the moment the water is so churned up we hit trouble as soon as the floor falls below a few hundred metres. Tom's looking at the tectonic plates and searching for fissures anywhere on the continental shelf up to a 5 kilometre radius. So far, he's found nothing significant.'

'Which implies no quake,' Mai commented. She was sitting at a secondary control station nearby, her white plastic chair swivelled round to study the screen.

Pete was perched on the corner of a table to Mai's left. 'I've run a scan for explosives,' he said. 'Nothing.'

'And I've had the computer search for any hull breaches other than the top of Alpha,' Mai said and tapped at her control panel. A new schematic appeared on the screen. 'There are some fissures, here and here,' she said, moving her fingers over the panel to control a pointer on the screen. 'But all those sections have automatically sealed themselves off.'

'Well, that's something,' Mark commented. 'So let's concentrate on how we can get the survivors out of there. We've made another satellite sweep of the hotel and, just as I feared, many of those warm red dots we saw on the thermograph at Base One have changed to blue – bodies grown cold.'

'How many are we talking about?' Mai asked.

'Tom's found the guest list for tonight's extravaganza. Ninety-five guests and 107 staff. More than 150 people were in Gamma, which was the worst hit dome. There are only 27 life signs there now. There are nine more in Beta and six in Alpha.'

'Just 42 survivors!'

'At the moment. It's impossible to tell how many of those will die from serious injuries.'

The room was silent except for the hum of the Big Mac's systems and, far off, the sound of waves lapping against the aircraft's hull.

Mark tapped at a virtual keyboard, a simple pattern of light on the surface of a plastic panel close to the screen. 'The Hunter is sending back some images,' he said, and the screen filled with a grey murk. It began to clear as the Hunter drew close to the domes and they could all see the sharp outline of the stricken hotel. Gradually, the definition improved and a digitally enhanced visual appeared, taken from the west of the hotel some 35 metres from Dome Alpha.

From this angle the damage did not appear too bad. They could see some holes in the outer casing of the enormous dome and the passage connecting it to Beta was buckled, but it had held. The Hunter, a sophisticated surveillance device that hovered over land, could withstand extremes of heat and cold and was also able to deal with the pressure up to an ocean depth of 2000 metres. It moved forward slowly, then swerved towards the south, giving the team a clear view of Beta and Gamma.

All the domes were blacked out with a few patches of dull radiance, but nothing of the inside of the hotel could be seen. There were large cracks in the casing of Beta and it had been twisted by the shock of whatever it was that had hit the building. The dome was tilted at an angle of approximately 5 degrees from the vertical. The walkway between Beta and Gamma was contorted. But this too had held, which meant all three domes were still connected.

Gamma was a real mess. It was leaning to the north. At the southern end, closest to the Hunter, parts of the dome's foundations had been wrenched away from the rock of the continental shelf. Two sections had been ripped from the main body of the structure, but emergency bulkheads had confined the damage and stopped water rushing into the rest of the building. The Hunter moved around the dome, skirting its base. From the north, the team in the Big Mac had a clearer view of the damage done to the top of the dome. The metal cap at the apex of the huge glass structure looked sturdy enough, but they could see fissures in the glass, dark jagged lines running down randomly from the cap. Some of these stretched almost halfway to the dome's base. From this angle, the Hunter was just able to pick out shifting patterns on the other side of the glass.

'Are they people moving around?' Mai asked, astonished.

Mark didn't answer. Instead, he let his fingers skitter over the plastic control panel and they could all see the image shift. The Hunter was moving closer.

'I don't want to alarm anyone,' Mark commented. 'So I think we shouldn't let the Hunter go too close. But there. Yes . . . human shapes.'

They could just make out the form of four men moving east across what remained of the banqueting suite. By ramping up the definition and shifting the lens on the Hunter to maximum magnification they could get some idea of the devastation inside the building. Metal beams dangled from the ceiling. Huge tables had been reduced to matchwood. There were heaps of rubble everywhere.

Mark touched the controls and instructed the Hunter to return to the Big Mac. Then he turned to the others. 'Looks like we've got our work cut out, guys.'

26

Dome Gamma

Michael Xavier peered through the gloom towards the east of the ballroom and pulled himself up onto a pile of rubble that had completely blocked the path to the emergency stairs. He slipped and almost went over. Bandonis, the engineer, just caught him. 'Thanks,' he said.

Michael was about to take a step forward when Bandonis grabbed his shoulder. 'Stop.'

'What?'

'An electric hum.'

'I can't hear . . . Yeah, there,' Johnny Xavier said as Bandonis descended the slope the other side of the pile of rubble. Xavier and the security man, Craig Deloray, watched as Bandonis bent down to an electrical cable. It was thrashing around like an angry snake. He grabbed it a foot from the live end and pulled it back, extracting a length of black plastic from the loose top layer of rubble. When it was a safe distance away, he lowered it to the ground, pinned it with a boulder and headed back up the slope. 'Nasty,' he said, reaching the others.

Beyond the pile of rubble, the area was clearer, with patches of floor just visible in the dim emergency lights.

'The stairs are straight ahead,' Michael said and led the others on. All around them, dust was falling like snow, and a constant creaking sound came from the outer rim of the ballroom. The infrastructure was groaning and straining.

They reached the door to the stairwell. It was different to the open one in the west of the dome. A narrow bridge crossed the pool on the edge of the dome. On the far side, close to the huge expanse of glass, a passage fell away to an access door 2 metres below floor level. Across the door were the words: 'EMERGENCY STAIRS'.

Michael tried the handle. It turned. He pushed. Nothing. The door would not move a millimetre. 'Help me,' he said to his brother. The two of them leaned on the door. Nothing. Michael ran at the door but only succeeded in bashing his shoulder. He yelped as pain shot up his neck and through his damaged ribcage.

'It's hopeless,' Johnny Xavier gasped. He looked defeated.

'Rubbish,' Michael snapped back. 'Miguel, Craig. Let's try again.' The three of them squeezed together across the width of the door and leaned their combined weight against it. They stopped to take a breath, then pushed again. It was obviously impossible. Whatever was behind the door was huge and heavy. They would never get it to open.

'Oh, great!' Johnny exclaimed. 'Told you it was hopeless.'

Craig Deloray looked away and sighed. Michael Xavier studiously ignored his brother, but Miguel Bandonis was suddenly brimming over with rage.

'Is that all you can say?' he exclaimed. 'Told you so!'

Johnny gave the man a contemptuous look. 'Why? You have some words of wisdom for us?'

The engineer was silent for a moment. Then he said, 'This is *your* fault.'

Michael Xavier and Craig Deloray stared at him. Johnny gazed down at the ground, grinding his teeth, his mouth clamped shut. He looked up, glaring at Bandonis.

Unflinching, Bandonis met Xavier's eyes. He knew his chances of getting out of this place alive were slender. He did not want to die still complicit in Xavier's crimes.

'What do you mean, Miguel?' Michael asked calmly, looking from his brother to the other man.

'Your brother here decided to cut back on the budget. He slashed the sensor numbers for the electronic units in Dome Alpha by two-thirds. We had a small fire in service conduit Number 6 earlier this evening. It shouldn't have caused any trouble, but obviously it wasn't picked up. No sensors in the unit, see.'

'But that's impossible,' Michael said, glaring at Bandonis. 'I've seen the inventories and the audits. Everything tallies.'

'He fixed it,' Bandonis hissed, nodding towards Johnny Xavier. 'Two inventories, two audits.'

'But . . . but, why?'

'He's lying, Mike.'

'It's the truth,' Bandonis snapped back. 'I've seen the cuts everywhere. The sensors are just one example. He pulled a lot of the fire retardant insulation, the communications net to the surface is compromised. And,' Bandonis concluded, with a new edge of disgust in his voice, '. . . at least two of the emergency subs are duds.'

'It's a lie!' Johnny Xavier exclaimed, and without warning he charged at the engineer, his eyes ablaze.

Bandonis was short, but exceptionally strong. He had also spent five years studying karate. As Johnny Xavier's fist flew towards his face, he dodged it and caught the man's arm, twisted it behind him, span him round and smashed his fist into the small of his back. Johnny crumpled. In a flash, Bandonis had his foot on Xavier's throat.

'Enough,' Michael barked and Bandonis reluctantly took his foot away.

Johnny staggered to his feet, rubbing his neck and gasping. Standing upright, he refused to look at the engineer.

Michael turned to his brother. 'Others had hinted at this,' he said. 'But I didn't believe them.'

'Oh come on, Mike.'

Michael Xavier had his hand up. 'Don't . . . don't.' For a moment, the older Xavier looked incredibly sad. 'I just hope you realise what you've done, Johnny.'

'I did not . . .'

With astonishing speed, Michael's left hand flew out and grabbed his brother by the throat.

Johnny froze. He had never seen his brother do anything remotely like this before. No one had. He was always such a placid, level-headed man. Michael's face was distorted by fury. Then he too froze, almost as though a shock had passed through him. 'We'll discuss this if we ever get out of here alive,' he spat. And Miguel and Craig could see the older Xavier's fingers whiten as his grip tightened about Johnny's throat. For the second time in a minute, Johnny was choking, his face darkening. Then Michael let his hand fall. He stepped back, turned, and without a word headed towards the small group of survivors gathered close to the centre of the ballroom.

27

Pacific Ocean, Fiji

The Big Mac floated stationary, directly above the Neptune Hotel. Mai and Pete had just left the flight deck to suit up when the comms sounded. Mark was sitting at the main control panel and looked up as Tom's face appeared on the screen in front of him.

'Tom. What's happenin'?'

'I don't want to worry anyone unduly, but we have a problem.'

Mark stared at him, saying nothing.

'Josh and Steph haven't made their last two designated call-ins.'

Mark looked down at the control panel and ran a hand over his cropped hair. 'You checked with BigEye?'

'No sign of them. The last comm was from Josh a while after taking off from Polar Base. He sent through their flight plan. That was almost an hour ago.'

'And the flight plan was pretty clear?'

'Yeah. What you'd expect – a course almost directly east and then south, avoiding anything controversial.'

Mark stared at the flight plan Tom had sent over and ran calculations through his head. 'I take it Josh was flying.'

'Yep.'

Mark sighed. 'You thinking what I'm thinking?'

'Probably, dude.'

Mark sighed again, heavily, then brought his hand down hard on the plastic panel, making Tom flinch. 'Fantastic, Josh. Thanks buddy.'

'That might be jumping to conclusions.'

'Bullshit.'

Tom fell silent.

'Could they be deliberately blocking the BigEye's detection frequencies? Trying to play hide-and-seek to stop us realising what damn fools they're being?'

Tom looked surprised. 'It's possible, I guess. But there's one other thing you should know, Mark.'

The team leader looked into Tom's face.

'I've lost their life signs. At best, their cybersuits are down.'

28

The *Narcis* and its twin, the *Drebbel*, were submarines like no other. In the days of E-Force's conception, when Mark Harrison had sat down with a team of engineers and designers from CARPA and thrashed out what would be needed by a rescue team, a super sub was close to the top of the wish list. After all, it made sense. The earth's surface is 71 per cent ocean, so there was a strong possibility the team would have to make underwater rescues pretty frequently.

The *Narcis,* sitting closest to the exit of the cargo bay in the bowels of the Big Mac, was named after the man who built the first submarine – the Catalan engineer and political radical, Narcis Monturiol. Twenty-five metres in length, it could carry a crew of six and, in an emergency, transport 23 passengers. However, if required, it could also be operated by a single submariner. Nuclear powered, the *Narcis* had a top speed of over 100 knots and could stay submerged indefinitely. It was incredibly manoeuvrable, and thanks to the carbonanotubes used in the honeycomb structure of its hull, the sub was capable of descending 4000 metres beneath the surface. It was transported in the cavernous hold of the Big Mac and was now poised, ready for launch.

Mai was in the pilot seat, Pete in the navigator's station beside her. The control modules of the *Narcis* were similar to those of the Silverbacks and the Big Mac. In front of Mai and Pete stood two long plastic panels. There were no switches or dials on the modules, just shifting patterns of light. Numbers and symbols flashed across the surface. In front of the pilot and navigator was a large holographic projection unit which produced a high-definition 3D image that floated above the control module. On the front wall, a screen projected images of the outside of the submarine taken from a dozen different microcameras dotted around the hull of the craft.

Mai ran her fingers over the guidance module, making last-minute checks. When she was satisfied, she glanced up at the screen. 'All systems green,' she said.

'Copy that, Mai,' Mark said from the flight deck of the Big Mac and he instructed the computer to open the main exit to the cargo hold.

Mai and Pete watched as the huge steel door lowered outwards slowly, forming a ramp from the end of the aircraft to the surface of the water. The submarine stood on a mechanical sled. Mai touched the controls and it began to slide forward, picking up speed as it went. In a moment, the *Narcis* reached the end of the ramp and slid smoothly into the water. Mai glided the sub into a sharp descent and made a quarter turn to bring it onto the pre-designated course to the hotel.

'ETA 83 seconds,' Mai announced. 'I'm going to take her straight down to Dome Alpha. Any updates from the Hunter, Mark?'

'The docking bay at the base of Alpha is pretty badly damaged. The sensors on the Hunter haven't managed to get a clear image because the water is churned up and the dock has been covered with debris and sediment. But you couldn't have used it anyway.'

'Why?'

As an answer, he sent over a schematic of the hotel. 'Close in on the dock,' he said.

Mai honed in on the lowest level of Dome Alpha, the docking bay. Pete came and stood beside her chair. She adjusted some controls and the 2D schematic was transferred to the holoscreen. It appeared as a set of green lines and shaded areas. They could both see that the door to the outer lock opened into a large cylindrical passage.

'Specially designed submarines from Suva travel through the doors into the opening,' Mark said. 'The outer door closes and the pressure differential is adjusted. A second docking station extends out from the far wall of the cylinder and hooks up with the nose of the sub. Passengers emerge through a short passageway into a pressurised inner lock. From there, an elevator takes them to the ground floor of Alpha and on to Reception. So, the dock is useless,' he concluded. 'It's all been designed to operate only with compatible components.'

Pete and Mai stared in silence at the image on the screen. Then Mai said, 'There must be a universal dock . . . in case of emergencies.'

'There is,' Mark responded. 'It's round the other side of the dome under the linkway to Beta. Head straight there. It's your best chance of getting into the hotel.'

For the next minute there was silence over the comms. Then Pete's voice cut through. 'We're at 96 metres, Mark,' he said. 'Heading south towards the linkway. We have a visual.'

On the screen, the lumpy, distorted shape of the hotel came into view.

'Taking us into grid ref 88976,' Pete said, his eyes darting over the control panel. He made minor adjustments to their course, then studied the screen again, watching as the hotel filled the view.

They passed under the linkway on the ground floor level between Domes Alpha and Beta. The linkway looked virtually untouched, the curved glass panels unscathed. The universal dock came into view as they turned towards the west and the lowest level of Alpha.

At first, the image was unclear. Then they realised the impression they had of the structural integrity of this part of the hotel had been overly optimistic. The linkway had not be compromised, but from where they were now positioned, Mai and Pete could see that a huge metal strut had come loose from the ground floor. It was one of four supporting beams that held up the linkway. The beam weighed more than 3 tonnes. At the linkway end it was hanging by a perilously small strip of twisted rivets. The bottom end of the beam had come to rest against the ocean floor, blocking the door to the universal dock. Any attempt to move it would bring the linkway crashing down.

'Damn it!' Mai exclaimed. 'I guess it's back to the first dock. It's our only hope.'

29

Gobi Desert, China

'Warning. Warning. Structural integrity at 5 per cent. Warning. Warning.'

The sound resonated around the cockpit of the Silverback at ear-splitting volume. But to Steph, it was little more than a whisper, a distant voice calling to her through a dense fog. She could see a light ahead, the welcoming glow of a cottage nestled in the woods. She could smell freshly baked bread. But then the cottage burst into flames and a red glow filled her vision.

Steph came to as hungry flames licked at her arm. She screamed, uncomprehending. She slapped at the flames along her arm, then reached for the control panel. It was shattered, a complete mess. When she tried turning to her left, a sharp pain shot down her neck and along her spine. The cockpit was beginning to fill with smoke.

'Warning. Warning. Life support failing. Structural integrity 4.5 per cent.' No longer a whisper, the computer's emergency alarm yelled at her.

Quelling the rising panic, Steph hit the canopy lock at her side. Nothing happened. She hit it again, harder, and there came a high-pitched whistle from deep inside the plane. She slammed her hand against the canopy and felt it move. It was only then she realised it had cracked. With lightning speed, she unbuckled herself. Stretching up, she found the opening in the canopy and pushed her fingers between the sheets of carboglass. The sharp edges cut into her and she pulled her fingers away quickly. Looking down at her cyber-suit she could see there were great rips in the fabric. A flap of material hung loose at her left wrist. She pulled at it and it came away. Then, not pausing for a second, she wrapped the cloth around her right hand and pushed back on the edge of the canopy. It was stuck fast. Taking a deep breath, Steph heaved at it with all her strength until it gave, suddenly, yawing up on a single buckled hinge.

Sticking her head above the edge of the cockpit, she saw a world that looked like an abstract painting. The plane was cast in an orange glow, but beyond this lay absolute black-ness. The Silverback was tilted to starboard. Its nose was buried, or torn off – it was hard to tell in the umbra. Both wings had been ripped away and a fire raged at the rear of the wrecked plane.

'Warning. Warning. Structural integrity 4 per cent.'

Steph scrambled out of the cockpit, pulling herself up onto the rim. Then she crawled forward to the pilot's compartment. The canopy had been ripped away and a terrible jolt of fear hit her. She could see nothing in the dull orange murk. Pulling herself along the hot metal of the plane, she reached the jagged edge of the pilot's compartment on the port side. Barely thinking, she stabbed at the controls on the wrist of the cyber-suit. Nothing would be working normally of course, but after the team's first mission at the California Conference Center in Los Angeles, their suits had been modified. An emergency backup system would kick in if the link to Base One was interrupted. It provided them with only a rudi-mentary internal network, but it could mean the differ-ence between life and death.

To Steph's huge relief, the emergency backup stuttered to life, a dull glow came from the miniature screen at her wrist. She tapped the screen and her helmet light came on. The beam was a sickly pale lemon, but as she moved her head, light fell across the cockpit and she could see Josh, his head down on the control panel, his arms limp at his sides.

'Josh!' Steph screamed. 'Josh!'

No reaction.

Steph ran her hand along Josh's neck, searching for a pulse. She found it. It was steady. She leaned in and tried to lift him under the arms, but he was stuck fast. Then she realised he was still buckled in. She leaned into the cockpit as far as she could and just reached the buckle with the tips of her fingers. Straining forward, she caught the release button on the restraint and the straps snapped apart. She pulled Josh back against the seat and levered her hands under his shoulders. Taking a deep breath, she yanked at him, but he was too heavy.

'Josh. Josh. You have to wake up. Josh!'

Nothing.

She steadied herself by gripping the edge of the cockpit with her left hand and slapped Josh with her right. His face lolled right, then left. But he was still unconscious.

'Josh!' Steph screamed and shook him. 'Wake up!'

Nothing.

'Warning. Warning. Rear hull temperature at critical. Eject! Eject!'

Steph was oblivious to the irony. She wasn't even listening.

She bunched her right fist and slammed it into Josh's jaw. Wincing as the shock of impact rippled up her arm, she slumped forward, tears welling in her eyes.

'Josh . . . please.'

She closed her eyes, her cheek against the rough fabric of his shredded cybersuit.

'Yeah? What is it, Steph?'

Steph lifted her head, stunned. She stared at Josh in disbelief. His eyes were closed. He smacked his lips and smiled as though he was having a pleasant dream.

Steph shook him and he opened his eyes. 'Get out of the plane, Josh. NOW!'

The smile vanished from Josh's face as he realised the cold reality of the situation. Then his eyes glazed over, his face contorted, and a wave of anguish shuddered across his features as the pain hit.

Steph couldn't give him a second to think. She pulled at him. 'GET OUT,' she shrieked. 'FOR GOD'S SAKE . . . !'

Josh pushed upwards and screamed. But he kept going. With a gargantuan effort, he made it to the edge of the canopy. Steph slithered down the side of the fuselage, pulling Josh with her.

'Warning. Warning. Structural integrity 1 per cent. Eject. Eject.'

Steph reached the sand a few seconds before Josh and tried to grab him around the waist. He reached the ground and collapsed. Steph's helmet light cast a sorrowful circle of orange onto the carpet of sand. Josh fell out of the light, and for a fleeting moment, he simply vanished.

'It's my right leg,' he said. 'Broken.'

She looked down, but could see almost nothing in the sallow helmet beam. She pulled herself up and under Josh's shoulder. 'Lean your weight on me,' she hissed, taking the strain and feeling every bone in her body scream at her. Finding strength she never knew she had, she managed to drag Josh's 110-kilo limp form 70 metres away from the plane.

When the explosion came, Steph felt the heat first; a scorching blast of hot air hit her back and seemed to envelop her like a shroud. Then came the sound – a gut-wrenching roar. She fell forward with Josh beneath her and heard him scream as her weight crushed his broken leg. Hot air whooshed over them. Steph tucked her head down and protected Josh as best she could, willing the pulsating heat and the ear-splitting noise to stop. But every second seemed to stretch to a minute . . . she felt trapped in a universe of thunder, heat and intense pain.

30

When Steph woke it was pitch black and freezing cold. The material of the destroyed plane was fire-retardant, so even though it had been blown into hundreds of pieces, those pieces did not burn for long. The insipid red of combusting fuselage had been snuffed out. So too had the beam from her helmet light. The battery only lasted an hour.

She pulled herself up, shivering, and as her eyes adjusted to the light, she could make out shapes. Josh's prone form in the gritty sand, pieces of ripped cybersuit and, eventually, her emergency backup belt, a sort of bum bag that was always worn over the cybersuit. It was a throwback, but another smart idea of Mark Harrison's from the earliest design days.

Steph grasped the belt and pulled it towards her. Inside was a Swiss Army knife, a box of matches, a whistle and a pocket torch. She flicked on the torch and swept it around her. Crouching down, she turned Josh over, dreading the worst. She felt for his pulse.

'Josh?' She shook him.

He opened his eyes. 'What the hell's . . . ?'

'We crashed . . . remember? You hijacked *Paul*. If you weren't injured and I wasn't a doctor, I'd smash your face in.'

He raised his eyebrows and let out a heavy sigh. Then he tried to move and cried out in pain.

Steph turned the beam to his leg. With expert fingers she gently prised away some of the fabric of the suit. His knee was a mess, bones protruded from ripped skin, blood had congealed around the wound. 'Looks like you've fractured your patella.'

'And no nanobots.'

'Not sure. They're integrated into the suits, remember.'

'Painkillers? They would be cool.' He winced.

'Let me see your wrist monitor.'

Josh lifted his left arm, trying to move as little as possible. Steph tapped at the screen, but it was dead. She checked her own wrist. It produced a pale blue light. 'Hang on,' she said, and scrolled through the information on the screen. 'Some systems are working. And, yes . . . I have signal transmission capacity over short distances. Which means . . .' she tapped a couple more times. 'I can instruct your suit to release the good stuff. There . . . it'll take a few seconds.'

'What about you, Steph? You hurt?'

'I'm fine,' she said, and for the first time realised just how fortunate she had been. She felt as though she had gone 10 rounds with a prize fighter and she was covered in cuts and bruises – but nothing serious.

She helped Josh remove his backpack, a unit only a couple of centimetres thick made from almost weightless carbon-iridium fibres. It was used in emergency situations to supply oxygen for up to 24 hours. It contained a chamber adjoined to the oxygen production tank which provided enough water and essential nutrients for a week. She placed the pack on the ground and helped Josh lie back with his head on the pack. He yelped in pain as his knee twisted, and Steph could see in the pale torchlight that his forehead was beaded in sweat.

'Wow,' Josh said as the painkillers kicked in. 'That's much better. Thank God for technology, eh?'

'Okay. Assessment,' Steph said. 'One: where are we?'

'What was the last position you recorded?' He sounded exhausted.

A glance at her wrist monitor told Steph where they had been when the CyberLink between the plane and her suit snapped: 117.45°E, 43.66°N.

'Well, we can't be too far from there. Not that it means much.'

'We have no comms. It looks like your suit is completely inoperable. Mine has limited capacity.'

'I'm freezing,' Josh said. The cold had only really hit him now the pain had been chemically dampened.

'Me too. The thermal regulators are offline and the internal temperature controls are obviously damaged in both suits.'

Steph tried the water tube connected to her backpack. It was fine. She tapped her wrist to see what the situation was with the emergency nutrients, only to find that the connection to her suit had been broken. She leaned over to test Josh's emergency water and nutrient tubes. They were dead. 'Okay, we've got water from my pack, but no nutrients.'

'The first priority is getting warm,' Josh responded and shivered. He looked up at the black sky. 'What time is it?'

Steph glanced at her watch. '19.33 local time.'

'It's going to get a lot colder.'

Steph simply nodded. She stood up and started scrambling in the sand.

'What you doing?'

'Basic survival, Josh. Remember Course 46? Surely you couldn't have forgotten that!'

'No.'

Steph clawed at the sand and began piling it onto Josh's body. 'It'll conserve the little body heat you have,' she said.

'And what about you?'

'I'm going to do a reccie while the torch lasts. See what I can find.'

A few moments later, Josh was covered from neck to toe in a mound of gritty sand. Steph crouched down beside his head. 'Here,' she said, plucking up a couple of scraps of cyber-suit material and placing them over Josh's head, leaving his eyes, ears and mouth exposed. 'You can lose over 50 per cent of body heat through your head.'

'I know,' Josh replied testily. 'I don't think I've ever felt so vulnerable . . . or so humiliated.'

'Oh shut up! I still haven't ruled out leaving you there after what you did,' Steph retorted. 'You'll be fine. I'll be back before you know it.'

31

The torch was weak, but its narrow beam lit up a surprisingly large area in the pitch darkness. Steph could smell burning plastic and rubber and followed her nose. The first thing she found was a Maxinium panel. The metal was almost untouched but it had been sheared from the plane along a join. Close by lay a chunk of carboglass, a piece of Silverback canopy. As she walked on she found more and more pieces of plane, modules with wires protruding, pieces of the plastic consoles, engine parts still smouldering in the sand. Then, she caught a flash of red.

She extinguished the torch. It was hard to tell how far away the fire was, but it was definitely fire. She flicked the torch on again and picked her way through the debris, sweeping the beam to left and right as she went.

The fire was small, enclosed in a bowl-shaped piece of Maxinium containing aviation fuel. Some flammable parts of the Silverback's interior had fallen into the liquid and kept the fire burning. It stank and Steph was forced to keep her free hand over her mouth. The flame would not last long – the fuel had almost gone and the flammable materials were almost used up.

Steph moved the torch around in a regular search pattern, scanning the sand for anything she could use to keep the fire going. There was nothing but lumps of twisted metal, electrical components and featureless plastic sheets. Widening the search, she paced out a square with the burning debris at the epicentre.

When she found it, she almost fell over it – a dried out shrub, a sagebrush perished in the cold. It was a rather pathetic specimen, little more than a bunch of tendrils sprouting from a central stem. It was about half a metre tall with a spindly trunk. She crouched down and yanked at the dead plant. It was stuck fast: 'Yep . . . roots have to go deep in a desert,' she said aloud.

After a second failed attempt, she sat back in the sand and took a deep exhausted breath. Unzipping her backup belt, she pulled out the Swiss Army knife, opened the blade and attacked the trunk of the dead plant, hacking at it with all the energy she could muster. The knife cut through the dry wood with surprising ease and she pulled the plant away.

Back at the burning wreckage, she snapped a large desiccated branch away from the trunk of the shrub and tossed it into the last of the burning fuel. It caught immediately, red tracers slithering along the dead fingers of wood. Steph then added three more pieces, and gradually, the area around her began to lighten. She flicked off her torch and tucked it into her backup belt. At the edge of the pool of light, she could see dozens of dead plants similar to the one she had just incinerated.

Thrusting a branch into the fuel, she held it above her head, and set off to explore the area. She followed a square search pattern as she had done before. This served two purposes. It would allow her to know where she was in the dim light, and it ensured she missed nothing.

Most of the wreckage was useless, but there were a few things that could mean the difference between life and death for her and Josh. Sheets of plastic for building a shelter, lengths of cabling and wires from the complex electrical systems of the Silverback that could be used as binding. But what she really wanted was a working radio or even one of the emergency beacons. She knew these were stowed in a specially constructed Maxinium box in the main body of the plane immediately beneath the cockpit. The trouble was, the wreckage from *Paul* was probably scattered for hundreds of metres around. The chances of finding a beacon were not good.

She gave it 10 minutes and decided she had to get back to Josh. Returning to the small fire she had nurtured, she threw the last twigs from the dead plant onto the pyre and ran over to where the other dried out shrubs stood. Five minutes later, she was back at the fire clutching two more bundles of dried wood. She threw a few branches onto the fire for good measure then, crouching down, she used some of the electrical cabling she had found to bind together the remaining branches. Using the last piece of wire, she tied it to the binding, made a loop at the other end, and with a blazing branch in her left hand, she dragged the wood across the sand, heading back towards her team mate.

The exertion of pulling along the bundle of wood started to warm her up, but she began to sweat and this cooled her down again. Her damaged suit clung to her and she shivered as she strode on. She had to get back and build a fire as soon as possible, or they would both die of hypothermia.

After a few minutes, the patch of light from the burning branch lit up a familiar rock formation and she knew she was almost back where she had left Josh. She lowered the branch to cast light onto the ground immediately ahead of her. Two steps on, and she glimpsed the mound of sand she had made 20 minutes earlier. But it looked different. Moving the flaming torch a little way to her left, she checked to see how Josh was doing.

Jolting backward, she almost dropped the branch. He had gone.

32

Base One, Tintara Island

Tom Erickson was in his quarters. In the eight months since Mark Harrison had recruited him and got him out of Aldermont Correctional Facility, Tom had been away from Tintara for a total of just five days. Two of those had been to visit Los Angeles for publicity, the other three were to visit his folks in Baltimore. As the only member of E-Force rooted to his post on the island, his bond with Base One was especially strong. He considered it home.

Tom had made his quarters the hub of his world. It was wired to Cyber Control in the main building so that all data streams and computing facilities could be accessed on a screen that took up an entire wall of Tom's room. Computers were Tom's life, and his room was his version of a cybersuit.

He wheeled his chair into the centre of the floor and faced the screen.

'Sybil,' he said. 'A detailed map of north-east Russia, Mongolia, north-east China please, in the range 77 degrees to 118 degrees east, 40 degrees to 50 degrees north.' The screen filled with the required portion of the earth's surface. At the very top of the picture, a red beacon shone – the location of Polar Base.

'So, what's the story then, Josh? Steph?' Tom said aloud. 'What happened after you left Semja Alexandry?' He stared at the screen, lost in thought. 'Syb? How long after takeoff from Semja was the last verbal communication from the Silverback?'

'Eighteen minutes 23 seconds.'

'So that would make it,' he did a quick mental calculation, '12.28 local time.'

'12.28.09.'

'Thanks! Do you have the transmission on file?'

'Of course.'

'What was their location?'

'110.48 east, 49.78 north,' Sybil replied immediately.

'And what time did the signals from the suits cut out?'

'12.32.23.'

'So that's just over four minutes flying time after the last verbal contact.'

'Four minutes, 14 seconds.'

'Which, at Mach 10, is about . . . 900 kilometres.'

'864.21 kilometres.'

'Sybil, project a circle onto the map centred at the coordinates of the last transmission.'

A circle appeared on the map, sweeping 360 degrees like a search pattern on an old-style radar screen. It covered a vast area, more than two million square kilometres. 'What was the Silverback's course at the time of the last transmission, Sybil?'

'Heading 149.34 degrees south-south-east.'

'Superimpose it on the map, please.'

A red dotted line appeared.

'So, let's make some assumptions. Suppose the plane crashed. Suppose that after the last transmission they didn't change speed or direction. That would bring them down just about . . .' And Tom tapped his virtual keyboard. 'There.'

A red flashing dot appeared on the map.

Tom read the coordinates. '115.45 east, 42.65 north. The Gobi Desert, just inside the Mongolian border.'

'You are making some very imprecise assumptions.'

'I know, Syb,' Tom responded, staring blankly at the screen. 'I know.'

33

Pacific Ocean

Pete and Mai decided not to retrace their route back to the main dock. Instead, they pushed south to circle the base of Dome Alpha from the opposite direction. It was a mistake that cost them 10 minutes – the route was strewn with pylons and flapping cables and they were forced to reduce speed to ensure they did not snag anything that might be keeping the dome stable.

As the *Narcis* approached the dock they could see that some of the dust and debris had settled. It afforded them a clearer view.

'I'm running a spectrum analysis,' Mai said, tapping at her control panel. A full sweep of the mangled dock with sensors on the *Narcis* would show them the stress lines and the precise way the dock had been damaged.

The results appeared simultaneously on their screen and on Mark's in the Big Mac. Pete studied the coloured stripes and the fracture lines.

'Twist fractures mainly,' Pete said. 'Produced when the dome wobbled and tilted. But something hit it too. See the pattern there, the concentric circles?'

Mai considered the image and closed in on the door of the dock. 'Okay, so what do you suggest?' she asked.

'The sonic drill would be the easiest thing. We could blow a hole through the door in a few seconds, but it would be dangerous.'

'Let me check,' Mark said from the Big Mac. Pete and Mai heard him talking to Sybil through the comms link with Tintara. His voice came over the speaker. 'You're right, Pete. Sybil has calculated that anything more than a millisecond sonic drill burst would create a wave front that will disturb Dome Alpha's fragile foundations. It could bring the whole thing down.'

'How long a burst of the drill would we need?' Mai asked.

'Too long,' Pete responded. 'We're going to have to blow a hole in the door the old-fashioned way, with explosives.'

'But won't that cause a similar disturbance and destabilise the dome?'

'Not the way I do it, lass,' Pete replied, his eyes sparkling.

Pete was suited up in under two minutes. The E-Force cybersuit doubled as a diving suit. He had to upgrade the helmet to one specially designed for high pressure environments and flippers were slipped over the skintight smart fabric of the suit's feet, but no oxygen tank was needed as the backpack of the suit served all requirements.

Pete opened the inner lock and entered a long, narrow, low-ceilinged passageway. A subaqua scooter stood close to the outer door. Checking his suit settings, he spoke into his comms. 'Ready, Mai.'

The chamber filled with water, the outer door slid open and Pete moved slowly through the hatch. He started up the scooter and studied a small screen between the handle grips. Depth 98.5 metres. Pressure 9.67 atmospheres. Water temperature 6.3 degrees Celsius.

The water all around the dome was churned up, as though a giant food mixer had been dipped in and switched on. Through the visor of his helmet, Pete could see the damaged dock door. Pushing the scooter to half speed, he shot forward, covering the hundred metres to the door in a couple of seconds. Mooring the scooter to a metal bar jutting from the side of the hotel, he swam over.

A quick inspection of the steel door confirmed Pete's impressions of how to blast it away with minimal disturbance to everything around it. From a pouch at his belt, he extricated a thumbnail-sized piece of explosive material nicknamed HELP – high explosive lithium plastic. It was a unique formulation which he had developed with CARPA scientists and the tech guys on Tintara. Blending his experience of explosives with the amazing new synthetic materials CARPA had in its labs, Pete had come up with an explosive that ticked every box. It was lightweight, extremely malleable and very powerful, so that only small amounts were needed for most jobs. It was also remarkably stable and therefore safe to transport.

Pete eyed the metal surface, running calculations through his head as he broke the tiny piece of plastic into half a dozen smaller bits, placing them in a seemingly random pattern on the distorted metal. He then ran a set of narrow wires between the lumps. The wires were connected to a metal box which he stuck to the door frame with a suction pad. A light flashed green on the sealed unit. At the last minute, he moved one of the pieces of explosive a couple of millimetres to the left. Satisfied, he returned to the scooter, stopping 50 metres away from the dock. Pete glanced at the monitor on the wrist of his cybersuit. Tapping a sequence on the tiny keyboard, he touched the screen and paused, looked at the door and took a breath before touching the monitor again.

There was a momentary flash of yellow. Burning lithium compounds from the knot of HELP flew out from the door, creating pale red and white streamers of fire that were quickly snuffed out. A pocket of air formed and grew, bursting into a thousand smaller bubbles. Pete felt a wave front of displaced water hit him, followed by a secondary vibration from ricocheted energy. A few moments later, the gases from the blast had dissipated and pieces of metal floated down to settle on the seabed under the bottom of the dock. Within a minute, the water had cleared and Pete could see a neat, metre-wide hole punched in the door. Beyond that lay a featureless black passageway leading to the inner door of the air lock.

'Well done, Pete,' Mark said through the comms. 'Mai's already on her way.'

Pete looked up to see the outer door of the *Narcis* open and Mai speeding towards him, her scooter churning through the water. He turned, flicked the accelerator of his scooter and headed for the opening in the dock. Tethering his machine to the hotel wall, he watched as Mai drew alongside.

'Neat work,' she said, studying the hole in the door.

'Yeah, I'm a neat freak when I blow things up,' Pete replied.

Mai anchored her scooter to the same spot and followed Pete as he swam into the newly formed opening.

It was pitch black inside, but their helmet lights were powerful and cut broad swatches of light in the passageway. The channel was about 35 metres in length, just big enough to hold the subs used to transport guests from Suva. Specially sealed electrical conduits ran the length of the dock. On the floor lay a pair of metal rails, and at one end stood a cradle for incoming subs.

'So far, so good,' Mark said from the flight deck of the Big Mac, 100 metres above their heads. 'Next step, try the pumps. The manual override switches are close to the inner door on the north wall.'

It took Mai and Pete only a few seconds to find the controls. They were sealed units with touch-sensitive screens. The screens were blank.

'No power, by the look of it,' Mai said.

'There should be a backup control,' Mark's voice emerged from their comms. 'Hang on.' They could hear him tapping at the virtual keyboard on the control panel of the aircraft. 'Okay, I've got the detailed schematic here. The backup control is a red metal lever to the right of the control box.'

'Got it,' Mai said. She pulled on the lever, it clicked into place and the dock filled with a tremendous noise. The water in the chamber began to churn violently. Mai slammed the lever back as fast as she could and the cacophony stopped abruptly. 'Whoa! Seems to be working!'

'Fantastic,' Mark responded. 'Better get the sheeting up.'

Pete and Mai swam back to the door and trod water. From a pocket in the leg of her suit, Mai removed a rectangular block of Morphadin. A white rubberlike material, Morphadin was another product of collaboration between Pete and the scientists at CARPA. It was a superstrong 'smart material' that could be morphed into any shape desired. In the lab, the inventors lightheartedly referred to it as playdough.

Mai started to mould the Morphadin with practised fingers, quickly stretching it into a tray-sized rectangle. Pete took one end, and between them, they opened out the material as though it were a sheet of well-chewed gum. Moving the rectangle into position close to the door, Mai and Pete pulled from each end and pushed the material hard up against the wall around the circular opening. As the Morphadin made contact with the metal it held fast, but when the fabric of the diver's cybersuits came into contact with it, a static charge from the suits altered the polarity of particles in the rubbery material, making it instantly malleable again.

After a few minor adjustments, Pete and Mai pulled back from the covering and trod water. The Morphadin hardened almost instantly to form a watertight seal. Pete lifted his hand and ran it in front of the sheet, scanning for imperfections by checking the monitor on his wrist.

Mai led the way back to the control panel at the far end of the chamber. 'Here we go,' she said, grasping the handle.

The water pumps started up, their noise filling the enclosed space of the dock as water began to swirl and churn. The Morphadin held perfectly. In less than 60 seconds, the water had been sucked out of the dock.

Mai returned the lever of the backup control to 'off' and nodded to Pete who was standing on the wet floor close to the manual override for the inner door. He turned a large handle that had been countersunk into the wall of the chamber and with a hiss of warm air, the door into the Neptune Hotel slowly opened.

Pete poked his head through the opening. Taking one step into the hotel, he almost tripped over a body on the floor. As Mai came up behind him, he crouched down on one knee, his helmet light illuminating the floor. It was a man in the red braided uniform worn by hotel staff. He lay on his back, his arms raised, his hands frozen into claws. His nails were ripped to shreds, fingers red raw, broken and covered with dried blood. The man's eyes were almost popping out of his head.

34

Dome Alpha

'Poor bugger,' Pete said, opening the visor of his helmet. Mai did the same then crouched down to inspect the body. Turning the corpse over onto its side, she and Pete both saw the wounds along the victim's back and legs. 'I reckon he was badly hurt by some sort of explosion, but tried to get out through this door. He must've lost his mind. There's no way out here, even if he could have got through the locked door.'

'Maybe he thought a sub was still docked.'

'Yeah, it's possible, I guess,' Mai replied, standing up.

The light from their helmets lit up part of a wide corridor. The floor was carpeted. There were paintings on the walls, all of them misaligned. It was eerily quiet. All they could hear was the creaking of metal straining against metal.

'We have to get some power on,' Mai said. 'There must be an emergency lighting circuit.'

Pete tapped the screen on his suit and pulled up the schematic of the hotel. Scrolling through the various images, he finally found the electrical systems diagram. 'Looks like there's an emergency backup. As you'd expect. But it should've come on automatically.'

'Obviously failed. There has to be a manual override. Can you find the access point?'

Pete tapped at the screen again. 'Follow me.'

He led them along the corridor, took a left and then a right. The passageway had been tastefully decorated. There were recessed lights in the ceiling, ornate light shades spaced along each wall of the corridor. The carpet, now soaked, was originally a plush red. This, Pete reflected, was the first view visitors had of the inside of the Neptune. It would have to make a good impression even if it was simply a connection from the dock to the main body of the hotel.

On the right stood a door. A sign read 'MAINTENANCE: AUTHORISED PERSONNEL ONLY'. It was locked. Mai stepped up to it and lifted her gloved hand. From her wristband a tiny tube extended – the business end of a vector-laser, a device that fired a beam produced by a high field-intensity laser built into the cybersuit. The beam width and power could be finely adjusted, allowing the vector-laser to perform a wide range of tasks. Mai touched her wrist monitor and a narrow blue beam hit the lock. It vaporised. The door swung out and Pete stepped in.

It was a cupboard, the walls covered with metal conduits and junction boxes. Wires led around the boxes. He tugged at the cover of a box close to the door. Inside was a series of switches and relays. Pete studied his screen, then looked at the circuits in front of him. He tapped his monitor and, using a cursor on the screen, turned the power of the vector-laser at his wrist to 'minimum'.

'Broken connection. There, see?' Pete said to Mai. 'Just needs a gentle touch.' An ultrafine, soft blue-green beam struck the circuit board. He moved his hand slightly and the broken connection between two printed circuits was sealed immediately. Switching off the laser, Pete stepped back and closed the lid of the junction box. Beside it was a switch that had flicked to 'off' when the circuit malfunctioned. Pete moved it up and the lights came on.

They stepped out into the hall now flooded with light. 'Eureka!' Mai exclaimed.

'What's that?'

'What?' Mai strained to hear. There was a faint sound coming from along the passage towards the submarine dock.

'Footsteps,' Pete said. Then his expression darkened. 'And what sounds like the safety catch coming off a weapon. You wait here, Mai.'

She nodded and Pete walked slowly along the corridor, retracing their steps back towards the dock. He could hear the shuffling of feet. The rustling of fabric. Irregular breathing. One person. Someone nervous.

Pete approached the corner slowly and edged round.

'Stop!' someone yelled. It was the hotel bellboy. He looked about 17. His red uniform was torn and stained and he had a cut across his forehead. He had blond, almost white hair, cropped short. It was matted with blood. He was holding a taser he had lifted from a dead security man, clasping it with both hands, his knuckles white. Pete could see the boy was shaking.

'We're here to help,' Pete said calmly.

'Oh yeah, and me old mum was the Prime Minister.' The boy's voice was pure cockney. He kept the taser trained on Pete.

'What's your name, son?'

'What's it to you?'

'I told you. We're here to help.' Pete took a step forward.

'No closer.'

Pete stopped 6 metres away from the kid. 'We're not a threat.'

'We? Who's that? Where you from? Up north by the sounds of ya.'

Pete couldn't resist a brief smile. 'I'm a Geordie, son. And you sound like the original cockney sparrow.'

'Yeah, and so what if I am?' The boy's expression was a blend of fear and pride.

Pete was about to reply when he caught a sudden movement behind the boy. Mai appeared a few metres away. She took a step towards him, plucked the taser from the kid's hands and grabbed his left arm, pulling it hard behind his back.

'Ow!' the boy yelped.

Pete took two steps towards him.

'Oh fuckin' 'ell,' the kid squealed. 'Okay, make it quick, mister.'

'What you talking about, lad?' Pete flicked a glance to Mai. 'Let him go. Poor sod's terrified.'

Mai released her grip on the boy's arm and slipped the taser into her belt. The boy looked around, obviously weighing up his chances of escape.

'Listen,' Pete said, extending a hand. 'Let's start again, shall we?'

The boy looked at Pete's palm. 'Who are you?' he said.

'My name's Peter Sherringham, and this is Maiko Buchanan. We're part of E-Force, a rescue . . .'

'E-Force? Fuck me! I've seen you in the papers. Wow! I see your badges now.'

'Okay. So, we're good?' Mai asked.

'Yeah! Shit, we need you, I can tell ya. Place is a fucking mess.'

'What's your name?'

'Me? I'm Archie Barnet. Don't like Arch, just Archie.'

'Okay, Archie. Have you seen anyone else?'

'Yeah, there're a few of us up in Reception. Some of 'em are buggered up proper. I've just got this scratch.' And he tapped his forehead.

'I guess the elevators are out?' Pete said.

'Yeah, but there're stairs. I know every nook and cranny of this place.'

'Well then, Archie, you'd better lead the way.'

35

Archie took them along the corridor to a wide door marked 'SERVICE STAIRS'. The sound of their footfalls echoed around the concrete walls. The stairs were narrow and spiralled up three flights to another door labelled 'RECEPTION'. It opened onto a narrow passageway. Mai and Pete followed Archie and they came out into the vast void of the main Reception of the Neptune Hotel.

Even after being shaken to its foundations, the place was still magnificent. The sculpture of Neptune stood imperiously, undamaged amid piles of debris. The four giant chandeliers that had been suspended above the sculpture had not fared so well. Each had crashed to the ground, shattering into tens of thousands of pieces. The white marble floor was covered with glass and slithers of metal. Two bodies lay in the wreckage, a man and a woman, each wearing a red uniform. The man's neck had snapped and his head was twisted at an obscene angle. The woman lay on her front, a field of glass shards protruded from her back; the deep red of her blood had soaked her uniform.

Archie, his face drained pale, looked at Mai and Pete. 'Yes, Trevor and Margo. They worked at the desk. I checked them earlier, but they're dead.' His voice cracked with emotion. Turning, he picked a way across the carpet of glass towards the curved dark wood counter. A computer screen lay on the floor immediately in front of the desk, the screen smashed. Papers and small office items were scattered

166

everywhere. As they approached, they could see the head and forearms of another body protruded from under the end of the counter.

Mai arrived first and went down on one knee. The victim was another woman, young, perhaps early twenties, her blonde hair wet with blood. A great gash ran across her face. Mai checked for a pulse. 'Natalia,' Archie said from where he was standing slightly behind Pete. 'It was her twenty-first today. We had a little party round the back there.' He pointed to a door close to the desk. 'While the posh do was goin' on in Gamma. We 'ad champagne and all . . .' He suddenly burst into tears, sobbing like a toddler.

Mai stood up and walked over to the boy, placing an arm around his shoulders. She let him sob for a few moments then she said, 'Archie. I know this is hard, but we really need your help. You said there were other survivors.'

He stopped crying as suddenly as he had begun and wiped his eyes with a grimy sleeve. Straightening his jacket, he cricked his neck theatrically. 'I'm fine,' he said unconvincingly. Then he cleared his throat. 'We 'ave a job to do. This way.'

He led them over to the other side of the desk and along a wide corridor that took them into another narrower passageway. At the end, a door stood ajar. Archie pushed on it.

There were four people in the room. They were all members of staff, three men and a woman, still in their red uniforms. The woman and two of the men lay on seat cushions on the floor, the fourth, a younger man, perhaps in his late twenties, was sitting in a chair, his arm bandaged from elbow to wrist. He looked alarmed as the two members of E-Force walked in.

'Don't worry, Ricky. Friends,' Archie announced to the man.

Mai walked over to the injured people lying on the floor and moved from one to the other. The men were unconscious. They were middle aged, each with gold stripes on the sleeves of their uniforms. After checking vital signs, Mai removed an electronic medscanner from a shoulder bag. The device, the shape and size of a ballpoint pen, bleeped and she surveyed the readings on her wrist monitor. She gave each of the men a shot of powerful painkiller and then moved on to the woman. Her face was bleached white and smeared with blood from a cut on her chin. The left side of her face was blackened by a bruise. She flinched as Mai approached.

'It's okay,' she said. 'What's your name?'

For a moment, the woman couldn't speak, then she cleared her throat and swallowed hard. 'Sandra . . . er, Sandra Rimmer.'

Mai ran the medscanner slowly across the woman's forehead, down each side of her face and neck and over her chest, checking the monitor as she went. 'You'll be fine,' she said. 'Head trauma, but not serious.'

Mai stood up, walked over to the man called Ricky and repeated the process. When she had finished, she strode across the room. 'Two of them have concussion,' she said quietly to Pete. 'One has two broken ribs. He'll be in a lot of pain when he regains consciousness. The guy in the chair, Ricky, has a fractured ulna. They all have glass lacerations, but nothing life-threatening. I've given them shots. You did all this, Archie?' Mai added, turning to the bellboy.

'St John's Ambulance Service, Leytonstone branch,' he said. 'Always thought it'd come in 'andy one day. I got the cushions from a couple of sofas. It's the staff recreational area through there.' He pointed to a doorway. 'Well buggered though. Managed to salvage the First Aid kit, the kettle, of course, and a couple of other things.'

Mai smiled. 'You did very well.'

One of the two unconscious men opened his eyes. Archie saw him looking at Mai and Pete, clearly terrified. The man gasped and clutched at his side. He looked horribly pale.

Archie turned to the four injured staff members. 'This is Maiko and Peter,' he said, waving towards the new arrivals. 'E-Force, would ya believe?' Then he turned to Mai. 'Ricky Bellamy,' he said, pointing to the man in the chair. 'Worked on the main desk with . . .' He pulled a face and turned to the three people on the floor. 'James Hornsby,' he said indicating the man with the broken ribs. 'Chief Concierge. Next to 'im is Hugh Gebbly, Assistant Chief Concierge, and Sandra . . . well, you've been introduced.'

'What's happened?' James Hornsby said. He was perhaps 50, heavily built, with greased-back hair dyed uniformly black. At first glance, he looked like an early 1970s Elvis, about the time the singer was turning to fat. 'We heard what sounded like a blast. The whole place shook and all hell broke loose. It's a terrorist attack, right?' he winced again. 'God Almighty . . . my side.'

'You've broken three ribs, James,' Mai said. 'But I've given you some powerful painkillers. They should start to work soon.'

'To be honest, we don't know what happened,' Pete said, looking around at the faces in front of him. 'It wasn't a bomb. Or at least, we're pretty sure it wasn't. But the hotel has been very badly damaged.'

'Dome Gamma?' Sandra said. There was an edge of panic in her voice.

'Not good,' Pete said. 'We know there are survivors, but not many.'

James stared at Pete, the others looked away, each lost in their own thoughts.

'So what do we do now?' James asked. 'You were going for a reccie, Archie.'

'Yeah, I did. Can't say it helped much.'

'We've run scans of the hotel structure,' Mai said. 'This dome is the least badly damaged, so you should stay put for the moment. We've got the docking bay dry, but we can't hook up our subs to the hotel.'

'What about the universal dock in Beta?' Ricky Bellamy asked.

'Tried that first. It's too unstable.'

'The emergency subs in Beta. Surely they would be a better option?'

'It looks like the way to Beta from here is extremely hazardous,' Pete replied. 'But, if we can't use the dock here, we'll be forced to try the Beta subs to get you out.'

Ricky Bellamy nodded.

'So,' Pete went on. 'What we're going to do is create a connector between the end of the dock we came through and our sub.'

'How on earth you going to do that?' James Hornsby asked.

'Don't worry about that,' Mai interrupted. 'We have some interesting materials that can be moulded any way we like. If we can get you guys out, Pete and I will go on to the other domes. Do you know if there are any other survivors in this dome, Archie?'

The boy shook his head. 'I ain't seen no one, but I can't be sure.'

'I'll run a scan,' Mai said, and glanced at Pete before heading for the door to the passageway back to Reception.

'So, we have to get over to the dock, right?' Hugh Gebbly said, watching Mai's retreating back.

Pete nodded and flicked on his comms. 'Mark?'

'Pete.'

'We've found five survivors in Dome Alpha. No serious injuries. Mai and I think the best plan would be to use Morphadin so we can dock the *Narcis* with the hotel. Now we've got the dock dry it should work well. Mai will go up to the surface with them and I'll press on. She'll rejoin me later.'

'You got enough Morphadin on the sub?'

'I'm pretty sure. I loaded some extra supplies just before we left the Big Mac. I had a feeling we'd need it.'

'Good. Well, it's a plan.'

'Mai's just gone back to Reception. She's going to run a scan of the dome to see if there's anyone else alive.'

'Okay, Pete. Keep in touch . . . and good luck.'

Pete turned to the five staff members and was about to explain the plan when the room shook violently. The lights went out. Sandra screamed in the dark. The lights stuttered on, then off, then on again. A roaring sound filled the room. There was a loud boom from beyond the passageway. It came from the direction of the Reception. The floor shook. Sandra screamed again. The rumbling stopped abruptly. Pete heard a sound like swishing swords. It was from close by. He span around and saw a metal beam come crashing through the ceiling. He dived to his left and the beam missed him by centimetres. Rolling onto his side, he crawled under a table close to where Ricky Bellamy had been sitting. The man was nowhere to be seen.

The table shook and Pete heard the thud of a heavy object crashing onto the table top above him. He covered his head with his arms. A second, heavier object slammed into the table top, knocking it aside. Pete whirled around and a piece of concrete the size of a football flew straight at his face.

36

Mengde Sun surveyed the main control room of the base at Hang Cheng and thought, not for the first time, how astonishingly it had all changed.

The original base, the one he had overseen, had been closed down in 1992, just when his experiments were beginning to bear fruit. He had always prided himself on his ability to manipulate politicians and the men who held the purse strings of state. He had given them the things they wanted. He had been a great scientific worker for the party. But he had not relied on such ephemera alone. He had always taken out insurance. He had known so many dirty secrets, he could barely manage the information. But it had been good insurance, great insurance, everyone, everyone had been scared of him.

But then the glorious but geriatric leader, Deng Xiaoping had handed over power to Jiang Zemin, the Eighth General Secretary of the Communist Party of China. And, for the first time in his life, Mengde had been unprepared. For reasons he still did not fully understand, Jiang hated him, and Mengde had nothing in the way of insurance, nothing with which to blackmail the man. Within a month of the handing over of power from Deng to Jiang, Base 44 at Hang Cheng had been closed down, stripped bare and bulldozed. The following week, Mengde was arrested and imprisoned without trial.

Mengde stared at the banks of sophisticated electronics, the plasma screens and the men in crisp white boiler suits. Then his gaze was drawn to a massive flat screen taking up an entire wall of the room. It reminded him of a time almost two decades earlier when a similar room had stood on this spot. There had been a wall-sized window, behind which experimental subjects had been mutilated and killed in terrible ways. He smiled to himself. He was back. He had served 12 years in China's worst political prison, Jing Shak. But General Secretary Jiang Zemin had been replaced, just as all leaders are, and he, Mengde Sun, was now back in favour. He had returned to his old job as Party Chief Scientist.

With the ascension of Jiang, in 1992, fate had dealt him a terrible blow. But the new leader was an old associate, and Mengde Sun knew a great deal about him. Within six months, the Chief Scientist's base at Hang Cheng had been rebuilt, and it was better than it could ever have been before. He was back, and with greater power than he had ever enjoyed. So much power in fact that he was completely autonomous. No one in Beijing had the slightest idea what experiments he was conducting. He had an almost limitless budget and zero accountability. He was a law unto himself, and he was exploiting it to the full. This was to be an über insurance policy. With work completed on his latest experiments he would be untouchable, and if he chose to, the total control of China, perhaps even the world, would be his.

'Relay station 1 online,' a technician announced.

'Relay station 2 online,' said another from across the room.

'Relay station 3 online,' declared a third technician.

The wall screen lit up. Mengde settled himself into a leather chair, a much bigger and better chair than he had used in the old days. A technician approached and the tingle of déjà vu passed through the Chief Scientist. But it was not his old lab manager, Yung Sing. Yung had been hanged in Ying Shak. His replacement was a fresh-faced youth, no more than 30, Mengde mused. His ID told the Chief Scientist the kid's name was Fu Tang. 'All is prepared, sir,' Fu said and pointed to a counter in the bottom right of the screen. Then, as Mengde watched, an image appeared. He knew what it was. He had been working on this project, supervising every detail of it for two years.

A bridge. A bridge half a kilometre long and crossing a series of swampy rivers. It was the Florida Road Bridge, a section of the I-75, 11 kilometres outside Miami. It was early morning, rush hour. The bridge, a 10-lane behemoth, was packed with cars, bumper to bumper, all crawling along at 30 kilometres per hour. The counter in the bottom right corner clicked on. It said: 00.20.

The room fell silent. The numbers ticked down.

Mengde felt supernaturally calm. He lived for these moments. These were the times he felt truly alive . . . just before he snatched the lives of others. There was an extra delicious frisson about this experiment – who knew how many would die? Who would they be? So-called innocents? Yes, women, children. Oh yes, lots of them, mummies and kiddies on the school run.

00.02.

00.01.

00.00.

For one and a half seconds it seemed as though nothing had happened, that nothing would happen, that the test had failed. Then the bridge started to vibrate. At first, the motion was almost imperceptible. But after three seconds, the entire structure started to shake and then to rock from side to side. Red taillights flicked on all along the bridge. From the other side of the world, the men in the laboratory at Hang Cheng could hear brakes squeal. Then came the thud of impact and car horns sounding.

The bridge snapped into three pieces. A middle section 100 metres long simply plunged 25 metres into the swamp, vanishing from sight and taking with it scores of cars. The southern section of the bridge shot up as though it were a drawbridge. Millions of tonnes of concrete and steel levered to the vertical. Cars flew backwards, cascading into others behind them. Trucks jack-knifed and tumbled like falling dominos. Within 10 seconds, the image on the screen was one of unimaginable carnage.

Except for the sounds coming from the I-75, 14,000 kilometres away, the room remained absolutely silent. Then Mengde pulled himself up from the chair and started to clap. The sound grew louder. Two of the men at the computers between the Chief Scientist and the wall-sized screen looked around. Turning back, they began to clap in time with Mengde. Soon, everyone in the room was applauding loudly. A technician started to whoop. He turned and embraced his colleague.

As hearts stopped and lungs collapsed, as heads were sliced from bodies and limbs were crushed to pulp on a Florida bridge, the laboratory at Hang Cheng erupted into ecstatic celebration.

37

Gobi Desert, China

'You must be Stephanie.'

She span around, the light from the beam of her torch darting about like a huge firefly. A man stood a few paces away. He was very tall, dressed in a tatty greatcoat over ragged jeans. His long hair and beard were streaked with grey. He was holding a lantern high in his left hand. It cast a sparse, greenish light across his face.

Steph instinctively adopted a defensive pose, brandishing the burning branch in front of her like a weapon.

'Forgive me. I didn't mean to startle you,' the man said. His voice was a baritone, pure Home Counties. It sounded so ridiculously incongruous, so out of place and time, it was almost comical.

'Who are you?' Steph said, keeping a tight grip on the burning wood. 'Where is my friend?'

'Josh? Oh, he's fine. Your plane crashed, yes? Made quite a racket, I might say! Certain to have woken the neighbours, dear girl.' He laughed suddenly. Two front teeth were missing.

Steph held his gaze. He appeared to be in his fifties, but he may have been younger; the beard and hair aged him. Steph weighed things up. His face was thin, the big greatcoat hung off him, he looked undernourished and unhealthy. Possibly unarmed. She could take him, if she needed to. The man seemed completely relaxed. He smiled and tilted his head.

'Who am I, you ask? Who are any of us? I've been trying to answer that one for 20 years. My name is Howard. You look cold, young lady. Come.'

'Come where?'

'My home is close by.'

'Home?' Steph asked, aghast.

He simply turned and walked away, leaving Steph little option but to follow. She kept her distance, the burning branch at arm's length.

It was dark, but Steph could just make out rocks, sand, dead plants, the occasional piece of tangled wreckage from *Paul*. She kept 3 or 4 metres back from Howard, eyeing him suspiciously. After a while, a pale light appeared in the distance. It grew and brightened as they approached.

Howard's home was an astonishing, amorphous thing. Steph's first impression was that it was something from the props department of a fantasy movie. The centrepiece was an old four-wheel-drive, a 30-year-old Toyota. The sides had been ripped away and canvas structures extended from each side. Where the driver's cabin had once been, the doors had been taken off and more box shapes stretched from the edges of the wagon to posts buried deep in the sand. Five metres from the Toyota stood a line of poles. Wrapped around the top of each were bundles of burning twigs. Together, these lit up the area with a pasty yellow luminescence, throwing weird shadows and black shapes against the canvas and tangled metal.

Howard stopped at the end of one of the canvas constructions that stretched from the mutilated Toyota. 'Welcome to Chez Howard,' he said with a smile, and dived inside.

For several moments, Steph stood alone, the burning branch in her hand. Howard's shape was just visible for a second behind the canvas structures. Discarding the burning wood, Steph removed the torch from her belt bag and gripped it tight. Pushing aside the canvas flap Howard had used, she took slow, cautious steps into the shadows and flicked on the torch. To her amazement, she saw a set of roughly hewn steps in front of her. It looked like a picture she had seen of Tutankhamen's tomb in the Valley of the Kings, a series of hand-cut blocks leading underground.

Ten steps down, she had no need for the torch. The steps led to a cavern some 8 metres square. The ceiling was low, but the walls glowed orange. Light came from a dozen lanterns in alcoves spaced around the room.

Howard stood a short distance away. 'Welcome,' he said.

In the centre of the strange subterranean room stood a byre made from bits of car and twisted wood. Josh lay on the bed, his head raised on a couple of pillows.

'Isn't this just so cool?' he said.

38

'How the hell did I end up here?' Howard asked, repeating Steph's question. 'Fate? Karma? Meticulous planning? Who knows?'

Josh was sitting up in the bed drinking a cup of steaming liquid, which Howard had told him was called Gung Ging tea. Steph cradled hers and took a few small sips. It wasn't half bad. She had topped up Josh's painkillers with supplies from her cybersuit. Josh looked surprisingly comfortable, but both of them knew the drugs would not last forever. The room was welcomingly warm, a fire burned in a metre square opening in the centre of one wall, the chimney had been cut into the wall and exited in the sand at ground level. Steph studied Howard's face. She had been wrong about his age, she decided. In the orange light of the subterranean room, he looked older, at least 60. His beard and long shaggy hair were more white than dark and his skin was leathery, worn and pitted. Steph could imagine each line and crag told a story. He had large, dark brown eyes, long lashes, a narrow mouth. He was probably once rather handsome, she concluded.

'You want the simple version?' Howard asked, looking from one of his guests to the other.

Josh nodded.

'Well, I was in my early twenties I guess, back in the seventies. Everyone was off on the magic bus, searching for enlightenment, tripping on acid in Goa. And I went along with them, straight out of university – Cambridge, Trinity, would you believe?' And he produced a rasping self-mocking laugh. 'I washed up on Goa's lovely warm shores too and I took my share of whatever drug was offered, in search of my spiritual guide. Didn't find one though. Then, one day, I had a minor epiphany. I looked around at all the people I had fallen in with and I thought to myself . . . Look at you. You're all trying to be so unorthodox, all trying to be so alternative, and what do you do? You all troupe off to India like a herd of sheep. How radical! How individualistic of you!'

'So you dropped back in?' Steph said.

'Oh very good,' Howard laughed. 'Yes, I did for a bit, Stephanie. I did. I went back to London. Got myself a job, got married and had two children.'

'So, what happened?' Josh said, wincing as he tried to move up in the bed.

'Melissa, my wife, and the two girls were killed in a car crash.'

'I'm sorry,' Steph began, but Howard had a palm raised.

'You shouldn't be. You didn't know them. Besides, it was over 30 years ago and, well, the world didn't stop moving in its orbit. But it was the pivotal event in my life. I realised I had gone to India for a reason. I really was uncomfortable with the orthodox life. I sold everything I had, gave up the job, bought a four-wheel-drive, loaded her up with supplies, tools everything I needed . . . and I drove.'

Steph shook her head. 'So you've been here for . . . ?'

'Not sure, my dear. What year is it?'

Steph gazed into his eyes and was about to reply.

'Actually, don't tell me,' Howard interrupted. 'It really doesn't matter . . . So, this E-Force is a rescue team?' he asked, quickly changing the subject. 'I saw your plane come down. It was getting dark, but I still saw it quite clearly. I know I've been away a long time, but it looked like a fine piece of kit, Stephanie.'

'It is . . . was.' Steph glanced over to Josh who had fallen asleep. He was snoring quietly.

'You're worried about your friend.'

'Well, yes. I've cleaned his wounds and we have painkillers available from my suit. Josh's was too badly damaged in the crash. But they're running out.'

'So, what do you plan to do?'

'Good question,' Steph responded. 'Our comms are out. You don't have a radio, I imagine?'

'I do, but it doesn't work any more, my dear.'

'No power, right?'

'It's not that. I have a solar power system. Which works rather well, I might add. I generate just enough for my needs, and until a few years ago, I had a working radio. I venture into Fung Ching Wa occasionally. It's a small town about 130 kilometres south-east of here. I stock up on replacement electrical components, new cooking utensils, anything I couldn't make myself. Anyway, the radio still works, but the signal is nothing but static.'

'What?'

'Look.' He took Steph over to an ancient-looking Rediffusion two-way valve set. Turning it on, Howard shifted the dial. Nothing but a stream of static tumbled from the tinny speaker. 'It happened suddenly, one night. I don't mind confessing that for some time I thought they'd finally dropped the bomb and civilisation was history.' He produced his raspy laugh again and his eyes shone. Steph looked at him, and for an instant she saw a new light there, an excitement, a flicker of wishful thoughts lost in disappointment. 'But, no. It was just the bloody Chinese,' Howard concluded.

'The Chinese?' Steph asked.

'Their base, Hang Cheng. It's about 60 kilometres north-west of here.' Howard was pointing across the room. 'I don't know what they're doing there of course. And to be honest, dear girl, I have absolutely no interest in knowing either. But, I must admit, I am rather peeved they've buggered up my radio.'

'You've seen this base?'

'Yes. You probably did too. You would have flown over it.'

Steph was nodding, lost in thought. Then she said, 'Well, that answers some questions, I guess. But, the long and short of it is that you can't contact the outside world . . . right?'

'Not any more. Sorry.'

'What medical supplies do you have?'

'You saw them. The kit I gave you to patch up Josh.'

'That's it?' Steph exclaimed. Then she sighed heavily. 'I'm sorry. I didn't mean to be rude.'

'It's quite all right. You've had a rather trying day. The fact is, I don't need anything more. If I hurt myself badly or I contract some horrible disease, I will simply die. My medical supplies are enough to help with a cut finger or a cold.' He looked at Steph. 'You're all in, young lady. Why don't you follow your friend's example and get some sleep?'

Steph sat down and ran a hand through her hair, then rested her fingertips on her temples. 'I can think of nothing nicer, but I have to find something in the wreckage to help us.'

'Well in that case, the best I can do is offer to keep you company. Lead the way.'

39

Howard had devised an ingenious torch. It was a glass box fashioned from pieces of Toyota window. He had covered five internal sides of the box with metal foil salvaged from the cooling system of the car's engine. In the centre was a chamber filled with the distillate of a shrub he cultivated in a vegetable garden beside the Toyota. It was the same plant that supplied the Gung Ging tea and, he confided to Steph, he refined it into a particularly potent hooch that he called Brain Cracker. The torch cast a powerful, diffuse beam and lit up the desert like a beacon.

Even close to Howard's camp they found pieces of metal and plastic, wires, glass fragments and bits of fabric. Fifty metres to the west, the ground rose suddenly and the sand gave way to a rocky outcrop. Craggy, wind-blasted stone rose from the coarse gravelly sand. Steph was about to lead them round the rocks to the south, but Howard put a gloved hand on her arm. 'We have to climb over,' he said. 'There are jagged rocks at least 3 metres high to the north and south. You can't get round either way.' He stepped ahead and began to clamber over the outcrop.

It was then they both saw the smashed up fuselage of the plane. Ripped into four pieces, it lay half-buried in the sand. Great holes exposed the insides of the shattered aircraft. From 40 metres away, the Silverback looked like a mutilated snake, ravaged by some predator that had ditched it in the sand and disappeared. All around lay smashed boxes, twisted metal, panels of Maxinium, and shards of glass glinting in the beam like diamonds on a velvet cloth.

They clambered down and Steph ran ahead, while Howard followed at a more sedate pace. Close to the plane, she crouched to inspect a metal cube about 30 centimetres on each side, partially buried in the sand. She turned it over and in the torchlight she could see it was nothing but a section of conduit. Tossing it aside, she stood up and headed straight for *Paul*. Howard caught up a few moments later.

'Best if you stay here,' Steph said. 'It wouldn't be a good idea to go poking around. I know this plane.'

Howard nodded and put out a hand to indicate Steph should go ahead.

It was hard to tell what was what inside the shell of the ravaged aircraft. It had been smashed around almost beyond recognition. But Steph knew what she was looking for. All she could do was pray it was where it should be.

She could see that the front section of the plane was almost totally obliterated. The nose was buried in the sand up to where the copilot's seat could just be seen. The seat was a mangled frame of metal. A few tatters of fabric and foam clung to it. Behind this was the midsection of the aircraft, a storage area for ancillary equipment, spares and backup units. Behind this was the computer centre, the brain of the aircraft. The blast had transformed it into a tangle of tubes, wires and melted plastic. Ducking low and taking exceptional care, Steph eased herself into an opening in the midsection of the Silverback.

She splashed the torch light around the inside of the cylinder of Maxinium. It was the least badly damaged part of the plane, probably because it was the section of the aircraft with the fewest electrical components and was some way from the engines and fuel cells.

To the left, the curved wall was pock-marked and cracked. On the righthand side of the chamber, Steph could see a line of storage bays. All but two of them were warped and the doors had caved in, shattering everything inside. Steph put the torch down on a high shelf of twisted metal on the left side of the fuselage, and pointed the light towards the storage units.

The first door she tried was stuck fast. She kicked it and yanked on the handle and it flew open, almost knocking her off her feet. Inside, she found flares, a box of tools, two boxes marked 'emergency rations'. On the floor lay a coil of reinforced carbonylon rope.

She pulled the items out and piled them on the floor of the gutted Silverback, then stepped up to the only other intact door. To her immense relief, it opened with a single yank on the handle. And there, crushed to one side of the storage unit by a pile of metal boxes, was the one thing in the whole world she most wanted to see – a backup cyber-suit.

Steph had the suit in her hand and was bending to pick up the other items when she heard the crack of gunshots. She grabbed the torch, eased her way along the treacherously narrow midsection and emerged into the freezing night through a jagged opening in the plane's outer shell. Howard was pulling himself up from a crouching position. He was breathing heavily, misty breath in front of his face. In his hand was an ancient-looking revolver. On the ground lay the twisted forms of two dead animals, one on its back, the other on its side. Close to the bodies the sand was soaked red.

'I forgot to tell you about the wolves,' Howard said. 'Nasty buggers.'

40

Steph woke Josh with a gentle shake of the shoulder. Howard strode over to the fire to put some more wood into the flames.

'Hey,' Josh said. 'What's new?'

'I have a present for you.' She held up the cybersuit. 'Complete with nanobots and your very own painkillers.'

'You're a miracle worker, Steph.'

'I know,' she shot back, and helped him remove the remnants of the old suit. Underneath, he was wearing an almost weightless, skintight carbofibre undergarment. Helping Josh get the suit over his injured knee was a struggle, but they both concluded pain now for the reparative properties of the nanobots was a fair exchange. Once it was on, Steph touched the wrist monitor on Josh's sleeve. He lay back trying to manage the pain as best he could while she altered parameters and reset the suit.

She looked up with a smile.

'Done. I've programmed the nanobots to concentrate on your shattered knee. Some stronger painkillers should hit any minute, and I reckon you'll be as good as new by morning. Now I think you need some rest.'

'Okay, doc. But you've discovered something else, haven't you? I can tell.'

Steph looked at him seriously. 'Howard has a radio.'

'That's good . . . right?'

'Would be. But he can't pick up a signal. A few years back,

But get this . . . The interference comes from a Chinese military base about 60 kilometres away.'

Josh looked startled for a second, then his eyes narrowed. 'That explains a thing or two.'

'It does.'

'So what now?'

She looked at him hard. 'We've no way of reaching the others. All we can do is hope Tom is a miracle worker too.'

41

Dome Gamma

Harry Flanders leaned on the door of the emergency exit, but it would not budge. He bent down and picked up a piece of concrete that was lying close by. Without hesitating, he smashed it into the glass panel above the handle. Pulling his sleeve down over his hand to protect himself from the glass shards left in the window frame, he put his hand through the opening and unlocked the door from the far side.

'Everyone okay to go on?' Harry asked, surveying the faces of the others. Alfred looked all in. He was sitting against the wall. Jim was beside him, with an arm around his shoulders. Kristy stood dejectedly, staring down at the wreckage of Dome Gamma. Her face was streaked with blood and makeup. Nick was sitting on his own, his head between his knees and Danny had wandered over to the railing of the mezzanine, gazing into the shadows at the smouldering debris and crushed bodies.

'Might be better if you leave me behind,' Alfred said, and started to cough.

'He stays, I stay,' Jim said, looking across to Harry.

'I'm not sure that would be wise,' Harry replied, taking a couple of paces towards the group. 'I reckon this dome is under a lot of strain. Look up there.' He pointed to the apex of the dome just visible past the ceiling of the mezzanine. They could all see shallow cracks spreading out from Gamma's metal cap.

'It's impossible to say,' Danny commented. 'That could hold for weeks. Rescuers could be here any minute.'

Kristy looked earnestly at Danny. 'You really think someone will rescue us?'

'Of course,' the old actor said. 'I have no doubts. The marines will be here, the US Navy.'

'The cavalry galloping over the hill at the last minute?' Harry said sarcastically. 'The good old US of A to the rescue.'

'Well there ain't going to be anyone else coming for us, is there, young fella?'

Harry shrugged. 'Yeah, but if they come, they'll be late . . . as usual.' He turned back to Alfred and Jim. 'Look. I really don't think you should stay here. There's no telling if Dome Beta is any better, but believe me, this place is going to go. I can feel it.'

'Okay,' Alfred said after a moment. 'I'm feeling better. I'm not ready to lie down and die just yet.'

'That's the spirit,' Harry replied. Then he walked over to Nick and gave the kid a hand up. The boy wiped his eyes. He'd been crying quietly but was trying his best to cover it up. 'Come on, Nick,' Harry said. 'You lead the way with me, yes?'

The door opened onto a dark stairwell.

'I say we go straight down to the bottom of the dome,' Harry said.

'Why?' Danny asked.

'Because that's where the connecting tunnel to Beta is.'

'If it's still there.'

'True,' Harry conceded. 'But put it this way, Danny. If it's not there, or it's impassable, we won't have many other options.'

'What have you got against going straight down?' Alfred asked the actor.

'Nothing, I guess. Let's go.'

The only source of light they had was the insipid glow from the top floor and that did not last long. After the third turn, the faint light disappeared altogether. They were in total darkness for two flights of the concrete access stairs. But then a new source of light appeared. It was a faint pinprick that grew rapidly as they took turn after turn of the stairs, descending through the floors of Dome Gamma. Approaching the light, they could see it was a dim single bulb illuminating the ground floor of the stairwell. It lit up a wide corridor. At the far end, they could see elevator doors, and beside them, a red rectangle of light, the call button. Harry took it slowly, picking his way forward, hugging the wall. It seemed to take an age to travel the 20 metres to the elevator doors, but they eventually all gathered there.

Harry punched the button forlornly. To no one's surprise, nothing happened.

'There are some stairs over there,' Nick said. 'They go down one more floor to the linkway.' He took a few paces to an opening in the wall on one side of the elevator. The steps were covered in dust and there were holes in the ceiling of the stairwell, but nothing lay in their way. Nick took the lead down the steps with Harry close behind. At the foot of the stairs, a narrow corridor curved sharply left and suddenly they were in the linkway between Gamma and Beta.

It was an inspiring sight. The linkway was a tube of specially reinforced glass cradled in a metal support frame. Three metres wide and about 25 metres long, it connected the two domes. Red carpet ran along a channel in the base of the tube. Sheer walls of glass swept up either side and curved overhead. It created the impression that by stepping into the tube you were actually walking into the ocean itself.

Huge multicoloured tendrils of coral and exotic ocean plants swayed in the current. On a normal day a bewildering array of sea creatures, anemone fish, blue ribbon eel and black tip reef sharks would dart and swarm round the tube. Some would peer into the glass as they swam by. Others were nervous and scattered as soon as there was any movement. For the moment, the fish had gone, scared off by whatever had rocked the hotel.

Nick Xavier ran along the tunnel, barely giving it a second look. He had seen the hotel grow. The project had dominated his childhood. But the others were still in awe of it. They had only seen it once before, earlier that evening, en route to Dome Gamma and the grand dinner.

'Come *on*,' Nick called, bringing them back to painful reality.

Harry was three-quarters of the way along the linkway when he heard the low rumble. They all stopped. The sound came again, much louder this time.

'Oh fuck! Not another tremor,' Jim exclaimed.

'Run!' Harry screamed.

A sound like a thunder clap ricocheted along the tunnel and they could all see the glass crack, random lines slithering down the sides. The tendrils shot past them as they ran. Harry slowed, almost stopping as he encouraged them all on. Jim and Alfred were trailing behind. He ran back to give Jim a hand. 'Come on,' he shouted above the noise. 'Just a few more steps.'

He grabbed Alfred's arm and helped drag the old man along the carpet.

A tremendous crash shuddered along the linkway and they could feel the glass tube wobble on its cradle. They were close to the far side. Nick dashed into a corridor, then pulled up sharp. He glanced back to make sure everyone was through the linkway and looked for the red security button on the wall. Panicking, he punched it and a thick metal door started to come down from the ceiling. Harry was still a couple of metres inside the tunnel. He pushed Alfred and Jim hard from behind. They stumbled forward, Alfred landing heavily on his partner, both yelping in pain.

The door was falling fast. Harry could sense it. His whole mind focused on propelling himself forward with every ounce of his being. Adrenalin shot through him like a surging wave, energising his muscles. He dived, slithering under the 2 tonnes of metal as it crashed downward. The door almost caught his feet, but he swivelled his legs round just in time. The steel barrier slammed to the floor, and Harry screamed involuntarily as it sliced through the heels of his shoes.

42

Dome Beta

'You okay?' Danny Preston was leaning over him. The air seemed to throb, a low hum. They could feel it rather than hear it. Then the corridor juddered. There was a great rush of sound, like nothing they had ever heard in their lives. It thundered down the corridor, the sound of tonnes of tempered glass shattering into millions of pieces.

Harry looked up, and for a moment, he could barely remember who he was. Danny had a hand out. He helped Harry up.

'So, what now?' Kristy said as the sound subsided.

Harry was about to reply when the walls started to shake again. He looked at the others, and then at the ground. The floor seemed to be buckling under his feet. It looked and felt utterly surreal, as though he were on a surfboard.

'Look out!' Alfred screamed.

Harry span around and saw a metal beam cut through the flimsy plaster of the ceiling. It thrust downward at a crazy angle. He yelled and dived forward as the ceiling came down in one great rush. He landed hard, his head slamming into a solid object. He turned to see cascading plaster, and just caught a glimpse of Danny and Kristy at the other end of the corridor. They were near the door to the doomed linkway. Something huge reared up from the ground lifting Harry into the air. He felt himself rise up towards the ceiling. Then, whatever it was suddenly slipped away and he crashed to the floor.

Jim Kemple was the first to recover. He opened his eyes and immediately started coughing. He sat up and looked around. Harry Flanders was next to him on his left, and he could see the young kid, Nick Xavier. The two of them were coming round. Where was Alfred? He suddenly felt a stab of panic. He stood up, took two steps and almost tripped over Alfred's legs. 'Al,' he sputtered, his mouth filled with dust. He lowered himself on his good knee, beside his partner.

'Jim,' the old man said. 'You okay?'

He pulled a face. 'I'm cool. What about you?' He leaned close and saw Alfred's shirt was ripped open, and a metal pole half a centimetre in diameter was sticking up from his abdomen. Jim started to gag, but managed to control himself.

'I'm dying, Jim.'

'No . . . no, you're not.'

'No, listen to me, Jim, listen. I *am* dying. I'm hurt bad, but I was already on my way out.'

Tears were welling up in Jim's eyes. At the periphery of his vision, he could see Harry and Nick pulling themselves to their feet. But they were a universe away in time and space. 'What do you *mean*?'

'Leukaemia. Bad prognosis.'

Jim didn't know what to say. He glanced up for a second as Harry stopped a few paces behind him. When he looked back, Alfred was motionless.

It took Jim a few seconds to realise what had happened, but even then, his brain could not process it. 'Alfred,' he said softly. 'Alfred, don't talk like that. We can beat this thing. We can . . .'

He stopped and stood up. Harry went to put a hand on Jim's shoulder but pulled back at the last moment. He simply watched him. Jim looked like a statue, completely motion-less. Before Harry could say anything, Jim took a step back, looked down at his dead partner and then slowly walked away, lowering himself into the far corner of the corridor.

'Nick? You all right?' Harry said to the boy.

'I think so. Just more cuts and bruises.'

Harry turned and walked over to where the corridor had been cut in two by falling rubble. 'We're cut off from the others. Kristy and Danny are on the other side,' he said.

'How do you know they're alive?'

'I don't. Come on.' He started scrambling at the barrier, lifting lumps of concrete and metal and tossing them to one side. Nick dug away at the foot of the barrier.

'Stop!' Harry yelled suddenly. 'Hear that?'

Nick held his breath. 'What?'

'Damn it.'

Then they both heard it. A single word. 'Help.' It was muffled by the barrier, but they could tell it was a girl's voice.

'Kristy,' Harry yelled.

'Yes . . . Yes. We're trapped.'

'Danny with you?'

'We're both caught between the door and the cave in. We're okay though.'

Harry threw himself at the piles of concrete and twisted metal. They cut into his palms, but he kept going. It was hot and stifling in the corridor. 'Nick. See if you can open the door at the end, get some air in here, yeah?' Nick sped off and Harry carried on, the sweat running off him. Just as the boy came back shaking his head, defeated, Harry felt a hand on his shoulder.

'Need some help?' Harry turned. It was Jim, his face as pale as death.

The three of them made more rapid headway, clawing at the heaped rubble, pulling out smashed chairs, chunks of metal, wooden table legs, papers and strips of carpet. Harry climbed into the hole they had made and scrambled at the detritus, passing it back to Nick and Jim. Pulling a lump of concrete aside, he saw a flicker of light.

'Kristy? Danny?'

Kristy's face appeared in the opening. She was sobbing.

'Clear your side,' Harry shouted. 'We've made a hole you can crawl through this end.'

The barrier was no more than 4 metres thick, but it was made from a motley collection of smashed and shattered wreckage.

'Who's going first?' Harry yelled through the hole. 'It'll be dangerous. Be very careful.'

Danny's face appeared. 'I'll try it.' He pulled himself up onto his side and clambered, head first, into the hole.

'Take it slowly,' Harry warned.

'Don't you worry, son. I will.'

Danny was surprisingly nimble and flexible. He clawed his way into the opening.

Harry reached in and took the old actor's wrist, and with his spare hand, Danny pushed against the sides of the opening. In a moment, his head emerged through the hole. Harry and Nick gripped him under each shoulder and helped him through the last metre or so.

'Jesus!' Danny exclaimed, dusting himself down.

Harry poked his head back into the hole. 'Okay, Kristy. Your turn.'

There was only silence from the other end of the opening.

'Kristy?'

The young woman's face appeared. She looked panic-stricken. 'I can't . . . I can't do it. I'll fall through and be impaled or something,' she said slowly, almost inaudibly. Then she dissolved into tears. Her face slid out of view.

'Shit!' Harry spat.

The others looked at him, confused.

'She can't do it. She's panicking.'

'All right,' Danny said, stepping towards the hole. 'I'll go back. Get her out. Then I'll crawl through.'

'What? You're crazy!' Jim burst out.

'Yeah, maybe I am,' he said, and moved Harry aside so he could reach into the opening. 'Wish me luck, though.'

They watched Danny disappear into the chasm and heard him crawling slowly and carefully over the jagged, twisted wreckage. Harry peered in and watched him descend the other side of the barrier. Then he saw Kristy's face appear again.

'You okay?' Harry called through.

'No.'

'Come on, Kristy. You can do it. You weigh nothing, after all.'

She was shaking, her face lathered with sweat.

'It's cooler this side,' Harry lied.

'Come on. I'll help you up,' Danny said, and put a gentle arm around the girl's shoulders. 'You'll be through in no time and I'll be right behind you.'

Kristy pulled herself up into the hole. They could hear her whimpering, her breath coming in irregular gasps.

'That's good,' Harry said. 'Great. The worst is over. Now, just put one hand in front of the other. Watch where you're putting your knees.'

She was moving incredibly slowly, so slowly it felt as though she would never emerge the other side. She stopped and let out a little cry.

'Nearly there,' Harry said gently. 'Three more steps.'

At first, the crashing sound seemed far off. Then it came roaring along the hole towards Harry, Jim and Nick. Kristy screamed and scrambled through the cavity, collapsing in a heap on the floor of the corridor. Harry clambered up the side of the barrier and dived for the opening as it filled with dust.

'Harry! Don't!' Jim screamed.

Harry pulled himself along the tunnel of debris, cutting his hands as he went. He put his knee on a length of plastic and he felt it slide away from him. The whole structure swayed. He stopped and tried to steady his breathing. Sweat ran into his eyes.

Harry waved at the air to try to see where he was going. But it was useless. His eyes were streaming and the dust felt as though it was cutting into his eyeballs. A metre further on he looked up and saw the opening into the far end of the corridor. And there, sprawled in the concrete and chunks of rubble, lay Danny's limp body, his head crushed under a slab of concrete.

43

'You stupid little bitch,' Harry screamed as he emerged from the hole close to where Kristy Sunshine lay in a heap, crying.

She pulled herself up and whirled on Harry, her face a mask of fury. 'How dare you talk to me like that . . . you . . . you . . . useless nothing!'

Harry's face turned pale. He looked at the floor for a moment and then to everyone's surprise, he laughed. It was a bitter laugh and it came from a seething rage. 'I feel genuinely sorry for you, Kristy. You are so deluded. You think you're something *really* special. But actually, you're just a silly little girl. You might think I'm a nothing, but you're certainly a something . . . A FUCKING AIRHEAD!'

Kristy flew at Harry, her fists flailing around.

Jim stepped in. 'Okay, guys. Cut it out.' He grabbed the singer's arms and pulled her back. Harry shook his head and laughed again, which only made Kristy Sunshine more angry. 'You retard!' she squealed and tried to pull away from Jim. He pinned her against the wall. 'Stop it! Stop it . . . NOW!'

She suddenly erupted into tears and slid to the floor, burying her head in her hands, her shoulders heaving.

Nick was looking on, confused. 'Shouldn't we get out of here?' he said quietly.

'At last. Someone talking sense,' Jim said. Then he walked over to his dead partner whose body lay close to the exit in the west end of the corridor. He knelt down beside him while the others kept a respectful distance. 'I have to go now, Al,' he said softly, and ran a hand through the old man's sparse white hair. Then he turned and walked towards the door.

The others were there in a few moments. The door was closed. Jim kicked at the lock, but it was useless. Harry ran back to the barrier and found a large chunk of concrete. Returning to the door, he heaved the concrete at the handle. After three blows, he was exhausted. Jim grabbed the lump of debris and slammed it against the wood of the door above the lock. It gave on the second attempt. The wood shattered, sending small shards into the air and revealing a ragged hole about 3 centimetres in diameter. Jim went to raise the chunk of concrete again. There was a loud crack and the door sheared in two. Water thundered through, sending wood and metal hurling towards them.

Harry landed on the floor and saw the other three fly through the air. Before he could even draw breath, a great wave of water crashed over them, propelling them along the corridor, back towards the barrier of rubble.

Somehow, they all managed to grab hold of something solid in the wall of wreckage that had cut the corridor in two. The water slammed into them, then it rolled back, giving them time to draw breath. It churned around the walls of the corridor, losing some of its momentum. It came up to Harry's waist. Nick had pulled himself up onto the barrier, his head a foot clear of the surface. They were all shocked into silence, grasping at the barrier for dear life, none of them knowing what to do next.

The flood began to slow.

'It's not a hull breech,' Harry spluttered. 'Water must've built up in a cavity.' He pushed away from the barrier.

'What're you doing?' Jim asked.

Harry said nothing, just waded through the waist-high water towards the shattered remains of the doorframe. Another corridor lay on the other side. It was narrower and shorter. At the far end stood another doorway. The door was gone, but the opening was completely blocked by rubble that had slid through from the far side.

It was then Harry noticed the water level was still rising.

He took a deep breath and ducked under the surface. He swam to the wall and pulled himself along, keeping his head under, trying to find where the water was coming in. He reached the blocked doorway without finding the source of the leak. Standing up, he waded over to the other side of the passageway and ducked under the surface again to inspect the far wall.

Three metres from the doorway, he found it. It was a roughly circular opening about a metre and a half wide. The flow had diminished thanks to a steel plate that had been pushed against the wall on the other side, blocking 70 per cent of the hole and leaving a gap about half a metre wide.

Harry's heart sank. They were trapped. They could try to block this hole but they couldn't just stay put in the corridor in the hope someone would rescue them before they died of hypothermia. The doorway at the end of the passageway was blocked, but water was gushing from an adjoining room. That meant that room must also be filled with water. Then he had a desperate thought. He resurfaced. The water was up to his chest now. Without wasting a second, he took another great gulp of air and dived under the water. He was just able to squeeze through the gap at the top of the opening in the wall. Once through to the other side, he swam a single stroke and reached for the surface.

There was a metre of space between the water and the ceiling. He looked around. It was a large room. Water was pouring into it through another hole in the far wall. Harry was about to swim over to the hole when he caught a glint of light to his left. He darted towards it.

It was the glass upper half of yet another door. He could see through to the other side. An archway led on to a wide open space. He could see a vast spiral staircase. It was the main stairs of Dome Beta. Diving under the water, he searched for anything he could find to smash the window. The first dive was fruitless. He resurfaced and took a gulp of stale air. Desperately, he shuffled along the floor of the room. He saw a grey shape in the murk, swung his arm around and felt a sharp stab of pain. Drawing back, he watched as a swirl of red enveloped his arm. Quelling the panic, he focused on the shape he had seen. It was a piece of metal shelving. One end was a sharp edge where it had broken away from the rest of the unit. He grasped at the shelf and pulled himself up through the water. Ignoring the pain in his arm and the red water at his chest, he gripped the door handle and crashed the piece of shelving into the window. It offered little resistance, shattering into dozens of pieces. One small shard flew into Harry's face and nicked his left ear. 'Fuck!' he exclaimed and felt blood trickle down his cheek. Using the shelf, he smashed away the remaining fragments of glass clinging to the frame. He noticed the water level had dropped quite a few centimetres. Diving back under the water, he turned and headed back to the hole in the wall and the corridor beyond. When he tried to regain his feet, the water came over his head.

'You can all swim, I hope,' Harry gasped as he pulled himself up the barrier. There was little more than half a metre of air above the surface now. Kristy, Jim and Nick had scrambled up the wreckage and were clinging on for dear life, barely managing to contain their panic. Nick had vomited, some of it was floating around his neck, and there was a line of yellow running from his mouth. His cheeks were deathly white.

'There's a hole,' Harry said. 'Leads to a way out. But it's a long swim, and I don't know if we'll have any air once we get into the next corridor. Come on, follow me.'

He swam to the doorframe, clinging to the wood for a few seconds then ducked down to peer into the adjoining corridor. The water was up the ceiling. He pulled his head back. 'Damn it!' he hissed. 'Okay, Jim. You go first. The hole is to your right. Once you're in the room and reach the surface you should be able to breathe, the water level is dropping there.'

Jim nodded and launched himself under the water. 'Nick, you next.'

The boy was paralysed with terror. 'Come on, Nick, you can do it.'

He stared at Harry. Then Kristy put her hand on the boy's shoulder. 'I'll be right behind you.'

Harry looked at her in surprise, but she simply glared at him.

Nick dived down, kicking furiously, churning the water. There was barely any air space now and Kristy and Harry had to tilt their heads to breathe. 'Follow me,' Harry said. Filling his lungs, he shot down under the water and he felt Kristy do the same a second after him.

Harry glimpsed Jim's feet as the American slid through the hole, and he saw Nick pull himself up along the wall, stick his head into the opening and propel himself forward. Swivelling around in the water, Harry was about to launch himself forward when he felt a rush of churning water. Something banged against his leg and twisted along his shin. He tried to kick it free, but it was stuck fast. He turned and went to reach down, but he couldn't move. He had put his foot through a smashed computer monitor and it had twisted around, trapping him.

Kristy was only 2 metres behind him. She saw Harry twist and caught sight of the plastic object wrapped around his foot. She was barely containing her panic. She had never been a strong swimmer. Her lungs were burning. Every fibre of her brain was telling her to go on, to push through the hole in the wall. She had to save herself. Nothing else mattered. But then, she caught a glimpse of Harry's face. He looked lost, overwhelmed, terrified. He gazed at her and she could see he believed he was going to die.

Pain rushed through Kristy's chest as she stopped, turned and clawed at the monitor. It was stuck fast. She yanked at it, feeling shards of glass rip her flesh, but it would not give. The pain in her chest was crushing her. The desire to open her mouth and breathe was almost overwhelming. She pulled again, and Harry twisted in agony as the glass cut him too. Then it gave, the plastic casing slid through Kristy's fingers and Harry's bloodied foot slipped free. She felt strong hands grabbing her by her wrists and pulling her. Then they were at the opening and Harry was shoving her through. She smashed her head against the edge of the hole and clawed at the jagged concrete of the damaged wall. With a last desperate effort, she pulled herself through and scrambled into the air, gasping as she saw Harry break the surface, his face blue and streaked with blood.

44

Dome Gamma

Michael Xavier approached the group of survivors in the Dome Gamma ballroom, and heard sobbing. A woman was on her knees leaning over a prone form. Taking two steps closer, he realised the woman was his wife. She was crouched beside an older woman. It was not until he bent down next to her he recognised one of the guests at their table, Sheila Hoffman, the wife of the architect who had designed the hotel.

Hilary moved her hand over the woman's face and closed her dead eyelids. Then she threw her head into her hands and wept. Michael put an arm around her shoulders and she melted into him. 'There,' he said softly. Hilary sobbed and clutched at his shirt.

'Why is this happening, Michael?' she managed to say.

Michael Xavier could not answer her. He knew that things had been made very much worse by the actions of his brother, but the man could hardly be blamed for the disaster. 'I wish I knew, Hilary,' he said and put a hand under her chin. She pulled away, but he insisted she look up at him. 'Come on. We have to focus, Hil.'

She surveyed his face, holding his earnest gaze, and clambered to her feet. 'What are we going to do?'

Michael kept his arm around his wife's shoulders and led her back towards the others gathered close by. Hilary sat down, and Michael stood in front of the group. There were 14 of them, including Hilary, Michael, Johnny, and the two men who had come with them to check out the stairs and the exit. They were all injured in one way or another.

'The staircase to the east of the building and the emergency stairs are both impassable,' Michael told them. 'It seems to me we have only one choice. We have to go down to the lowest level using the escalators. There are three emergency subs there. Also, if any rescue attempt is to be made from the surface, a sub will have to hook up with the universal dock in Beta. Failing that, a sub may be able to dock with Dome Alpha. The only route to any of these is via the lowest level and the linkways.'

'That's madness,' Johnny Xavier burst out. He had been sitting on a pile of debris close to the others. Standing, he walked over to his brother. 'I know this building as well as anyone,' he said to the group. 'You've all seen the devastation up here. It'll be far worse down there.' And he pointed towards the floor. 'Besides, the escalators don't work and may well be severely damaged.' He started to pace in front of the group. 'We have to stay put up here. Any rescue attempt will be made through one or other of the docks, but they will know we are up here and get through to us. If we go down they'll never find us.'

There was a heavy silence broken only by the crackle of electrical cables close by and the constant dripping of water.

'The top of the dome won't last much longer,' Michael reasoned, letting his words fall like lead weights. 'Stay here and you'll drown or be crushed to death. Going down is our only hope. The emergency bulkheads will cut off the top of the dome if pressure on the glass reaches a critical level. Johnny, you know that.'

'What does he mean?' It was Hilary. She glared at Johnny, then turned towards her husband. 'What do you *mean*, Michael?'

'What I said. Look for yourself, Hil. All of you. Look at the cap.'

Heads turned towards the apex of the dome. It was just visible in the gloom. They could all see the cracks running down the sides of the dome.

'It's designed to take the stress,' Johnny insisted. He turned to the gathering. 'Believe me. Going down is suicide. None of us have any idea what is down there. The cap will hold.'

Michael whirled on his brother. 'Why are you doing this, Johnny?'

Johnny turned away from the others and took a step towards Michael. 'I know you find it hard to accept that you might be wrong about *anything*, Mike. But why should any of us believe you? Tell me that, brother. You built this hotel, you brought us all here tonight.' And he waved a hand back towards the others. 'Why should any of us trust your judgement?'

Michael fixed his brother's eyes. Johnny broke away and spun on his heel. 'It's up to each of you to decide what to do,' he said.

Michael had a hand to his forehead, his eyes closed. Then he looked up and walked over to Hilary. Their daughter, Emily, was next to her. Hilary had an arm around the girl's shoulder. Mother and daughter stared at Michael as he approached.

'I'd like you to trust me,' he said.

Hilary flicked Johnny a glance then looked at the ground for a second. Pulling Emily with her, she strode forward and threw her arms around Michael's waist. He kissed her, then crouched to kiss Emily.

'I believe we have to go down, and now,' Michael said, turning to the group. 'But as my brother says, it's up to each of you to decide what's best for you.'

Craig Deloray, the Australian security man, stepped forward. He had improvised a sling from a strip of fabric. He was followed by two others, the engineer, Miguel Bandonis, and the financier, Sigmund de Silva.

'Johnny,' Michael said, turning to his brother. 'Please. You're making a mistake.'

'I don't think I am, Michael. I think you are.'

'Is that your final word?'

Johnny did not reply, just walked back towards those who had decided to stay.

Michael watched him. Then he took a deep breath, turned and never looked back.

45

The two escalators descended directly from the banqueting hall. But Johnny Xavier was right, they had stopped working. They were also cast in darkness.

'Here, I've got this,' Bandonis said, pulling a torch from the back of his belt. He swept the beam over the top of the right-hand escalator. It lit up the first 5 metres, then petered out. 'Let's go then,' he added, gripping the rail and stepping onto the steel tread. It was wet with water.

The light spilling back from the torch was so faint it barely did any good at all, but gradually their eyes began to adjust. Hilary held Emily's hand tightly with her left hand and grasped the rubber handrail with her right. She felt a horrible sense of dread deep in the pit of her stomach, but knew she had to project the illusion of remaining calm. After two steps on the wet metal, she stopped, pulled off her high heels and tossed them over the railing onto the parallel escalator.

Michael was close behind Hilary and Emily. He took a step down to join them.

'You okay?' he asked his wife.

'Oh yes!' Hilary declared. 'Reminds me of a holiday in St Tropez.'

Michael looked pained.

'I'm sorry,' Hilary said suddenly. Then she did something she had not done for a long time. Taking her hand from the rail, she put it on Michael's cheek, feeling the soft warmth and revelling in it for a second.

'I'm so sorry about . . .' Michael began.

Hilary shook her head.

Craig Deloray and Sigmund de Silva, who had been a few steps behind, approached them. Michael looked up at their vague shapes emerging from the gloom. Then he squeezed Hilary's hand.

The escalators ran in three stages from the top floor of the dome to ground. The first led down to the second floor where the cinema and theatre were located. Another set connected the second floor to the first level which was dominated by a set of conference rooms. The final escalator hooked up with the ground floor, and the casino, Poseidon's Gold. From there, a wide, carpeted staircase descended one level to the lower ground floor.

'Miguel? Can you see anything?' Michael called.

'Looks like the escalator is in one piece, sir,' he called back.

Then Michael noticed the torch beam wobble.

'Miguel?'

There was no reply.

The light moved downwards, casting strange shadows across the wall, a silhouette of the engineer, crouching down.

'Miguel? What is it?' Michael repeated, and edged his way carefully in front of Hilary and Emily. They had frozen to the spot.

Michael came up behind the engineer. Bandonis turned as his boss approached. In the light from the torch, Michael could see the mangled body on the metal steps. It was a man in a tux. His dead face was blackened. There was a huge red and grey opening running from his left temple to his lips. His legs were twisted under him. One arm hung from a few sinews.

'My God!' Michael exclaimed.

Bandonis rose unsteadily. Michael took four steps back up the escalator to where Hilary and Emily were standing outside the circle of light.

'There's a dead body a few steps down,' he said.

Hilary put a hand to her mouth. The two men, Sigmund de Silva and Craig Deloray, had come up behind Hilary and Emily. 'Miguel and I will move the body to the right side of the escalator.'

Michael disappeared for a few moments. The others heard a heavy weight being shifted over the wet metal steps and then Xavier was back, his face pale.

'Hil, you cover Em's eyes and help her past, okay?'

Hilary Xavier nodded.

Michael took Emily's right hand, Hilary turned her daughter's head away holding her against her hip. Slowly, carefully they crept down the frigid steps of the escalator. Hilary tried hard not to look, but morbid curiosity overwhelmed her. She glanced to the right as they passed the body. The dead man's blind eyes were staring straight at her, his mouth slack and open. She recognised him . . . just. Unable to contain herself any longer, Hilary gasped. She had seen the man earlier. He had been alive and well and tending to his famous charge. Now Kristy Sunshine's manager, Brett Littleton, was as dead as dead could be, a mutilated corpse on the icy steel steps.

46

A few minutes after leaving the banqueting hall, they had reached the second floor of Dome Gamma. It was pitch black. Michael and Hilary Xavier, with their daughter and Craig Deloray, followed Miguel Bandonis and Sigmund de Silva. Bandonis held the torch as steady as he could. The carpet was sodden and water had gathered in puddles in the lush fabric. And it stank – a blend of food, the crisp ozone of electrical activity and the stench of the ocean floor, a rich salty compost odour.

Bandonis swept the torch around the walls and into the dark recesses of the landing. The walls ran with water. Part of the ceiling had collapsed and a metre square piece of plasterboard hung down from one edge. The torch revealed electrical wiring and a brightly coloured plastic conduit running along the cavity above their heads.

'There's an emergency override for the ceiling lights here somewhere,' Michael said. He looked over to Bandonis.

The man was shaking his head. 'There should be.'

Michael held his gaze then closed his eyes for a second and sighed.

'There're a couple of floor lights,' Bandonis offered.

'Forget it. What about the lower floors? What are the cuts there?'

'Not sure, sir. I think emergency lighting for the casino was untouched.'

Michael Xavier looked at the engineer. 'Well, that's something at least.' He turned to the others. No one spoke. 'After you, Miguel,' Michael said.

The next pair of escalators were shorter, and they all reached the conference suite level without incident. Michael took the torch from Bandonis and walked half a dozen paces over to a wall panel adjacent to the doors to Conference Room 1. From his pocket, he removed a credit card-sized piece of black plastic and ran it down a slot to the right of the panel. Nothing happened.

Bandonis was at Michael's shoulder. 'It's down too,' he said. He pulled a penknife from his pocket. 'Here, let me try this.' He leaned in and ran the knife along the slot. Stopping about two-thirds of the way down, he pulled the knife back towards him a fraction of a millimetre. There was a quiet click and the panel swung outwards. Michael Xavier held the torch while Bandonis fiddled with a collection of wires. The engineer tugged on a red lead, unthreading it from the others and slotted the copper end into the opening of a junction box. He flicked a switch to one side and the lights came on.

'So, what now?' Craig Deloray asked as Michael and Miguel approached. His face was wreathed with sweat. Michael had forgotten how badly injured the man was.

'You okay to go on?'

'Don't have a choice, do I?' Deloray replied and forced a half-smile.

'What *is* the plan, precisely?' Sigmund de Silva asked. He was sitting on a low wall that surrounded a flowerbed in the centre of the hall close to the foot of the escalators. He looked exhausted. Like the others, his face was smeared with sweat and dust and blood.

Michael took a deep breath. 'We have to get to the emergency subs on the lower ground level.'

'And if they're not working?'

'Then we have to head that way.' He pointed to his left, the west side of the building. 'The linkway to Beta is on the same floor. If we can get to Beta, there is another set of emergency subs. We can try to reach the universal dock or press on to Alpha and the other dock. I'm assuming any rescue effort will use the *Cousteau* or one of the other subs.'

'But Miguel, you reckoned half the subs were duds,' de Silva said.

Bandonis nodded. 'Yes, but the other half aren't.'

'Okay, but then, Michael,' de Silva went on, turning back to Xavier, 'your brother was telling the truth about one thing, wasn't he? If the linkway is impassable or destroyed, we'll be trapped.'

'There's always that possibility,' Michael conceded. He looked from face to face. 'But I'm hoping we won't need the linkway.'

Emily Xavier was the first to hear the strange hissing sound. 'Dad, what's that?' she asked suddenly.

'What's what?'

'That sound?'

'Hissing,' Craig Deloray said. 'It's coming from up there.' He pointed to the ceiling a few metres across the hall towards the escalators that fell away to the first floor. He walked over, staring at the ceiling. 'It's a gas leak,' he called to the others. 'Methane, I think.'

No one saw where the flame came from. The first anyone knew about it was when a sheet of fire shot out from the ceiling. From a few metres away, it looked like a powerful jet spewing from a hose, a deadly cascade of orange and yellow flame. It caught Craig's left side and enveloped him. He screamed. His clothes caught alight instantly and his hair burst into a mass of sizzling black. The stink hit the others before they could even comprehend what was happening.

Sigmund was the first to react. He was the only one of the men still wearing a dinner jacket. He pulled it off in one smooth movement as he ran towards the stricken security man.

Deloray was blown off his feet by the force of the blast. Screeching in agony, he landed in a fiery heap. They all heard a fizz as his body hit the sodden carpet. It sounded like a pork chop being thrown onto a barbecue. He writhed and rolled over the wet carpet trying to put out the fire.

Sigmund grabbed the man's kicking right leg, keeping as far away as possible from the still gushing flame. Deloray was smothered in fire now, his clothes peeling away, his hair a charred mess. Clear of the gaseous burst, Sigmund repeatedly smacked his jacket onto Deloray's body, but it was making very little difference.

De Silva looked up as a burst of fire-retardant foam showered down. Michael was holding a fire extinguisher and frantically spraying it in a wide arch over the burning security man. In a few moments, the fire was out. Sigmund slammed the jacket down a few more times for good measure. They both noticed Craig Deloray had stopped screaming. He was lying still on his front.

Michael got down on his knees and gingerly turned Craig over. His face was frozen in a horrible grimace. Half of the flesh had been ripped away by the flames, his teeth and jaw bone were exposed on one side. The remaining skin had been charred black, bubbled and fried.

'MICHAEL!' Hilary screamed.

He span around to see his wife clutching their daughter and pointing towards the ceiling. Her eyes reflected the bright yellow slurry of fire sweeping across the ceiling towards the escalators.

'Run!' Michael yelled. 'Go!'

He jumped to his feet and saw that Sigmund was already dashing after Hilary and Emily. Miguel Bandonis was only metres away and had just seen the fire. Without thinking, acting purely on impulse, Michael Xavier ran as fast as he could across the squelching carpet towards the top of the escalator. He could see Hilary and Emily had made it to the top step and were running down as fast as they dared. He was about to shout to them again when he slipped, his feet sliding awkwardly on the soaked floor. He fell backwards, banging his head on the floor. A terrible pain shot down his spine. He tried to pull himself up and felt strong arms grabbing him under the shoulders. He saw Sigmund in front of him, heading down the escalator, and felt a burst of heat on the back of his neck. He cried out in panic. The smell of burning hair filled his nostrils.

He was stumbling, falling again. Then he caught himself, snatched at the rubber handrail and felt a hand grip his free arm, glimpsing Miguel Bandonis beside him on the escalator.

Lights streamed past. Another burst of heat came from directly overhead. He heard Hilary scream and his stomach felt like it was falling out of his body. Then he saw his wife and daughter. A sheet of flame shot down from the sloping ceiling above the frozen metal steps. It missed them by centimetres and was sucked back into a panel overhead. The escalator stairs seemed to rear up. He collided with Miguel. An elbow slammed into his damaged side sending a flood of pain through his body. He waited for the crunch of impact, saw blurred steel, a flash of black rubber railing, the soiled white of his shirt sleeve. But the bone-shattering landing never came. He fell onto his side, hitting a hard floor covered with soft carpet. He rolled away just as Miguel crashed down beside him. Pulling himself up, Michael looked down to see the engineer lying on his front, groaning into the carpet. Michael helped him to his feet and looked up. Hilary was standing just up ahead of them, her face a picture of terror. Xavier was about to ask what had happened when he saw for himself. The staircase down to the lower ground floor was completely blocked with burning rubble.

47

'The casino,' Michael yelled, grabbing his wife and daughter and shoving them towards a set of heavy double doors. He turned back to Miguel. The man was getting to his feet, grasping his side, clearly in agony and barely able to walk. Sigmund was there in a second, and between them they helped the injured man towards the casino.

The sound of the fire filled the hall as flames found new material, new fuel. Superheated air rushed across the ceiling and embers dropped and fizzed on the wet carpet. In a few moments, the three men had traversed the short distance to the doors and dived through. Dumping Miguel on the carpet just inside the casino, Michael and Sigmund rushed back to the doors and heaved them shut.

Hilary collapsed to her knees. Emily was gasping for air. Michael went over to them. 'You okay?'

Hilary nodded.

'We have a few minutes,' Michael said. 'Those are fire doors. They'll hold back the flames for a bit.' He walked over to Miguel. The man's shirt was wet with blood. He crouched beside him and gently lifted the wet fabric. There was a deep gash in his side. Standing up, Xavier ran over to the office of the casino close to the doors. Rifling through a cupboard beside a desk to one side of the room, he found a First Aid kit and dashed back to the others.

Throwing open the box, Michael found antiseptic cream, wipes, iodine, pads, plasters and bandages. 'This will hurt,' he told Miguel. The man nodded. Michael cleaned the wound, smeared it with antiseptic and pressed a pad onto it. Miguel yelped.

'Sorry.'

Michael stuck the pad to Miguel's abdomen with two large plasters then wrapped bandage around his waist.

'Thank you,' Miguel said, between gritted teeth.

'So, how're we going to get down to the subs?' Sigmund asked. He was standing beside them breathing heavily.

Michael said nothing, just gazed around the vast space, his expression desperate. Then they all heard a sound. It was familiar, but wildly incongruous, a clanking of metal against metal, a tumbling of coins.

Michael and Sigmund took a couple of paces in the direction of the sound. Turning into an aisle of slot machines, they saw a man in a dirty dinner suit and a Stetson standing at a machine. He had just yanked the handle and was watching the spinning wheels intently. He seemed completely oblivious to them.

Michael and Sigmund approached slowly. They were almost at the man's side before he glanced round and produced a crooked smile. 'I'm just having the best run. Friggin' unbelievable.' His voice was a heavy Texan drawl. He was a short, overweight man of about 50. Neither Michael nor Sigmund recognised him. His dinner suit was ripped and covered in dust, the Stetson was powdered grey. He had a dark bruise on his left cheek and his upper lip was swollen.

'I'm Michael Xavier, and this is Sigmund de Silva,' Michael said, unable to keep the bemusement from his voice.

'Yes, I know who you are,' the man said, keeping his eyes fixed on the spinning wheels.

'What's your name?'

'Gil,' he said. 'Gil Tallow.'

Michael vaguely recognised the name – one of Johnny's business pals.

'What're you doing here?' Sigmund asked.

The man did not take his eyes from the wheels. 'Winning!' he said. 'I'm winning.' Then he turned to face the two men square-on, pushed the hat back up his forehead and beamed. 'It's sooo darn exciting!'

'Why are you here?' Michael persisted. 'I didn't see you at dinner.'

'No. Damn pissed about that.' And he looked into Michael's eyes, his face suddenly serious. 'Martha was so friggin' late. We came through the linkway from the other dome, what's it called?'

'Beta.'

'Yeah, that's it. Beta. We're headed for the banquet when the whole friggin' place starts a-shakin'. One wild ride,' he added with a grin, and turned back to the machine.

'Where's Martha?' Michael asked.

'Oh, she's dead,' Gil responded without looking away from the slot machine.

Michael glanced at Sigmund, who looked completely lost. Then he noticed how Gil's hand was shaking so much it took him a few moments to slip a coin into the slot at the top of the machine.

'So . . . so, Gil,' Michael said. 'How did you get here?'

'Back stairs,' he replied and turned to give Michael a puzzled look. 'Over there.' He pointed to the far wall of the huge open space. 'Ain't that obvious? The main stairs are backed up worse than an old lady on a cheese diet.' Then he gave a manic laugh. 'Thought that was pretty friggin' apparent.'

'Gil, there's been a terrible accident,' Sigmund began.

'We've got to try to get down to the lower ground floor. It's our best chance of survival.'

Gil ignored him.

'Gil?' Michael said and placed a hand on the man's shoulder.

'Don't you friggin' touch me,' Gil Tallow spat. For the first time, he took his hand from the arm of the machine, and span on his heel. 'I know your game, mister,' he hissed, his eyes narrowing to slits. 'Oh, yeah.' He snarled. 'Oh, yeah.'

Michael pulled back, speechless.

'You wanna piece of the action, don't ya? That's your friggin' trick, ain't it?' Tallow's voice was little more than a whisper. 'WELL YOU AIN'T HAVING NONE!' he yelled suddenly, his eyes ablaze. Before Michael could realise what was happening, the man pulled a length of metal pipe from the far side of the slot machine. Gripping it in his right hand, he swung it round. The pipe cut the air, missing Michael by a centimetre. He leapt to the side and fell over his own feet, landing with his back against another slot machine on the other side of the aisle.

Stunned, Sigmund had frozen to the spot. Gil Tallow looked at them and laughed, let the pipe slip through his twitching fingers and turned back to the machine. 'Darn farm hands,' he exclaimed and spat on the floor between them. 'Bunch of friggin' pussies.'

Sigmund did not waste a second. He pulled Michael to his feet and gripped him by the shoulders. 'Don't say another word, Michael,' he said under his breath. 'The crazy fucker's helped us more than he'll ever know.'

48

Gobi Desert, China

Steph worked her way through the material she had collected from the wreckage of the Silverback. Very little of it was useable. Almost all the components of the aircraft were sealed units and highly specialised. They did not lend themselves naturally to being cannibalised. What she had salvaged lay on a rickety table close to the fire. Howard was cooking up some food in the kitchen just a few metres away. It smelled surprisingly good.

On the table lay a bunch of different coloured wires, a power pack from a coolant unit, a solar power cell and some parts from a shattered communication console. Beside the pile of smashed equipment stood Howard's old radio.

Using a miniature screwdriver from the toolkit she had found in the wrecked plane, Steph prised open the back of a small metal unit. Inside lay a deceptively simple array of wires and plastic rectangles placed in a regular arrangement. Although it looked no more complex than the sort of device a young techno enthusiast might build with his first electronic design kit, it was a machine with the computing power of a TV station.

The CARPA eggheads who designed the module used components so small that they had reached the effective limit for miniaturisation at which a fundamental principle of quantum theory called Heisenberg's Uncertainty began to interfere with the functioning of the device. This meant that the innards of any form of processor could get no smaller unless, that is, quantum computing mechanisms were used. (This was how Sybil operated and it gave the Base One computer extraordinary processing power. Unfortunately, this could still only be achieved with a large machine such as Sybil – a computer that took up a huge room in the lowest level of Base One on Tintara. Even the scientists at CARPA were a long way from building miniature quantum computers.)

Steph studied the inside of the module and suddenly felt overwhelmed by the task she had set herself. A surge of anger erupted inside her and she slammed down the metal box, rocking the old handmade table so that it almost toppled over.

'What're you hoping to achieve?' It was Josh. He was pulling himself up on some animal skins that had been rolled up to form a pillow.

'Hi,' Steph responded. 'How're you feeling?'

'I was fine . . . until the alarm call,' he declared, glancing at the box Steph had brought down on the table.

'Sorry about that.'

'I'm actually feeling a million times better.' He went to move his legs. 'Ow!'

'Easy tiger.'

'No, it's just pins and needles, Steph. The knee is feeling . . . well almost bearable,' he said and grinned. 'So, you going to tell me?' And he nodded to the muddle of objects on the table.

'Howard lent us his radio. Says it's no good to him as it is. It's actually working fine. It's just that any signal it could pick up is jammed.'

'So, what good is it to us?'

'It occurred to me that if the range of the interference is limited, then we might still pick up a signal from Tom. Or we could send a high frequency signal to him. E-Force comms work on ultra high frequency radio waves, remember.'

'So you're hoping the Chinese jamming won't reach such high frequencies?'

'Exactly.'

'But then, if the Chinese jamming signal doesn't reach that part of the radio spectrum, why haven't you been able to pick up anything from Base One?'

'Because this dear old thing,' and she patted the wooden casing of the radio affectionately, '. . . would not be able to operate at that range, unmodified.'

'Hence that lot.' Josh nodded towards the pile of salvaged components. 'Anything I can do?'

Steph ran her fingers over her chin. 'I'm not so sure either of us can, Josh.' She lifted up a metal box about 5 centimetres square. It had three red leads coming from its underside. Apart from that it was featureless.

'A comms modulator,' Josh said.

'Yeah, found it in this piece of console.' Steph pointed to a length of shattered plastic about 30 centimetres long and 15 centimetres wide to which three similar metal boxes were attached. 'It should boost the signal to cover either end of the range of the old radio.'

Howard walked in, wiping his hands on an old rag. 'Ah, how's the patient?'

'Feeling much better, thanks.'

Howard shook his head. 'Steph was trying to explain about the nanowhatsits. I know I've lost touch living out here, but that's pretty amazing.'

'Yes, it is,' Josh said, nodding. 'I wouldn't worry. I still find it incredible.'

224

'So, what are you trying to do with my old radio, Steph?'

She repeated what she had told Josh.

'That's good . . . isn't it?'

'Would be, except I can't power the modulator.'

'What about my generator? It's as ancient as the radio, but it has a fair old kick.'

Steph smiled. 'I'm sure it does, Howard, but it has to be a very precise power signature, or the components will fry – assuming the modulator is still working, of course.'

Howard sat down in the only other chair, close to the end of Josh's bier.

'God! How dumb am I?' Josh said suddenly. 'The cyber-suit. We could use its powerpack.'

'Nice idea, Josh, but it won't work. The suit has an entirely different modulation system.'

'Damn it, I knew that.'

'You're forgiven,' Steph said with a smile.

Howard stood up and walked over to a pair of shelves cut into the wall close to the exit. He rummaged around for a few moments, mumbling to himself. Steph turned back to the pile of components on the table. Josh closed his eyes for a second. When he opened them again, Howard was walking back towards them. 'Will this help?' On the table, he placed an ugly-looking mess of wires and bulbous clumps of insulation tape that sprouted from a small, lidless wooden box.

'Er . . . what is it?'

'A transformer, of sorts.'

Steph stared at it. Josh was leaning up on one elbow peering over towards the table.

'Made it from bits of the original Toyota and other odds and ends I've found over the years.'

'But why?'

'I'll have you know it's extremely useful.'

Steph and Josh looked at him doubtfully.

'Almost every electrical device I brought with me has long since gone the journey,' Howard said. 'Any replacements I've managed to procure have been by bartering with nomads who pass by occasionally, or from the market in Fung Ching Wa. I discovered quite early on though that only rarely do two devices work on the same voltage. Most of them are Chinese, Russian, American and a few European products, and by the time I get them they've almost always been mauled by the locals. So, I built this.' He looked down at the contraption with pride. 'A transformer. It can handle most voltage changes. You could hook it up to its operator and get the power signature you need'

'Well, I don't know what to say,' Steph said looking up from the box of tricks Howard had placed on the table. She studied the man's face. 'You really are a most remarkable man, Howard.'

'Why thank you,' he replied with a bashful smile and went off to the kitchen.

49

It took Steph another half hour of wire-fiddling to rig up the circuitry for the modulator on the kitchen bench. The generator stood at one end of the room. The equipment was an amorphous heap of metal boxes, wires, relays and lengths of plastic. At one end was the modulator looking totally incongruous among the piles of homemade electrical gadgets and devices that belonged in a museum. Steph had soldered together most of the components, but some wires were wound together and covered with insulation tape. The final step was to connect the leads to Howard's ancient generator. She uncoiled two rubber-sheathed lengths of wire, clamped one end to the output pads of the transformer and the other to electrodes on the generator.

Howard came into the kitchen as Steph was finishing off with the connections and checking everything through. Josh was sitting up in bed nearby, watching with interest.

'How's it going, Steph?' Howard asked. 'Looks horrendously complicated.'

'Well, it looks worse than it is,' she replied. 'I've just connected the generator to the transformer and from there the power goes to the modulator. I've hooked up the modulator to the main transmitter in your radio. If we can get enough juice from the generator, we should be able to push the radio frequency range beyond the interference region, and maybe, just maybe, get a message out.'

'Fingers crossed,' Howard said and stepped back.

'You want to do the honours?' Steph asked, pointing at the switch close to the modulator.

Howard had his hands up. 'No . . . Your machine. You do it.'

Steph shrugged and leaned over the bench, held her fingers on the switch for a moment and then clicked it to 'on'.

At first, nothing happened. Then the modulator began to hum and a dull green light appeared inside it and started to pulse. Steph leaned towards a slider close to the main switch. 'I'm going to gradually increase the power to the modulator,' she said. 'We need to get the transmission signal up to at least 102 gigahertz, the bottom end of the range E-Force operates in. If we make that, we just have to pray the interference band doesn't go that far.'

Steph moved the slider slowly. With each increment, the hum shifted to a higher pitch and the light inside the modulator pulsed a little faster. With the slider halfway along its groove, Steph stopped to check the frequency. It was at 30.3 gigahertz. Good, but still nowhere near the frequency she needed.

Josh appeared in the doorway. 'How's it going?'

'You should be in bed,' Steph said, without taking her eyes from the mess of tangled electrical components on the kitchen bench.

'I'm feeling much better.'

Steph pushed the slider to the three-quarter mark, and the hum increased in pitch again, turning into an irritating squeal. She checked the frequency. 57.8 gigahertz. 'Damn it,' she exclaimed.

'What?' Howard asked.

'Should be 75 to 80 gigahertz by now.' She shook her head and sighed. Then she adjusted a couple of the controls on the radio. 'Ow!' she exclaimed. 'That's hot.'

'Perhaps, we should . . .' Howard began quietly.

Steph ignored him. 'So close . . .' she announced and tapped the slider, nudging it a millimetre. Glancing at the frequency meter, she cursed and went to nudge the slider again. There was a loud crack and a spark flew from the modulator. At the same moment, the generator started to crackle where the leads had been attached to the electrodes. A wire connecting the radio to the modulator snapped, burst into flames, flew up into the air and hit the low compacted sand ceiling. It rebounded and shot back to the bench, missing Steph's hand by millimetres. A low fizz emanated from the radio and the whole arrangement of components shut down as though a switch had been thrown to 'off'.

50

Base One, Tintara Island

'So, you can't reach Pete or Mai in Dome Alpha?' Tom said. An image of Mark at the controls of the Big Mac filled the screen in his quarters.

'No. Comms between here and the hotel are completely down. You got anything on your monitors?'

'I lost the link at the same time as you, Mark. BigEye has traces for each of them on infrared. Mai had just separated from a small group, leaving Pete behind. Their traces show they're still in Alpha, but infrared doesn't mean much.'

Mark knew precisely what Tom meant. Both Pete and Mai could be dead, but they would still have some residual heat in their bodies. For a while at least. He pushed the thought aside and focused. 'Tom, I want you to make a detailed scan of the structure of the three domes.'

'What're you thinking of doing?'

'I'm going in.'

'But how're you going to dock?' Tom asked, surveying Mark's face on the screen.

'That's why I want the information on the structural integrity. I'm going to have to cut my way in.'

Tom nodded.

'Anything more on Steph and Josh?' Mark asked.

Tom looked pained. 'Oh, I've narrowed it down . . . to an area about the size of New Jersey,' he said, and looked at his control panel. 'BigEye 17 is sweeping the area in a standard search pattern. I'm due an update in a few minutes.' He looked up. 'If they are alive I'm sure Steph and Josh will make their presence known somehow.'

'Okay, Tom. Let me have those stats on the hotel asap, yeah?'

Tom set to work straight away. He had the most recent BigEye images of the stricken hotel on his screen, ones taken after the second tremor that had broken the comms link with Pete and Mai.

'Sybil, can you bring up the stress pattern for each of the domes? Start with Alpha.'

The image focused in on the most westerly dome. It filled the screen and rotated slowly to show all angles. A series of coloured lines appeared. They looked like the lattice work of veins in a human body, or the filaments of fat in a side of meat. The top of the dome was shattered and closely packed fissures ran from the cap along the west side almost to the second floor. The clearest region was on the first floor on the east side.

'Dome Beta please, Sybil.'

An almost identical picture appeared. Dome Beta. It rotated slowly on the screen. The west side had fewer stress lines, and they were less closely packed than those for Alpha. The cap was holding up well, but this would be the worst place to try to enter the hotel. The glass was at its thickest and under the most stress from tension.

Tom ran his hand over the virtual keyboard on the top of his desk and the image shifted to the east side of Beta. This was severely damaged, the stress lines packed tight and running halfway down the side of the dome. He took a deep breath and exhaled through his nose. 'Gamma please.'

Dome Gamma appeared on the screen. The top of the structure was such a mess of fault lines, Tom was amazed the cap had not given way. The fissures ran down the dome in every direction. But, below these, the structure was remarkably undamaged. Tom closed in on the image, following fault lines from the top of the dome until they petered out. Then, moving down to the base of the structure, he could see that a small section at the east end of the linkway was still connected to the west side of Dome Gamma, but the corridor was completely unusable. The other end had snapped away from Beta.

Tom shifted the image again to study the most easterly side of the dome. Here the structure was the most stable of any section of the hotel. If any part could sustain Mark's effort to cut into the glass, this would be it. He turned to the control panel and sent the information over to Mark in the Big Mac.

A signal sounded. It was the update from BigEye 17. Tom span his electric chair round and leaned over the plastic top of the console, not daring to hope the satellite would deliver some positive news. He flicked the signal to the main screen. The image was clouded with lines of static. Tom waited for the image to clear, but it would not shift. All he could see was a background of orange covered with streaks of distortion and jagged white bands. From the speaker came nothing but white noise.

51

Dome Alpha

Pete awoke to a horrible silence, and for a moment he could not move. He tried to sit up but was stopped by a heavy object across his chest. He looked down and saw a steel beam. It had come within centimetres of crushing him. Pete pushed against it. It was incredibly heavy and had stuck fast. Taking a deep breath, he pushed again with every ounce of his strength. The beam shifted. He lifted it away from his chest and pulled himself out from underneath.

He sat up and felt a sharp pain across his forehead. His right leg was stiff, and when he moved it, his nerves screamed at him. He brought his arm up and stared at his wrist monitor. It glowed warmly in the dark. Tapping the screen, he checked the integrity of his suit. It was unscathed. Next, he instructed the suit to release painkillers. A glance at the medistats on the screen showed that he had torn a ligament in his right ankle, but nothing was broken. A few taps on the screen and several million nanobots were on their way to the damaged area to repair the tissue. Until that was fixed, he would just have to make do with the painkillers. He checked the time. He had been out for no more than a couple of minutes.

Wincing, he stood up. His helmet light illuminated the room. The ceiling had caved in. Two steel girders lay on top of a heap of rubble. He picked his way to where the injured had been lying. Gazing down at the monitor on his wrist, he checked for life signs, then using his cochlear implants, he listened for heartbeats. Other than his own, there were two. They were both strong and steady. He touched a control at the side of the screen.

'Mai? Mai? Come in, Mai.'

Nothing.

'Mark? This is Pete calling Big Mac. Do you read me?'

Nothing.

Pete cursed and lowered his wrist to his side. Then he heard a voice.

'Pete?'

He turned towards the sound. The beam from his helmet seared through the dark and lit up a pale face a couple of metres away. It was Archie Barnet.

'Can you help get this thing off me?' the boy called.

The remains of a table lay across Archie's body, a chunk of concrete with metal rods sticking from it at odd angles lay on top. Pete bent down and lifted the concrete, resting it on the floor beside him. Then he levered up the table with his left hand and helped Archie up with his right.

'You hurt?' Pete asked.

Archie patted himself, then put a hand to his head. His cut had reopened and blood was running down his cheek. His face was blackened with dirt and dust. 'I'm okay . . . I think.'

Pete turned as he heard a whimper. Taking two paces across the room, he found Sandra Rimmer. She was pulling herself from under a pile of debris. Pete took her wrist and she clambered to her feet. Her right sleeve was red with blood, the fabric clinging to her. Pete helped her over the rubble into a clear area. He ripped open the woman's sleeve and studied the laceration.

'Here,' Archie said. He pulled off his jacket, tossed it to the ground and tore a strip of fabric from one of his shirt tails.

Pete took it and wrapped it around Sandra's arm just above the cut. 'That'll stop the bleeding,' he said, and looked into the woman's face. 'You all right otherwise?'

She nodded.

'She's shaking,' Archie said. ''Ere, Sand, love.' He plucked up his jacket and put it over the woman's shoulders. She gave him a weak smile.

Pete left them and checked to see if anyone else was alive. It took him only a few minutes. Sandra and Archie both watched him as he picked his way back through the debris. He simply shook his head, and Sandra burst into tears.

'Come on,' Pete said.

'Where?' Archie asked.

'First we find Mai. Then we stick to the original plan. Try to get you to the dock.'

He turned, and the other two followed him through the door and along the passageway. He stopped and lifted his wrist. 'Mark? Mark, Pete here. Do you read me? Mai? Mai?' He paused and tried again.

Nothing but a quiet hiss of interference.

At the end of the passage, the floor was strewn with rubble. They clambered over it and turned into Reception.

It had been hit hard. The desk was reduced to firewood. A curved line of metal stumps were all that remained of it. At first glance, the sculpture of Neptune looked untouched, but even this had been blasted. The god's toes on his left foot had been blown away, steel rods protruded from the feet. All along the left side of the sculpture there were pits and marks, and Neptune's nose had been snapped off.

Mai lay with her back propped up against the plinth. Her legs were spread and her arms hung limp at her sides. The god towered over her.

'Mai,' Pete yelled and dashed over. He slipped on some loose plaster, almost went down, but just managed to keep his balance.

'Mai.' He crouched beside her. She opened her eyes, taking a few seconds to focus.

'Pete! What . . . ?'

Pete scanned her with his wrist monitor, running it over her torso, her head and then along her limbs. 'Anything hurting?' he asked.

Mai shook her head and looked round as Archie and Sandra appeared to her right. 'The others?' she asked.

'Dead,' Pete said. 'Come on, up you get. You seem to be in one piece, lass.'

Mai leaned on Pete's arm and pulled herself to her feet. 'Wow! Do I have a headache.'

'I'd think yourself lucky.'

'Oh, don't worry, I do,' she retorted and glanced at her wrist monitor. 'According to my sensors, the aftershock was less powerful than the first, but it's caused some serious damage. Bound to have weakened the hotel's infrastructure.'

Pete nodded and tried his comms again, but the system was still down. 'We have to get to the dock.'

'Lead the way.'

The floor was treacherous. Covered with shards of glass and rubble, there were great holes in the marble, and some parts of the floor that looked intact were little more than a crust of tile with nothing under them.

It took them several minutes to cross Reception. From where they stood, the view of the exit was obscured by a giant mound of masonry, twisted metal and shattered tiles. They picked their way towards the obstruction and then around it to the left. They could see a clear space stretching towards the door to the service stairs. Then, 2 metres in front of it, the ceiling had collapsed, bringing down a second, larger mound of rubble. It blocked the door, making it completely impassable.

'Well I guess that narrows our options to one,' Pete said, turning to the others. 'We'll have to press on to Beta.'

52

Dome Beta

Harry, Kristy, Jim and Nick tumbled through the smashed glass panel one after the other, collapsing onto the floor and gasping for air. Water was only a couple of centimetres deep here, and that was draining away into some hidden hole or invisible opening. Harry tried to pull himself up, but his knees gave way. He was chilled to the bone and shaking. It was several minutes before he could roll over and sit up, his back against the wall. He looked down and blood ran into his mouth. His left foot was throbbing. He tugged gingerly at the lace of his shoe and loosened it carefully. The pain screamed through him and he gasped. Very slowly, he pulled the shoe away from his foot, removed the sock and stared at his foot. It was torn to ribbons, great cuts ran along the top of it and along both sides. The sock coloured the puddle of water pink.

He turned to the others. They were in little better shape. They looked like drowned rats. Kristy's stage costume was in tatters, the bandana long-gone, and the silver jumpsuit soiled and ripped. Nick was the closest to him and seemed to be the least injured by the trauma of their escape.

'You're hurt,' he said.

'Looks very much like it,' Harry replied.

Jim turned to them, saw Harry's injury and pulled himself to his feet. He came over and slumped down against the wall next to him. 'Let me see,' he said and bent forward to study Harry's wounds. 'You're losing a lot of blood,' he said. He staggered to his feet and pulled a length of black fabric from his trouser pocket. 'Don't think I'll be needing this for some time,' he said, holding up his bow tie. He settled himself unsteadily on one knee and, with great care, wrapped the tie tight around Harry's ankle, just above the uppermost laceration. 'Best I can do, I'm afraid.'

Harry smiled at him. 'It's Armani, isn't it, Jim?'

'Certainly is. Cost a fortune at Barney's.'

'Well, thanks. And thank Barney for me,' he quipped. Without missing a beat, he pulled himself up. Holding onto the wall for support, he managed to keep his injured foot off the ground. 'I'm going to have to improvise a crutch or at least a walking stick,' he said. 'Without that, I'm, going absolutely nowhere.'

Jim glanced around. 'Hang on,' he said. 'Nick, I can see a metal rod over there. It's stuck under that smashed up table. Can you see it?'

The boy nodded and headed over. He could just squeeze through an opening in the rubble covering the remains of a mahogany table that had once stood close to the foot of the grand staircase. Pushing his head and shoulders through, he emerged a couple of seconds later with a metal pole about a metre long. Beaming, he walked back to the others.

'Perfect,' Harry said and leaned his weight onto it. He caught Kristy's eye. She was sitting against a sturdy metal box that had somehow found its way into the hall. Harry limped over and, leaning on the stick, he offered the singer his right hand. She looked at it for several moments and then glanced up at Harry's expressionless face, before she slipped her small hand into his. She was so light, it took little effort to pull her to her feet in one smooth movement. She let out a quiet groan as she straightened.

'You're injured,' Harry said.

'I'm cool. Just ache, like . . . all over.'

Harry produced a faint smile. 'I owe you an apology,' he said gently. 'And, I also owe you my thanks.'

Kristy looked startled, as though no one had ever spoken to her in this genuine way before. And it was only at that moment Harry and the others saw the singer for who she really was – a confused, lost little girl, a child who was never treated with any *real* respect. To some, Kristy was a vile bitch who had to be sucked up to, to others she was a golden goose, a piece of meat. To many more, she was a mythical creature, an object to be adored, copied, loved. No one any longer treated her simply as a human being.

Tears welled up in the girl's eyes and she went to pull her hand away. Harry held it firm and fixed her with a sincerity and clarity she had rarely seen. 'You're welcome,' she said finally, slipping her fingers from his and looking away.

There was a sound from across the hall. All four of them turned in unison. They heard footsteps, people running towards them, the sound muffled by the thick carpet. A door opened slowly. Harry, Kristy, Nick and Jim were rooted to the spot, staring at the door as it swung out into the hall. A woman wearing what looked like a skin-tight futuristic space suit appeared in the opening. For a second, she seemed surprised to see them. Then she took a step into the hall.

'Hi,' she said. 'I'm Maiko Buchanan . . . E-Force.'

53

Harry lay on the wet floor at the foot of the main staircase. The massive marble edifice took up half the hall. Plush red carpet ran up the centre of each tread, fastened to the stone with brass runners. It was mottled and stained with oil and dust. The marble looked untouched by disaster, an incongruous symbol of stoicism surrounded by death and destruction.

Mai replaced the makeshift tourniquet Pete had put on Sandra's arm, cleaned the wound, gave her a shot of painkiller and applied a special material called SkinGloo which could seal lacerations temporarily. Then she transferred her attention to Harry, running a medscanner over his injured foot. 'Nasty cuts,' she said and used the Vasjet, a needleless hypodermic delivery system, to give him some strong pain relief before cleaning his wounds and applying the same sealant.

Harry looked down at Mai as she worked. 'This is all getting a little surreal,' he commented.

'A very normal reaction, Mr Flanders,' she replied.

'Please. Not Mr Flanders! That's my grandfather. It's Harry.'

Mai smiled. 'Well, Harry, it's to be expected. This sort of thing doesn't happen every day. Thank God!'

'Yes, but you do find yourself in these situations more often than the average person.'

'True. But you never get used to it. Let's just say that, to me, it doesn't feel quite so surreal as it must do to you.'

Harry nodded. 'I also have to say, the pictures I've seen of you don't do you justice.'

'Really.' She gave him a cynical smile. 'Now is that a fact? Perhaps, Harry, you don't need the painkillers after all.'

He gave her a mock horrified look. 'Oh no, keep them coming, please. I was just being friendly!'

Mai laughed and helped him to his feet. He leaned on the metal pole Nick had found for him. Pete approached. 'The emergency subs are not far from here,' he said, studying his wrist monitor displaying a schematic of the dome.

'There's a quicker way,' Archie said. He'd been standing beside Pete, staring in fascination at the wrist monitor. 'Through there,' he went on, pointing to the far wall beyond the staircase. 'There's a service point for unloading supplies. It's all hidden away, on the north side of the dome. The two emergency subs are docked right by there.'

Pete studied the boy's earnest face. 'Okay, lad,' he said and turned to the others. 'Archie here knows a quick way to the emergency subs. Is everyone up to moving on?' He looked from one to the other and thought, what a bedraggled bunch they were. He walked over to Sandra who appeared to be the most exhausted and frightened. 'Come on,' Pete said, helping her to her feet.

Archie led the group across the marble floor to a pair of oak doors. He pushed them open and headed through to a long, carpeted corridor that ran directly north. Doors led off left and right. It was disturbingly quiet. Even the creaking and groaning of the infrastructure of the hotel was inaudible here. It was a sound they had become so accustomed to it was only when it stopped they noticed it was missing.

They traversed the length of the corridor as fast as they could. At the end there was a metal door. Beside it, on the wall, was a sign that said: 'SERVICE AREA. STAFF ONLY'.

Archie pushed on the handle and opened the door outwards, holding it in place for everyone to file through.

The first thing they sensed on the other side of the door was the cold. The floor and walls were rough concrete. The light was duller than outside in the corridor. A single fluorescent strip ran along the ceiling. In a space about 5 metres square, half the floor was taken up with piles of cardboard boxes. There was a wall of metal shelving and on the shelves stood more boxes.

'Through 'ere,' Archie said, letting the door swing shut and pushing past the others towards the gap between the towers of boxes and the metal racks. At the end of the room, a short flight of stairs stretched up to a gantry. They all trooped up. 'Along there,' Archie said, pointing east towards an opening. 'It's the staff access corridor above the main passenger collection point. Down some stairs and we're there.'

Through the opening they could make out a brightly lit area. The corridor Archie had described was just out of sight, with only a reflected glow breaking through the gloom of the storage area. It lit up the expressions of relief and optimism on their faces.

Archie turned quickly and Pete walked on, following close behind. Jim, Nick and Kristy were next. Harry and Sandra did their best to keep up. Mai held back a few paces.

A row of huge windows ran along the north wall of the corridor. Beyond the windows lay the stunning vista of the Pacific Ocean – dark blue, streaked with multicoloured coral banks and hundreds of fish caught in the light from the hotel. But at that moment, the beauty of the sight meant absolutely nothing. A dozen metres away were the two emergency subs. One of them lay on its side, a rip in the hull running from bridge to starboard engine. The other was crushed under a rock the size of a London bus.

54

'Pete? Mai? Come in. Mark calling Pete. Mark calling Mai. Please respond.'

The two members of E-Force were so stunned by the sight of the emergency subs shattered on the ocean floor, it took them a few moments to realise Mark Harrison was calling them.

'Mark,' Pete and Mai said in unison.

'Thank God,' Mark exclaimed. 'Comms were down your end. I guess it had something to do with the second shock.'

'I wouldn't be surprised. The aftershock has caused serious damage. But it's good to hear you, man,' Pete responded. 'We only have audio, no visual comms.'

'I know. I'm working on that. I had to go to emergency backup transmission. My link with Tom is fine, so it must be something local. Anyway, what's the story?'

Pete brought Mark up to speed. There was a long silence the other end. Pete surveyed the faces of the others in the corridor. They ranged from expressions of shock to total despair. He flicked his wrist comm to speaker mode.

'Our options are kinda running low,' Mai said eventually.

'I've just had the computer bring up another schematic of the Neptune. It's more detailed than the one you saw earlier on the Big Mac,' Mark said. They could hear him moving around the control console as a series of buzzes came through the comms. 'Zeroing in,' said the onboard computer.

'Right . . . got it,' Mark said.

Pete and Mai waited as Mark worked things through.

Harry came over to Pete. 'What's going on?'

'We're in touch with the main aircraft on the surface. Mark Harrison is our team leader. He's working on an alternative route out.'

Harry raised an eyebrow, but said nothing.

'Okay,' Mark said finally. 'Looks like your only hope is Dome Gamma.'

Harry shook his head. 'The linkway is down.'

'Who's that?' Mark asked.

Harry stepped forward unnecessarily. 'Harry Flanders,' he said. 'I was in the banqueting hall in Gamma. We got through the linkway into Beta. But it collapsed. Nearly took my foot off.'

'Yes,' Mark replied after a moment. He glanced at a monitor displaying images from the two Hunters still circling the hotel. 'I can see it now. But I think there's an alternative. A tunnel runs from Beta to one of the power supply domes to the north of the main structure of the hotel. Another runs back from there to Gamma. It's not going to be easy, but it's the only way left.'

'But what's the point of going back to Gamma?' Jim asked, approaching the pair from E-Force. 'We've just come from there.'

'Two reasons,' Mark replied crisply. 'First there are two more emergency subs docked on the Lower Ground Level. I would imagine anyone trapped in Gamma would be making their way there. The other is that I'm taking a sub down to cut a way into the base of the dome.'

'What!' Harry exclaimed. 'How on earth . . . ?'

'Leave the logistics to us, Mr Flanders,' Mark replied. 'Now, Pete, I can't send you the schematic, but . . .'

Pete's comms suddenly emitted a high-pitched whine.

'Mark?'

No response.

Pete stared at his wrist monitor, then tapped it twice. 'Mark?'

Nothing.

He lowered his wrist and took a pace towards Mai who was staring at her own wrist monitor.

'Oh, fantastic!' she exclaimed.

'What?' Harry began.

'Pete? Mai? Come in.'

'Mark . . . What the hell's going on?' Pete said.

'Another comms drop out. Must be unstable electromagnetic fields from damaged electrical circuits. Where was I?'

'You were going to tell us how to reach the tunnel over to the power supply dome.'

'I know the way,' Archie interrupted.

'Who's talking now?'

'Archie Barnet at your service, sir,' the boy said brightening up for the first time since they had arrived in the corridor.

'Pete?'

'Archie is the bellboy,' Pete said. 'We found him in Alpha.'

'I've made it my business to know every nook and cranny of this bloody place,' Archie added, leaning in towards Pete's wrist.

Pete put a hand to Archie's shoulder, pushing him back. 'You'll blow Mark's ears off, Archie.'

The boy looked embarrassed and stepped back. 'Sorry! Er . . . you're thinking of the primary power conduit on this side, aren't you?'

'That's correct.'

'It's really narrow, guvnor.'

'One hundred and five point seven centimetres in diameter, to be precise.'

'But it's lined with electrical whatnots.'

'I'm sure it is,' Mark replied.

'But, yeah, it's the last option, so . . .' Archie mused.

'Correct again. Now, you know how to get there?'

'It's close. Just down the corridor to the east of 'ere. Just past the assembly point for the emergency subs.'

'That's right, Archie,' Mark confirmed. 'Looks like we're in your hands for the moment.'

'Won't let you down, sir,' he said earnestly. Then he grinned at Pete. 'Gordon Bennet, if I'd known being a bellboy would be like this, I'd 'ave stayed in Leytonstone with Aunty Sharon!'

55

The hatchway into the tunnel stood at waist height and was accessed by a circular metal door with a security lock. Archie did not know the security code, but Mai's vector laser made short work of the lock and Pete pulled the door outwards. He turned to the group. 'This isn't going to be easy. But it really is our only way out. I'll lead the way. I know your instinct will be to get through the tunnel as fast as possible, but that would be a bad move. We have to take it slowly and carefully. You all understand?' He climbed in and started to edge forward. One by one, the others clambered after him, a few seconds behind each other. Harry, Kristy and Mai were left outside the entrance.

'I can't do it,' Kristy said suddenly, looking from Harry to Mai.

'Kristy, you can. I'll be close behind,' Mai said.

'No, you don't understand. I *really* can't.' She looked petrified. 'I'm claustrophobic.'

Harry looked at Mai and raised his eyebrows. 'Give me a second,' he said. He took Kristy's arm and pulled her away gently to a spot a few metres along the corridor.

'Kristy, you *can* do this.'

Kristy was shaking her head. 'No, no. That's why I . . . I froze earlier. That's why Danny died. It was my fault. I know it was. I can't go in there.'

'You can,' Harry insisted.

The girl was rooted to the spot, head down. She couldn't look Harry in the eye. She just shook her head.

'Kristy.' Harry lifted her chin. 'Kristy. You can beat this.'

'But, I'll panic again . . . and.'

'No you won't. Concentrate on pleasant thoughts. Think about how you feel on stage, when the audience is with you. Think of your favourite moments – the lights are up, the music is loud. You feel consumed. Think of that, Kristy.'

She looked at him doubtfully. Then she closed her eyes. A tear welled up between her eyelashes and ran down her cheek. 'Just leave me,' she said finally, and looked away.

Harry pursed his lips and shook his head. 'Can't do that, Kristy.'

She met his eye. 'You're a stubborn . . .'

'I know.' And he walked back to Mai who signalled to him to climb up to the opening. He looked back at Kristy, and she strode towards them.

'I figure I owe Danny one,' she said, pushing Harry aside and clambering up the wall to the tunnel entrance.

The tunnel was illuminated by recessed florescent bulbs running in a channel above their heads. Half of the lights were broken, but the tunnel was still over-lit. The floor was hard and scattered with bits of debris, pieces of plastic and glass from broken components shaken from their fittings. They could just move along the tunnel by crouching low, heads down.

Pete was 10 metres from the end when his alarm went off. For a heartbeat, he wasn't sure what it meant. But then it increased in pitch and he signalled to Archie and Jim behind him to slow down. Pete studied his wrist monitor. A red light was blinking on the tiny flat screen. A line of writing appeared. 'Danger: Unstable electrical field'.

Pete screwed up his face, trying to figure out exactly what it meant. There came a loud crack. He span around in the direction of the sound. Sandra, crouching low a few feet behind Jim, screamed as a clamp holding a black electrical cable snapped open and the cable slithered away from the wall beside her. Sparks flew from the end, crackling and stinking of ozone. A clip popped and shot away. The cable unfurled another metre. Two more clips disintegrated and the cable slipped to the floor. It looked like a sea serpent thrashing through the air, or a hose pipe filled with water left to shimmy on the lawn.

The cable seemed to have a mind of its own. Sandra fell back instinctively, knocking her head against a metal box. She squealed in pain and stumbled, her left leg slipping on the wet floor. The cable flicked up . . . and brushed her with the gentlest touch. Thirty amps of electricity shot through her. She flew backwards and her body lit up as though a flare had gone off inside her. Slamming into the wall, she crumbled. Steam shot from her mouth, her eyeballs melted and ran down her fried cheeks.

Pete was the first to react. He grabbed the cable half a metre back from the live end, found the holder it had slipped from and jammed it back in. His suit protected him against the current as sparks flew through the air and landed ineffectually on his arms. With the cable returned to its housing, he tugged back the clamp designed to keep it in place. A horrible fizzing sound came from Sandra's charred remains.

'Archie,' he shouted, snapping the boy back to reality. 'Get out the end. Quick!' He pushed him along the tunnel and turned to Jim. 'You too!'

The others approached one after the other. 'Keep going,' Pete yelled, trying to shield Sandra's corpse as best he could.

Mai approached. 'What?'

'Sandra Rimmer,' he said.

She sighed and Pete followed her the remaining few metres to the end of the tunnel.

They were in a bare, low-ceilinged room. On the concrete wall, a sign read: 'MAIN GENERATOR. DANGER. NO ADMITTANCE. HIGH VOLTAGES'. To the right of this stood a door. It opened onto a small room. In the far wall was a circular hatch similar to one they had just emerged through.

The group was silent, shocked, unable to fully comprehend what was happening to them. Nick leaned his back against the wall and slid to the floor, sobbing into his palms. Mai walked over to console him. Pete stepped away from the others and touched the screen on his wrist. 'Mark?'

'Pete. Status?'

'We've made it to the power dome. We lost one of the party.'

'How?'

Pete described the incident and Mark was silent for a second, tapping at the control panel in the Big Mac.

'I've been analysing the infrastructure of the tunnel back to Gamma,' he said.

'And?'

A pause. 'It's not good, Pete. For a start, the tunnel is much narrower than the one you've just come through. But more importantly, it wasn't designed to bear much weight. It's just a conduit. You'll have to go one at a time, or the tunnel will collapse.'

'Ah!'

'It's built in three self-sealing sections. If the structure is compromised at all, that section will close off at one end. It's designed to protect the electrical systems as much as possible.'

'All right.'

'The other thing is, you'll need to unlock the door at the far end where it opens into Gamma. You can't blow it out or even use the laser – it's too dangerous. I have the lock code. I'll send it to both you and Mai. Good luck.'

Pete walked back to the others. Mai had managed to calm Nick down. Pete took her by the arm and told her what Mark had said.

Glancing at her wrist, Mai saw the code had been sent through. 'I'll go first,' she said. 'Get the door open. I suggest you keep to the back.'

'So, what's happening?' Harry asked, stepping up to Pete and Mai.

Pete explained the situation to the group.

'This is a fucking nightmare,' Jim said slowly, shaking his head.

'You're right there,' Archie nodded. Then he took Nick's hand. 'Come on, matey boy. Let's get you over to see ya mum and dad, right?'

Mai swung open the hatch and squeezed through. 'I'll call you from the other end,' she told Pete, and headed off.

They all waited in silence, straining to hear any indication that Mai had reached the far end of the tunnel some 80 metres away. Time seemed to slow. It felt as though an hour had passed before they heard Mai's voice coming through Pete's comms. 'I'm at the far end,' she said. 'Just entering the code.' They heard a click and Mai turning a handle. Then came the sound of metal grinding against metal as the door swung outward. 'Through,' she said. 'Next one.'

Pete and Archie lifted Nick into the opening and gave him a gentle push. He scrambled along faster than Mai. Kristy was next up. This time she did not hesitate, just plunged into the darkness, breathing heavily.

She had been gone 20 seconds when Mark's voice came over Pete's comms. 'Pete? Problem.'

Harry was about to say something. Pete held up a hand to stop him. 'Structural integrity is going.'

'What do you mean?' Jim exclaimed, stepping forward.

'It's not designed to take the stress we're putting it under. It could go at any second.'

'I see,' Pete said calmly.

'Kristy's through,' Mai said over the comms.

'Right, Archie. You next,' Pete said.

'But . . .'

'No buts . . . Get in there. You're wasting time.'

The boy turned and dived into the hole.

'Want to draw lots?' Harry said and glanced at Jim. The American stared back at him. 'No, Harry. I'm through gambling. What will be, will be.'

Harry gave him a wan smile and was about to reply when Mai's voice broke in. 'Next.'

Harry limped over to the portal and Pete helped him through the opening. 'Go,' he said and turned to Jim.

'Pete . . . Integrity reaching critical,' Mark said through the comms. 'How you going?'

'Nearly there, Mark,' Pete responded and caught Jim's eye. The man looked resigned, supernaturally calm. 'You lost your partner back there?' Pete said.

'Yes.'

'All the more reason for you to keep going, man.'

'Yeah? And why would that be?' Jim looked away for a moment.

'Who else is going to tell people what a great guy he was?'

Jim stared at Pete for a moment, his face completely expressionless. Then he looked up at the ceiling and sighed heavily.

Pete heard his comms come alive and didn't pause for a second. Squeezing Jim's shoulder he nudged him towards the hole in the wall. 'Make it fast, man. I don't want to be left here too long.'

Alone in the power dome, Pete felt absolutely isolated from the human race, but he was oddly calm. He had known this feeling before. In the army, when he had been staring a bomb in the face. He would have the clippers poised to cut a wire, and had no choice but to believe in himself. He had to convince himself he knew which wire to cut first. But in those moments, he felt suspended outside of reality, the sole inhabitant of a private world. He and the bomb were one. There was nothing else.

Mai's voice sounded in his comms, and for a split second he could not hear it. She was calling from another world. Then he sprang into action. He was in the tunnel in a flash, turning in the narrow tube and pulling the door shut behind him to seal off the power dome. All his senses were at max. He could hear creaking and straining and the movement of water currents outside the tunnel. From far off came the sound of the others. He shuffled forward as fast as he could.

A loud crunch.

He cried out involuntarily, but kept going.

There was a high-pitched whistle as a steel door slammed down a few feet behind him. The whole tunnel shuddered. He knew what that meant. The first compartment had gone, the safety door had come down. He could only hope it was enough, that the rest of structure would now hold.

He sprang forward, grasping at the floor, propelling himself on as fast as he could go.

'Pete! It's breaking up!' Mark's voice screamed from the comms. 'GO, MAN. GO!'

Pete could barely hear him. His heart was pounding, his breathing coming in desperate gasps as he pushed back on the floor.

CRUNCH!

The second compartment went a fraction of a second after Pete made it to the third and last portion of the tunnel. He could see the door ahead and Mai leaning in. 'Come on,' she yelled.

She was only half a dozen metres away, but Pete knew she would close the door if she had to. She could not leave it too late, because, if the tunnel went, then water would flood into Gamma. He put everything he had into moving through the tunnel. His boots somehow found purchase on the slippery, uneven metal floor. He grasped at cables and junction boxes lining the walls. With his enhanced hearing, he could just discern the metal framework around him start to buckle. Tether lines snapping. Electrical cables fizz and shear.

Three metres.

Two.

He could almost touch the door. He felt the walls shake. The floor under him split and he caught a glimpse of pipes and steel mesh. Steam shot up into his face. He recoiled, but did not miss a beat. Scrambling for dear life, his hand was a metre from the door. Mai was reaching out to grasp him. Then he felt her glove in his and he pushed with all his strength, tumbling forward into the opening, feeling the steel door slam shut millimetres from his toes. The room shuddered, as the tunnel crumpled like tinsel.

56

Pacific Ocean, Fiji

Mark clicked off the comm link to Pete and Mai and let out a sigh of relief. 'None of this got any easier,' he thought.

He jumped up from his seat and headed for the control room door. 'Computer,' he said, 'is the *Drebbel* prepped and ready to go?'

'Affirmative.'

Mark walked quickly along the corridor leading from the control room to the elevator. It was a wide passageway with curved walls and windows looking out to the featureless black of the ocean. He checked his watch. It was 03.08.

The elevator travelled three storeys down to the cargo hold. Mark took a right out of the elevator and strode through a pair of swing doors. The *Drebbel*, a sub identical to the *Narcis* and named after another great engineer linked to the invention of the submarine, Cornelius Drebbel, stood in the docking area. Mark punched in a code on a flat pad close to the door of the sub and a steel panel opened.

The sub was primed, all systems online. It was ready to do Mark's bidding. He dropped into the pilot's seat and ran his hands over the smooth plastic surface. Applying pressure to key points on the panel, he activated the controls. Perched on a short monorail, the sub slipped through a set of doors into the dock. The doors closed silently behind it.

'Pressure equalisation complete,' the computer announced after a few moments. A hatch on the outer skin of the Big Mac opened and the submarine was poised ready to go.

A light came on in the centre of Mark's display and the comms sprang to life. 'This is the Fijian naval vessel, *Lambasa*. Stand down. Repeat. Stand down. We are about to board your vessel.'

Mark was stunned for a second, then he stabbed at the comms control. 'The hell you will,' he snapped. Then to the computer: 'Emergency shut down. Security code: 646348gryh#.'

'Code accepted. Shut down activated,' the onboard computer replied immediately.

'To whom do I have the pleasure of speaking?' Mark said.

There was a pause. Then a new voice came over the line. 'Mr Harrison, yes?'

'That's correct.'

'I am Acting Admiral Ratu Naivalurua.'

'I spoke earlier to Admiral Sir Joni Madraiwiwi.'

'Yes, the honourable admiral is . . . indisposed. I am in command of the naval task force assigned to the Neptune Hotel.'

'I see. So, why are you hindering our rescue operation?'

'That will become clear later, Mr Harrison. But right now I'm afraid we have to board your vessel.'

'I don't think so.'

'Mr Harrison, I . . . '

'Look . . . I'm here to save lives. I don't have time to argue.'

Another pause. Longer. 'My officers are on their way.'

'Okay, Acting Admiral Naivalurua. You will not be able to board my vehicle. That is completely out of the question,'

Mark said coolly. 'However, E-Force are bound by law to cooperate with local authorities. You're doubtless aware that if I don't have the full support of my hosts, I can't act unilaterally. I can only appeal to you on humanitarian grounds. There are many people down there who need help. We're the only ones able to rescue them. Why are you hindering our mission?'

The Fijian commander liked pauses, but eventually the comms came to life. 'My officers are close to your vehicle. Please surrender and you will be treated with the utmost respect.'

Now it was Mark's turn to pause. He felt like saying, 'Do your worst, *Acting* Admiral.' He knew the officers of the Fijian navy could not get into the Big Mac if they had a thousand years to try it, but he also knew the rules E-Force operated under. He had written those rules.

'Exactly what is it you want, Acting Admiral?'

'We are impounding your vessel and taking you into custody.'

'On what grounds?'

'Trespassing into Fijian waters.'

'But we had clearance.'

'That was granted by the former government.'

'I see,' Mark said slowly, realising what had happened. 'Okay. I can see we're going to have to strike a deal here.'

'No deals.'

Mark cut the comms, folded his arms and sat back. He was burning up with anger. People might be dying down there and this buffoon was interfering. He steadied his breathing and waited. The minutes passed and Mark's anger grew exponentially, but he was a disciplined ex-military officer. He knew what he was doing.

The comms sounded. Mark ignored it. It kept going. After a dozen rings, Mark tapped the control panel.

'Mr Harrison.' The Fijian commander's voice spilled into the control room.

'Acting Admiral.'

'It seems we *have* reached an impasse.'

'It does.'

'You want to get down there, yes? Well, that will not be happening.' There was real menace in the man's voice.

Mark remained silent.

'There will be no deals,' Naivalurua said. 'But these are my . . . instructions.'

Mark said nothing.

'You want to rescue the unfortunates trapped in the hotel. We are not convinced your intentions are pure. After all, these are . . . trying times, are they not? We wish to check your credentials. Will you allow us aboard?'

Mark knew he had little room to manoeuvre. He could not simply launch the *Drebbel*. That would be breaking the rules binding E-Force to international law. Nor could he just sit tight and wait. That would do nothing to help the people trapped in the Neptune. He leaned into the comms, running a hand over his temple and breathing steadily. 'Withdraw your boat to the *Lambasa*,' he said. 'I'll come to you.'

57

Pacific Ocean

The *Lambasa* effectively was the Fijian navy, and they were very proud of it. A 52-year-old minesweeper which had been modified with a single Soviet 4.37 millimetre gun taken from a Russian sweeper type T-44, it was a preloved vessel from the French navy that had been sold on to the Argentineans in the late 1970s. After they had thrashed the thing, including taking a hammering from British Harriers in the Falklands War, the junta passed it on down the line to the Fijians.

Mark sent an encoded message to Tom at Base One and pulled away from the Big Mac on a jet ski. He had left everything of value behind and exchanged his cybersuit for a blue jumpsuit and flak jacket. Apart from a conventional radio, he had no comms, and he was completely unarmed. Dead ahead bobbed the launch the Acting Admiral had mentioned. As agreed, it was holding steady at a point 100 metres from his aircraft. Two men dressed in black military fatigues and brandishing AK47s stood aft. A third man was at the wheel. Mark followed the launch back to the grey minesweeper. As he drew close, he could see streaks of rust along the hull and a broken window on the bridge. It was a sorry excuse for a military vessel. As the launch pulled alongside the *Lambasa*, a stairway was lowered into the water and the black-clad figures climbed up to the deck. Mark tethered the jet ski to the stairs and flicked on the defence shield, a tamper-proof system that produced an electric shock if anyone decided to get too close to the machine. Reaching the top of the steps, he pulled himself up onto the deck.

The Acting Admiral was a short, rotund man in a white uniform. An impressive array of medals hung across his left breast. His head was the shape and size of a ripe watermelon. Perched on his hairless pate was a stiff white cap smothered in gold braid. He had small, black, darting eyes and a flat nose. More figures in black stood either side of him, their machine guns at waist height.

They all stared at Mark intently. Even without his E-Force uniform, he looked an imposing figure. A head taller than any of the crew, he was powerfully built and carried himself with a poise that came from a blend of many years of military training and an innate self-confidence. He took half a dozen paces towards the Acting Admiral. 'Mark Harrison, E-Force,' he said.

Ratu Naivalurua stared at him and walked forward, stopping so close, Mark could feel the man's breath on him. And before Mark could react, the Acting Admiral's fist flew into the E-Force leader's solar plexus. Mark collapsed in a heap, clutching his abdomen. Naivalurua clicked his fingers and the two armed sailors ran forward. Mark shot a hand out to grab the ankle of the Fijian commander. He felt an intense stab of pain as the butt of a machine gun crashed down on his head and he tumbled into blackness.

58

Dome Gamma

The service stairs at the back of the casino were almost unscathed, but filled with acrid smoke. Something was burning a flight or two up from where they were and it didn't smell good. They closed the door to the casino behind them to provide another level of protection against the approaching fire, and Sigmund led the way, the others close behind. Michael Xavier followed two steps back.

A mean light came from a few surviving florescent strips and it was hard to make out one step from the other. 'Keep going,' Michael called from the back and watched the shapes ahead shuffling down the stairs. 'There should be four flights down to Lower Ground.'

A scream rang out. Emily. Her legs went from under her. Michael dashed forward, but was too slow. She hit the concrete with a thud. Hilary was there just before him. The kid burst into tears. Hilary pulled her close, almost going down herself as her feet slid on a patch of oil.

'Up we come,' Michael said, taking Emily's hand and giving her an encouraging smile. She clambered to her feet, rubbing the back of her head. Michael lifted her chin. 'Gotta be brave. You can be brave? Can't you, Em?'

The girl wiped the tears from her eyes and managed a brief smile. Michael was suddenly filled with a terrible sense of guilt. It was his fault they were all in this horrible situation, a voice screamed in his head. He felt a welling panic and forced it away. Yes, this might have been his fault, he reasoned, but if he crumbled now it would make everything 10 times worse. It was his responsibility to get his family out of this place, even if he died trying. He gripped Emily about the shoulder and caught Hilary staring at him. Her expression was almost serene. Michael couldn't remember the last time she had looked that way. It lasted only a moment and was quickly smothered with anxiety and pain. She grabbed Emily's arm and pulled her on, down the stairs.

Sigmund reached lower ground level first and almost fell over a shape on the floor. The others piled down behind him. He raised a hand and they stopped. Crouching down, he saw a body. It was a man dressed in a security guard's uniform. He was lying on his side. He smelt of burned flesh and incinerated hair. Sigmund covered his mouth and pulled the man over onto his back. His jacket was shredded and streaked with carbon. His face was a black husk, unrecognisable as human.

Emily and Hilary turned away. Michael and Miguel stepped forward. A red light was flashing at the dead man's waist. Miguel lifted the bottom of the security guard's jacket. They could see a radio hooked to his belt. Beside that, a plastic ID. It had melted around the edge, but they could just make out the name: Epeli Uluivuda.

'I knew him,' Miguel said. 'Wife and kids in Suva.'

A loud buzz came from the radio. At first, they were so startled, none of them could understand where the sound was coming from. Then Michael bent down on one knee, carefully plucked the radio from Uluivuda's belt and stared at it as though it were an alien thing. Then he put it to his ear, and depressed a button on the side. 'Hello,' he said, feeling slightly ridiculous.

A crackle. Then a voice. 'Hello. This is Base One, Tintara. Over.'

59

Dome Gamma

'What's your status?'

'Base One? What's Base One? Are you on Fiji?' Michael asked.

'No, sir. My name's Tom Erickson. I'm a member of E-Force . . . the rescue organisation?'

'E-Force?'

The others stared at Michael in astonishment.

'Sir, we don't have any time to waste. May I have your name?'

'Yes, yes, of course. My name is Michael Xavier. Some of my family are here – my wife Hilary and daughter Emily. There are two others in the party Miguel Bandonis and Sigmund de Silva.'

'Right. The satellite tells me you're on the lower ground level of Gamma.'

'How can you . . . ? No, it doesn't matter. Yes, we've just got down from the casino.'

'Mr Xavier, there's another group of survivors who've just reached Gamma and are close to you. Your son is with them.'

'Nick? Oh, thank God.'

Hilary was at his side. 'What's happened?'

Michael turned from the radio. 'Nick's safe. He's close by.' Xavier turned back to the radio. 'They came through the linkway?'

'No. It's been destroyed.'

'Oh, Christ! That means we only have one chance . . .'

BOOM.

The sound was like a low note on a bass guitar played at excruciating volume. Michael felt Hilary grab his arm. 'What was that?' he exclaimed.

There was a silence from the radio. 'Hello, er . . . Tom?'

'Mr Xavier,' Tom said calmly. 'You have auto-isolation systems in the hotel, yes?'

'Yes, we do . . . Oh my God! No!'

'What? What is it, Michael?' Hilary tightened her grip on his arm. He could feel her nails digging into him. Her face was millimetres away from his, panic in her eyes. He stared at her, speechless. He opened his mouth to reply but was cut off. The stairwell shook, sending them all sprawling across the floor. The radio flew from Michael's fingers and clattered across the concrete. Hilary and Emily screamed.

The shaking stopped abruptly. Crumbled concrete cascaded from the roof, pellets falling to the floor.

They picked themselves up. 'Everyone okay?' Michael asked. He looked round and saw they were all standing, shaken, but no more harm had been done. He could hear Tom's voice and walked over to the radio, plucked it from the floor and brought it to his ear. 'The top of the dome has gone, hasn't it?'

There was a long pause, then Tom said, 'I'm afraid so, Mr Xavier.'

Michael lowered the radio and stared at the others, his face drained of blood. Hilary's hands flew to her face. Tears began to stream down Emily's cheeks.

'All those people,' Miguel said, almost to himself.

'Mr Xavier? Come in please. Mr Xavier?'

Michael lifted the radio back to his ear.

266

'Sir, you have to keep moving.'

Michael was staring into space, barely able to register where he was or what was happening. His brother was dead. Johnny was dead. He glanced at Hilary, catching her eye. She stared straight back at him, distraught. In that moment, she suddenly realised that her husband knew all about her and Johnny.

Michael looked away and felt his daughter Emily beside him. She clasped his hand and leaned against him. He glanced down at her filthy, tear-streaked face. Her dark hair was tangled and matted with dirt and dust, her silk gown smeared with grime and spatters of blood. 'Okay, Tom,' Michael said into the radio. 'We're heading for the emergency subs.'

'That's a good plan.' Tom replied. 'Sir, could you flick on the speaker, please?'

Michael depressed the switch.

'The other party are almost at the dock.' Tom's voice echoed around the stairwell. 'From where you are, there are two possible routes. One's blocked.'

'Right. So, which way?'

'Leave the stairwell straight ahead and take a left.'

Michael glanced at the others and they followed him across the landing. The door opened onto a corridor. The walls ran with water, the carpet was sodden. They sped past closed doors to left and right, the carpet squelching under their feet. The corridor curved right. They took the corner and almost fell over a cleaner's trolley blocking the way. It was on its side. The floor was strewn with toilet rolls, bars of soap, cleaning fluids and linen. The cleaner lay on her back close to the trolley, crushed by a large lump of plaster. Pieces of masonry and crumbs of light blue plaster lay scattered all around. In the ceiling, a gaping hole exposed pipe work and cabling. Michael crouched down to check that the woman was dead. He found no pulse and her skin was cold.

They edged their way around the obstruction and headed on down the passageway to a lobby. An empty desk stood to one side. A small table lay smashed on the carpet, pieces of broken vase and bits of flowers scattered in an arc about it.

They all stopped suddenly as a door opened on the other side of the lobby. A head came round the edge. Pete Sherringham stepped forward. Behind him, a bedraggled group stumbled into the reception area.

'Nick!' Hilary Xavier screamed and ran towards her son.

60

'Pete? Mai?' It was Tom's voice in their comms. They were standing to one side of the civilians gathered in Dome Gamma, checking their equipment. 'We have a problem.'

Pete and Mai looked at each other and wandered further away from the others, towards the lobby desk.

'What is it?' Pete said quietly into his comms.

'I've lost Mark.'

'What!'

'He called in 10 minutes ago to say he'd hit a bureaucratic problem. There's been some political trouble on Fiji. The administration that gave us clearance has been . . . superseded.'

'Oh wonderful!' Mai exclaimed.

'Mark said he had agreed to go aboard a ship called the *Lambasa* that had dropped anchor close to the Big Mac.'

'And he went?' Pete said in disbelief.

'I told him I thought it was a bad idea. But he pointed out that until he sorted things out he could do nothing to help with the mission. He was about to launch the *Drebbel*. I think he had a plan for getting you all out of Gamma.'

'Yes, he did. And, of course, he would have gone over there without any E-Force equipment, just in case,' Pete said, half to himself.

'Precisely. He had a radio, but that's now dead.'

'Well, we can only assume the worst, Tom. You have to call on some political muscle. Contact Mark's old buddy, Senator Mitchell.'

'I was just about to,' Tom replied. 'And er . . . there's something else.'

Pete and Mai said nothing.

'Josh and Steph have vanished.'

'Vanished!' Pete stated.

'They took off from Polar Base on schedule. The last communication we had with them was 18 minutes into the flight.'

'Mark knows about this?' Mai said.

'Yes, of course he does,' Tom retorted. 'We've known for a few hours. I guess Mark didn't want to add to your troubles. I'm doing everything I can to trace them. I've narrowed the site to the eastern region of the Gobi Desert, but it's a pretty big area.'

'Anything from BigEye?'

'Well that's the odd thing. I've just had an update from BigEye 17.'

'And?'

'Nothing but interference.'

'Interference? In the Gobi Desert?'

'I know. I don't get it either. I've tried everything to clean up the image, but without any luck. I don't think there's a problem with our equipment.'

'What else can it be?'

'There's obviously an external source. Something down there jamming signals across a very wide frequency range.'

'So there's nothing you can do?'

'I didn't say that,' Tom replied. 'Do please remember who you're dealing with, people.'

Pete couldn't help smiling. 'Of course. Sorry!'

'I accept your apology, Peter. And I'll commence reprogramming the BigEye to sweep the interference and get an analysis. I hope to have something in a few minutes.'

'Well okay, Tom. I guess there's nothing we can do from down here. Keep us posted, yeah?'

Tom flicked off the comms and Pete turned to Mai. 'God, this operation is turning into a night out in Newcastle gone wrong!'

61

Base One, Tintara Island

Tom was in Cyber Control studying the machine code flashing down the screen. 'Syb,' he said to the base computer, 'can you run a Level One diagnostic on this?'

Sybil's quantum processors worked silently and took less than a millisecond to run the required analysis on the 3 terabytes of code from BigEye 17. 'Diagnostic complete.'

'So what's happenin'?' Tom declared.

'Please rephrase, Tom.'

Tom smiled to himself. 'Sorry, Syb. What's the frequency range of the interference?'

'35.45 to 36.12 hertz.'

Tom whistled. 'No kidding? That's very low. Okay, remodulate the signal for the satellite. I want to go over and under their range simultaneously, see what's most effective.'

'Processing,' Sybil responded.

Tom studied the big screen as it started to clear. 'Excellent, Sybil,' he said. 'Right. Now let's get down to business.' He span in his chair and wheeled over to a control panel where two technicians were working.

'Jeff,' Tom said to the nearest of the pair. 'I want a signal sent out across this range.' He showed him the figures on the holoscreen of his laptop. 'The message is the standard E-Force call, encoded to Level Four, please. If they're there and have some sort of receiver, they should pick it up.' He turned to the other tech. 'Maddie. I want BigEye to sweep this part of the desert.' He sent over to her computer a set of parameters – the area the size of New Jersey he had reported to Pete and Mai. 'Do the analysis across the entire range, and over every level of magnification. If there's a thread of a cybersuit or a crumb of emergency rations down there I want to see it. You got that?'

The tech nodded and Tom wheeled back towards the screen.

'Sybil,' Tom said to the air. 'Put a call through to Senator Evan Mitchell, priority red. And patch it through to my room, please.'

62

Dome Gamma

'I hate to spoil the party,' Pete said, 'but we have to go.' He'd wandered over to the group on the other side of the lobby.

Michael turned from hugging his son and stared at the ID patch on Pete's cybersuit. 'Quite right, Mr . . . Sherringham.'

'You know the way from here, I take it?'

Michael nodded. 'There's only one route. Straight through there and down.' He pointed to an archway on the other side of the lobby.

'Tom?' Pete said into his comms. 'There's only one way from here to the dock. I hope it's not blocked.'

'No. All clear,' Tom responded.

'Well that's something.' Pete turned to Mai, who was standing close by. 'Same arrangement, Mai. You come up behind the others, yeah?'

She nodded, and Pete edged past Miguel Bandonis and headed towards a pair of doors close to the empty lobby desk. A staircase descended into shadow. All the lights were out. Pete and Mai flicked on their helmet beams and Bandonis held back to take up a place in the middle of the group, using his torch to cut through the gloom.

There were only two short flights, but they had to be careful of loose cables or other obstructions. A door at the foot of the stairs opened out onto a hallway. Ahead they could see a wall of glass. It was similar to the emergency submarine dock in Dome Beta.

They ran over to the window. Two subs lay close to the side of the hotel. They looked unscathed. Flexitubes connected the hatches of the subs to doors in the Neptune, and to the right of the huge windows was a locked door that opened onto a short set of stairs down to the flexitube. On the wall was a control panel to unlock the door in case of emergency. The code worked in conjunction with a plastic pass carried by every member of staff.

Michael stepped forward and removed the card from his trouser pocket. He slid the plastic along a groove on the edge of the control panel. Then, pausing for a second to gather his thoughts, he leaned in towards the panel and tapped at the keypad.

Nothing happened.

He tried the card again and retyped the numbers.

Nothing.

'Hell!'

'What is it?' Pete asked.

'The control panel isn't responding.' He stepped back, trying to remain calm and stared at the keypad.

'Tom?' Pete called into his comms. 'We have a problem here. The control panel for the doors isn't responding. Can you check the network?'

'I'll try,' he replied. 'But the hotel's system is pretty shot.'

Miguel Bandonis stepped up. 'Let me have a go,' he said, and slid his own card through the groove, then keyed in the code.

Again, nothing.

Bandonis pushed 'cancel', then typed in an alphanumeric sequence.

'What're you doing?' Michael asked.

'Running a diagnostic, sir,' he replied. 'This smells bad.'

'What do you mean?'

'I'm not sure.' A line of type appeared on a small screen above the control panel: 'DOORS NOT RESPONDING'.

'Well, we know that!' Bandonis exclaimed and screwed up his mouth. He tapped in more numbers and letters. A second later, the screen changed: 'LINK TO MAINFRAME LOST'.

'Christ!' Bandonis spat.

Michael Xavier grabbed the engineer's shoulder. 'Miguel. What is it?'

'These doors will never open again, sir,' he said.

63

The Lambasa

The room stank . . . old fish, and damp. Mark opened his
eyes. He was in a tiny space, little more than a cupboard.
He tried to move and realised his arms were tied behind his
back. He sat up and cracked his head on a pipe. Cursing, he
shuffled towards a chink of light that came from under the
door. He listened, straining his cochlear implants, but all he
could hear was the ship's engine ticking over.

He felt completely powerless, and he hated it. In fact,
it was just about the sensation he detested most. But his
military training was deeply ingrained – rather than getting
angry, he got analytical. This was time given to him by his
captors, he reasoned. It was valuable and must not be squan-
dered. He had no way of telling the hour or how long he
had been there, far less what this whole thing was about,
but he had to formulate some sort of plan. There could be
people dying 100 metres beneath this ship, and there were
two members of his team down there.

Mark concentrated on the binding around his wrists.
They had used plastic ties, the sort gardeners employed to
keep saplings attached to supports. They were impossible
to snap with bare hands. His eyes were gradually growing
used to the dark and he could see the room was a featureless rectangle. No windows, one door, a low ceiling. Pipes
hung low and traversed the ceiling in parallel lines. The

walls and floor were old steel, and water ran down the wall close to his back. His jumpsuit was soaked through. He shivered suddenly, and became aware of just how cold he was.

There was a sound at the end of the corridor. Two distinct footfalls – boots on steel, coming towards the door. Mark heard one of the men speak to the other but he could not understand what he said. Then he heard the sound of keys rattling on a metal chain. The door swung inward and the room was flooded with light from the corridor. Mark squinted. He was grabbed roughly under each arm and dragged to his feet. He did not try to resist. There was no point. Best to conserve energy.

The two men said nothing. They were in the same black uniforms as the ones Mark had seen earlier. Both were short and stocky, good in a fight, he imagined.

'Where're you taking me?' Mark asked.

They said nothing, just pushed him through the opening into the corridor. One of them nudged the barrel of an AK47 into Mark's ribs as he walked ahead, his arms still tied behind his back. They guided him along a narrow passage towards an open door. He was led into another featureless room about 4 metres square – probably the biggest room on the boat, he thought. Naivalurua sat in a metal chair close to the centre.

'Mr Harrison. I take it you had a nice rest,' the Acting Admiral said, eyeing him. Mark stared back at the man in silence.

'We have been busy,' Naivalurua went on. 'Making a very close study of your remarkable vehicles. Quite unsporting of you to put those defence shields up, though. Gave a couple of my men quite a shock.'

'That's their purpose,' Mark replied evenly.

Naivalurua produced a faint, humourless smile and interlinked his fingers on his lap as he studied Mark Harrison.
The Fijian played the silence for a few moments, fixing Mark
with cold, intent eyes. 'So, let me explain the situation,' the
Acting Admiral began. 'I have limited time to achieve my
goal. I'm sure you have realised by now that I want access
to your vehicles. Immediate, unrestricted access. I have
analysed E-Force technology and I know that you control
the defence shields with alphanumeric codes and that there
are other codes to activate the vehicles. I want those codes.
There are two ways I can obtain them quickly. The first way,
which I think would make us all a lot happier, is by you
giving them to me. In return, I will leave you with a launch
and you can make your way to Fiji. The other path is altogether messier. I will be forced to torture you.'

Mark was stunned. A part of him wanted to laugh, but a
stronger voice in his head was telling him that this was far
more serious than he had realised. This was no joke.

'Who do you work for?' he said after a long pause. 'I
cannot believe the Fijian government would sanction this.'

'It's not for you to ask questions, Mr Harrison. That's my
job. Now, the question uppermost in my mind is this. What
are the code sequences I require?'

Mark shook his head and looked down at the floor. He
could feel the plastic ties about his wrists biting into him,
but pushed the pain away. 'You know it's impossible for me
to give you that information.'

'Impossible? Nothing is impossible, Mr Harrison.' Naivalurua stood up quickly, not once taking his eyes from Mark's
face. 'I am a fair man,' he said. 'I will give you another chance.
You know, Mr Harrison, I realise Fiji is a tiny country, a mere
pinprick on the map. And as a consequence, you may doubt
that I would have acquired the skills necessary to make a

man such as yourself divulge any information he would not want to divulge. But I feel duty bound to assure you that this is certainly not the case. I was born here on Fiji, but I have had some of the best instructors in many areas of learning, not all of which are sanctioned by the United Nations or fall within the limitations of international law. You understand me?'

Mark said nothing.

'Very well.' Naivalurua clicked his fingers. The two guards who had brought Mark into the room stepped forward and grabbed him, pushing him ahead of them across the room. Mark stayed passive, conserving his strength, mentally preparing himself for the ordeal ahead.

A table stood against the wall. It was about 2 metres long, 1 metre wide. Ropes hung limp at each end. A cloth mask lay on the table. Close to one of the table legs stood a pair of buckets filled with water. A black-uniformed sailor stepped forward. He cut the ties at Mark's wrists and then roughly yanked down the zip of Mark's jump suit, pulling the fabric over his shoulders. Then he untied Mark's boots, levered them off and flung them to one side. Mark stood shivering, dressed only in a pair of boxer shorts. No more than 2 metres away, two AK47s were trained on his head. Naivalurua stepped forward. He barely came to Mark's shoulder. 'I'm sure you recognise this equipment,' he said. 'Your government was very fond of using it on Al-Qaeda suspects.

'Now, I will ask you one last time. Save us all a great deal of unpleasantness and simply give me the codes. We're not talking about secret military hardware here, Mr Harrison. No one need suffer.'

Mark fixed the little man with his most withering look, and for a moment the Acting Admiral seemed to lose his poise, flinching almost imperceptibly.

Mark was yanked backwards. The hood was tugged roughly over his head and he was spun around, pushed in the chest and tripped from behind. He landed heavily on the table, his head smashing on the wood. A ripple of excruciating pain shot down his spine. His arms were yanked above his head, hands bound to the end of the table by ropes. His feet were lassoed and wrenched down so hard the ropes cut into his flesh.

Hands grabbed Mark's face, one at his chin, one at his forehead. His head was yanked back at an angle, his mouth forced open. He tried to focus, tried to force himself to breathe steadily, to control the panic he could feel welling up inside him. He had been trained by the best. He had experienced waterboarding before, during exercises at the Special Forces training centre at Fort Bragg in North Carolina. But that was many years ago . . . and it had been a training exercise. He had never been captured during tours of duty in Iraq and Bosnia. Never been subjected to torture by the enemy. But he could not dwell on these facts. Instead, he tried to purge himself of all negative thoughts, fears, doubts.

And then the water hit.

It ran over his chin and into his mouth, filling his mouth, running over his nose and filling that, and then on, over his eyes. He gagged, and shook. His hands and feet strained against the ropes burning into him, but that did not matter. Nothing mattered but the water. 'I'M NOT DROWNING,' he screamed to himself. 'I'M NOT DROWNING.' But he was choking. The water kept coming. His whole world felt as though it was filled with water. It was swamping him, pulling him under. The water was killing him.

64

Mark stared at the faint parallel lines of pipes in the ceiling of his dark, cupboard-sized prison. The searing memory of the torture filled his mind, and his body screamed at him. It felt as though every muscle had been stretched. His head throbbed, his wrists and ankles screamed, and he was freezing cold. He lay on the metal floor, wearing nothing but boxer shorts, his hands bound behind him again.

In the dark, it was hard to keep a handle on the passing of time. He could not tell with any certainty how long he lay there looking at the pipes. It could have been minutes, it may have been hours. All the while, he was trying to rationalise, trying to find answers to some very difficult questions. But they were questions he could not answer. Was anyone still alive in the Neptune? Were Pete and Mai safe? Tom knew about the minesweeper. What had he done about it? Who were these maniacs, holding him and torturing him?

He must have dozed off because the next thing he knew a key was rattling in the lock and the door swung open. It was the same two guards. The brightness of the corridor stung his eyes, just as it had before. Again, the guards said nothing, simply pulled him upright. He tried to turn away from the painful light, but they frogmarched him from the room into the neon glow of the passageway.

They followed a different path this time. Through a door, they led him up a flight of stairs and suddenly they were on the deck of the *Lambasa*. He could see the rear end of the

Big Mac a few hundred metres away. Close by, *Ringo* bobbed gently on the water. The sun was bright in the sky. An orange glow swept over the ocean. For a few seconds, Mark felt the warm fingers of the sun. Then they were heading for a hatch. He was pushed down, a firm hand on the top of his head. He took the rungs of the ladder as slowly as he could. He was hurting all over, his head spinning. He felt nauseous, but managed to force back the vomit rising in his throat.

Along another narrow corridor and through a doorway and he was back in the torture room. It was as though nothing had changed. Naivalurua was in his chair, one leg crossed over the other. He looked up as Mark was led into the room. 'Good morning,' he said, quietly.

Mark looked away, focusing on a spot in the ceiling above the Fijian commander's head. Naivalurua stood up and walked over to the E-Force leader. He grabbed Mark's jaw and forced his head down to look at him. Mark stared at the floor.

'Look at me or I'll have your eyes gouged out,' the Acting Admiral hissed.

Mark lifted his gaze from the floor to meet the man's and felt a sudden burst of pain as Naivalurua landed a punch into his solar plexus, hitting precisely the same spot as before. Mark gasped.

'That's better. Now, I'm rather hoping you have reconsidered your position, Mr Harrison.'

Mark did not make a sound.

'Well, that is a pity.' Naivalurua glanced at the guards a few paces behind him. They stepped forward and spun Mark around. Ahead of him stood a small metal trolley. A box stood on top of the trolley. A lead ran from the back to a mains socket in the wall. Two thick wires, one red, one black hung down from the box. Each wire had a clip on the end.

Mark was pushed over to the trolley. This time, they kept his hands bound. A guard stepped up to him. In a single movement, he yanked Mark's boxers to his ankles. The guard straightened up, took a step over to the trolley, grabbed the two leads attached to the machine, and turned back. At a sign from Naivalurua, he bent down and attached one of the clamps to the prisoner's left testicle. Mark yelled in agony, the sound escaping from him in spite of all his efforts to hold it in. The guard attached the second clamp. Mark started to shake involuntarily.

Naivalurua walked over, stopping a foot in front of his prisoner. 'We can stop all this right now,' he said matter-of-factly. He stared into Mark's face. It was streaked with sweat, the agony clear in his eyes. The muscles of his neck had tensed and his jaw muscles protruded. He said nothing.

Naivalurua looked down and shook his head. Then he nodded to the man who had connected the clamps. The man leaned over the trolley and placed his hand on a large white slider.

'Drop your weapons!'

They all turned towards the voice. A man in the uniform of a Royal Navy commander stood in the doorway. He was holding an M16, the barrel pointed at Naivalurua's head.

One of the Fijian guards raised his gun.

'Don't!' the Royal Navy officer snapped, and moved a little to his left as six Royal Marines of 40 Commando in full combat gear and armed with BMG assault weapons slid into the room. They fanned out, guns poised, ready for anything.

65

Mark emerged onto the deck of the *Lambasa* sandwiched between two Royal Navy officers, who led him aft where a launch was waiting for them. He checked his watch. It was 09.23. The sky was a dazzling blue, the sun, a great yellow orb. He shaded his eyes and took in great lungfuls of warm, salty air. It felt as though he had been kept in the dark for weeks.

The commander of the operation, Captain James Heathcote, stepped forward, offered his hand and introduced himself. 'Pleasure to meet you, Mr Harrison.'

'Believe me, Captain Heathcote,' Mark retorted, 'the pleasure is all mine.'

Heathcote indicated Mark should take a seat and buckle up, and the launch sped away from the rusty Fijian naval vessel.

'Do you have any idea what the hell is going on?'

Heathcote shook his head and gave a brief smile. 'A coup, and a counter-coup, Mr Harrison. I believe they have them on a regular basis here. Particularly bad timing, this one.'

'So, who's in power now?'

'The bunch who gave you free passage. When we heard you had gone missing, we presented the deposed government with a deal. Let us have free rein getting you off that old tub . . .' he nodded towards the *Lambasa*, 'and we'd offer background muscle for them to regain control of the island.'

'So, one of my team, Tom Erickson, reached you?'

'Well, by a convoluted path, yes. My orders came from Whitehall. As I understand it, one of your military bigwigs contacted one of ours through the UN. Wheels within wheels, Mr Harrison. Always the way. Still, it worked, that's the important thing.'

'Yes, it did. So, what happens to the Acting Admiral now?'

'Well he's no longer an "Acting anything". My men will escort the crew to Suva and they'll be held in custody. I'm sure you'll be required to provide a statement at some point. But in the meantime, I imagine, you have a job to finish.' He looked straight into Mark's eyes, his face expressionless.

'Yes, I do,' Mark replied. 'And I've had plenty of time to work out just how to go about it.'

66

Pacific Ocean

'I can't believe that!' Tom exclaimed as Mark described what had happened to him.

'Well, I guess I wouldn't if it hadn't happened to me, Tom. I'm just really pissed at the waste of time. But what's done is done. I'm here. In one piece. And I have you to thank for that.'

'Me? I just put through a call.'

'Yeah, but it was a very good call! So, what's the situation in the Neptune?'

'I made contact with two groups. They've met up. There are 10 survivors plus Pete and Mai in the base of Gamma. That's the good news.'

'And the bad?'

'They can't get out. The computer systems have shut down and they can't reach the subs.'

'What state are the civilians in?'

'Some broken bones and serious lacerations but nothing life threatening. The one good thing about your delay is that they've all had a chance to rest for a few hours. But I don't know if many of them have actually slept.'

'Okay, can you get me the latest from the BigEyes?'

'Sure.'

'Anything from Josh or Steph?'

Tom told him about the interference around where he

thought the Silverback had come down. 'One of the techs here is reprogramming the BigEye to search in the far ends of the spectrum. It's a huge job. We're trying to get round the interference the best we can.'

'Okay, Tom, keep me informed. And get me those sat images asap.'

Still furious that the team had lost close to five hours thanks to his imprisonment, Mark wasted no time getting kitted out in his cybersuit and re-prepping the *Drebbel*. He checked his fuel levels, then ran an analysis of the Neptune, matching the images Tom had sent from the BigEyes with data from the Hunters, and set a course for the stricken hotel. He brought the sub back up to the outer door of the internal dock, instructed the computer to unlock the portal and let the *Drebbel* slide under the Pacific waves.

He dived on a diagonal course from the north. The hotel was visible on the sub's monitors as soon as the vehicle submerged, the image growing clearer as he approached. Fifty-three metres beneath the surface Mark changed course, heading west and then south to bring the sub around Dome Alpha. A few moments later, he could see *Narcis* where Pete and Mai had moored it. It lay some 20 metres from the base level of Dome Alpha. Bringing his speed down, Mark opened comms with Dome Gamma.

'I'm approaching the *Narcis*,' he told Pete and Mai. 'I should be close to Gamma in under two minutes.'

'Copy that, Mark,' Pete replied. 'Good to hear you're back with us, man. That's the longest night I've ever had . . .'

Manoeuvring along the south side of the hotel was a delicate operation. There were loose beams and cables that were only visible at very close range. The sensors on the sub were set to 'max' as Mark guided the vehicle a few metres above the ocean floor.

Passing close to the linkway between Beta and Gamma, he could see the extent of the devastation. About one-third of the glass tunnel had shattered. The Beta end was no more, and the seabed was strewn with fragments of glass. Mark could see that the connection at the other end was undamaged. He pulled the *Drebbel* away and around, approaching the base of Dome Gamma square-on from the south.

Twenty metres from the dome, he could just make out human shapes on the other side of large glass panels in the Lower Ground Floor Level. He cut the thrusters to minimum, allowing the sub to drift slowly towards the hotel. Ten metres from the dome, he cut the power completely. He could see the unmistakable forms of Pete and Mai at the huge glass window, and beside them, a few of the survivors.

'Good to see you, Mark,' Mai said, her voice booming through the speakers in the control room of the *Drebbel*.

'Tom tells me you've hooked up with the survivors from Dome Gamma. I can see some of you from here. There're 12 of you, right?'

'Yes.'

'What's your status, Mai?'

'Pretty good, considering. We've had a few hours rest – fretful rest – but the two kids slept. We have some severe lacerations, broken ribs, mild concussions. I've given almost everyone painkilling shots and sealed up cuts. I've used SkinGloo on Harry Flanders' foot and Michael Xavier's leg – they were both pretty badly cut. No one is seriously injured, but . . .' and she lowered her voice, 'they're frightened, Mark.'

'Understandable. So, Mai, this is what we're going to do . . .'

67

Base One, Tintara Island

Tom lay on his bunk staring up at a holographic image hovering in the air about half a metre above his head. He needed to get out of his chair sometimes, needed to lie flat on his back and let his mind churn through things. He had adapted the holoprojector on his laptop so that he could move the image away from the computer and let it float anywhere within 4 metres of the processor. It was completely hands-free because he could instruct Sybil verbally. He had Neil Young's 'After the Gold Rush' playing quietly in the background.

'Sybil, display the seismic readouts for all tremors affecting the hotel.'

'There have been three disturbances during the past 12 hours. The first was the largest. This occurred at 20.04.13 local time.' The image of a graph appeared in the air above Tom's bunk. It showed a jagged line running horizontally, time displayed on the x-axis, strength of tremor on the y-axis. At 20.04.13 there was a spike, showing a tremor strength of 6.3. This was followed by several smaller peaks.'

Tom looked at the figures and ran through a set of calculations in his head. 'Okay, Sybil. The second and third tremors.'

'The first aftershock occurred at 02.10.19 local time. It was weaker than the original tremor, but it still caused substantial damage.' A second graph appeared. It was strikingly similar to the first, but the tremor was less powerful. 'The third tremor was relatively minor. It did not cause any structural damage and may not have been felt by many of the survivors.'

A third graph appeared. It was almost identical to the first and second, but the peak showing the power of the tremor was less than a twentieth the size of the first aftershock.

'When was the second aftershock, Sybil?'

'02.51.34.'

'Sybil?' Tom said. 'Mark lost his comms link to the hotel a couple of times back there. When exactly were those radio drop-outs, please?'

'The first lasted more than 35 minutes. It began at 02.10.21.'

'And the second?'

'02.51.36.'

68

Gobi Desert, China

Steph lay wide awake on a collection of cushions in front of the fire.

She was wrapped in a wolf hide, listening to Josh and Howard snoring quietly. She had not slept since leaving Polar Base, but felt unnaturally energised. The thing she hated most in the world was being beaten. It was, a distant part of her realised, one of the things that made her special. Her inability to accept defeat had driven her through medical school, and it had kept her sane when her husband, Ted, was killed in Afghanistan. It was the same determination to succeed at any cost that had made her such an indispensible member of E-Force. But now – now she was facing defeat. This appeared to be one battle she simply could not win.

She pulled the hide away and sat up. Without making a sound, she tugged on her boots, found Howard's homemade torch, and felt her way to the steps that led up to the surface.

Outside, it was blacker than anything she had ever known. Then, as her eyes adjusted to the all-embracing night, the stars began to appear: hundreds of millions of stars – the cool strip of light that made up the Milky Way, stretching from the flat horizon halfway up the sky. It looked like a jet trail. She had loved astronomy as a kid, and suddenly a long-lost memory came into her mind. She was standing in the

292

garden of the family home in Sydney. Her father was beside her, patiently adjusting the focus on a cheap telescope she had been given for her birthday. When he was done, he beckoned her to come, to peer down into the eyepiece. 'Close one eye, Steph,' he'd said. She lowered her eye to the rubber rim of the eyepiece. At first, she could see nothing – she had closed both eyes. Sensing what had happened, her father gently nudged her. 'Just close the left eye,' he whispered conspiratorially. She had smiled to herself and opened her right eye to see the surface of the moon as she had never even imagined it. She could see craters, mountains, light and shade. The earth's closest neighbour, just as Galileo had seen it centuries before.

Stephanie suddenly snapped back to reality and turned away from the splendid vista of the distant stars. She lit the fuel in the torch she had borrowed and it cut a strip of lemon light through the vacant night. She had her bearings from the earlier trip with Howard and headed straight for the crash site. She had no idea what she was doing, but she knew she could not simply lie in the dark running through her failings any longer. She had to do something, anything, no matter how futile it seemed.

No more than a few paces from Howard's home, Stephanie began to see pieces of wreckage, strips of metal and plastic caught in the torchlight. She took the same route she had followed earlier with Howard, skirting the mound some 50 metres to the west of the Toyota. Holding the torch at head height and sweeping the horizon, she spotted the fuselage of the Silverback, nose down and tilted at a precarious angle in the sand.

She paused for a moment, turning 360 degrees. Straining her cochlear implants, she listened hard. The silence was almost total. Leaves on desiccated plants rubbed together,

293

creating a faint rustling sound. She could hear a few insects scratching in the sand, and from far off, from the direction of Howard's strange home, plastic sheeting flapped in the light breeze.

She pushed on, taking slow, careful steps towards the shattered aircraft. Using her enhanced vision, Stephanie surveyed the sand as she walked. She had no real idea what she was looking for. In fact, she wondered if she would even recognise anything useful if she stumbled upon it – the plane had been blasted from the sky by some strange force their instruments could not understand. Tonnes of fuel had gone up in the ensuing explosion. It was a miracle they had walked away from the crash. Miracles, Stephanie knew, were not in great supply. Perhaps they had already had more than their fair share.

Then she saw it.

It was almost unrecognisable, just a copper disc no more than 3 or 4 centimetres in diameter, lying in the sand. She stopped, her heart pounding, and dived to the ground, scrabbling in the sand with both hands. In a second, she had the cylindrical metal object clasped between her fingers. At one end, the end that had been protruding from the sand, she could see a flat copper surface. At the other end was a small glass dome. Stephanie turned the object round so the glass portion pointed towards her face. Behind the glass she could see a red bulb. It was dull, lifeless. Around the circumference of the tube, just beneath the glass dome were the words: 'E-FORCE. EMERGENCY BEACON'.

She could hardly believe what she was seeing. Her fingers were shaking as she lowered her gaze to a point just below the strip of writing. There was a tiny switch countersunk into the metal cylinder. It was in the 'off' position. She had used the emergency beacon only once before, on a survival exercise at Polar Base. It seemed like a lifetime ago. The beacon was a standard piece of kit, the sort of thing the military had used for decades – it sent out a signal across a broad spectrum.

For several moments, Stephanie stared at it. She could not bring herself to look at the tiny strip of clear glass inside the copper base that would tell her the power level of the device. A bead of sweat ran down her spine and she swallowed hard, making a supreme effort to steady her breathing. Then she ran her index finger along the cylinder, resting it lightly on the plastic switch. 'On three,' she said aloud. 'One, two . . .'

She slid the switch down.

At first, nothing happened. Then the red bulb under the glass dome at the end of the cylinder flickered into life. The beacon emitted a high frequency whine, a single pulse. Then the light switched off and the beacon died.

69

Base One, Tintara Island

'Ah . . . right,' Tom said quietly as he stared at the graphs floating above his head. 'So, Sybil? Was there any sort of radiation burst? Interference pattern? Anything to coincide with the signal breakdown?'

'Each tremor was associated with a burst of ELF waves in the vicinity of the Neptune.'

'No shit!' Tom exclaimed and sat up suddenly. The holoscreen moved away, keeping the same distance from his face. 'Of course! Extremely Low Frequencies. That would explain it.' He realised he was breathing hard and made a conscious effort to calm down. 'Sybil, what's the range of the ELF bursts?'

'35.45 to 36.12 hertz.'

'The same frequency range as the interference over the Gobi Desert,' Tom said. 'Sybil, the ELF burst near the hotel. Was it a natural phenomenon?'

'It was not.'

'Where did it come from?'

'It originated 1.36 kilometres north-east of the hotel.'

Tom stared at the holoscreen. It had flicked to a screensaver of swirling colours. 'So, what's there?' he said finally.

'Insufficient data.'

'Why?'

'The continental shelf falls away a little over half a kilo-metre from the Neptune in the direction of the source. The epicentre is located on the slope of the shelf, approximately 1400 metres beneath the surface. BigEye is not able to detect a structure there and all other radiation effects have been masked by the depth of water. It is effectively invisible.'

'Okay, Sybil, give me the lowdown on ELF radiation, please.'

'Lowdown?'

'Just Wikipedia level, Syb.'

'The very basics, Tom?'

'Yeah, the basics,' Tom replied testily. 'I skipped lectures that day, okay?'

A few paragraphs of text appeared in the air. Tom quickly read through the material.

ELF (Extremely Low Frequencies) are those in the lowest known region of the electromagnetic spectrum. First discovered in the early part of the 20th century, ELF are in the range 1 to 100 hertz. They include the little understood Schumann Resonance, a natural frequency produced by the earth itself. This has a frequency of 7.5 hertz.

ELF have been peripherally linked with earthquakes. In particular, the Loma Prieta Earthquake, California, 1989. Extremely Low Frequencies were detected close to the epicentre of the quake shortly before it struck.

It is known that several military powers are experimenting with ELF in the creation of what is known as acoustic weapons, but it is believed that little progress has been made and that the

US, Russia and the UK have stepped down research in recent years.

Internet rumours continue to circulate that acoustic weapons are on the wish list of several high-profile terrorist groups. Some have even suggested such a weapon has already been used. (see: Florida Bridge Collapse, 2007.)

'I remember that,' Tom said to himself. 'Sybil, bring up the link to the bridge collapse, please.'

Fresh text replaced the earlier report.

The I-75 Florida Road Bridge collapsed during the morning rush hour on 22 June 2007, killing 173 people and injuring many more. According to independent researchers in the United States, the Siberian State Radio Telescope (SSRT) at Russia's Institute of Solar-Terrestrial Physics in Irkutsk, Siberia detected a massive ELF burst moments before the bridge collapse. So far there has been little corroborative evidence to support claims of a link between the two events, but research is ongoing.

Tom looked away from the screen, lost in thought. He felt a vague tingling in the pit of his stomach. 'Sybil,' he said finally. 'What was the epicentre of the ELF burst that was picked up by the Siberian radio telescope?'

'116.23 degrees east, 42.55 degrees north.'

'The Gobi Desert,' Tom said slowly.

70

'So what exactly are you saying, Tom?'

'We're dealing with terrorists, or some rogue military scheme.'

'Because of this radiation burst?' Mark replied. He was in the control room of the *Drebbel*, running figures through the onboard computer, prepping the sub for its approach to Dome Gamma.

'Well, yeah.'

'And it couldn't be a coincidence? Or a natural phenomenon? All this stuff about the bridge in Florida – sounds a bit vague. You sure it's not some crackpot internet theory?'

'Well which way do you want it, Mark?' Tom snapped. 'You've given me three ways to explain it right there – which one you want me to pick, man?'

There was a momentary silence from the other end of the line.

'All right,' Mark replied finally. 'So, let's get this straight. You're suggesting that someone or something over a kilometre from here is sending out a beam of ELF radiation. This radiation has produced the tremors and destroyed the Neptune. You're also claiming this is linked to Steph and Josh disappearing over the Gobi Desert. That there's another source of ELF radiation there that caused them to crash.'

'Another source with precisely the same frequency, Mark.'

'Okay, but why, Tom?'

'Why what?'

'Why would some military power or terrorist group aim a weapon like that at a hotel?'

'Oh, come on, Mark! Why would anyone fly a couple of commercial jets into the Twin Towers?'

'Okay, okay,' Mark retorted, an edge of irritation in his voice. 'This is getting us nowhere. Theories won't help me get these people out of the hotel. If there's any substance to the idea we can contact the authorities after we're outta here.'

'What about Steph and Josh?'

'Tom, you're chasing shadows. What have you got? An internet rumour that a burst of radiation projected from a site in the Gobi Desert destroyed a bridge in Florida?'

'The area around the point where Josh and Steph would have come down is shrouded by the same interference.'

'Okay. Let Sybil investigate.'

Tom was about to respond when a voice broke through the comms. 'Sorry to interrupt, Tom.' It was Jeff Tolders, one of the techs working in Cyber Control. 'We just received a signal.'

'A signal?'

'A single, short burst, really weak. We've traced it back to a point within the search area for Steph and Josh. It was sent from an E-Force emergency beacon.'

71

Hang Cheng, Gobi Desert, 22 June 2007

As Mengde Sun was escorted away from his laboratory by two guards, he felt euphoric. Watching the American bridge collapse like a pack of cards was the greatest experience of his life. He had succeeded. He would become a legend. Turning, he saw a young man running along the passage towards him. The guards span around, guns raised. Mengde shook his head and they lowered their weapons. The man stopped a few metres away. It was the technician, Fu Tang. Mengde looked at him blankly. 'What do you want, Fu?'

'I'm sorry, sir. I did not want to speak in front of the others.' And he inclined his head very slightly back toward the lab.

'Speak about what?'

'An idea I have, sir.'

'An idea?'

'May I have one minute of your time?'

They were in a conference room that led off the corridor. The guards had been told to wait outside. Fu stood at a smartboard at one end of a long table. He had slotted a CD into the drive and the board had lit up with a series of equations, line drawings and schematics. Mengde looked at them in silence.

'Sir, today was a wonderful success. I congratulate you on your achievement. But I have been thinking for some time about other ways of utilising the beam.'

Mengde looked into Fu's eyes. A faint smile played across the

Chief Scientist's lips. 'Oh, you have, have you, Fu?'

Fu licked his lips and turned back to the smartboard. 'I've made a study of how to use the beam through water.'

'Through water?' Mengde said, surprised. It was a notion that had never occurred to him.

'Well, sir, it's just that, as you of course know, if a ground- or air-based beam transmitter fires the beam through water, there is so much distortion produced, the beam becomes almost completely useless. It cannot be focused or modulated.'

Mengde was nodding. 'But why would we need to pass the beam through water?'

'Simply because NATO possesses more than 100 nuclear submarines, which between them carry close to 2000 ballistic missiles. Our great nation has only a dozen comparable vessels.'

Mengde looked at the young man, and for a second his earnest face reminded him of his own, half a lifetime ago. The realisation made him feel momentarily nauseous. 'So, what do you propose?'

Fu seemed happy with the question. 'I think we should build an experimental station on the ocean floor where we can develop a version of the beam that will work under water,' he said confidently. 'I think I have found the perfect location for such a base. It lies in international waters, a region in which no one would expect to find us.' He pointed to the smartboard. It now showed a map of the Pacific Ocean, around the island of Fiji.

72

Gobi Desert, China

Steph stared down at the silent beacon. It was nothing more than a mute lump of metal and plastic, utterly useless. Frustration and anger welled up and she flung the thing as far as she could. It somersaulted through the freezing night air and disappeared into the blackness. Leaning forward with her palms on her knees, she closed her eyes for a second.

Thanks to her implants, Steph heard the chopper blades several minutes before the sound reached the auditory range of the average person. She strained to listen, trying to detect anything about the noise that would help her figure out what sort of helicopter it was. All she could tell was that it was a conventional chopper – twin turbo, with a five-blade main rotor and a three-blade tail rotor.

It was coming towards her.

She span around and dashed for the cover of the wrecked Silverback, reaching the mid-section of the fuselage just as a pair of searchlights at the front of the chopper pierced the crisp dark. She ducked under a protruding sheet of Maxinium as the light reached her. The chopper slowed and hovered overhead, kicking up sand and loose vegetation. She could separate out the sounds coming from overhead. Overlaying everything was the roar of the rotor blades scything the air, but beneath that, there was the lower tone of the turbines. Just within audible range came the voice of the pilot. He was speaking excitedly in Chinese.

The helicopter pulled away for a moment, making a wider sweep of the area. Steph risked peeking around the side of the Maxinium sheet. She could identify the aircraft immediately. It was a Russian-made Mi17/171, a favourite of the Chinese. But it carried no official military insignia.

The chopper swung back around and took up position directly over the wreckage of the Silverback. It'll be taking pictures, Steph thought to herself. Good luck to them – they'll see nothing but a blur. But, she reasoned, the base was only a few minutes flying time away. Now the wreckage had been spotted, there would be more than one chopper hanging over the place before too long.

Steph stayed very still and waited it out. After what seemed like an eternity, she heard the pitch of the rotors change and the chopper moved off. She stayed where she was for another 60 seconds, making sure the helicopter was not simply banking around. Satisfied, she pulled herself clear of the fuselage, jumped down to the cold sand and ran as fast as she could back to Howard's camp.

She shook Josh awake and started to explain what she had seen. Howard stirred and sat up. 'What's happened?' the older man asked, pulling himself, fully dressed, from under an animal skin.

'Chinese,' Steph said. She was breathing steadily, bringing her heart rate back down quickly. 'A chopper.'

'It didn't see you . . . ?' Josh began.

Steph gave him a withering look.

'I'll take that as a "no". They flew off again?'

'Yes. North-west.'

'The base at Hang Cheng,' Howard said, almost to himself. 'They'll be back. My home will be destroyed, they don't care about anything.'

Steph glanced at Josh. 'Howard, I'm sorry . . .'

Howard walked over to the stairs that led up to the surface. Leaning against the wall close to the first step, he was staring at the floor. 'It's all right,' he mumbled without looking up. 'Not your fault.'

There was a heavy silence for a moment. Howard kept staring at the floor as though lost in thought.

'We've got to get moving,' Steph said quietly.

Howard turned. 'Why?'

'You said it yourself, they'll be straight back with reinforcements. They've seen the wreckage.'

'Not immediately, they won't.' Howard looked from Steph to Josh. 'They'll wait till daybreak. Then they'll put soldiers on the ground to go over everything.'

'How do you know that?' Josh asked, looking concerned.

'I haven't survived here this long without learning something about how the Chinese work,' he said. 'I told you where I got most of the electrical bits and bobs you were using. The market in Fung Ching Wa attracts all sorts. You pick up some useful information when you live the way I do.'

'I don't know,' Steph said, shaking her head. 'My instincts tell me they're on their way.'

Howard shrugged. 'Well, put it this way, my dear. If you're right, we're done for anyway. If *I'm* right, we have . . .' And he paused to look at an old clock on a shelf close by, 'About an hour until first light.'

'But, Steph, what can we do anyway?' Josh asked.

She didn't know what to say and simply stared at the two men. Then she sighed heavily and flopped onto the edge of Josh's bed.

'It's not as if we can start walking,' Josh added unnecessarily. 'The game's up.'

Steph was silent for a moment, staring at her palms lying in her lap. Then her head shot up. 'You're right, Josh. The game *is* up. Which means, we don't have to keep our heads down any longer.'

'What do you mean?' Howard asked.

'We can make a big show of being here, can't we? We didn't want to attract unwanted attention before . . . Now, it doesn't matter.'

73

Base One, Tintara Island

Cyber Control was abuzz, and seated at the centre of the maelstrom was Tom Erickson. He was in his element. The atmosphere was charged, techs rushing around, the giant screen on the wall flickering with images. They had spent the past few hours using remote systems on Tintara to try to improve the images from BigEye 17. It was a delicate operation, but a necessary one. The interference affecting the region of the Gobi Desert in which they believed the Silverback might be located was proving resistant to E-Force probes and sensors. They had started to lose hope. Then one of the technicians, Madeleine Alexander, had thought of realigning the imaging filters.

'The picture is clearing,' Madeleine said excitedly. She was running her expert fingers over the control panel in front of her and watching a hovering holographic image as it flickered and flashed.

Tom span his chair to face the screen. The picture began to clear revealing a perfect, high definition image.

'Transfer it to the wall screen, please, Maddie,' Tom said.

It was just after 6 am and still dark in this part of the Gobi Desert, but the cameras on the BigEye could pick up radiation across a wide range, and shift it to the visible spectrum almost instantaneously. This meant that the picture beamed to Tintara could be viewed in any way the team wished. By adjusting the settings on the panel in front of her, Madeleine Alexander was able to shift the image into the visible part of the spectrum and the desert suddenly lit up as though it were noon.

They could all see a fragmented landscape, unlike any other desert on earth – 2000 square kilometres of the south-eastern Gobi, a vast swath of orange flecked with brown and grey and patches of green, as seen by the satellite.

'Okay, Martin,' Tom said, turning to a tech sitting at a workstation close to the back of the room. 'Set the search parameters on the BigEye to detect the largest manmade structures in the area.'

The technician adjusted a set of controls and stared at a holographic image in front of him. 'There are two that have come in on the first sweep, Tom.'

'Take the biggest first,' Tom replied.

'Position: 116.23 degrees east, 42.55 degrees north.'

'Well, whaddya know?' Tom exclaimed. 'Smack on the money.'

'Close in,' Tom said crisply, and the camera on BigEye 17 slowly modulated the image. The edges of the picture tumbled over the rim of the screen and vanished. Tom watched a set of figures on the edge of the picture change. The numbers displayed the longitude and latitude of the centre point of the image. Slowly, the 2000 square kilometres on the display reduced to 500, then 100.

Gradually, a set of rectangular shapes appeared in the centre of the image. As the camera zoomed in, the shapes became clearer. It was obviously a military-style base. A set of half a dozen camouflaged buildings. One was much larger than the others. The compound was surrounded by a 5 metre high wire fence with guard towers at each corner. A road ran east from the base and disappeared off the edge of the image. There was a helipad close to the centre of the compound. Two choppers stood close by, another occupied the pad itself. A bank of ground-to-air missiles had been positioned along the western perimeter. There was a rectangular patch of tarmac close to the eastern edge of the camp. A set of military vehicles was visible – three armoured cars, four large troop carriers and a motley collection of supply trucks. As the camera moved in from directly overhead, those working in Cyber Control could just make out human figures moving around, walking from building to building. A truck came into view from the far eastern rim of the picture and went through the camp gates.

'What do we have on this place?' Tom asked.

'Nothing,' one of the techs responded.

'Nothing?'

'Not on the Chinese military database, Tom.'

'Sybil,' Tom asked. 'What can you make out from the images?'

'Chinese military-style compound,' the computer replied. 'Not in any official party records. The area is known as Hang Cheng, a desolate plateau in the desert. There is no record of any habitation in the area. Only official mention of this patch of desert is in a 1933 survey. There used to be a small town on the site.'

'Well it ain't there now,' Tom remarked.

'The compound area is approximately 1.2 square kilometres. Building area is . . . '

'Okay, Sybil. Thanks,' Tom interrupted. 'How far is this from the nearest centre of population?'

'The nearest community is Fung Ching Wa, 193 kilometres south-east of the military base. Population at time of last census in 1969 was 1345. The nearest population centre with more than 50,000 inhabitants is . . .'

'Cool, thanks,' Tom said and Sybil fell silent. 'Okay, Martin,' he added, turning back towards the technician. 'So much for the biggest manmade structure. What's the second largest?'

The image shifted, a smudge of colour ran down the screen as the camera on BigEye 17 tilted a fraction to show a 20-kilometre wide strip running south-east of the military base. In a few seconds, it slowed and stopped. They could all see a new shape on the screen. The image began to grow and fall away at the edges.

'This lies just over 60 kilometres south-east of Hang Cheng,' Martin reported.

At first, they could not fully understand what they were seeing. It was a uniform shape, a manmade structure as Tom had requested. Nothing in the natural world could have produced so regular a configuration among such desolation. Tom raised a hand. 'Slow the zoom,' he commanded.

The techs in Cyber Control all stood rigid, staring at the screen. Tom was the only one moving. His motorised chair whirred and he circumvented a control module to approach the wall. Then he stopped a few metres from the screen, his head moving almost imperceptibly left, right, up, then down. From the centre of the vast room, he looked puny against the massive image towering over him.

He turned his chair to face the others and broke into a smile. 'That, guys,' he said pointing back, ' . . . is one hell of an advertisement.'

The image showed a cross, 100 metres wide, made from bits of Silverback wreckage.

74

Dome Gamma

Mark opened the forward cargo hatch of the sub and equalised the pressure differential. A rail ran the length of the hold. It was used as a platform for launching mini-subs and subaqua scooters. Now, though, there was a metal sled on the rail and on top of the sled lay a 2-metre wide hoop of Morphadin, the multipurpose rubber-like material devised by CARPA that could be moulded into any shape one wished.

There was an extra feature built into this particular piece of Morphadin. It contained 400 million nanobots, give or take a few.

The whole science of nanotechnology had been advanced incredibly by CARPA. Indeed, from an outsider's perspective, it was probably the greatest single achievement of the organisation. And it was an amazing resource for E-Force. Its earliest days were back in the 1950s when it had been postulated by great minds like that of Richard Feynman who had a completely fresh approach to physics. He made the prophetic statement: 'There's plenty of room at the bottom'. By this he meant: how about starting with the basic building blocks? Would it be possible to put atoms together one by one? To link individual molecules to build something bigger, and to grow outwards from there?

Nice idea, but in the 1950s it was as fantastic as interstellar travel. It was only half a century later that conventional science had caught up with the concept and had started the basic experiments to put Feynman's fantasy into practice. Meanwhile, secretly, the scientists at CARPA had already constructed nanobots and had a fully fledged nanotechnology capability.

By the time E-Force was established, CARPA eggheads could build simple machines atom by atom in vats in the lab. Indeed, some of the tools used by the team on Tintara had been constructed by nanobots, 'from the bottom up'. And now, Mark was going to use the same technology.

The sled rolled along the rail and the hoop of Morphadin shot out of the hatch and somersaulted the 10 metres from the end of the sub to the wall of Dome Gamma. A few seconds later, watched by the small group of survivors at the window, the hoop came to rest flat on the side of the hotel, 3 metres away from the window.

'Looks good,' Mai said into her comms.

'Sure does. Now the bots have to do their bit,' Mark replied, and ran his fingertips over the control module in front of him.

For a few moments, it seemed nothing was happening. The hoop was stuck fast to the metal shell of the hotel. It was bright red and caught the light from the beams of the sub. But then, as all of them watched, the hoop began to shimmer and vibrate. It took a few more seconds for the first signs of expansion to become visible, but it soon became obvious what was happening – the hoop was growing outwards from the shell of the Neptune. Gradually, the flat hoop began to form the beginnings of a cylinder. After a few minutes, the shape had transformed. It was now a red tube half a metre high, stuck to the hotel wall. As it grew, it maintained its cylindrical shape and supporting struts appeared around its circumference, giving it the appearance of oversized airconditioner ducting. After five minutes, the tube was 3 metres long and its growth rate seemed to keep increasing.

Ten minutes after the hoop landed on the skin of the Neptune the tunnel had almost reached the submarine positioned 10 metres from the hotel. The end of the tube swayed gently in the underwater current, making it look like a gigantic hydra. But the nanobots knew what they were doing. They were following a program written by the onboard computer of the submarine and were snapped into action by a high frequency signal, their minuscule self-contained power systems coming to life. They worked like a colossal ant colony.

The end of the tube grew molecular hooks that locked into receptors in the outer skin of the submarine, and millions of nanobots positioned on the rim of the tube meshed with the docking port of the *Drebbel*. A minute later, the hotel was linked to the sub.

'Connection complete,' Mark announced through the comms.

Pete looked around at the faces of the survivors. They showed a blend of awe and confusion. 'Excellent work, Mark.'

'I'm on my way down to open the connection,' Mark said and headed for the tube. He was there in 30 seconds. 'Make sure everyone's well away from the wall,' he told them through his comms. 'Oh . . . and prepare them for a bit of noise!'

The sound began as a dull rumble from the outer wall of the hotel.

'What's happening?' Michael Xavier asked Pete.

'Mark is using a machine called a Sonic Drill. He'll punch a hole in the skin of the hotel.'

'And that thing . . .' Kristy Sunshine said, waving a hand at the view of the ocean through the window, 'is meant to stop the ocean rushing in?'

'It certainly will,' Mai interjected. 'Better still, it will hold our weight and we can get through it to the sub.'

Kristy turned pale and looked away.

'Bloody amazing,' Archie Barnet exclaimed. 'You lot are just the dog's boll . . .'

'Okay,' Pete interrupted with a grin. 'Let's save it for when we're all safely aboard the sub, shall we, Archie?'

Suddenly, the pitch of the sound from the Sonic Drill changed dramatically, shooting up half a dozen octaves to a piercing screech. Then came the crash of masonry and metal cascading onto a hard surface. A hole appeared in the wall and the sound stopped as suddenly as it had started. A man in an E-Force cybersuit appeared in the opening, ducked as he pushed through the gaping hole, took a step into the room and straightened.

'Okay, people,' he said. 'Let's get you the hell outta here.'

75

Mark led the way back through the opening, with Mai and Pete at the rear of the group. The structure of the tunnel was amazingly rigid. It did not even move in the water now that it was fixed at each end. The floor was flat and level, and it was easy to run along. None of them wanted to hang around.

Mark arrived at the sub a long way ahead of the others. He kept going along the corridor, headed straight for main control. As he pulled himself into the pilot's seat, the voice of the onboard computer came over the speakers. 'Attention, attention. Unidentified vehicles approaching at high speed.'

'On screen.'

The monitor burst into life. At first, it showed nothing more than a hazy blue-black. A school of yellow fish slithered past the lens of the starboard external camera. Then two dark shapes appeared out of the gloom, slowing as they approached.

'Computer. Identify the vessels.'

'Checking . . . No identifying marks.'

'What type of subs are they?'

'Dyong Class nuclear submarines. Chinese-made.'

Mark stabbed at the plastic control panel. 'Base One. Come in. This is Mark Harrison aboard the *Drebbel*.'

The line was dead.

'Tom? You there?'

Nothing.

'Must be blocking our comms,' Mark mumbled to himself. He went to speak again then changed his mind. 'Computer. See if you can open a channel to the commander of each vessel.' He paused for a moment and heard a click as a radio link was established. 'Interesting!' he said under his breath. 'This is Mark Harrison, E-Force. We are currently in the middle of a rescue operation. Please identify yourselves.'

The blast came as Mark finished the sentence. He was thrown across the control room, smashing his head against a leg of one of the panels. For a second, he thought he was going to lose consciousness, but he pulled himself to his feet, gripping the plastic panel to steady himself. He heard a scream from the corridor beyond the control room. Michael Xavier and his son Nick appeared at the opening and Mark could see Hilary Xavier and Emily clinging to the back wall of the passageway.

Then the second blast hit, and they were all thrown to the floor again.

Mark pulled himself up.

'Grip something solid,' Michael shouted to his family. Kristy and Jim appeared in the corridor. Behind them came the remaining survivors. Mai and Peter pushed through the group and ran over to join Mark at the main control panel.

'What the hell's happening?' Pete said.

Mark nodded towards the screen. 'We have visitors. And they don't seem terribly friendly.' He turned away. 'This is Mark Harrison of E-Force. We have a group of survivors from the Neptune aboard our sub. Why are you firing at us?'

The sub rocked again. This time the shock was more violent.

'Depth charges,' Pete said. 'They're not trying to hit us, just shake us up.'

'But why?' Mai said, anger clear in her face.

Mark was about to reply when a voice cut through the comms. 'Prepare to be boarded.'

'You called Tom?' Pete asked.

'Comms are down again. I think our friends have blocked them.'

'Excellent!'

'But they're working ship-to-ship.'

'Yeah, I think that's about the extent of it,' Mark replied. He turned back to the console. 'That won't be possible,' he said, responding to the command from the other sub. 'We've accomplished this phase of our mission. Just let us be on our way.'

Silence.

'Prepare to be boarded.'

Another blast. Much closer this time. The sub shook violently. Archie Barnet yelled and tripped over a box bolted to the floor. He landed hard against the wall of the control room, groaning. Harry hobbled over to him. 'You okay, son?' he asked and helped the boy sit up. Archie shook his head and put his fingers to a new cut just over his right eyebrow.

'Yeah, must be getting used to this malarkey. Either that or I 'ave a steel 'ead,' he said and Harry ruffled his hair before offering a hand up.

Across the room, Mark was growing angry. 'Please explain. Why are you attacking us?'

When the next blast came, they were expecting it. It was becoming a little predictable. This time everyone had a grip on something, or someone.

'Prepare to be boarded.'

Mark looked at Mai and Pete and shook his head slowly. 'I think they mean business, Mark,' Mai said gravely.

'Yeah, so do I.'

'We could try to outrun them,' Pete offered.

Mark gave him a sceptical look.

A loud thud echoed throughout the sub. It made the vessel shake violently.

'Shit! What was that?' Kristy Sunshine screamed. She was clinging to a pillar close to the centre of the room, a look of terror on her face.

A second loud thud. It came from the other side of the submarine. Mark stabbed at the control panel. The cameras outside swivelled round. They could all see the 10 centimetre thick metal cables that had shot out from the strange visitors. Moving the cameras to look along the hull of the *Drebbel*, the source of the loud thuds became clear. Huge clamps had been secured to the outer shell of the E-Force vessel. These were connected to the metal cables which stretched a few dozen metres through the churning water and disappeared into openings in the side of the intruder subs.

They heard a loud crack as the tunnel from the Neptune snapped and felt a jolt as the *Drebbel* started to move. On the screen, they could see the outlines of the two huge nuclear subs and hear the engines change pitch. The pair of black shapes turned in unison. The *Drebbel* began to accelerate, heading north-east, away from the hotel.

76

Pacific Ocean

The view through the cameras showed a churning mass of dark water. They began to pick up speed and after a few minutes the images from the outside grew progressively darker. They could feel from the movement of the submarine that they were descending, following the ocean floor on its downward incline as the continental shelf began to slip away.

Mark and Pete had stopped watching the screen and were studying the instruments.

'Heading north-east,' Mark said. 'Now steady at 37 knots.'

Pete was running programs through the sub's computer system, trying to get sensor readings from the other subs. 'Pretty regular Chinese Navy subs,' he said. 'I've done an infrared sweep. Twelve crew on each. Neither vessel is carrying nukes. I'm getting low-res images of the sub's ID.'

He turned away from the panel for a second. 'Computer. Designation of port vessel is DFCD-768R. The starboard vessel is DFCD-744N.'

'No known vessels in database.'

'Check online. All NATO and non-NATO information hubs.'

A few seconds passed.

'No internet connection.'

Pete turned to Mark. 'What the hell are we dealing with here?'

'Not the Chinese military. Or any regular military on the planet, that's for sure.'

Then the power went off.

One of the women screamed.

'Must have picked up our scans. Cut us off,' Pete commented.

Michael Xavier appeared at Mark's elbow. 'Is everything down?' he asked.

Mark ignored him for a moment, tried bringing the dead plastic control panel to life by tapping at a few key points, but nothing happened. 'The engine is off-line,' he replied. 'Generators are down.' He glanced at his wrist where the monitor of his cybersuit glowed lemon in the dark. 'Our suits run independently of the ship's systems,' Mark went on. 'I'm picking up a very low frequency transmission.'

'What does that mean?' Michael asked.

Mai approached and stood next to Michael Xavier. 'Yeah, what does it mean?' she interjected.

'The last time I spoke to Tom was when I was approaching Dome Gamma. He had figured out what had caused the quake.'

Michael stared at him, muscles in his cheeks protruding slightly as he clenched his teeth.

'He believes it was caused by Extremely Low Frequency vibrations originating just over a kilometre from the hotel. He couldn't pinpoint the source, or how the vibration beam had been used, but he was convinced it was the cause.'

Mark turned to Mai and Pete. 'He also believes the same sort of beam brought Josh and Steph's plane down in the Gobi Desert. He's pretty sure it's some sort of weapon. Most probably Chinese.'

'Military research into Extremely Low Frequency radiation has been going on for decades,' Mai said.

The three men stared at her. 'NASA had a leaked memo from the Pentagon. I saw it years ago. We've been developing ELF weapons since the 1960s. So have the Brits, the Russians, French and Chinese. It's generally assumed no one's got very far with it.'

'Well, it looks like that assessment may have to change,' Mark commented.

'So, let me get this straight,' Michael said, his face expressionless. 'You're telling me my hotel has been destroyed and hundreds of lives lost because of a weapons test gone wrong?'

'We don't know . . .'

'The Chinese?' Michael's face began to change, anger flaring up in his eyes. He took a deep breath.

'We don't know enough yet, Mr Xavier,' Mark said calmly. The Englishman turned and walked back to the others, lowered himself against the wall, too lost in confusion and fury to speak.

Mai left Pete and Mark at the control panel and crossed the room to where the survivors were huddled together. They were all filthy, hungry and scared. Hilary was clutching her children close to her. The three of them looked petrified. Michael had sat down beside his wife.

'You guys must be hungry,' Mai said to the two children. 'Would you like to help me get some food and drink for everyone? I've got a torch and there's emergency lighting in the other rooms and the corridor.'

The kids looked at their mother. For a second, Hilary didn't know what to say. Then she relaxed and managed a brief smile. She turned to Michael, who appeared to be in another world, put a hand on his arm and squeezed it gently.

'You go,' she said, turning back to Nick and Emily. Mai helped the children to their feet and led them out of the control room.

The others were almost as despondent as Michael Xavier, each of them seemingly lost in their own thoughts. Harry had his back to a metal pillar, head between his knees. The pain in his foot had turned to a dull ache, thanks to the powerful drugs Mai had given him. He ran his fingers over the super-lightweight bandage wrapped around his foot and ankle and recalled how Mai had sealed his wound with that stuff she had called SkinGloo. Incongruously he thought how, if he ever got out of here alive, he would make a documentary about the advanced technology E-Force used. Kristy had sat down beside him, speechless, her face a blank. Jim was staring into space. Miguel and Sigmund had been talking, comparing notes, but had fallen quiet. Archie pulled himself to his feet and wandered over to Pete and Mark.

'Where're they taking us?' he asked. 'Who are they?'

Mark turned and put a hand on the young man's shoulder. 'I wish I knew, Archie. But at least we're safe for the moment.'

'Yeah, I guess you're right there, mister. Gotta be better than a collapsing hotel, ain't it?'

They all felt the sub start to slow.

They could see nothing of the outside, the vessel was windowless and the cameras had gone down when the power was cut. The deceleration was rapid, and in a few minutes they had almost stopped moving. They heard a loud clanging sound as the clamps were released. Then came the grinding of metal against metal. The sub juddered before stopping dead.

'What's happening?' It was Harry Flanders. He had pulled himself up and crossed to the control console.

'I think we may have reached our destination,' Pete replied.

'What're we going to do?' Jim asked, standing up and walking unsteadily into the middle of the room.

Mark and Pete stood in front of the panel. Mai stood at the back of the room. Mark sighed. 'We have no choice but to let them board,' he said.

'But they could kill us.' Kristy said, her eyes wide with fear.

'I thought your vessels were impregnable,' Archie declared. 'Least that's what I read.'

'They are, to a degree,' Pete responded. 'But we have no power, no comms to the surface.'

'But your base. The rest of the team . . . won't they be able to get here and sort things out?'

'Maybe. But I don't think we have time. The air will run out, and without power, it's going to get very cold in here very quickly.'

It was only then the others seemed to notice the temperature had already dropped several degrees.

'Whoever is responsible for this probably knows that. They can wait it out.'

Mark gazed around the room. They all looked sullen, defeated. Michael Xavier pulled himself up from where he had been sitting in silence. 'Mr Harrison is right,' he said, easing himself to the front of the group. 'We don't have a choice. Worse case scenario, they kill us. Might be preferable to slowly suffocating.'

There was a silence in the sub. It was broken by a distant voice, coming from a speaker beyond the hull of the sub.

'Prepare to be boarded,' the voice said, the English heavily accented. A loud bang rang along the corridor beyond the control room. Someone was bashing the Maximium shell of the sub with what sounded like a hammer.

'Everyone stay here,' Mark said. He walked into the corridor and turned right. On the wall was a box containing two stun pistols. They were the only weapons E-Force carried. He stepped back into the control room for a second and tossed one of the guns over to Pete.

Pete turned to Mai. 'You still have the taser you took from Archie, right?'

She nodded.

'Wait here,' Mark said and ducked back into the corridor, priming the stun pistol as he ran.

The banging grew louder. It was coming from the other side of the main exit, a sealed metal door at the far end of the corridor. Mark stood still. 'Who are you?'

'Prepare to be boarded.'

'That's not good enough.'

'Prepare to be boarded.'

Mark opened a small metal sliding panel to the side of the door. Inside was a large red plastic handle. Above this was written: 'Emergency Door Release'. He pulled it down and quickly took a step back, assuming the power stance, brandishing the stun pistol in both hands.

The door flew open. A soldier holding a QBB-97 light machine gun capable of firing ten 42 mm shells per second charged through the opening. He was wearing a gas mask.

'Drop weapon,' he said in English, his voice muffled by the mask. Mark lowered the stun pistol. The soldier took two steps forward and smashed the barrel of the gun across Mark's left temple, sending him to the metal floor.

Turning, the soldier pulled the pin on a canister of M99, a powerful synthetic opiate. The nozzle burst open and vapour billowed along the corridor of the sub.

77

Base One, Tintara Island

'Tom?'

'Madeleine,' Tom replied, studying the tech's face in his holoscreen.

'The planes are on their way from Polar Base.'

'Cool. What's their ETA?'

'They've sent a Silverback ahead at top speed to make contact with Josh and Steph.'

'I thought Josh and Steph had the only Silverback there – *Paul*.'

'No, the base has two of its own, *Mick* and *Keith*.'

'Okay. What else?'

'A Hummingbird is right behind *Mick*.'

'And they've been told the top priority after getting the guys outta there is to dissolve every piece of wreckage on the ground?'

'Of course.'

'All right, thanks, Maddie.' Tom turned back to his laptop. He was on the balcony above Cyber Control. The warm afternoon sun lit up the bright jungle colours of Tintara and the ocean spread out below. He liked coming up here on his own, loved gazing at the glorious tropical vista, feeling the natural warmth on his face. 'Okay, computer,' he said, and clicked his knuckles before splaying his fingers over the virtual keys in front of him. 'We have work to do.'

78

Gobi Desert, China

The sun came up over a line of hills to the east of the crash site. It was huge and orange and it threw warm shafts of colour across the speckled desert. But it was the last thing Josh, Steph and Howard wanted to see.

Josh was up and walking, almost mended. He had his cybersuit on, running on its lowest power settings – just enough to keep him warm and the nanobots functioning. Howard was wearing his greatcoat, ragged old jeans and walking boots he had bought in England in another life. He had loaned Steph a wolf fur jacket he had made himself, which she wore over her almost redundant cybersuit. They looked an odd group, as though an interstellar traveller had gone on a field trip with a couple of hippies.

They stopped next to the fuselage of the downed Silver-back. Steph lowered herself onto a metal cylinder, part of one of the plane's engines. She was exhausted. She had not slept for over 24 hours. Every muscle in her body ached from the exertion of making the cross in the sand from pieces of wreckage and debris. She looked over at Josh sitting against the fuselage. 'How you bearing up, Josh?' she asked.

'I feel better than you look.'

'Oh, thanks, buddy,' she laughed. 'Whereas you, of course, look ridiculously well.'

'Good old nanobots. Love 'em.'

They had tried to persuade Howard to stay behind, but he would have none of it, claiming he could not rely on them to save his home. He leaned against a section of wing that had gone edge-first into the sand when the plane had exploded the night before. Pulling out his old army revolver, a Webley Mark VI, he checked it was fully loaded. 'My father's,' he said, patting the weapon proudly. 'Used this at El Alamein. Colonel, 50th Northumbrian Infantry Division. We have this to thank for the furs.' He grinned.

Steph raised a hand suddenly.

'What is it?' Howard asked, cocking the firing pin.

'Sssh.' Steph and Josh both strained to hear.

'Choppers. Three of them.'

'Coming from the north,' Josh added.

They ducked down, using the fuselage and the morning shadow to keep out of sight. They knew it was not a serious hiding place – the choppers would have infrared sensors.

The first helicopter came in low and swooped over the fuselage no more than 20 metres above the ground. Two others hovered overhead about 100 metres up.

'We'll have to surrender,' Josh said. 'Otherwise we have a very strong chance of getting ourselves shot.'

'Yeah, but they may just kill us anyway. Who would ever know?' Howard replied.

'That's a possibility,' Josh agreed. 'But there's a chance we won't be shot if we surrender. There's nowhere to run. With respect Howard, your father's World War II pistol won't do us much good.'

The first chopper was making a tight circle over the wreckage and started to bank back around towards the crash site. Steph stood up, raised her arms above her head and walked slowly away from the fuselage of the Silverback. Josh came up behind her. Howard pushed himself away from the wing and followed suit.

The chopper hovered directly overhead, kicking up great clouds of sand. The powerful rotors were incredibly loud, slicing the air as the engines roared, keeping the chopper in a holding pattern. The three figures on the ground could do nothing but close their eyes, keeping their hands in clear view above their heads.

A second chopper began to descend as the first one prepared to land. It was then they heard an incredibly loud shriek. Howard tried to open one eye to see through the sand gusts. He lowered a hand to shade his eyes, but all he saw was a flash of green streak low overhead at incredible speed.

Josh and Steph had no need to look. They knew what the sound meant. The Silverback screeched over the sand and the wreckage in a tiny fraction of a second, moving so fast it was almost impossible to follow it with the eye.

Two hundred metres beyond the edge of the crash site, the Silverback named *Mick* pulled up and soared into the sky at almost 500 metres per second, faster than a bullet. Dimitri Godska, E-Force's only Ukrainian pilot, rolled the plane, bringing it horizontal and heading due south-south-west, ready for a second run.

'My God!' Howard exclaimed.

'Come on,' Steph snapped, and pulled Howard towards her. Josh turned on his heel and all three of them ran as fast as they could back to the fuselage.

The Chinese chopper crews were too stunned by the Silverback to pay any attention to the three people on the ground. The two helicopters close to the ground rose up, their engines roaring, kicking up sand and loose debris.

Steph, Josh and Howard made it to cover just as the

Silverback came back around, even lower than before. Steph stepped out from the shadow of the twisted metal of the fuselage as far as she dared, waving frantically.

The Silverback slowed and in little over a second and a half came to a dead stop directly over its smashed up twin, hovering 30 metres in the air.

There was a momentary crackle, then a voice came over a speaker mounted on the front of the Silverback.

'Steph, Josh,' Dimitri Godska said. 'I'm dropping you a comms set. A Hummingbird is right behind me. ETA . . . 65 seconds.' A small door on the underside of the Silverback slid open and a metal box about 30 centimetres square fell out and plunged to the ground. It landed close to the wreckage and the sleek E-Force jet climbed, rolled and shot off at a diagonal, rising 2000 metres in the blink of an eye.

Josh pulled the box over to the relative safety of the fuselage. Its Maxinium case looked like the day it came off the production line – not a scratch on it. Josh opened the latches on each side and pulled the lid back. He grabbed the handset and flicked it on. For a few seconds all they could hear was static, then a voice cut through the cold morning air.

'This is Omar Deseau on Hummingbird 3. Steph? Josh? Come in please.'

'Josh here, Hummingbird 3. Great to hear your voice, Omar.'

'What's your status, please?'

'Steph and I are fine. We have a civilian with us. We're being buzzed by three Chinese helicopters.'

'Okay, we're a few seconds away.'

'What's the plan?' Steph asked.

'We get you out, then we have to USAM the whole area.'

'Copy,' Josh said and looked at Steph.

'What the hell is USAM?' Howard asked.

'It's . . .' Josh began and looked at the ground.

'Ultra Sound All Materials,' Steph interrupted.

'And that means?'

'Howard, it means one of our planes will fly low over this area and turn everything to powder with ultrasound radiation.'

Howard looked at them, horrified. 'Even my home?'

'We can't leave a trace . . .'

The air was filled with the crack of machine gun fire. A chopper swept low overhead and banked as the Silverback, *Mick*, came around for a third time. The E-Force jet shot past and there was more gunfire. Then a chopper was landing directly in front of Steph, Josh and Howard, so close they could see inside. The pilot turned to them. Directly behind him, a second soldier swung a mounted machine gun, the barrel pointed straight at them.

They scrambled for cover. There was a sound like rocks cascading down a mountainside, an ear-splitting roar. The earth shook, pieces of wreckage rattled where they lay. The fuselage of the downed Silverback shuddered, flakes of Maxinium tumbled to the sand.

Steph had thrown herself behind a steel sheet, not daring to lift her head above the rim. She could hear Chinese voices raised in panic. Barked orders. She felt a rush of air and sand spraying everywhere. Then came the unmistakeable change in pitch as the chopper climbed and pulled away.

'Steph?' It was Josh. She pulled herself up and he was leaning down to help her out. Howard was behind him. The three of them crouched close together. They were covered in sand and dust, their faces almost black. The sand had found its way into their mouths and up their noses. Their eyes stung.

'It's the Hummingbird,' Josh cried above the noise.

A voice came through the comms. 'Hummingbird here. Guys, you ready to move out?'

'Where have you put down?'

'We're approximately 30 metres directly east of your position. We couldn't get any closer because we thought it would destabilise the wreckage.'

'But the choppers–'

'Dimitri is doing his best to distract them,' Omar replied. 'But we have to move . . . now.'

'Steph. I'll go first. Then Howard. You okay with that?' Josh looked from one to the other. They both nodded and scrambled to the edge of the fuselage. Josh looked out. He could see two of the choppers in the distance. Dimitri was playing with them, swooping close then ducking away at phenomenal speed. The helicopter crews could not have any clue what the hell was going on. He turned to Steph and Howard, took a deep breath and ran as fast as he could into the open.

It felt as though he was running for hours. His knee had been repaired, but he was still stiff and sore. The sand rushed past. He could see the ramp of the Hummingbird descending from the underbelly of the enormous aircraft. At the top of the slope stood a figure in black fatigues encouraging him on. The new morning seemed superbright. Colours streamed past. Sounds bounced around. He felt the sand giving way under his boots. He made it to the ramp, the hard Maxinium floor so very different to the sand. He almost stumbled, but managed to stay on his feet.

Then he was running up the slope into the safety of the plane. He stopped and turned. Howard was halfway across the stretch of sand, his greatcoat flapping about him, his long, grey hair flying around his face.

A chopper lowered itself into view no more than 20 metres beyond the fuselage, directly behind Howard. Steph had dashed out from the wreckage to follow Howard. Josh watched, horrified, as the machine rose up a few metres and sped forward, directly toward the Hummingbird. Steph and Howard were caught in the open.

Steph saw the chopper, but kept going. Howard was running as fast as he could, gasping for breath as he went. He was a dozen metres from the ramp when the rattle of machine gun fire split the air. Josh could see the end of the 12.7 mm barrel flare orange and yellow. The bullets thudded into Howard's back, exiting through his abdomen and sending a fountain of blood in front of him.

Josh dashed out into the open again. The man at the top of the ramp cried out, but Josh ignored him. Steph was there first, almost falling over Howard and sliding to one side in the sand. The chopper roared overhead. Bullets spat from the machine gun, thumping into the sand. A few more hit the fuselage of the Hummingbird, not even denting the Maxinium.

Josh and Steph grabbed an arm each and dragged Howard towards the ramp. The man in the black fatigues ran down the ramp towards them. He helped them up onto the metal slope and yelled into his comms.

They had just reached the top of the ramp when they all felt the Hummingbird start to rise up from the desert. The ramp came up, slithering into its recess with a loud hiss. Another door opened in front of them and they all fell into a corridor as a pair of E-Force paramedics rounded the corner directly ahead and dashed towards them.

79

'I'm fine. It's okay,' Steph said, as one of the paramedics helped her to her feet.

Josh was standing, one hand gripping a rail running along the wall.

'Josh, you go and help up top,' Steph said. 'Here.' She snatched a mobile comms set from one of the paramedics and tossed it over to him. He caught it, stood up and raced along the corridor.

Steph crouched down beside Howard. He was lying on his back, unconscious, a pool of blood spreading out from under him across the metal floor. Steph checked for a pulse. It was weak. She ripped open Howard's shirt and started performing CPR. There were gaping wounds in his chest and abdomen, exit wounds caked with splinters of bone and blobs of tissue. One of the medics ran a scanner over the injured man's body.

'Roll him over . . . gently,' Steph snapped.

Suddenly, the plane shuddered and dropped altitude. The paramedics were thrown across the corridor. Steph managed to grasp the handrail just in time. Howard rolled forward and then onto his back again. It lasted only a second or two, and then the plane's stabilisers kicked in. But in those moments, Steph could see the extent of Howard's injuries. His back was completely ripped open, his spine shredded.

'Heart's stopped,' the paramedic said.

'All right, step back,' Steph said. 'Give me the defrib pads.'

333

She snatched at two plastic discs and slapped them onto Howard's exposed chest. Unlike the old-style machines, these worked by sending an infrared pulse from a small box in the paramedic's belt to activate the pads and zap the patient's heart with an automatically adjusted electric shock.

'Clear.'

Howard convulsed, his back arching. He slumped onto the metal floor and Steph leaned in to give him mouth to mouth. 'Clear,' she yelled again pulling back and pushing down on the pads. Howard convulsed a second time.

'Still no rhythm,' the paramedic said.

'Damn it! . . . Clear.'

Howard's body arched up a third time, then slumped to the floor. Steph pushed the pads aside and went back to pumping the man's chest with her hands, bending forward to administer mouth to mouth. After a few seconds, she paused and looked at the paramedic. The man shook his head.

Steph thumped Howard's chest as hard as she could. His body bounced on the metal. She hit him again, and again. Paused. Took a deep breath and began pumping again, getting oxygen into his lungs, desperately trying to kick-start his heart.

'Howard!'

'Steph.' The other paramedic had crouched down next to her.

She ignored him. 'Howard! Howard!' Steph shouted at the prone body. 'Come on, Howard!'

'Steph.'

She stopped and sobbed into her palms. Howard's head lolled to one side.

80

Josh was halfway along the main corridor leading to the elevator when the plane shuddered and dropped altitude suddenly. He was sent tumbling forward. He managed to roll with the fall and came up against a support column, bashing his left cheek against the metal.

The plane stabilised before he could pull himself up. Ignoring the pain in his face, he ran for the elevator and opened a channel on the mobile comms set. 'Omar. This is Josh. Come in.'

'Josh. You okay?'

'I'm fine. Listen. The Chinese have some sort of disruptor weapon.'

'What?'

'Look. I'm on my way to the flight deck. Watch your flight guidance systems. And, Omar. Call Dimitri. Now. Tell him.'

'Will do. Out.'

Josh ran into the elevator and punched in a call to Base One. 'Tom.'

'Josh. What's . . . ?'

'Tom, this is priority red. The Chinese brought *Paul* down with some sort of interference beam. It was way down in the low frequency end of the spectrum. Cut right through the shields as though they weren't there. It attacked the guidance systems and then disrupted almost every part of the plane. I think they'll try to do the same here, now, with the Hummingbird and *Mick*.'

'Yeah, I know they're experimenting with ELF radiation,' Tom said. 'What was the exact time of the attack? Do you know?'

'Engraved in my memory, Tom. We felt the first shock precisely 21 minutes and six seconds after takeoff.'

'Okay. Leave it with me. I'll see what I can do to block it . . . somehow.'

The elevator shot up three floors, the doors parted and Josh dashed out into another corridor that curved gently to the left. He ran as fast as he could. As he reached the door to the flightdeck, it opened automatically and he sped over to the bank of control panels where Omar and his copilot, Gillian Fernandez, sat.

He had just reached them when the plane shuddered again. A computer voice broke in over the comms system.

'Warning. Unidentified object. One point nine kilometres north-north-east.'

'On screen,' Fernandez commanded.

'Not possible at this time.'

'What!'

Josh reached the control station and stepped between the two pilots. 'It's happening again,' he said.

81

A high-pitched whistle burst through the comm speakers.

'What's happening?' Omar yelled.

'Warning. Warning,' the onboard computer cut through the shrill noise.

'It's a low frequency energy burst,' Josh shouted. 'It's the same thing that brought us down. Omar, take us up. We'll have to try to get out of range.' The copilot offered Josh her seat and strode over to a secondary control console the other side of the flight deck.

Josh yanked on a helmet and his fingers flew over the control panel.

'What about the shields?' Omar said.

The plane shuddered.

Josh did not reply for a moment, he was concentrating on the holodisplay before his eyes. 'Cuts through them,' he said after a moment, and punched in a set of parameters for the computer. The plane banked to port and they could feel it start to gain altitude. Josh flicked his eyes over the 3D display. They were climbing fast. Ten thousand metres, 20,000, 25,000.

'Warning. Engine One efficiency down to 63 per cent.'

Josh cursed and glanced over to Omar, who was focusing all his attention on helping to control the plane.

'We have to get out of range or cut the engines, Omar,' Josh declared.

'What?'

'Get outta here or cut them. The ELF radiation will completely fuse them.'

'Yes, but we might not be able to bring them back online.'

'Omar, if we don't shut them down now, there'll be nothing to bring back online.'

'I'll get us out of range.'

A voice came over the comms. 'Hummingbird, this is Silverback *Mick*. Come in.'

'Dimitri,' Omar said, trying to keep calm. 'What's your status?'

'I caught a faint trace of an unidentified object in my remote scanner a few moments ago. I saw you pick up Josh and Steph, so I took off. I've climbed to 33,000 metres and I'm 94 kilometres from the crash site, bearing 74.6 degrees. The object has fallen out of range.'

'Good!'

'Kind of.'

'What do you mean?'

'I have to get back there to get rid of the wreckage with the ultrasound emitter.'

'It'll have to wait.'

'Afraid not, Omar. The computer's just intercepted comms from the base and translated for me. The three choppers are returning to base, but the Chinese have sent a transport jet to parachute in a salvage team. Their ETA is under three minutes. I'm going to have to go down . . . now.'

82

Base One, Tintara Island

Tom's holoscreen was ablaze with colour. He moved his fingers over the keyboard and the colours were replaced with text.

Without taking his eyes from the screen, he said, 'Sybil, go back over the monitor records from BigEye 17. Time scale: 20 to 22 minutes after the Silverback took off from Semja Alexandry. Full spectrum analysis.'

'Done.'

'What sort of emission was it?'

'Extremely Low Frequency. 35.45 to 36.12 hertz.'

'Yes!' Tom exclaimed and hit his palm on the armrest of his chair. 'I knew it. Okay, Sybil, how was the disruption controlled? Was it from the missile, the jet or the base?'

'No information available. It was all under the interference.'

'Yes, of course,' Tom remarked and let out a deep sigh. 'Okay,' he said to the air. 'Have to work on a hunch. My guess would be that the disruptor beam is generated at the base and the jet simply launches a missile that acts as a relay. The Florida Bridge attack wasn't so long ago. I can't believe the Chinese would have perfected the equipment to the point where they can miniaturise it to fit in a missile. Sybil, I'll need instantaneous Chinese-English and English-Chinese translation for all visual and audio.'

'Ready.'

Five seconds later, Tom was into the military mainframe in Beijing. He had been there many times before, and he knew the protocols inside out. The passwords had changed a hundred times since his last visit, but he knew how the Chinese computer designers thought. It had been a simple matter to shift a few of the parameters, to substitute key cultural terms for others and to outwit his opponent. That was his special skill, the skill that had landed him in goal two years before. The skill that had earned him a place in E-Force.

Getting into the mainframe was one step on the way, but there were plenty more doors to open before he could have a chance of finding what it was he was after. What did he need to track down? He had to pause for a second to remind himself. He gazed past his holoscreen, out towards the sparkling expanse of the Pacific Ocean. The Chinese had obviously developed a way of using Extremely Low Frequency radiation as an effective weapon. Or at least they were a long way along the road to developing one. It may have been the Chinese who had been responsible for the bridge collapse in Florida, or that may just have been a coincidence. Tom hated the crackpot amateurs who smothered the internet with their ridiculous conspiracy theories, but it was extremely odd that there had been a burst of ELF radiation originating in the Gobi Desert, at the precise coordinates of Hang Cheng immediately before a bridge plunged into the water in Florida. And, there had never been any form of official reason given for the collapse.

'But,' Tom said aloud, 'if they're building this weapon in the Gobi, why are we getting bursts off Fiji? Has that just been chosen randomly as their latest target?'

He turned back to the screen and typed in 'ELF research'.

A data stream flowed down the holoscreen.

'Sybil,' he said to the air. 'How many files are there in this folder?'

'Two thousand, three hundred and nineteen.'

'Please extricate anything mentioning Hang Cheng.'

'There are no files mentioning that name in this folder.'

'What?'

'There are . . .'

'Okay, Syb, babe. I get it.' Tom paused for a moment and looked out to the ocean again. 'That can only mean one of two things,' he said aloud. 'Either Hang Cheng is so secret there are no records or files on it. Which I find pretty unlikely. Or . . .' And he tapped at the rim of his laptop absent-mindedly. 'That base is not an official Chinese military centre.' He span his electric wheelchair around and sped over to the door and the passageway leading back to Cyber Control. 'Sybil,' he said as he accelerated along the corridor. 'I think it's time we rolled out the CyberLink.'

83

Tom had just turned into Cyber Control when Josh's face appeared in the holoscreen floating above the laptop on his electric wheelchair.

'Josh.'

'Tom, things are worse than I thought here. The Chinese have just launched a transport plane. We're pretty sure they're going to drop troops into the crash site and we haven't been able to USAM the area.'

'How long?'

'Dimitri is about to make a low run over the site. He reckons we have less than three minutes before there're men on the ground.'

'Okay. What's your status? The ELF radiation?'

'We managed to pull out of range . . . just. We're headed south-south-east to get out of Chinese airspace and we're at . . .' There was a momentary pause, '32,000 metres. The sensors show we're outrunning the beam, and it's weakening. But it's not us I'm worried about, it's Dimitri. You have to cut the link from the base to the missile.'

'Yeah, I know, Josh. I'm going to use the CyberLink.'

'But you've only had it up and running for a short time . . .'

'You got any better ideas?'

A pause. 'No.'

'Right, well I gotta go,' Tom snapped, cutting the comms and spinning his chair around, easing his head back as a tech fitted him with a tight plastic headset. The tech tapped a sensor on the side of the cap then walked back to one of the control panels. 'Ready.'

'Go,' Tom commanded.

It was nothing like the 'real world'. At least not in any aesthetic sense. Tom's senses were limited. He could see, but only outlines, some patches coloured in, some not. He could hear, but couldn't smell anything. Although he could interact with the outlines around him, he had no sense of touch as he had in the 'solid world'.

'I'm in,' he said, his voice spilling from the speakers in Cyber Control.

He looked down at himself. He was Tommy Boy, his avatar. In this cyber world Tom had legs that worked. He could walk and run and do everything he could do before his accident. He had adopted the cyber persona of Tommy Boy years earlier when he was a teenage computer geek obsessed with games. During the mission to save Senator Kyle Foreman, he had used his avatar to defend Base One against a cyber attack from an old gaming adversary, Francine Gygax. Now, he had only minutes to save this mission.

He looked around. Colours, bright tubes of light. They formed the outlines of a corridor. There were patches of light on the floor. He knew they were parcels of data. They shot past him, away along the corridors and through the walls before disappearing just as a new batch arrived at his feet.

Then he heard a crack, like a whip. He span around and a black amorphous shape appeared at the end of the corridor. It morphed before his eyes, taking on the shape of a sword, slicing the air. The sword sped towards him.

'Okay, the first layer of defence,' Tom said to himself. The sword somersaulted along the corridor as though it had been thrown by a giant hand. Tommy Boy lifted his arm and saw he was brandishing a large metal shield. The sword struck the shield and with lightning reflexes, he grabbed the hilt before it could flip away. It tried to slip through his fingers, but he held it tight and brought it down, flat to his thigh. It snapped in two and he threw the shards to the illuminated floor. He laughed. 'Bring it on, baby.'

'Tom? You okay?' It was the voice of a tech, Noel Brannigan, on Tintara.

'Everything's cool, Noel. Just met the welcoming committee . . . Shit!'

'What?'

Tommy Boy ignored him. The floor ahead of him had vanished. He was sliding over patches of light. There was nothing to grip on to. He began to accelerate. Colours rushed past, and he plummeted into blackness.

The panic hit, but at the same time he could not deny it felt really good. He had not known such freedom since his last sojourn in the cyber world. This universe of bits and bytes was a place out of time and space and so different to the physical world in which he was confined to a wheelchair.

He was tumbling head-over-heels through the void. Bright bands of colour shot up to meet him. He saw outlines of components, wires. He was inside a chip, weightless. He had no size, no mass. He was barely there, just a shadow, an intelligence. Then he landed in liquid. He had not experienced such a thing since he was a young boy. At first, he could not quite understand what had happened. Then instinct took over and he started to tread water.

The place lay in semi-darkness. He could see curved metal walls, a domed roof. Wall-to-wall water. There was nothing to swim towards. It was as though he were a flea that had landed in a cup of coffee. He started to swim, regardless.

There was nothing else he could do. That's when the fear started to grow. What was under the water? What unspeakable thing could be lurking there, ready to attack?

He swam faster and faster, but the rim of the liquid kept moving away, as though the room was growing, the edge forever receding beyond his grasp. He kicked his legs and felt a tiny flash of relief, almost pleasure, at the fact he could do such a thing.

Snap.

The unmistakable sound of jaws slamming together, teeth grating.

He did not stop to look, did not stop to think. Just moved, thrusting forward, thrashing through the water and into the air.

Snap.

His fingertips brushed something solid. Some sort of platform. He grasped at it and felt a rail. He shook his head, letting the liquid fly off him. He could see the rail . . . and steps. He swung his legs through the air, pulling himself up with all his strength. A huge black shape soared out of the liquid.

Snap.

He felt the air rush past his legs as the jaws closed centimetres from his ankles, then a loud splash as the creature fell back into the water.

Tommy Boy pulled himself to his feet and flung himself as far from the edge of the lake as he could. He stumbled and, as he caught himself, he twisted, his legs almost buckling under him. He just managed to keep his balance, and straightened.

The barrel of a machine gun was poised 3 centimetres from his nose.

He turned very slowly. Three more guns were pointing at his head.

'Don't move!'

He swivelled his eyes, made a slight turn of the head.

'DON'T MOVE!'

He obeyed.

'You are not welcome here.'

'You don't say!'

He heard the click of a trigger release.

'Now look . . .'

'Silence!'

Tommy Boy closed his eyes. He could not die here, but his avatar would be destroyed and he would be instantly snapped back to the 'real' world, his efforts wasted.

But there was no gunfire. He heard a strange sound. Heavy weights hitting metal.

He opened his eyes.

The four Chinese soldiers lay on the floor in a crumpled heap.

'Tom? What's happening?' It was Cyber Control.

He did not answer immediately. He crouched down and inspected the closest body, rolling the man over. His face was contorted in pain. Green lines had spread along his cheeks, a latticework that grew as Tom watched. Then the soldier's face caved in like a soufflé gone wrong.

Tom pulled himself up. 'A virus,' he said to the air.

'What?'

'A virus,' Tom repeated. 'I must have brought something in with me.'

'Well that's fantastic!'

'Yes, it is,' Tom replied thoughtfully and stared round at the other three collapsed bodies, now mere piles of rags. A sound came from the lake of liquid. A huge black shape rose to the surface. It bobbed for a second and emitted a low growl. Then it rolled over and dissolved.

346

'The virus is spreading,' Tom said.

'That should do it,' Noel Brannigan said. 'Shouldn't it?'

'Maybe, maybe not,' Tom replied. 'I've still got to make sure.' He turned at a sound from behind him. A flight of stone stairs had appeared in the wall close to the edge of the lake. Without a second thought, he dashed towards them.

84

Gobi Desert, China

The Hummingbird hovered just out of range of the ELF beam. The missile relaying the destructive pulse from the Chinese base was circling around the crash site 85 kilometres west of their position. From images beamed to them by BigEye 17, they had a clear view of the area on the wall screen in the main control room of the giant aircraft.

Dimitri in the Silverback was directly above the crash site, descending very fast. 'Target locked,' he said through the comms, his voice booming out of the speakers. 'I'm going for a 2 square kilometre sweep with the ultrasound. Prepped and ready.'

'Copy that,' Josh replied. 'Make it quick, Dimitri.'

'Don't you worry, my friend. I plan to.'

They watched the sleek jet twist over the wreckage, 21,000 metres above the frigid sand of the Gobi. The sun sparkled off its green fuselage as it plummeted. Then, pulling up, Dimitri levelled off at 10,000 metres, changed course to a heading of 67.44 degrees and set the controls ready for the dive.

It would take all the man's skill to pull off this delicate operation. He would have to swoop down at Mach 2, twice the speed of a bullet, level off at an altitude no greater than 300 metres, purge the area with ultrasound, then pull up and climb to a safe altitude while all the time avoiding the Chinese disruptor beam.

'Okay, Hummingbird. I've levelled off.'

'You're well clear of the beam.'

'Good. All systems check green.'

'Copy that here.'

'Anything from Tintara?'

'Tom's doing his best, Dimitri. Remember . . . top speed Mach 2. Go a fraction faster and you'll risk losing trim and . . .'

'I know, Josh.'

'Yeah, sorry, man.'

'All right.' Dimitri's voice spilled from the speakers. 'Let's do this.'

85

Everywhere and nowhere

Bundles of information pulsed along the tube. Tommy Boy stared at them zipping past his feet. They glowed every colour imaginable and some he had never conceived of before. Then he leapt forward, grabbed hold and rode the information stream.

He found he could steer the bundles simply by thinking where he wanted to go. And he knew where he was aiming for – the central processor. The fact that information bundles were still moving meant the system was still operating. His mission was not yet accomplished. He had to get to the core of the Chinese computer and take it out.

A fraction of a microsecond and he was there. The outline of the processor grew on the horizon. The information bundle hurtled towards it. Tommy Boy jumped off his ride with precision timing and flew into the heart of the machine, tumbling onto a hard metal floor and rolling over.

'Get up,' said a voice.

Tommy Boy lifted his head. An old man was standing in front of him. He was leaning on a gnarled staff made from some exotic pale wood. Behind him stood the central processor for the Chinese computer system. It hummed quietly. Bundles of information were streaming in and out of it. Tom's avatar pulled himself to his feet.

'I am the guardian. It was unwise of you to come here,' the old man said.

Tommy Boy stared at him, silent.

'Your virus has weakened us. I cannot destroy you. But I can stop you from controlling the processor.'

Tommy Boy ignored the old man and dashed towards the processor. He slammed into some sort of invisible barrier and fell back in a heap on the metal floor.

The old man cackled, shaking his head slowly. 'Ah, the folly of youth.'

Tommy Boy pulled himself up. Time was running out. He took another run at the processor and was thrown back again. Then he turned on the old man and swung his arm round to smash his fist into the guardian's face. Instead, he found himself sprawling on the floor again.

In Cyber Control, Tom shook in his chair. His heart was racing, eyelids twitching.

Tommy Boy went for the old man again. This time, he caught hold of his tunic. The guardian swung around as nimble as a young boy. Tommy Boy clung on and tightened his grip. New strength came from desperation. He managed to pull the old man towards him and they fell to the floor in a confusion of limbs. Tommy Boy clawed and grasped, never letting up. The old man folded under him, his wooden staff flying away. Tommy Boy punched him hard in the face. He went to hit him again and the old man laughed. Tom's avatar held back, fist poised in midair.

'You'll never break into the processor,' the old man gasped.

'That's what you think.'

'It is what I *know*. Consider the prime factors of that number . . . there.' And he pointed to the processor. The machine was daubed with a number dozens of digits long. The old man laughed again and wriggled out from under

Tommy Boy. Grabbing for his staff, he stood over him, beaming.

Tommy Boy lowered his fist, and in Cyber Control, a shudder passed through Tom's body. Now he understood. The processor was protected by pure mathematics. Finding the prime factors of such a large number as this was almost impossible.

Tommy Boy looked at the metal floor, let out a sigh and took a deep breath.

'You realise, yes?' the old man said, his voice even, totally in control. 'To break into the processor you must find two prime numbers that multiply together to give you this number. Perhaps you should go now. Return to your friends. Let us get on with our duties.'

Tommy Boy continued to look at the metal. And as he did so, the fear fell away from him. The old man was right. Finding the prime factors of this huge number was almost impossible. It would take a computer thousands of years to calculate. But the old man obviously had no notion of Sybil, the quantum computer. When Tom raised his head, it was he who was smiling.

The old man fixed him with a serene look.

Tommy Boy was about to speak to Cyber Control when the guardian lifted a hand. He looked straight into the avatar's eyes.

'Oh . . . and no cheating,' he said, and Tom felt the comm link with Sybil snap.

86

Base One, Tintara Island

'Shit! What's happened?' Noel Brannigan exclaimed and span around, staring at Tom slumped in his chair. The CyberLink was still attached, his eyelids flickering.

'We've lost the comm connection between Tom and Sybil,' one of the techs responded. 'Every other system is up and Tom's getting sensory information in the cyber world. But that's it.'

Noel Brannigan closed his eyes tight and screwed up his face.

'What do we do?' the tech asked.

Noel opened his eyes and stared around the room. 'I have absolutely no idea.'

87

Gobi Desert, China

On the Hummingbird screen, Josh and the others could see the Silverback making its final turn 6000 metres above the desert. As they watched, it dropped like a stone out of the bright blue sky, moving so fast the cameras on BigEye could barely keep up.

'Ultrasound coils set,' Dimitri said through the speakers. 'Final systems check A-okay. Four seconds to range.'

They all heard the squalling sound from inside the Silverback. It was so loud it almost blew the speakers in the Hummingbird's control room. Then a computer voice aboard *Mick* cut through the sound. 'Warning, warning. Unidentified electromagnetic disturbance. Abort, abort.'

Omar span in his chair to face Josh. 'His starboard engine is hit.'

'How bad?'

'Fifty per cent efficiency and dropping. Forty per cent.'

'Dimitri, pull up,' Josh yelled into his headset.

No reply.

'His comms are down,' Omar said.

'Aggh,' Josh screamed and hit the control panel with the palm of his hand.

'Port engine hit,' Omar reported. 'Seventy per cent efficiency.'

A crackle came over the comms and Dimitri's voice could

be heard, fragmented, distorted. 'Hummingbird . . . get the damn thing . . . I'm . . . try . . .'

'Warning, warning,' came the metallic rasp of the computer aboard the Silverback. 'Electro . . . serious . . . compromi . . . abor . . .'

On the screen, they could see the Silverback levelling off no more than 100 metres above the desert. It screamed over the wreckage, and somehow Dimitri was keeping control of the plane. But they could all see what a struggle it was – the wings kept dipping, and every few seconds the Silverback juddered. The plane started to climb.

'Starboard engine down to 10 per cent.'

Then suddenly the interference over the comms vanished and the squalling sound disappeared.

'Dimitri,' Josh shouted.

'Hummingbird.'

'Get out, Dimitri.'

'Couldn't get the ultrasound online,' he said.

Looking at the big screen, Josh saw the plane bank around and start to make a second run.

'Dimitri. Get out. That's an order!'

Dimitri's reply came as fractured words. Then the ear-splitting squall crashed through the speakers louder than before.

88

Everywhere and nowhere

Tommy Boy stared in disbelief at the old man. He could feel the panic rising inside him but knew that to react to it would be fatal for the mission. Instead, he tried with all his strength to calm his breathing, to steady the shaking in his hands, to think clearly, analyse, analyse. That's what he did best.

The old man's smile was infuriating. Tommy Boy felt an overwhelming desire to smash the wizened face with his fist, pummel it to nothing. He could not win this battle, but he could smash up the old bastard good. It would be a hollow gesture and achieve nothing. He knew that. He also knew how hard it would be to calculate the prime factors of this number himself. It would take a human being without the benefit of a computer longer than the lifespan of the universe. Whatever Tommy Boy did, the old man would win.

The guardian sighed and narrowed his eyes. Then he broke into a laugh, a triumphant cynical laugh. And it was at that precise moment that Tommy Boy had a brilliant idea.

The old man gave him an odd look as the avatar lowered himself to the floor cross-legged, arms behind him, palms flat to the metal floor.

Hands out of sight, Tommy Boy began to tap.

89

Base One, Tintara Island

'We've gotta unhook him,' exclaimed Madeleine Alexander standing beside Tom's chair.

'No, that would be disastrous,' Noel shouted leaping from his seat. 'Both for Tom and Sybil.'

'Well, what then?'

Noel ran a hand through his hair and stared around the room, desperate for some clue, some answer.

'What's he doing?' It was one of the techs on the other side of Tom's wheelchair.

Noel and Madeleine both looked at the tech, and then round at Tom. 'What do you mean . . . ?'

'There. He's tapping his fingers.'

Noel took a step forward and crouched down beside Tom slumped in his wheelchair. The young man's head was tilted to one side, the CyberLink headset clung to his scalp. His eyes were closed, but they could see his eyeballs moving, his lids flicking rapidly as though he were in REM sleep. Glancing down to where Tom's hand was resting on the leather armrest, they could all see his fingers moving, drumming out a rhythm.

'What . . . ?'

'It's Morse Code.' It was Madeleine's voice. She was standing behind Noel, staring at Tom's fingers.

'Morse . . . ?'

357

'He's tapping out a message. Get me a pad and pen,' she snapped turning towards the nearest panel. 'Quick!' A tech ran forward and Madeleine stared scribbling.

'What the hell's he saying?'

'Sssh.'

They fell silent.

'It's part way through. Just numbers. Start again, Tom,' Madeleine urged, knowing he could not hear her but needing to say it.

'Words,' she said as she scribbled.

'What words?'

'He's saying . . . Prime factors. He wants prime factors. Must be a security barrier. Hang on, the numbers again.' She scribbled more digits onto the notepaper in her hand, flicked the page, writing frantically, knowing she could not afford a single mistake. 'Yes . . . yes, I'm back to where I was,' she said triumphantly. 'Got it.'

She dashed over to the control panel, tapping at it and talking twenty to the dozen. 'It's a bloody huge number. More than 40 digits.'

'But Sybil can do it.' One of the techs interrupted.

'That's why their defence system cut the link,' Noel replied. 'They can't stop Tom being there, but they can stop him getting into the central processor which must be guarded with this "insoluble" problem. Well done Tom!'

'There,' Madeleine said, and stepped back from the console. 'Now it's up to Sybil.'

'How long?' Noel asked.

'That's harder to answer than the problem,' Madeleine retorted.

90

Gobi Desert, China

On the big screen, the jet was just a blur as it streaked down vertically through the crisp desert air.

'Warning . . . warning.'

'Same thing,' Josh hissed. 'Same fucking thing. God!'

Omar was in the seat beside him, staring at the screen.

Again Dimitri's distorted voice crackled over the speakers. 'Ultrasound primed,' he said. 'Altitude . . . ousand metres . . . level . . .'

'Warning. Warning. Abort . . . ystems . . . criti . . . Abo . . .'

The plane levelled off.

'Both engines down to 11 per cent,' Omar said. 'Damn it!'

'What?'

'ELF signal power is increasing.'

Josh stared at him and bit his lower lip.

'Humming . . . I'm losing . . . '

'Warn . . . arning . . . Ab . . .'

'Unidentified aircraft approaching crash site.' It was a clear voice – the Hummingbird's onboard computer.

Josh swung around to face the control panel, and there in the holoscreen he could see the shape of a transport aircraft.

'What's its ETA?'

'Thirty-five seconds.'

'Come on, Tom!' Josh said under his breath. 'Come on!'

91

Base One, Tintara Island

'Come on, Sybil!' Madeleine said and glanced at Tom. Unaware they had got the message, he was still tapping out the same rhythm on the armrest.

'Do you want to find out how long . . . ?'

'No, save the processing power.'

'But it could take weeks,' Noel Brannigan persisted.

'In which case, we don't have a hope anyway.'

Brannigan sighed and stared at the screen. Colours flashed across its plasma cells. And then it lit up.

'Prime factors calculated,' Sybil said.

92

The Silverback shook violently, span 360 degrees on its axis and dropped another hundred metres. It was now no more than 70 metres above the wreckage. There was a roaring sound in Dimitri's ears, and his vision was blurred. Keeping his grip on the flight control handset with his left hand, he reached out with his right to touch the main control panel, but he could not reach it. A plastic support had slipped under the tremendous g-force trapping his arms, pushing them down and back. The only way he could release it was to climb and allow the plane to spin again so he could push the support back into place. Right now, though, that was impossible.

'Warning. Critical. Structural integrity at 16 per cent. Eject. Eject.'

He could not eject, even if he wanted to. He could not reach the release control. He stretched his fingers, forcing his arm forward, millimetre by millimetre. He knew the controls like the back of his own hand. He did not need to see them. He knew his fingertips were hovering close to the panel.

'Agggh!' he yelled, making his ears ring as he put everything he had into moving his fingers.

He felt the plastic beneath the tip of his middle finger. The control was touch-sensitive. It responded instantly.

'Ultrasound engaged,' the onboard computer said.

Sixty-five metres beneath the undercarriage of the Silverback, a burst of high frequency cyclic sound pressure, beyond the limit of human hearing, pulsated over the crash site.

'Structural integrity 7 per cent. Critical. Eject. Eject,' came the calm, dispassionate voice of the computer.

Dimitri pulled back on the control handset, feeling the plane roll. He could see in his helmet holoscreen that the Silverback had plunged to less than 30 metres above the ground. The orange sand and the blue sky swirled into one as the aircraft turned on its lateral axis.

The jet shuddered. An explosion to port rocked the plane as the ultrasound clipped it, and Dimitri saw a fireball envelop the engine. Pieces of Maxinium and plastic smashed against the canopy and bounced off. A great red streak of fire shot from the wing and the plane went into a spin. Dimitri fought to regain control, but nothing was responding. The control panel was dead.

93

Base One, Tintara Island

'Wow!' Madeleine exclaimed, watching as two large prime numbers appeared on the big screen. 'Wow!'

'Now what?' Noel asked.

Madeleine snapped away from the screen and stared into her colleague's eyes. For a second she looked completely lost. Then she broke into a smile and dashed over to Tom in his wheelchair. He was still frantically tapping. Madeleine ripped a plastic badge from her boilersuit, twisted the pin outwards and without wasting a second crouched down beside Tom. 'Really sorry about this,' she said, and stuck the pin into the top of his hand.

94

Everywhere and nowhere

The pain hit him like a flash of lightning out of the dark void of night, but a second later it was replaced with euphoria.

Tommy Boy jumped to his feet. The old man made a show of not reacting and stayed rooted to the spot leaning on his gnarled staff, surveying the avatar with his black, mirthful eyes.

'One, six, zero, three,' Tommy Boy began.

The old man gave him a surprised look and started to laugh. Tommy Boy kept shouting numbers. 'Four, zero, three, four, six, nine, two.'

The old man roared with laughter, his eyes glinting.

'Seven, eight, four, two, one, one, two, eight, seven, eight.'

The old man's laughter stopped, but his face remained creased with humour, the lines seemed to be etched into his old skin.

'Five, five, four, nine, zero.'

The smile faded.

'Two, two, four, zero, five.'

The old man rushed towards Tommy Boy. He seemed to have shed a thousand years in a microsecond. With stunning agility, he flew though the air. Tommy Boy managed to sidestep the guardian with a fraction of a second to spare. He kept on shouting numbers. 'Nine, nine, four, zero, two.'

The old man's face had transformed into a horror mask, his eyes blazing, mouth red and gaping, rotten old teeth snarling. His staff whistled through the air, missing Tommy Boy by a millimetre.

'Nine, one, two, one, four, three.'

The old man roared and swung the staff again. Tommy Boy caught it and kept hold as the guardian yanked at it with incredible strength.

'Four, four, two.'

The old man froze.

'Six, six, five, one, zero, three.' Tommy Boy swung the staff, missing the guardian and slicing the air.

'Six, five, one,' Tommy Boy went on, not missing a beat.

The old man stared straight ahead, unmoving, ignoring the arc of the staff as Tommy Boy brought it around. The wood slammed into the frail figure, smashing him across the side of the head. He collapsed in a heap.

Tommy Boy took a step forward, looked down at the old man bleeding on the metal floor. 'Seven,' he said and lifted the wood to deliver the coup de grâce.

The lights snapped off.

Silence.

95

Gobi Desert, China

Josh and Omar stared at the screen, their faces frozen in horror. The Silverback had made its cleansing run, and beneath it on the desert floor, the wreckage of *Paul* and every other material thing within a kilometre radius simply turned to microfine powder. But then the Silverback started to roll and shudder.

Josh had flown these planes a thousand times. He knew them intimately and he had experienced the terror when the ELF beam struck. The sense of powerlessness it brought. He turned from the screen, no longer able to watch the terrible scene unfolding. Throwing his head into his hands he tried to obliterate the horrible reality. 'Oh God,' he mumbled. 'Oh, God.'

'Hummingbird 3. Come in, Hummingbird 3.'

It took Josh a few seconds to realise the crazy truth. The voice was Dimitri's.

'Hummingbird 3. This is Dimitri. Come in.'

Josh lifted his head and saw Omar as he broke through his own moment of disbelief and shock. They both snapped around to gape at the screen. The Silverback *Mick* was climbing into the blue. Its port wing was blackened, the engine had disintegrated, but the onboard systems had compensated – nanobots were already at work patching up the wing, and the computer was automatically stabilising the jet.

'Dimitri. This is Hummingbird 3,' Josh managed to say. 'God, it's good to hear your voice, man.'

'Not half as good as it is to hear yours, my friend,' Dimitri replied.

96

Subaqua Chinese Base, 13.5 kilometres off Fiji

'Mark . . . Wake up.'

The voice seemed far off. He opened his eyes and saw Mai leaning over him. For several seconds he could not remember what had happened or even who he was. He moved his leg and a ripple of pain shot along his spine. His head felt like it was splitting in two. Mai helped him sit up.

The room lay in semi-darkness. As he looked around, he saw other human shapes in the gloom. Some of them were beginning to stir. The place stank of damp and sweat.

'You okay?' Mai asked.

'I guess.'

They saw Pete struggle to his feet on the far side of the room and walk over to him.

'You all right?' Mark asked.

'Yeah, apart from the bastard with the hammer who keeps hitting me.'

'I saw one of the intruders. He was wearing a gas mask. I think they knocked us out with a nerve agent, some sort of opiate.'

'So much for Chinese hospitality!' Mai added, rubbing her head with the palm of her hand.

Then Mark noticed what the other two were wearing. Their cybersuits had been replaced with green one-piece boilersuits. He looked down at himself and sighed. 'The weapons have gone of course.'

Pete nodded.

'Fabulous!'

There was a sound from the middle of the room. Mark turned to see Harry Flanders clambering to his feet and wincing with pain.

'Okay,' Mark said to Pete and Mai. 'Assessment. First check that everyone's here.'

Two minutes later, all the survivors were awake and accounted for. Everyone felt bruised but there were no serious injuries.

Mark paced the circumference of the room. It was about 5 metres square, the size of a double garage. There were no windows. Metal shelves had been built into three of the walls. They were all empty. In the fourth wall, the outline of a door, sealed tightly shut. No markings on the inside. He surmised it had some sort of electronic lock.

'It's a storeroom,' Mark said to Pete, sitting down on the floor beside him.

'So, what now?'

Mark shook his head. 'Comms are nonexistent. We have no idea who our captors are. We have no weapons. We're basically at their mercy.'

Pete looked at the floor between his feet. 'And we have no idea if there are any other survivors in the hotel, what's happening on Tintara, or what the hell has happened to Steph and Josh.'

There was a sound from across the room and the door in the far wall slid open. Two Chinese soldiers ran in and took up positions either side of the door. They covered the room with their machine guns. A third Chinese man in civilian clothes stepped in and stood close to the entrance. He was wearing black spectacles and had a round, chubby face. He turned to one of the guards, barked something in Mandarin and the soldier dashed straight for Mark Harrison, dragging him roughly to his feet.

Pete made to get up, but the soldier shouted at him and brought his gun around. Pete put up his hands. 'Oki dokie. I get the message, man.'

Michael Xavier, who had been sitting against the wall close to the door, sprang up. 'What *are* you people doing?' he yelled. The second guard at the door turned on him, swinging his gun, ready to smash it across Xavier's face. Harry Flanders suddenly appeared in front of Michael, pushing the hotel owner aside. The guard was about to land a blow on Harry's unprotected temple. The man at the door roared an order and the soldier froze. He lowered the gun and retreated backwards to the door. Mark was pushed out into the corridor, the barrel of a gun in his back. One of the soldiers pulled a black hood roughly over his head and the door slammed shut.

97

It was only a short walk, but Mark could not see where he was going, so he kept stumbling and tripping. One of the guards guided him around bends in the corridor but cared little if Mark hit his knees or bashed his shoulders into protruding objects along the way.

He heard a door slide open and fell forward, hitting the floor. Someone ripped off the hood.

'Stand up.'

Mark looked up. It was the man in civilian clothes. His English was perfect.

Mark clambered to his feet.

They were in a luxuriously furnished office. The walls were teak panelled. Book cases filled with leather-bound volumes lined two of the walls. Directly in front of him stood a huge old-fashioned mahogany desk. A Chinese man sat behind the desk. He had his elbows resting on the leather-trimmed top, fingers interlinked in front of his face. His index fingers were placed together to form a spire at his lips.

'Leave us,' he snapped to the guards.

The man in civilian clothes and black-rimmed spectacles lowered himself into an armchair to Mark's left.

'I don't know who the hell you people are, but you're interfering in a civilian rescue mission. You will be accountable for any harm done to us,' Mark said, his voice even and controlled.

The man behind the desk lowered his hands, placing them flat to the desk. He stood up and began to pace, hands behind his back. He was unusually tall and stick thin. He was wearing a dark blue uniform that Mark knew was not standard Chinese military. The man frowned, wrinkling his entire, bony face as though the skin was too taut. He picked up an E-Force stun pistol from where it lay on his desk and waved it in the air nonchalantly. 'This is a funny little thing,' he said. 'Toy guns! Why do you people insist on using such things?' He placed it back on the desk. 'That said, I do admire you, Mr Harrison. You've worked hard to establish your . . .' He puckered his lips, 'interesting organi-sation. It is simply that you have . . . how should I put it? Trodden on our toes.'

'Look, we're just trying to do our job. Let us be on our way. We're not interested in politics or whatever it is you're doing here.'

The man frowned again and glanced at his friend in the armchair. 'That's noble of you, Mr Harrison. I would expect nothing less. After all, you are a man of great integrity. I have followed your career and that of your associates with very keen interest.'

'Who are you?'

The man looked a little perturbed at the question. 'Forgive me, I've been very rude. My name is Mengde Sun. My friend here is Fu Tang.'

Mark stared at the older man, his face expressionless. He went to speak, but Mengde raised a hand. 'No, just listen. I don't have time to waste on small talk, Mr Harrison. We have our own agenda here. This base serves an extremely important role. You'll understand if I cannot go into specif-ics. The Neptune Hotel has got in the way of our work. It is very unfortunate. We did not want to take so many lives. It was quite unnecessary, but our warnings were left unheeded. You see, this is a research base, we have work to do. We have schedules to follow. If people ignore our requests to cease and desist then we are not responsible for any damage caused by the testing of our equipment. Of course, we did not bank on you people turning up. But that has, in fact, been a pleasant surprise. I never let an opportunity pass without taking full advantage of it. You are here, with your rather wonderful machines.'

Mark shook his head, the facts finally falling into place.

'But how did you build a base without being noticed?'

Mengde Sun touched his nose and smiled. 'We Chinese are clever people. This station is very deep – way beyond the range of conventional sensors. We transported everything here by long-range nuclear submarine. It took several years and meticulous planning. I admit it was not at all easy. But then, nothing worthwhile is. You'd appreciate that, Mr Harrison.'

'And you expect me to believe this is all sanctioned by your government?'

'Did I imply that? If I did I'm sorry for misleading you, Mr Harrison. This has nothing to do with Beijing. The Chinese government know nothing of my work, but they pay for it. I do precisely what I like. You might say I'm the real power behind the throne. Many years ago I allowed myself to be controlled by the glorious leader of the time, Jiang Zemin, the Eighth General Secretary of the Communist Party of China. In those days I was idealistic, loyal to our great government. But 12 years in Jing Shak Prison changed all that. You've heard of Jing Shak, of course.' His face suddenly drained of blood, his eyes glazed. 'No, this is my project. Call it an insurance policy, an ace up my sleeve. I'm happy to be the puppet master, for the moment. But things can always change.' He sighed and seemed to snap back to the moment. 'So, Mr Harrison, we will continue with our project, but as you were so kind to drop by, we will gladly relieve you of your equipment. We tried and failed to obtain the E-Force codes to take advantage of your technology . . .'

'The Fijian coup,' Mark interrupted.

'It would have been so much easier if you had cooperated then rather than having Her Majesty's Royal Navy intervening.'

'I suppose you're going to torture me too. It didn't work before.'

Mengde fixed Mark with a blank face. 'Let me assure you, Mr Harrison, if I wanted to acquire information using torture I would get it. But no, I work in very different ways.' And he glanced again at his colleague, Fu Tang. 'There are 13 of you. Every 10 minutes, I will kill one of you until you provide the codes.'

Mark was speechless. He stared back at Mengde, keeping the flood of his emotions to himself.

Mengde glanced at Fu. The man pulled himself up from the armchair and paced to the door.

'You're a very interesting man,' Mengde said as the door to the room closed behind Fu. 'A soldier, a computer expert. You're multilingual, an athlete with an Oxford education. *Very* impressive, Mr Harrison. Yet you go and expend your energies on a *rescue* organisation.' Mengde shook his head. 'What a terrible waste.'

Mark said nothing, just stared fixedly at his gaoler.

'You see,' Mengde went on, 'such a notion as E-Force goes completely against all that I believe in. Your toy guns sum it up.' He glanced at the stun pistol on the desk. 'My view is that if people are so stupid as to find themselves in a disaster, then they should be left to die. Or, if they are strong and find themselves in the midst of a catastrophe, they will find their own way out.'

Mengde seemed to expect a response from Mark, but none came. He was quite aware of the game the man was playing.

There was a sound from beyond the door. A soldier shouted. It was followed by a muffled response. Mark thought he could recognise the voice. The door flew open and Fu led the way. Behind him, the soldiers escorted a man wearing a black hood. One of the soldiers removed the hood. The financier, Sigmund de Silva, stood, dazed, blinking under the bright lights.

Mengde looked at de Silva, then looked again at Mark. 'So, Mr Harrison. The codes.'

Mark said nothing.

There was a sound at the door. It slid open and a soldier bowed and stepped in. 'Apologies, Commander,' he said in Mandarin. Then he paced over to say something quietly in Mengde's left ear.

Mark heard it clearly, and he understood Mandarin. The man said: 'Another plane has landed on the surface, sir.'

Mengde span round to face the soldier. 'What sort of plane?'

'A very large aircraft, sir. It is another E-Force jet.'

Mengde held the soldier's eyes for several beats. 'Prepare the beam,' he said, then turned away quickly, flicking his fingers to dismiss the man. The soldier bowed and left the room.

Mengde took a step closer to Mark. 'The codes.'

Mark said nothing.

Mengde nodded to the soldiers. Between them they pushed Sigmund de Silva to his knees. One of them bound the man's hands behind his back.

'What the fuck is this all about?' de Silva screamed. 'Mark? What . . . ?'

'Shut up,' Mengde snapped and kicked de Silva in the face. Sigmund's head jarred back, blood spraying from his smashed nose. He looked pleadingly at Mark.

With a supreme effort, Mark stood rigid, showing no emotion.

'Oh, you're such a good man, Mr Harrison,' Mengde said, and gave Mark a contemptuous look. 'No doubt you are thinking of the greater good. This man may be sacrificed for your precious technology because that technology will allow you to save many more lives in the future. Am I right, Mr Harrison?'

'Sacrifice? . . . What?' Sigmund screamed. He was shaking, his eyes were massive and black and they held Mark's.

Mengde nodded again and one of the soldiers grabbed Sigmund's sparse white hair. Yanking his head back, with his spare hand he pulled out a Commando knife – 20 centimetres of gleaming stainless steel. With lightning speed, he brought the blade down to Sigmund's neck, lining up the edge with the man's jugular.

'Last chance, Mr Harrison.'

Mark still did not move.

Mengde started to turn back to the soldier.

'Okay,' Mark hissed.

'I'm sorry?'

'Okay. You win. I'll give you the codes.'

Mengde tilted his head slightly, and flicked his palms up. 'Well?'

'Let him go first.'

'Oh, Mr Harrison, I wasn't aware of your talent for comedy. Another thing to add to your impressive CV.'

Mark said nothing.

Mengde's face fell, suddenly expressionless. 'No, it doesn't work that way. Codes first.'

Mark looked at the floor. 'Give me pen and paper.'

Mengde turned to the desk and plucked up a sheet of watermarked paper and a Mont Blanc pen. The soldier with the gun took a step forward nervously. Mark could see his trigger finger whitening slightly.

Mark grasped the pen and wrote down a series of numbers and letters. He handed the paper and pen to Mengde.

'Very good,' the Commander said. 'But of course, I will have to have these checked.' Then he gave the merest hint of a nod to the man holding de Silva. The soldier drew the knife across the financier's neck, cutting into his throat almost to the vertebra. Blood spurted in a great fountain and Sigmund's head fell back, a gaping red and grey wound grinning like an open mouth. His eyes rolled up and the soldier let him fall sideways, blood siphoning into a puddle.

Mark was so shocked he did not move even when Sigmund's blood sprayed across his face. And then everything suddenly seemed to shift into fast motion. There was a blaring sound, a screaming from a speaker in the ceiling. It took him a second to realise it was a voice, a metallic rasp. 'Warning. Station under cyber attack. Warning.'

Mengde turned his eyes from the terrible scene and looked at the ceiling, momentarily confused. The soldier with the machine gun let the barrel droop. Mark snapped out of his horrified stupor, and instinct and years of training took over. In a millisecond, he was leaping forward, diving headlong towards the soldier.

The guard fell backwards, spraying bullets around the room. In a fifth of second, two 42 mm shells struck Fu Tang in the forehead, splitting open his skull. Brains and blood shot into the air, cascading down over his falling body.

Mark smashed his elbow into the guard's face, breaking his nose and knocking him unconscious. Spinning on his heel, he slammed his fist into the side of the other guard's face. The man fell backwards, cracking his head on the edge of Mengde's desk.

Mark straightened, surveyed the scene with disgust and just caught a movement at the edge of his vision. Commander Mengde Sun had made it to the door and was disappearing into the corridor beyond.

98

Mark picked up the QBB-97 machine gun and threw the strap over his shoulder, then he yanked an NP42 pistol from the guard's holster, turned to the desk and pocketed the E-Force stun pistol. E-Force did not carry deadly weapons. He knew that of course. He had written the rule. But his training and his sense of self was a more powerful impulse. The gun offered him a feeling of security. He ran for the door.

'Warning. Station under cyber attack. Warning.' The metallic voice boomed out of speakers along the passageway leading away from Mengde's blood-drenched office. It made him feel good to hear it. It meant Tom was getting into the computer systems of the base. He knew that Tom would eat up the mainframe and spit out the bones. And getting control of the computer network was half the battle.

He ran along the corridor, retracing the steps he had taken as a hooded prisoner. Stopping at the end, he edged slowly round the corner. It was all clear. Twenty seconds later, he was at the door to the storeroom where the others were held. He hit the button on the wall and the door slid open.

'Christ, Mark!' Pete exclaimed. 'What the fuck happened?'

'No time now. Come with me.' Then he turned to Mai, pulled the machine gun from his shoulder and tossed it to her. 'You stay here with everyone. Keep that gun trained on the door.'

She looked a little confused.

'I know, E-Force doesn't do guns, but if soldiers come here intent on killing civilians, it's us or them. We can discuss the morality of it all later . . . yeah?'

Mai gave him a weak smile. 'It's a date, Mark.' Then she said quietly, 'Sigmund?'

Mark just shook his head, turned to Pete, tossed him the stun pistol and led the way out.

99

Pacific Ocean, 21.7 kilometres off Fiji

The Hummingbird came in low over the water. The late afternoon sun was hot and bright. Josh and Omar took the huge plane in a tight circle and then lowered it to the surface of the ocean. The aircraft settled onto the water directly above the Chinese subaqua base. Tom had located it using automatic beacons built into the cybersuits.

'So what's Tom got from BigEye?' Steph asked.

They were sitting in the Ops Room behind the flightdeck. Josh flicked a control and a wall screen lit up. 'The techs at Base One have managed to boost the sensors on BigEye 9. They've got some images of a structure on the ocean floor. It's located at the exact coordinates Sybil found for the source of the tremors. Some sort of subaqua base.'

It was constructed from a collection of 24 cylinders arranged as a flat, elongated cube lying on the floor of the ocean. They could see the E-Force sub *Drebbel* docked to one of the short ends of the building. On each side lay the black shapes of the Chinese nuclear subs. They were docked to the base with fuel lines and power cables running from the wall of the building.

'There are three cybersuits here,' Josh remarked, and a cluster of three red dots appeared on the screen. 'Infrared scanners show there are 26 human life signs on the station. A group of them are concentrated in this area.' He pointed to a spot in the western section of the base. 'I would guess it's some sort of holding cell.'

'Okay, so I imagine you've already worked out a plan, Josh.'

He looked unusually serious. 'Well, we still have a few advantages. It's quite possible sensors on the base have detected the Hummingbird, but I think they would have trouble picking up a personal sub.'

'What makes you so sure?'

'Tom's breaking into their network as we speak. He's trying to target key control systems. He can't just cut all power – or everyone in the building would suffocate. He's disrupted their sonar and other sensor systems, so if they saw the Hummingbird come in, they won't see it any more.'

'So we could take a sub down and they would never know we were there.'

Josh smiled and nodded.

'And you think you're back to 100 per cent fitness?'

'One hundred and 10 per cent.'

She gave him a sceptical look and shook her head. 'All right, Josh. Lead the way.'

100

Subaqua Base

Mark and Pete ran along the passageway. Mark had pulled the NP42 handgun from his pocket.

The computerised voice started up again. 'Warning. Station under cyber attack. Warning.'

'I love you, Tom!' Pete exclaimed as they ran.

Mark stopped and turned to something on the wall halfway along the corridor.

'What is it?'

He was staring at a laminated rectangle pinned to the wall. 'It's a schematic of the station.'

Pete stood next to him. 'My Chinese is a little rusty.'

'There,' Mark said after a moment. 'Down this corridor.' He pointed to his left. 'Right, left, second right . . . Let's go.'

Mark led the way while Pete guarded their rear, eyeing the corridor behind as they ran, sweeping it with the stun pistol. They saw no one and reached the room they were looking for in a few moments. The sign on the door was written in simple Chinese characters: 'COMMUNICATIONS CENTRE'.

Mark stepped forward, stabbed a metal pad on the wall and the door slid open. All they could hear from inside was the electronic hum of computers and comms equipment. They clung to the wall either side of the opening, listening intently, their weapons raised in front of their noses.

Their cochlear implants could pick up nothing to suggest the room was manned.

The computer warning sounded again: 'Warning. Station under cyber attack. Warning.' The last word echoed along the corridor, and suddenly Mark heard something. Two different people in the Communications Centre. They were trying not to make a sound, but he could just hear them breathing. Pete caught it too. He nodded to Mark, and ducking low they swivelled into the Communications Centre.

One of the soldiers had a pistol drawn. He fired and missed. Pete pulled the trigger of his stun pistol and a beam of intense electromagnetic energy hit the man in the chest. He fell back, unconscious.

The second soldier had more time. He span around, went to fire, but the gun flew out of his hand. It pirouetted in the air and smashed into a control panel close by. He yelped as two of his fingers dislocated. Then a second beam from the stun pistol hit him square in the chest and he was out cold.

'Sharp shooting, man,' Pete said.

'Not so bad yourself, Pete. Here, help me tie them up.' Mark had yanked a phone from a cradle on the wall close to the door. He ripped the receiver out of its socket and threw the rest to Pete. The severed mains lead dangled from its rear end. Mark used the coiled lead with the receiver still attached to bind the first soldier's hands behind his back. Pete tugged at the phone end of the mains lead and the wire came free. Dragging the second soldier along the floor, he positioned him against the leg of a bench and tied him to it with the lead. He stood up and slapped his palms together as though cleaning dust from them. 'There,' he said. 'Very neat, even if I say so meself.'

Mark was already over at the main desk. 'Pete, guard the

door. Don't hesitate to use the stun pistol.' The console was covered in Chinese symbols, but that did not present a problem for him. He flicked a switch and a crackling sound came from a speaker in the control panel. He leaned in towards a microphone on a flexible stand protruding from the console.

'E-Force. Come in.'

Nothing but the crackling sound.

'Tom? You there?'

'Mark.'

'Steph!'

'What's your status, Mark?'

'I only have a few seconds. Pete and Mai are safe. We have nine survivors from the Neptune. We've been taken captive by some sort of renegade group – Chinese, but I'm sure they're not official military. They're a bunch of murderers led by a man named Mengde Sun. You got that? Mengde Sun.'

'Yeah, Mark . . .'

'Let me finish. Might lose comms any second. Tom's in the middle of a cyber attack – you probably know that. Great distraction, but we need more. If we don't get out of here, Mengde's people will kill all of us. We're going to try to get the survivors back to the *Drebbel*.'

'Someone's coming,' Pete hissed.

'Gotta go, Steph,' Mark snapped and cut the comms link.

101

Subaqua Base

It was a tiny, two-seater sub, nicknamed the Hot Dog. It was nimble, very fast and almost totally undetectable by conventional sonar. The fact that Tom had culled the system in the Chinese base at Hang Cheng was a welcome bonus.

The Hot Dog dropped out of the Hummingbird. Its single, 900 horsepower engine kicked in and the compact little vessel shot into a diagonal dive, headed straight for the base. Steph was at the controls this time. She had refused point blank to have it any other way and Josh could hardly argue. She manoeuvred the vehicle with consummate skill derived from many hours of practice, and within 60 seconds they were 350 metres below the Pacific. In their cockpits they could each see the base on their screens. The place looked uncomfortable on the ocean floor, a typically ugly communist edifice; all substance, no style.

'Drop site located,' Steph said, and the sub pulled rapidly to starboard, turned and dived incredibly quickly. A moment later, it was purring along, 3 metres above the ocean floor, following the contours of the strange marine landscape. They stopped 15 metres from the north-east corner of the base, cut the engines and floated silently.

Josh's fingers played over the controls of the Hot Dog and a panel opened in its underside. A retractable metal arm slid out. Nestled in the metal claw at the end of the arm was a cylinder about a metre long, half a metre in diameter. It was a Distractor – a box of electronics that could simulate any form of seismic disruption required. It was a classic decoy. All you had to do was assign it a disruption level, set the timer, put it in place, and let it do its job. And best of all, it caused no real damage, just a lot of fuss and noise.

The retractable metal arm lowered the Distractor to the seabed and folded itself back into the underside of the sub. The door of the little sub's cargo hold slid shut, and for a moment nothing more happened. Then slowly the cylinder lifted a few centimetres from the ocean floor, hung there for a second and moved towards the wall of the base.

A metre from the wall, a steel tube shot out from the end of the Distractor. A sucker unfolded itself from the end. It looked for all the world like a very hi-tech toilet plunger. The pad attached itself to the wall and the device stuck fast.

'Excellent,' Steph said into the comms. 'Couldn't have done it better myself, Josh.'

'I know that!' he retorted. 'It's set for six minutes. Let's get into position.'

The Hot Dog sped away from the drop site and swung around the edge of the base, its powerful motor churning the water as it went.

'The door is dead ahead,' Steph said into her comms.

Within two minutes they were suited up. They let the Hot Dog hover a few metres from the base and jumped on a two-seater scooter attached to the outside of the mini-sub. Reaching the door to the base, they killed the engine of the scooter, slid off and held onto a pair of handles cut into the wall.

'Let's hope Tom's done his bit,' Steph said.

Josh turned a lever on the door and pulled on the handle. It swung outwards.

Inside the lock, they sealed the door. On the wall was an electronic panel countersunk into a rubber rectangle. The buttons were rubber. Josh tapped in a combination he had downloaded from Tintara and the water started to drain from the chamber.

It took three minutes to empty. A signal sounded, a high-pitched whistle to indicate the chamber was ready to be unlocked. Steph stabbed at a pad on the inner door, and it slid open.

They were inside the base.

102

Subaqua Base

The voices were coming from the passageway to the right of the exit from the Communications Centre. Mark and Pete dashed along the corridor in the opposite direction, back towards the storeroom and the others.

They reached the end of the corridor, hung a left and found themselves in a long passageway with doors leading off to each side. The storeroom was ahead, around a bend to the left.

'Pete?' They both stopped in the corridor. 'You go back to the room with the others. Get them ready to move out.'

'What're you doing?'

'I need to find the cybersuits.'

'I should come too.'

'No. Mai needs help. There are nine survivors. It'll be easier for me to move on my own. Besides, I don't want both of us running the risk of getting caught.'

Pete held Mark's eyes for a moment then nodded. He turned and sped down the corridor. Stopping at the end, he peered around, then ran on, stun gun ready, gripped in both hands.

Mark had remembered the schematic of the base down to the last detail. He was in what translated to Corridor B. He raced on, past the turning that led to the storeroom. The passageway curved to the right. A short way along, he stopped, then took a left. The Main Control Room lay directly ahead.

He could hear voices – half a dozen different people. There were other sounds too, machines whirring, computer crosstalk, a man pacing. Then, cutting over it all, the warning from the computer blared again. Mark leaned back against the wall to the right of the sliding door, and took a deep breath. His left hand was poised over the door's release button. He gripped the pistol with his right. Pushing away from the wall, he thumped the release.

'Drop the gun,' a voice shouted in Chinese.

Mark turned and saw a soldier at the corner. The man ran straight towards him keeping his machine gun trained on Mark. Two more men emerged from the room. Behind them stood Mengde Sun. 'Oh dear,' he said in English.

103

The door slammed behind him as Mark was shoved into the store-cum-prison. He tripped and landed heavily. Pete walked over and helped him up. Mark gazed around the room and saw all the survivors were there. The Xavier children looked petrified. Hilary was holding Nick close to her and Michael had his arm about Emily's shoulders, whispering words of comfort. Kristy sat against the far wall, her head down on her raised knees. Harry, Miguel, Jim and Archie formed a small group close to the door. They looked utterly drained.

'You've still got the weapons?' Mark asked urgently.

Pete patted his hip and Mai nodded towards the machine gun on the shelf at the back of the room.

'I thought I said you should use it, Mai.'

'I know you did. But I didn't, Mark. Okay?'

Mark gazed at the floor. 'I got a message out,' he said.

'Yeah, I know.' She nodded at Pete.

'What's that?'

'What's what?'

Then Pete and Mai heard it.

Mark turned and saw vapour appearing from under the shelving unit in the wall furthest from the door. Harry Flanders had seen it too. 'What the fuck's that?' he exclaimed.

Mark and Mai strode over to the shelves and crouched low near the source of the vapour, trying to find the inlet. They both started coughing and pulled back.

'Oh fuck,' Jim said. He looked round at the others. 'They're poisoning us!'

Everyone started talking at once.

'Okay, people,' Mark snapped and raised his hands. They quietened down, but he could see in their faces they were all petrified. They had been through so much, the strain was showing.

'I know it's hard, but we have to keep calm. Try to not to breathe any more than you have to. My colleagues are on their way. Please, try . . . try to remain calm.'

Mark ripped at the sleeve of his boilersuit, and Pete took his lead. Mai found a bottle of water that had been left with some food a couple of hours earlier. The sleeves were ripped into smaller strips, Mai drenched them with water and handed them out.

Hilary Xavier, her face drawn, almost skeletal with stress, took two lengths of cloth and told Emily and Nick to put the fabric over their mouths.

'Any idea what the gas is, Pete? Mai?' Mark asked.

They shook their heads.

'Odourless, just about visible as a white vapour. Could be anything,' Pete concluded.

'It's lighter than air,' Mai added and nodded towards a wispy trail ascending to the ceiling. 'Buys us a little time.'

Michael and Jim started to cough.

'Get to the floor . . . Everyone,' Mark commanded. Hilary pulled the kids down. Emily started to cry. Hilary shushed her. 'Don't, Em . . . please.'

'Okay, everyone, breathe only when necessary. Shallow breaths,' Mai told them and threw herself to the floor.

Mark scrambled under the shelving at the back of the room. He had a damp cloth pushed up against his nose and mouth, but the vapour was still getting through. He waved the gas away, searching for the inlet. He shuffled forward on his belly, alternately pushing himself against the floor and trying to clear his vision with his spare hand. His eyes were streaming.

His whole body was under the shelving unit before he found the source and, when he did, his heart sank. It was not a single opening, but dozens of small nozzles tucked up inside a cavity under the crossbeam of the shelving support. There was nothing they could do to stop the gas coming in. He swung around, coughing into the damp rag. Pete was crouching down and helped him out.

'Hopeless,' Mark said, his voice muffled by the wet cloth.

Pete nodded towards the floor. The civilians were all unconscious.

Mark felt a movement behind him. He turned just in time to see Mai's head slump to one side. He lowered her gently, making sure the wet cloth was tight about her nose and mouth. Then, straightening, he shuffled towards the door, his head swimming. He caught a glimpse of Pete drop unconscious beside him. His vision started to go and he felt the room start to shake. Was he imagining it?

'Fight it!' Mark mumbled. 'Fight it . . .'

104

The first thing Steph and Josh heard as they entered the base was the blared warning telling them the place was under cyber attack.

'On the ball, this computer,' Josh said.

'Yeah, but don't get too cocky,' Steph retorted and led him to the left along a corridor. They had their stun pistols drawn and were moving along the passageway commando style, crouching low, listening intently. Josh checked his watch. He nodded to Steph and they stopped and pulled back to the wall.

A low hum filled the corridor and the entire base began to shake. The hum changed into a growl and started to build. Then came a horrible grating sound, a screech and a loud bang.

'Well, the Distractor's working,' Josh said. 'Come on.'

They took the first bend carefully, hugging the wall and slithering around the corner, stun guns poised.

They knew where they were going thanks to the schematic of the base Tom had uploaded. A right at the end of the corridor, then a left and they could see the final turn that would take them to the storeroom.

Steph led and eased herself along the wall. The cacophony from the Distractor was deafening. Then another alarm sounded, a high-pitched wail that resonated along the corridor cutting through the racket. The floor shook and Josh almost lost balance. He grabbed at the wall to steady himself. Steph peeked around the corner and pulled back. 'One guard,' she said. Then, before Josh could respond, she had taken a step forward, crouched and fired her stun gun. The guard collapsed, unconscious.

Steph tugged at the handle to the storeroom. It was locked. Tom obviously had not managed to deactivate the security systems this far in. She stepped back, touched a control at the wrist of her cybersuit. The vector-laser slithered out of her suit. She touched a control on her wrist again and a high energy beam hit the lock and vaporised it in a millisecond.

Josh kicked the door and it flew inwards.

Steph almost fell over a body lying close to the entrance. She caught herself and crouched down. It was Harry Flanders. He was unconscious.

Steph looked up and saw Josh run across the room to where two children lay on their backs, damp rags over their mouths. Then she saw Mark staggering towards her. He looked terrible. 'Help me get them into the hall,' he gasped.

Steph caught a glimpse of Pete. He was leaning over Mai, bringing her round and helping her to her feet. Turning, Steph helped two more survivors into the corridor, checked each of them with the medscanner and got them to sip some water. Then she went back into the storeroom. Pete and Mai were stumbling towards her, each helping out a semiconscious survivor. Pete had his stun pistol in his spare hand. The machine gun was slung over Mai's left shoulder.

Within 20 seconds, everyone was out except Michael Xavier and Miguel Bandonis. Josh ran back into the room. He crouched down beside the two unconscious men, then straightened and grabbed each of them by a leg, sliding them roughly across the metal floor. Mark appeared at his side, gasping into the wet cloth at his mouth.

'I'm okay, Mark. Get out,' he said. But the E-Force leader ignored him, dragged Bandonis out through the door as Josh pulled Michael Xavier clear of the room.

The screech of the alarm ricocheted along the passageway. The survivors lay where they had collapsed on the floor, coughing and wheezing, eyes streaming. Steph was crouched down between Emily and Nick. She ran a medscanner across the girl's head and down her body then repeated the action with Nick. They were both coming to. Nick tried to sit up.

'Sssh,' Steph said gently. 'Take it easy.'

'My mum and dad . . .'

Steph looked around and saw Hilary sitting up against the wall a few feet away, coughing. Mark was helping Michael to his feet. 'They're going to be fine.'

Mark approached. 'Good timing, Steph,' he said. 'Now, we've got to get these people out.' He led the way, helping Michael Xavier. The others took two civilians each.

The Distractor stopped suddenly, and a moment later the base alarm cut out abruptly.

They all froze.

A deathly silence.

Then a new computerised message started up. 'Base will self-destruct in five minutes.'

105

Mark didn't say a word. He just ran on along the corridor as fast as he could.

Michael pulled away from Mark's grip. 'I'm okay,' he said. 'My family . . .'

'They're all right,' Mark said and stole a glance back to see Pete immediately behind him with Hilary Xavier and Kristy Sunshine. Further back, the two children were stumbling along. Mark let Michael go and ran on to the next bend. He stopped. The others all came up behind.

'Four minutes 30 seconds to self-destruct,' said the metallic voice.

'Stay here,' Mark whispered to Pete, and slid around the wall. A few metres along the passageway there was another turn. Mark stopped before the bend and peered round. Directly ahead was a door marked: 'DOCKING BAYS'. The door was slightly ajar. There was no one to be seen. He turned and crept back to the others.

'What's the situation?' Michael Xavier asked.

'The docking bays are just around the next bend. I couldn't see anyone.'

'Let's go then.'

Mark put a restraining hand on Michael's shoulder. 'Not so fast. Just because I didn't see anyone . . .'

Michael nodded and hung back. Mark dashed to Josh, who had been helping Archie and Miguel. 'Josh, try Tom. See if he can do anything to stop the self-destruct program.'

Josh nodded and touched a control at his wrist. 'Tom? Come in, Tom.'

'Josh. This is Madeleine Alexander.'

'Madeleine. We need Tom.'

'He's on the CyberLink.'

'He has to get to the self-destruct program.'

'The self-destru . . . ?'

'We have less than four . . .'

'I wouldn't bother, gentlemen.'

Josh and Mark snapped round. Mengde Sun was standing at the corner. He had a pistol gripped in his hands. 'You must be the redoubtable Professor Josh Thompson. It's . . .'

'Cut the crap, Mengde,' Mark barked. The Chief Scientist looked startled. 'You going to try to shoot us all?'

'Well, yes. I suppose so. Then I'll deactivate the self-destruct. I'm not the self-sacrificing type.' He took a step towards them. Michael Xavier stepped forward. Mai came up beside him and started to raise the machine gun.

'Don't be silly, Ms Buchanan,' Mengde said. 'Mr Harrison would be dead before you could get the gun horizontal.' He turned back to Mark.

Mai stopped moving.

Michael Xavier span round, and with lightning reflexes he grabbed Mai's gun.

Mengde was so startled, he turned from Mark, swinging his gun around.

Michael fired.

Bullets sprayed around the corridor.

Hilary and Kristy screamed. They fell to the floor, hands over their heads.

'Warning: three minutes to self-destruct.'

A single shell smashed into Mengde's right eye sending him sprawling backwards along the corridor. Blood, like a dark fountain, cascaded through the air. The Chief Scientist landed against the wall in a heap and started to scream.

'Come on!' Josh cried and pulled at two of the civilians. Pete dashed forward, helping Archie along the corridor.

The others ran on. Josh and Pete led the way, with Mark and Mai shepherding the survivors from the rear. Steph held back and crouched down beside Mengde's writhing body. She grabbed his chin to stop him moving. A quarter of his face was wrecked, the right eye gone. There was a groove 5 centimetres wide in the side of his head. He stopped moving.

Steph leaned in to check his pulse and Mengde suddenly jolted up, his hand at her throat.

Mark turned. Lifted his pistol and shot four bullets into Mengde's head.

106

'Two minutes to self-destruct.'

Pete ran at the door to the docking bays, almost knocking it off its hinges.

Hilary and the two children were stumbling along a few paces back, with Josh close behind, helping Harry. 'Madeleine!' Josh screamed into his comms.

'Tom's onto it, Josh,' she replied.

The airlock lay directly ahead. Pete ran up to it. It was electronically sealed. He span round as Mai crashed through the door to the docking area with a group of survivors. Michael Xavier was behind her, his face white, expressionless. Hilary ran over to him and they gripped each other tight. Michael sobbed into his wife's shoulder.

'It's over, Michael. It's over,' she said softly.

'Josh. Your vector-laser,' Pete called over.

Josh dashed across the corridor, tapping at his wrist as he went.

'Self-destruct in 90 seconds.'

'Stand back,' Josh said, and put his hand out. A bright light shot from his wrist and hit the lock, melting it instantly.

Steph appeared around the corner just outside the door to the docking bay. Mark followed her. They could see everyone had gathered at the lock. Josh leaned on the door and it swung inwards. A few seconds later, they were all inside.

'Self-destruct in 60 seconds.'

'Madeleine!' Josh shouted into his comms.

'I don't think . . .'

Mark dived for the inner door, and then on through the hatch into the *Drebbel*. 'Everyone, get in . . . NOW!' he yelled.

Steph led the others into the main passenger area. 'Strap yourselves in, quick!' she said. 'It's going to be a bumpy ride.' She helped Nick and Emily with their belts.

'Self-destruct in 30 seconds.'

Josh ran after Mark, crashed into the control room and threw himself into the copilot's seat. Mark barely noticed him. He was running his fingers across the touch-sensitive panels. Two screens lit up showing the E-Force emblem. A hum came from the main engines. Mark depressed a control and the submarine started vibrating. The hum rose in pitch. He touched another control and the screens showed the external view. They were hooked up to the side of the base by two docking clamps. Ahead of them lay the open water.

'How're we going to decouple?' Josh asked.

Mark ignored him for a second as he gave all his attention to the controls. Then he glanced at Josh. 'Let's just pray Tom got this far into their system . . .'

'Self-destruct in 15 seconds.'

Mark pulled back on a control and touched a pad on the right of the panel. There were two small explosions in quick succession. The sub juddered, and a deep, heart-shaking roar came from the rear of the vessel. The *Drebbel* shot forward, turned sharply to port and accelerated away from the Chinese base.

They felt the shock of the explosion 1.4 seconds after the base ripped itself apart. A great bubble of expanding air smashed into the rear of the *Drebbel*. It slithered along its sleek

Maxinium outer shell and broke into random turbulence which the sub shot through with barely a vibration. Then came the debris, clumps of metal and plastic sprayed out from the heart of the explosion, spiralling through the water, and slowing. A piece of metal wall, half a desk and a door panel slammed into the covered engines of the *Drebbel*. They bounced off, leaving barely a scratch. Eleven seconds after detaching from the base, the E-Force sub was almost 200 metres away from the shattered complex.

Mark set the controls to 'auto' and threw himself back in the pilot's seat. 'Man, that was close,' he said.

107

Base One, Tintara Island, two days later

'So what's this? The post-mortem post-mortem?' Josh said lightly as he followed Mark into the E-Force leader's office. They had just left a meeting to run through the Neptune mission with all six members and some of the senior ancillary crew.

Mark indicated a chair in front of his desk and perched on the corner close to Josh. Josh crossed his arms and looked directly at Mark.

'It's about the incident over China.'

'Ah, yes, of course.'

'I had a very long conversation with Senator Mitchell.'

'Oh, how is my friend, Evan?'

'He's pissed, Josh.'

Josh stared him out.

'He's had an ear-bashing from Tito Manchetti, the Chief Moderator of the Security Council. Manchetti had been given a similar ear-bashing by the Chinese Ambassador, Mao Ying.'

'Look . . . Mark.'

Mark raised a hand, pulled himself to his feet, walked round his desk and sat down. 'Josh, I could put it down to a spur of the moment impulsive action, but would that make things any better?'

Josh made to answer, but Mark cut in over him. 'Steph has been trying to play it all down, claiming you only clipped

Chinese airspace. But that's not what the BigEye records tell us. Furthermore, because of your actions a civilian, Howard, died, and we almost lost several more lives, yours and Steph's included. I won't even go into the loss of a $100 million Silverback. Most importantly, you very nearly destroyed the rescue mission, which would have cost more lives.'

'But I didn't jeopardise the mission,' Josh managed to say. 'I saved it.'

There was a silence for a moment, then Mark leaned forward on the desk. 'But that's not the point, Josh, is it? You lucked out this time.'

Josh took a deep breath, feeling his anger build.

'You know the rules, Josh,' Mark went on. 'Why do you insist on flouting them?'

'I put the mission first. I always do.'

'But that's irrational. What you did undermines E-Force's image, its reputation. It not only endangered this mission, it endangered future rescues.'

'That's absurd.'

Mark shook his head. 'It is not absurd. E-Force survives on trust. We need the governments of the world on our side. They must be there to help us, to let us fly over their territory, to allow us free reign to do our job.'

'The Chinese don't.'

'No, they don't. But they are one of a tiny handful of nations that won't play ball. Some others are less than keen. I could name a dozen states teetering on the brink of withdrawing their cooperation. The Chinese are clearly unhappy about what you did and they are not going to keep quiet about it. I imagine you have noticed there is a little tension between China and the West at the moment.'

'Don't be so patronising . . .'

'And don't you be so ridiculous,' Mark snapped angrily.

'I would've thought the Chinese might be glad a renegade like Mengde Sun was exposed.'

'Oh yeah, Josh! They're thrilled! Makes them look great!'

Josh said nothing.

'Besides, the research base at Hang Cheng is not the only facility in the empty wastelands of the Chinese-Mongolian border. It was a coincidence you were brought down by the beam. But not a major one. If it hadn't been that, it could have been something else – the area is littered with secret military establishments. Even ignoring that, you could have been picked up on radar. Questions would have been asked. It's a hot zone, Josh. Very hot. Why do you think the Chinese don't want us flying into their airspace?'

'Okay,' Josh said slowly and calmly. 'Then maybe, Mark, this issue should be brought out in the open.'

Mark was shaking his head, making a great effort to control his anger. 'That's not your job.'

Josh stared at him, his own fury finally bursting through. 'Oh, I see. So, it's just dandy for me and the others to risk our lives, to put ourselves in danger purely to save others, but it's not okay for us to have any say in politics. Is that how it is?'

'Josh, you're being childish.'

'But grown up enough to keep putting my life at risk?' he spat back.

Mark let the silence between them linger for a few moments. 'I'm going to have to take disciplinary action,' he said eventually.

Josh stared at him, his mouth open. 'Disciplinary action? What? Lines? Something for the silly child?'

'You'll be replaced by a temporary backup for the next mission. One of the B-team is almost up to speed. I'm also docking your salary for three months.'

Josh looked at him, stunned. He produced an uncertain smile. 'You're joking, right?'

Mark shook his head slowly. 'I wish I could say I was, Josh. I hate having to do this, but you have to understand there are parameters to our behaviour. There are limitations, both for you and for me. We all have our masters.'

Josh shook his head. Then he stood up suddenly and brought his hand to his forehead as though pained. 'Well . . . nobody can say being part of E-Force is ever dull.' He took a deep breath. 'But you know, Mark, I don't think I want to be part of all this any more.' He removed his E-Force ID badge and tossed it onto Mark's desk, watching it slide across the highly polished surface.

'I quit,' he said.

Epilogue

The Hilton, Suva, Fiji, the same day

Afternoon sunlight streamed through the huge windows of the hotel lounge. Gentle jazz piano notes drifted over from somewhere near the bar and a TV in the corner showed soundless images of Chinese and Western diplomats facing each other across a huge conference table.

Harry Flanders looked up to see his producer, Natasha Young, walking across the room towards him. She had flown in the previous evening, claiming she wanted to see how he was. Harry had been in the business long enough to know she was there for other reasons. She wanted to be ready with an open chequebook, ready for the exclusive of a lifetime.

Harry was still in a state of numb confusion. The last few days had been like something straight out of a Hollywood movie. He knew it would take him a long, long time to get over it.

The members of E-Force had not stayed around too long. They had returned to the Neptune but found no other survivors. Mark had succeeded in keeping the press at bay by volunteering to give a full account of what had happened to the hotel if the survivors were left to recover in peace. The deal had worked.

The day before, Harry had said his goodbyes to Jim Kimble and Kristy Sunshine. The singer had given him her address and mobile number, and made him promise he would look her up if he was ever in LA.

After that, he had some time to himself. Time to reflect, to pick a route slowly along the beach with the help of a new walking stick, to look out over the Pacific Ocean.

That morning, Michael Xavier had held a press conference in which he had declared his intention to retire from business altogether so that he could spend a great deal more time with his wife and children. The hotel would be left where it was, at least in the short term – it would be unfeasibly expensive to repair it or to dismantle it. He had gone on to shower praise on E-Force for their professionalism, their skill and their immense bravery. To warm applause, he then described his fellow survivors as 'heroes'. Each of them, he said, had gone to the hotel as ordinary people and had shown themselves to be extraordinary.

After the talk, Harry had a quick work with Michael and learned that Miguel Bandonis had accepted a job as Chief Technical Consultant for one of the Xavier family's US-Based companies, on a very large salary. Archie Barnet had booked a flight back to London and had taken a five-figure offer from a British national paper for his story.

Harry had sat at the back of the room packed with hundreds of his fellow journalists. A week earlier, he could have been one of them, he thought, another hack trying to get a slant on a story, grasping at the air for any morsel of information.

Afterwards, he thought long and hard about what Michael Xavier had said and wondered whether it was true about himself. Was he brave? Was he a hero? He didn't think he was. He had just done what he had needed to do. He hadn't been given any choices. People were only heroes, he concluded, if they had a choice and took a decision to risk their lives to save others.

And had any of it changed him? It was probably too early to tell. He knew that; knew it would take time for the weirdness to filter through, for his mind to process it all. But then, a few hours later, he had been struck by a startling thought. For a year now he had been pining for his ex-wife, Jane. He had been blaming himself for letting their marriage crumble and he had felt only self-disgust. It was the thing that had driven him to find consolation in the bottom of a bottle. It had almost destroyed his career, almost destroyed him. But, as events had unfolded in the Neptune, he had not once thought about Jane. A part of him had risen above his obsession. He had found inner strength, new purpose. The will to survive had transformed him.

'You look relaxed, Harry,' Natasha said, plonking herself into a huge armchair.

'Do I? What's that?' he asked, noticing for the first time a package in her hand.

She looked down. 'Someone handed it to me in Reception. It's addressed to you.'

'Me?'

She passed it to him. It was a small, light package. On the front in lime green marker pen was written: 'HARRY FLANDERS, ROOM 610'. He ripped it open at the top.

A waiter approached with a tray of drinks and paused next to Harry's chair. Harry put his hand inside the package and pulled out a CD and a card. He gazed at the cover of the CD, a huge grin spreading across his face.

'What is it?' Natasha asked, and leaned forward to take a closer look.

'It's from Kristy,' Harry replied. 'A special extended mix of her first single.' And he burst out laughing. Opening the card, he read the line of writing: 'Harry. Thank you for helping me find myself again.' The words shocked him. What had he actually done for Kristy? Nothing more than anyone else would have done in the same circumstances. But it didn't matter, he thought. Like him, Kristy was trying to find some meaning in what had happened. He closed the card, looked up at Natasha's nosy expression, pursed his lips and shook his head slowly.

'Sir?' the waiter said. 'May I interest you in a glass of champagne?'

Harry looked up at him, tears welling in his eyes. 'You know, I don't think I will, thanks,' he said, and turned back to re-read Kristy's card.